THE
·
ETERNAL
·
ENEMY

THE
ETERNAL
ENEMY

Michael
Berlyn

**William Morrow
and Company, Inc.
New York**

Library of Congress Cataloging-in-Publication Data

Berlyn, Michael.
  The eternal enemy.

  I. Title.
PS3552.E72495E8   1990   813'.54   89-13834
ISBN 1-88795-963-3

Printed in the United States of America

First Edition

1 2 3 4 5 6 7 8 9 10

BOOK DESIGN BY RICHARD ORIOLO

AS ALWAYS,
FOR M. M. McCLUNG

Man is nothing more than what he makes himself.
—Jean-Paul Sartre

Part One
MARKOS

1

The grips on the plastic handles were slippery with sweat even though the screamer's air conditioning blasted him. He tried to keep the muscles in his forearms and his hands from cramping—controlling the screamer was a delicate task and any sudden, jerky move could be his last. The screamer continued its level flight, just missing the carpet of treetops two meters below the belly of the craft. He knew the risks he took, flying this low just under the speed of sound, and he knew he had no choice.

If they caught him, there was no telling what they might do. What Van Pelt might do.

He glanced at the rear viewscreen and saw some mendils take to the air, a line almost a kilometer long, filling the sky like a roostertail wake. Their alien bodies disturbed him, spotted and mottled with clashing reds, greens, oranges, and blues, skin stretched so tightly he thought they should burst. And still the sight was more tolerable than looking into Van Pelt's eyes.

He needed to wipe his forehead on his sleeve, to shut his burning eyes for a few moments, to scratch the tip of his nose. He yearned for the massager bunk, the unit that lulled him to sleep each night, deep massaging every muscle in his solid, large frame. He wanted to feel the ground beneath his feet, to have this insane flight over, to be at rest on the planet's surface. To have this whole thing done with, Markos thought, to feel a resolution.

It was stupid to run. Stupid, but necessary, he realized. What other choice was there after what Van Pelt had done?

If there were only some kind of safety, some refuge to which he could flee. Still, he had a goal of sorts—distance between himself and the ship, a large settlement of native sentient creatures, the Habers, in which to hide. If he could manage that, he would have time to plan, to think, to help.

Less than two kilometers ahead the trees ended. He could see the expansive yellow plain stretching out to the towering mountains on the haze-filled horizon.

His fevered hope was to find a village hidden on the plain, sheltered by the high weeds. The Habers would be friendly—they knew nothing else. He could set the screamer down a few kilometers from a settlement and make his exit. Yes. Set it down, then adjust the autopilot for a thirty-second delay, have the screamer take off at full throttle. The empty screamer would do a good enough job until it hit the mountains.

If someone were following him, as he suspected, it would buy him the time he needed.

The forest dwindled, disappeared behind him, becoming a low, solid wall in the rear viewscreen. A tone chimed, synchronized with a flashing red light above the detection screen.

Markos knew what the chase screamer looked like—blue like his own, like all those from the *Paladin*. He had no time to look. This was the horrible confirmation for which he was waiting.

The screamer flew a high course, making it easier for whoever was piloting it to detect his screamer. And Markos knew that if he'd detected the chase ship, the chase ship had detected him.

Markos's mind split between fighting the other screamer and fleeing, dropping even lower, closer to the ground to evade the chase screamer's detection devices.

Markos knew what his mistake had been. He should never have confronted Van Pelt. He should have stayed aboard the *Paladin* and worked from within, talking to the other crew members, showing them how truly insane their captain had become. What kind of xeno-biologist was he? How could he help the Habers now?

He had to clear his mind, make a decision—the right one. Van Pelt had probably sent Wilhelm after him. Wilhelm was the best screamer pilot around, capable of staying with just about any maneuver, and just as afraid of shooting down Markos's screamer as Markos was of shooting down Wilhelm's. So, then, there was little point in climbing and dueling it out up there, high above this alien world.

The handles eased forward as Markos applied slight pressure, praying his hands wouldn't slip. He cursed the designer of the control handles—how stupid to leave the plastic smooth.

As the craft lowered, the high grass seemed to bend to either side of the screamer, and then Markos realized he was too low, just above the tips of the grass. His eyes were wide open, paralyzed by the overwhelming sight of the grass speeding toward him. A few seconds of terror made him force his eyes away, glance at the overhead screens, the detection devices, and let go of the right handle long enough to throw a switch putting an added detection circuit into play.

He knew how important his flight was. If Wilhelm managed to catch him and bring him back, there was no telling what Van Pelt would do. And if Wilhelm caught him, the Habers would most likely be history.

Just the slight contact the crew of the *Paladin* had had with the aliens had triggered off a string of rapid mutations in the Habers. Only their oldest rites were surviving. They had developed sound-speech a few days after the *Paladin* had landed, dropping their method of communicating through prismatic displays of light. If the Habers weren't helped, they would mutate toward more human forms. He knew that as they changed physically, they would change culturally, too.

The readouts on the control panel showed that Wilhelm was almost five kilometers behind, right at the detection limit. With a few lucky maneuvers he could make the needed distance.

The radio chirped repeatedly, distracting Markos, its pulsating sound cutting through his ears. He knew it was Wilhelm, trying to establish contact, an attempt to talk him out of his flight.

Good, he thought. Ignore the signal and concentrate on losing him.

A thump from the bottom of the craft tensed every muscle in his body. At this speed, running into the tops of the wild grass could be fatal. He clenched the handles tightly, easing them back ever so slightly, rising above the grass a little more. A tiny grayish-brown pebble in his path grew to monstrous size in less time than it took him to open his mouth to scream.

He yanked back hard just as the screamer struck the boulder.

The space program had been nothing like what he'd dreamed of as a boy, but that never stopped him from dreaming. Blazing rockets, ray guns strapped to hips clad in silver lamé, a beautiful and competent female copilot beside him, rushing headlong through the Solar System at incomprehensible speeds, dashing from planet to planet to help colonists over mysterious plagues and diseases.

Markos had known the difference between reality and fantasy, had known what the space program was really about when he was five, when the first wave of manned exploratory pods had left the Solar System on their long, solitary journeys.

But he still dreamed.

He'd taken the first battery of tests for NASA 2. He'd filled in answer after answer on the exams. He'd been poked and prodded, and he'd wondered whether or not he was doing the right thing by applying. But what else was there for him? It was as close to his dream as he'd ever get.

His parents were dead, his interactions with both sexes strained, bordering on nonexistent. When he did manage to make a friend, Markos latched onto him as if the person were an object or a possession. He always feared the new friend would leave for parts unknown for some inscrutable reason. And they all fulfilled his fears, never staying long enough to tell him why they left.

He'd had only one relationship with a woman, Theresa, and that had ended when she explained to him, "If I'm in the shower, you want to be there, too. If I'm dreaming, you'll want to get into the dream. Give me some room. You're suffocating me."

He never really understood, so he applied to NASA 2 and prayed they would take him regardless of the realities of deep space. He considered NASA 1 first, but they were limited to projects within the Solar System and overseeing colonization—all mundane chores learned through the training geltanks. NASA 2 was reshaping personalities as well as training minds for their missions, conditioning them to interact on a social and professional level, something that looked extremely attractive to him.

When one of the manned exploratory pods sent back a message from Tau Ceti, NASA 2 moved quickly, starting to build a larger ship to follow up what they thought had to be contact with an alien race.

With Theresa gone, all the Earth held was a slow, boring, lonely life. With NASA 2 he saw the chance to do something, to explore, interact, live.

Live.

He opened his eyes.

A Haber stood a few meters away, watching. It was 120 centimeters high, humanoid, with well-defined features. The outermost layer of skin on its face was transparent; the upper portion revealed small beads of organic crystals, clustered like clear pomegranate seeds, traced by a thin network of connecting fibers. There were fewer crystals in the Haber's face than he'd expected—most probably another mutation toward sound-speech, away from cold-light generation.

It had small hands, complete with opposable thumbs and jointed, stubby fingers. More mutations. Its body was covered with a gray, skinlike layer, an integral part of the creature. From its small size, Markos figured it was in or nearing its final cycle, something that made little sense to him.

The *Paladin* hadn't been on this planet long enough for a mutated Haber to be this old.

They were alone in the darkened room with walls of carved stone. There was a faint musty smell in the air. Markos did his best to ignore the odd, painful jolts shooting through his body as he tried to push himself up into a sitting position. His head pounded and the room spun. He fell back to the bed of native grass and tried to orient himself, tried to overcome the nausea. From what he could make out, they were in an underground cavern or a cave.

He concentrated, trying to remember where he was, where the Haber had come from, why he felt ill. He closed his eyes and the pain increased. An image of an immense figure took shape in his mind, towering over him, the image and thoughts temporarily blocking out the physical pain.

It was Van Pelt.

The pain rushed back in a wave.

He could see the way Van Pelt had paced before the whole crew, hands clenching and unclenching behind his back. His sandy hair was long and shaggy, unlike the shorter, almost military style he'd worn over most of their journey. The top two buttons on his gray worksuit were open, his feet bare, his gray eyes sunken, rimmed with black circles.

"I need more information before I reach a decision," Van Pelt said.

The crew remained silent. They had quickly learned not to offer information or opinions anymore. Markos had seen Van Pelt's degeneration start while they were still orbiting Gandji. The artifact had been there, just as the pod had reported, and Van Pelt had started to change. The way he pinched his bottom lip when deep in thought, the way he jiggled his foot when he crossed his legs, the way he cracked his neck by pivoting it around and around—his mannerisms seemed to be taking him over, as if he were fighting some inner battle and losing.

The pressure on Van Pelt had increased after they'd landed and encountered some of the Habers. Markos had led the examination of the enigmatic creatures, and with every new discovery he related to Van Pelt, Van Pelt only seemed to get more and more upset.

Only one other ship had made contact with the Habers, and that contact had occurred a long time ago. The manned pod had never returned to Earth and had never sent a second message.

"Well? Anybody?"

Still nothing.

Van Pelt had grown more haggard, had aged too quickly even though he had received the geltank treatments.

"Markos? You're the closest thing to an expert we've got. What about these creatures? What are our real chances?"

All eyes turned to Markos. He licked his lips, glanced at Van Pelt's wild eyes, then at the deck. This was insane. "Well, Captain, we're, uhm . . . we're not really in a serious situation. The Habers pose no threat to us at all. They don't have the technology that could have put that artifact in space around this star—"

"A threat!" Van Pelt said.

"No, Captain, *no* threat. They're more peaceful in their philosophy, though definitely human in intelligence."

"So you say, Markos. So you say. But you still haven't answered. Just what are our chances?"

"I'm not sure I understand," Markos said, stalling, trying to formulate the safest way possible to answer.

"Will they fight? Yes or no? It's that simple. Your opinion?"

Will they? From everything Markos knew of the race, the Habers would never fight. Say yes, he told himself. Say yes, and maybe Van Pelt will fear a real confrontation, come to his senses, reestablish contact with NASA 2, report what he's discovered. Maybe he'll drop this ridiculous plan and follow procedures. But then again, he might not. He's strange enough to try anything. Strange enough to use the slightest hint of a threat as a justification for wiping them out. They have no weapons and they wouldn't know how to use them if we gave them some. If I tell him they won't fight, he might spare them. He might stop seeing them as a threat.

"Well?" Van Pelt demanded.

"I'm not sure," he said.

A gleam lit Van Pelt's eyes as he stopped pacing and stared at Markos. "Then they won't fight?"

"There's no way to be sure."

"Not sure?"

Markos shrugged. "They're Habers, Captain—not people."

"Not sure? You're the one who's spent the most time with them, dragging them in and out of the lab, running tests, wasting our resources on these things, these creatures. Don't you realize what you've done? You've shown them the layout of our ship. We're in constant danger now. There's no telling when the attack will come."

Only because it somehow fits your fears, Markos thought. Only because it makes it easier for you. You won't have to deal with these creatures.

"Well? What about the rest of you?" Van Pelt asked. "With Markos leading the campaign—he should be able to whip up something horrible and appropriate—we can handle them easily."

A vote followed, a mockery, a sham ruled by their fear of Van Pelt's insanity. Everyone knew why the vote was requested: Van Pelt could see which crew members bore watching. Markos proved to be the only one foolish enough to vote against Van Pelt. If the others had stood up to him, had united against his plan, he could have been handled. NASA 2's training had proven out—the psychologists had programmed the xenobiologist to feel for the creatures, while the crew was programmed to care about getting back, getting on with it, following the Captain's orders. Sure, Markos thought, only what happened to the Captain's programming?

No one mentioned Markos's having taken a stand. No one went out of his way to avoid him, but no one talked to Markos unless he'd been addressed. No one was willing to take the chance.

Markos's duties increased in quantity and decreased in quality; he had to stand additional long, boring watches. What little free time his duties allowed was spent in the bunk massager as he attempted to sleep. He never had time for the geltanks.

Van Pelt got stranger as the first months on Gandji passed. He seemed plagued by doubts and uncertainty about the Habers but for one point: He was certain they posed a real threat to Mankind. The crew walked on tiptoes, staying as far out of Van Pelt's way as possible, while Cathy Straka, the only other person with xenobiology training, made extremely slow progress carrying out Van Pelt's plan.

Markos was kept away, but he knew what was going on. A

biological solution was much preferred by Van Pelt. Not even he was insane enough to try to burn the entire race out of existence. Engineering a little virus, one that would multiply quickly and easily, was a much easier and cleaner way of handling "the problem," as Van Pelt called it.

Straka knew enough about the Habers' biology to attempt a mass genocide. She had been there for most of the examinations and had witnessed them reproducing. Three Habers were required for mating—there were no real sexes until mating had begun. One Haber in the group performed as a flow-bridge. The flow-bridge was the most delicate and important of the three during mating. The two Habers would stand on either side of the neuter Haber and establish physical contact with it. Chemical components and genetic materials flowed from the two Habers by an osmoticlike pressure and met in the flow-bridge, mingling, mixing together. From what Markos could surmise by viewing the process through every instrument available and studying the holograms he made, the central Haber, the flow-bridge, could then consciously alter the genetic material, make any genetic-engineering changes it felt were necessary, then push the altered, fertile materials back into the other two Habers. Gestation was fairly quick—three months—and the two impregnated Habers gave birth to between one and three offspring each.

Markos knew that damaging the chain at its middle point, the Haber acting as flow-bridge, could wipe out the entire race. But he also realized they were mutating rapidly and he hoped their system of reproduction might be changed by the time Van Pelt got his plan into motion.

The following day, while Markos was standing watch, he spotted a group of first-cycle Habers, an odd combination of youthful bodies and graceful movements. Van Pelt appeared by his side, weapon in hand.

"Saw them approaching on the screens."

Markos nodded. "Just a young group, curious about us."

"You're mistaken. Ask Straka. She'll tell you this is a scouting party, no doubt carrying concealed weapons."

Markos was about to laugh at the Captain's attempt at humor when he saw Van Pelt raise his weapon to the firing position.

"They're not armed!" Markos said.

"Sure they are. See the one on the end there?" he asked, flicking the weapon toward it.

Markos looked but saw nothing irregular.

"Not only are they armed, but they're closing in on us."

Van Pelt's weapon emitted a bright, tight beam of emerald light, and the Habers toppled to the ground, sliced in half one by one, in a few horrifying instants. The grass in the area smoldered. Van Pelt returned to the ship as the breeze carried the scent of charred meat to Markos's nostrils.

He was sick to his stomach.

There had been talk, rumors, probably started by Van Pelt, of taking over and exploiting the planet once the Habers were gone. He'd made noises about cutting in all the crew members for shares. Markos no longer cared if the rumors were true. He'd seen enough to know Van Pelt meant business. He threw down his weapon and ran for one of the screamers, then headed for the mountains at top speed.

And then Markos remembered the rest and sat up on the bed in the cavern. Memories rushed back in one tremendous, painful surge —the boulder! The impact and explosion, then blackness. But he couldn't have survived that crash.

He started to tremble.

"What's—" he started to ask but stopped when he heard his own voice. It was a rough, gravelly rasp—bubbling and liquid, totally different from what his voice should have been. He was shocked, and a hot flash, like a river of molten metal, ran diagonally through his chest.

He looked at his hands. They were different too. Deformed. Ugly. Wrinkled and cracked and the wrong kind of skin and mottled and spotted with reds, greens, and oranges and blues and he could see right through the skin and into his arms and legs and chest.

He screamed a frothing, gargled, piteous wail.

2.

Markos waited. It was what he did best. He figured that if there were ever prizes awarded for having the most patience, he would probably win one. Waiting. That was all NASA 2 was about.

They'd told him he would get a chance to meet alien creatures. They told him he would get the chance to fly in the first and only faster-than-light ship ever developed. They told him he could go to Tau Ceti and find out what happened to that missing guy, the one who disappeared in that pod.

But all they had done so far was stick Markos in a geltank and have their computers throw all different kinds of imaginary aliens at him to see if he were xenophobic.

He sat on the edge of his bunk, looking across the small room at Jackson, one of the others "handpicked" to make the trip on the *Paladin*. How do you select people to man a ship that might blow up the instant the f-t-l drive is engaged? Do you pick expendable people? Or qualified ones? And what if they don't come back?

Markos picked up the magazine he'd placed on the bedstand, the one he'd bought in the spaceport on Earth. The voice chips printed on the magazine's cover had said something that caught his attention, something about an exposé and NASA 2. It was some fifty years after the pod had left, but the arrival of the telemetered information from the pod made this guy, Jacob Galley, news again. It also implied that the NASA 2 selection criteria were not exactly what might be expected.

Markos read it. . . .

Jacob Galley started life like most city children, but somewhere in the process of personality development, something special happened. His parents had always considered themselves lucky to be able to afford a private apartment in a good neighborhood, even though they earned the right by each working two jobs. The other four families who lived in the apartment considered themselves equally fortunate. Fifteen people shared meals, entertainment, and living space in a happy communal spirit until Jacob was four.

It started innocently enough. Jacob took to hiding under the furniture instead of playing in the common areas, locked in his own little world. And there were times he would sit in dark closets, huddled in a corner, eyes closed. Everyone thought it a little strange but since his odd behavior violated no laws, no formal complaints were registered. If his parents had had the extra money, they could have sent him to a clinic to be cured, but the extra money was simply never there.

As he grew, he went to school like all other children. He had a good time there, sitting in his private cubicle, headset plugged into the teacher, absorbing knowledge and developing understanding. He stayed later than most children, in no rush to get home to spend time with his extended family. By the time he reached his teens, Jacob's personality was set.

He had developed into a loner, and yet people liked him well enough. He was an attractive young man with a genuine, disarming smile, soft-spoken and intelligent. He just didn't socialize well. He graduated a chemical engi-

neer, near the top of his class, and his parents were proud. The fourteen other people he lived with were proud, too, and they all attended his graduation. His real problems started after he left school, though.

Work didn't afford him the time or opportunity for privacy, and his living quarters were even more crowded and difficult for him than his family's apartment had been. His desire for solitude was interpreted as unhappiness by the people he lived with and the people he worked with. Each group did its best to pull him out of his quiet retreats into their own realities. Jacob appreciated their well-meaning intentions and realized he was fighting a losing battle.

When the company for which he worked landed a contract with the government, the opportunity for a transfer to the space colony arose. He was well qualified for the job, and the people he worked with recommended his transfer with great enthusiasm thinking it was a solution to the problem of how to deal with him. His eagerness to go into space was due solely to the living arrangements aboard the colony—he would have to share his living quarters with only three other people.

While Jacob lived his quiet life, NASA 2 was created. NASA had grown too large to be properly managed; their responsibilities included the space colony, attempts to mine asteroids, and other projects limited to the Solar System. NASA 2 was formed to explore deep space, to venture out beyond the gravitational field of Sol and determine if there really was any life out there.

NASA 2 searched for two years and three months until they found just the right people to man their deep-space probes. The psychologists had designed a model of the perfect personality, a personality capable of handling the elastic years of solitude, the enforced sense of mission, and the tremendous responsibility that went along with the mission's potential.

When they met Jacob Galley, they knew they had a potential match.

He had been working on board the space colony. He was found hiding in the lower levels, cramped into a tiny locker, when his roommates reported him missing. The doctors who examined him saw that his disorder was easily treated and filed a standard fitness report. NASA saw the report and brought it to the attention of NASA 2.

NASA 2 ordered a few intensive treatments in the geltanks. Their doctors regressed him, unwound his experiences, then regressed him some more, but when they brought him forward, they eliminated the negative associations of *being a loner, eliminated the social stigma. The doctors took care to keep the things that made Jacob different.*

While he was in the geltank, completely submerged in the fluid vat, the psychologists modified him to bring his personality closer to the ideal. They provided him with a reinforced sense of self-importance and memories of people, places, and things that had never existed for him, experiences that would have been impossible for him but necessary to survive the empty years that lay ahead.

There were lies, false memories of training sessions in NASA 2's non-existent underground complex on the Moon. There was a memory of a man created within Jacob, a Brian Taggert, a man who was Jacob's roommate in this fiction the psychologists wove. There were interactions with people of all nationalities, sexes, and physical abnormalities added to his memory. There was a theoretical and practical knowledge and understanding of all human language, a knowledge burned into his synaptical connections. In the years of solitude Jacob was submerged in the ship's geltank, the ship could use these memories to stimulate him, to ward off the inevitable return of solitude.

By the time they were finished with Jacob, his new memories fit him comfortably. When he stepped out of the training geltank, he felt as if he were the same person he'd always been.

Jacob Galley was perfect for the mission NASA 2 needed done, for the years of solitude and enforced self-discipline.

Six sectors of space demanded exploration and explorers. There were planetary bodies circling nearby stars, and these needed to be visited by a human being. The stars were all neighbors: Tau Ceti, Alpha Centauri A and B, Epsilon Eridani, 61 Cygni A, 61 Cygni B, and Epsilon Indi. The drive units NASA 2 had developed were capable of reaching the farthest of these, capable of speeds slightly in excess of 0.25 c, 46,500 miles per second. The pods would accelerate until this speed was achieved and then "coast" until arrival. The trip to Tau Ceti could be made in under fifty years. Everything was falling into place for NASA 2—exploring the neighboring stars with a human being along for the ride, just in case.

Just in case the exploratory pod ran across something the instruments might not be able to interpret properly, just in case immediate action was called for, just in case the pod ran across something unexpected, something for which NASA 2 hoped and prayed, Jacob Galley would be there.

They were prepared for this eventuality. NASA 2 left little to chance, least of all Jacob Galley.

If contact were established, the ship would activate a sequence and Jacob would lose some of the artificially layered personality the psychologists and geltank had provided. After all, they didn't want an emissary of Earth to appear more alien than any life-form he might run across. Like a clockwork mechanism, like a posthypnotic suggestion, Jacob was two people—one who could deal with the immense distances and time of the trip, the other one waiting, invisible until needed.

Jacob and five others like him left. Only five of the six returned, and Jacob was not one of them. . . .

Markos put the dramatized version of Galley's biography aside and picked up the NASA 2 "official" transcription. NASA 2 would not say anything regarding the Galley biography, and after reading it, Markos felt he understood why. It didn't make them look too good at all, and it made Galley look a little stranger than he probably was.

He picked up the report by his bedstand. It was titled "Transcription and Interpretation of Telemetered Data from Pod 6, Manned by Jacob Galley, Assumed Lost."

"We're here," Galley said. (Transmissions reveal the strain in his voice.)

"Approaching, anyway, but there is more," the ship said.

"More what?" (Fear audible in Galley's voice.) *"Increase magnification,"* Galley said.

"Magnification is logarithmic and at maximum," it said.

"It looks like a planet—the one we've been looking for?"

"It is. If this were all there were to it, I wouldn't have left you in the tank. There is more."

"More what? More planets?"

"Yes, there are more planets. But there is also a small body, well under planetary mass, traveling the exact orbit of the planet, forty-five degrees above the ecliptic."

"Give me visual confirmation," Galley said.

(A commanding tone could be detected in his voice at this point.

His entire personality firmed, a result of the geltank training and imprinting.)

"Impossible. Albedo is less than ten percent, and at this distance, resolution from background radiation is impossible."

*"Graphics, then. Give me some*thing!*"*

"Screen three," it said.

(Telemetered data showed that the third screen held a computer graphic of a large disk, Tau Ceti, and a smaller disk toward the right edge, the planet. Above the graphic of the planet was a point of light, surrounded by a circle.)

"The object in question is within the circle. Scale is nonrepresentational."

"What do you make of it?" Jacob asked.

"It is one of two things: an astronomical anomaly in direct contradiction to all presently accepted models for solar system evolution, or it is an artifact of non-Terran origin."

"Which do you think?"

"Be serious. The odds against it being a natural phenomenon are high enough to rule that out as a possibility."

"Then why did you keep me in the tank? I should have been out here the second the object was spotted."

"I thought you enjoyed spending time in the tank," the ship said. *"You have always argued for more time and more frequent immersions."*

"That's irrelevant, and you know it." (An audible sigh, let out slowly.) *"Forget it. Have you gathered any data on the planet yet?"*

"Yes. We are still too far away for our more sensitive analysis equipment to be effective, so whatever data I have are incomplete. Screen four."

(Preliminary report on the planet scrolled on screen four. Most of the spaces for information had "UNKN" in place of numbers. The planet was 0.92 Earth mass, rotated every 21 hours, and was just under 0.79 AUs from Tau Ceti. The planet's albedo was 0.32. From the raw data the ship telemetered, the planet seems Terran enough.)

"An additional piece of pertinent data," the ship said.

"What is it?"

"The smaller body is sending a beam of coherent green light to the planet's surface."

(This rules out the natural-phenomenon theory proposed by the antiexploration and antiterraforming lobbies. Coherent light doesn't beam down to a planet's surface in nature. This was sufficient evidence to get funding for the *Paladin* expedition.)

"*It appears as if we've activated some sort of warning system,*" the ship said.

"*Possibly. Recommendations?*"

"*None,*" it said.

"*You sure are a lot of help when you want to be,*" Jacob said.

"*As you've been over the last four decades,*" the ship said.

"*More information. Just give me more information. I've got to know what's going on. You're not telling me much of anything.*"

"*I do what I can. I have very little data on which to base recommendations or draw conclusions.*"

"*What makes you think it's an early-warning system? Couldn't it be a ship?*"

"*You asked for conclusions based on raw data. The primary consideration used was our approach. We have entered the Tau Ceti system and are being considerably influenced by Tau Ceti's gravity well. As soon as this influence was significant, the green light appeared.*"

(This reasoning is sound.)

"*With our present position, course, and speed, you have under two hours to make your decision,*" the ship said.

"*I know.*"

"*Have you decided, then?*"

"*Two hours,*" Jacob said. "*You said so yourself. Don't push me or I'll pull your plug.*"

"*You can't.*"

"*Don't tempt me. If I can't, I'll still try, and probably end up doing irreparable damage.*"

"*One hour, fifty-nine minutes, thirty-five seconds.*"

"*Stop the countdown. Just tell me how much time is left every fifteen minutes.*"

(Galley faced the following decisions: return to Earth, or alter his course. The pods were designed to have some advanced science contact them—not to initiate contact, so they were limited in fuel. This decision to limit fuel enabled us to get these exploratory missions funded. Actually there was most probably enough fuel for deceleration into a stable orbit around Tau Ceti and for limited course corrections when reentering our Solar System. But there was a limit to the fuel, and that put a definite limit on the number of course corrections available, and the psychologists stressed the importance of contact. We stacked the odds in favor of his deciding to opt for contact.

If he chose to ignore the possible contact and simply waited another forty-odd years until the pod reentered the Solar System, he would have a safe amount of fuel to adjust his angle of entry and decelerate into a stable orbit around Sol. He would be picked up by a NASA 1 shuttle.

At this point the lights, instruments, and life-support systems shut down for two seconds. End of first telemetry and transcription.)

"How many times you gonna read that?" Jackson asked.

"Huh?" Markos asked, looking up from the papers. "What?"

"I asked how many times you were gonna read that stupid thing. Nothing changes in there, does it? It's not one of those interactive articles."

Markos shook his head. "That's not the point," he said. "I read it so I can understand what this guy went through, what he ran into. Maybe it'll help when *we* get there."

"*If* we get there, you mean."

"Come on, man. It's not that risky."

"Yeah? Then where *is* this guy? How come he never came back?"

"I don't know," Markos said. "That's what we're going there to find out."

Markos sighed and put the transcription on his nightstand. The guy in the pod, Jacob Galley, had gone a little around the bend. Markos slipped his hands behind his head to stare at the ceiling. Perhaps some of the answers of what really happened to the pod, why it was the only one not to return, would appear there, written in the fused, dull plastic.

"I hear Van Pelt's in the tank now," Jackson said.

"Yeah. Better him than me," Markos said. "I didn't test out as a leader, so I don't have to worry about that."

"You and me both, man. You hear where they found him?"

"I heard. You know the name of the prison?"

Jackson smiled. "Some maximum-security place. That's all I know. That's all he'd say."

"Straka said that Van Pelt's a psychopath. A real criminal genius."

"If he makes it out of that tank, he'll be normal enough," Jackson said.

Markos shook his head, then rolled onto his side so that he could face Jackson. For some reason the tall black man looked even taller when lying down. "You hear how many they carted out of there in a straitjacket?"

"I heard seven so far."

"Get serious, man. Two or three, tops," Markos said.

"That's not what Straka says."

"Don't listen to her. She has a flair for the dramatic."

Jackson laughed. "You can still go for the testing, become a captain of the first f-t-l ship ever."

"Yeah, I could. I could also be number eight on the fried-brain list."

Jackson laughed again.

But Markos hadn't really meant it as a joke. He thought about Van Pelt, a nice enough guy, considering, submerged within the gel-tank, wired up to a couple of computers, all to find out whether he could withstand the pressures of command. The programs were designed to put you through your paces, and the biofeedback loops made everything seem real enough. When Markos had gone through the xenobiological training procedures, such as they were, he could have sworn he'd actually met and talked to the ridiculous creatures the computers had summoned up. Of course, since no one had ever met an alien creature or even confirmed any alien creature's existence, the training was all pretty fictional in nature.

He wondered what kind of mind trips they were putting Van Pelt through. If the guy was really that smart and that good a leader, then maybe they could fix what made him a psycho. Still, Markos figured, they might end up doing him more harm than good. He was glad he wasn't a shrink and didn't have to deal with those kinds of problems. All he had to do was sit and wait for the rest of the crew to be selected. And after the *Paladin* left the Solar System, all he'd have to do was wait, take orders, and do what was expected. Which was probably wait.

He wasn't a leader, and he didn't need to be one. Markos knew how to wait.

3.

The Haber stood a few meters away, waiting, watching.

Markos rose unsteadily to his feet, felt stabs of needle-sharp pain running through the soles of his feet, and advanced on the Haber. Immediately its face emitted pulsating combinations of colors. The patterns were organized and geometric, each pulse with its own color scheme and rhythm. Points of light within the Haber's face sparkled, danced before Markos's eyes in a rapturous display. He stood transfixed, gently swaying in time to the light pulses. The rhythms were soothing and hypnotic, but more importantly, draining away the pain and agony.

The Haber pointed to the bed of grass.

Still staring at its face, Markos backed up and sat on the bed. His body still twitched as its alien biology tried to balance itself.

"What's ... going ... on?" he asked, trying to ignore the vile sounds he made, but not succeeding.

"You died and then we, we brought you back."

Brought back? Back to life?

Markos said nothing. A diagonal slash of heat ran through his chest. What was there to say? It was bad enough thinking it, fearing it, seeing it as the only possible answer for what had happened, but it was another thing to hear it spoken aloud, to have his worst fears confirmed.

Dead.

Dead, but alive again—an accomplishment beyond Terran technology. His life had been extended before the journey; due to the prolonging effects of the geltank, he could have lived for centuries, barring accidental death. But piecing together a human being, a body, a corpse, after it had smashed into a boulder at the speed of sound? Impossible. If there hadn't been an explosion—his body jerked and spasmed—he should have been nothing more than protoplasmic goop.

"How?" Markos demanded. He had to shut his mouth with his hand. For some reason it didn't close on its own that time.

"It was not that difficult for us, us to do. The form of a mendil supplied us, us with some of the needed materials for your new body. Your skin had burned off ..."

A mendil? One of those obscene birdlike creatures? He thought he shuddered at the thought, but then realized his body did something else—his palms felt cold. He shook his head to try to think this insanity through. How could the Habers do that? He'd never seen any Haber technology. But if the artifact existed, which it did, then there could have been some technology hidden somewhere.

"I can't believe you," Markos said, wincing at the sound of his voice. "It's your speech and what your eyes did that's convinced me. I know I haven't really changed at all."

"No," the Haber said.

"Then where are your machines? Your instruments?" he shouted.

"They are here, all around us, us and here," the Haber said, touching its chest, "within us, us."

"I don't see anything," Markos said.

"You will. As your eyes develop, you will see more."

"Let me touch something, then. Hold some of your instruments out for me to feel."

"No," the Haber said. "They do not exist in that physical sense. They do exist, though, as a part of us, us. As we, we have learned by touching and helping you, just as we, we touched and helped another of your kind many years ago, your life is based on a single molecule, a chain that is what you are. And you are what it is."

"DNA," Markos said.

"All life on our, our planet is based on a different complex molecule and we, we can mold and shape life through it. The mendil supplied some of its pieces, as did some molecules from your old body, as did some other life-forms, all evolved from the same source, the same molecule as yours. Interesting that one of our own volunteered to have his, his base molecule altered to reflect yours and supply you with your basic form."

"I don't believe this. This has to be some kind of trick."

"You as well as we, we remember what has happened to you. You abandoned your friends to help us, us."

Markos's eyes stung and he found it harder and harder to follow what the Haber was talking about. Something was happening to him physically, bathing him in chemicals that didn't quite fit together in a way he could easily deal with. Disordered thoughts raced through his mind, mixing pain with relief, curiosity with detachment, reality with paranoid fantasies. For all he knew, he could be in a geltank on board the *Paladin*, with mind-altering chemicals mixed in with the gel. His body twitched, spasmed, then was still.

"If I did die, then why did you bring me back?"

A short prismatic flash of blue, softened and textured by surrounding, complementary colors, pulsed through the Haber's face. "Do you want me, me to reverse the process? Would you prefer being as you were? Dead? Eternally quiet?"

Markos swallowed and stared at the dirt floor.

"It would be no difficulty," the Haber said. "The mendil would be happy to get back its form, as would the other, other. Only it seemed so important to you—this living and helping. I, I thought you would have been pleased."

Pleased? Pleased? If it weren't so revolting, Markos might have laughed. If he could still laugh. A patchwork creature—that's what he was now, where all the pain in this . . . body came from. He would have been better off dead and forgotten, his atoms mingled with the soil of Gandji, fertilizer for the plants, food for the alien worms. He was alive. But in this body, that meant almost nothing.

He couldn't go back to the ship now, even if he wanted to. Not like this. Van Pelt would probably have him shot on sight as a Haber, a new and dangerous mutation. Markos's life work was finished. No more alien cultures to observe, no more watching Van Pelt slip over the edge of reason, no more all-night sessions with Straka and Wilhelm trying to figure out similarities and differences between Terran and Haber cultures. No more wrestling with his conscience over disrupting an alien civilization.

Earth held nothing for him—it never had—and yet he felt a loss, knowing he could never go back, never interact with people again. He was, in the true sense of the word, dead. All the things he'd ever held important were now only memories.

And what the hell was he good for now? An amusement for the aliens? A horrible freak show for the Terrans?

"The form I'm in doesn't please me," he said, trying to sound calm, in control.

"I, I don't understand. Forms are mutable, are they not? You live now, do you not? Things change. What else matters?"

What else matters? What was the use in trying to explain it? It would be like trying to explain piety to a hedonist, space travel to a slug. The Habers, as well as himself, were finished. It was over. Van Pelt would act as soon as Straka came up with the answer to blocking the flow-bridge, and they'd wipe the planet clean of Habers. He and the crew would carve out a fortune by destroying Gandji. And Van Pelt would be in charge of the exploitation; whatever Gandji offered that could be of use to Terra and her colonies would pass under his watchful eyes. A finder's fee, NASA 2 had called it.

He found it ironic that he would still be around, alive, to witness the end.

Markos sat on a soft cushion of flattened-down grass watching the semicircle of Habers watch him. Parts of his body burned with heat that should have blistered his leathery skin, while other parts of his body burned with cutting frostbite. A section of his abdomen right below skin level itched incessantly; scratching it did no good. Tiny, sharp, pinpricks of pain covered the rest of his body like a thorny blanket, throbbing with each erratic, irregular beat of his nonhuman heart.

Breathing was no longer an automatic reflex; his breaths were shallow, sometimes within seconds of each other, sometimes long minutes apart. Each inhalation with its new, odd smells and sensations made him instantly aware of the soil, the grass, and himself. Even the air tasted different, a strange, almost cloying mixture of sweetness and spice, stimulating him, heightening what little appreciation for Gandji he could muster.

His eyes had changed, too; despite their constant irritation, their burning and itching, they revealed inexplicable shifts in colors and forms that were distracting in a new, semipleasant way. The Habers, their deceptively simple dwellings, and the surrounding wall of waving grass exposed visual patterns, an organic geometry, a solid foundation for his new view of the universe.

He was adjusting to his new body slowly, painfully, doing his best to accept the repulsive transformation. Less than a man, less than a Haber. A freak to both civilizations. His physique was that of a Haber—humanoid enough—but his skin was a horrifying tapestry of mendil and haber flesh. The *Paladin*'s crew was trained by the geltanks to deal with all the life-forms the psychologists at NASA 2 could create. Some had been beautiful, some had been ugly, and all had been imaginary. Markos knew that no preparation would be good enough for the crew to handle seeing him. The vestiges of his human self added horror to his form, the horror any Terran might feel when the jolt of recognition hit—*that thing had once been human*. Interacting on a one-to-one level would be impossible.

And what about the Habers? Were they cringing beneath their inscrutable faces? What did they expect from him?

"What are you staring at?" he asked in his liquid voice.

A Haber, old and very small, flashed a reply. The order and color of light he generated with the beads of his eyes made Markos uncomfortable. They were different from any he'd seen before.

A metallic taste bit his tongue. "Can't you talk, for God's sake?"

"I, I can," the old Haber said.

The metallic taste increased as a pounding started in his head. "Tell me what you're staring at."

The Haber said nothing.

"Speak, dammit. Please speak."

"I, I will speak, but only to explain. Speaking takes too much energy," the old Haber said. "It is easier for the young, for those of us, us born changed. I, I am trying to prepare for death—not for communication."

"What did you say with your eyes? Tell me," Markos asked.

"I, I said to be still. Death will come soon enough."

Markos spat the metallic taste to the gray-brown earth before him, then glared at the old Haber with searing eyes. "Sooner than you think, old one. You creatures make me ill. Have you got any idea about what's happening?"

"We, we are aware," one of the young ones said. "When you were changed, we, we learned what might happen."

"And you sit here, waiting for the end?"

"Yes."

"Why?"

Silence.

"Why don't you *do* something?"

"What is there to do that hasn't already been done?" the young one asked. "Would you have us, us march on your ship? Touch and change the crew? We, we could not. We, we understand change and how to accept it.

"Change," the Haber said, "is as real and as important as life, as death. Things will never be the same, but they will continue. Even if we, we are not there to watch."

In unison the group of Habers flashed a pulse of red through the area around their eyes, a sign of agreement and support. Markos shook his head. These creatures were no more than ambulatory vegetables. He felt cheated, robbed of the things he'd held important—ideals, principles, and basic rights for which he'd been willing to sacrifice himself. They wouldn't fight. Not for themselves, their civilization, their planet. They couldn't do a thing to stop Van Pelt and had killed Markos's chances of dealing with the Captain. And this was the race of sentient beings for which he'd given his life.

By trying to help these creatures he'd been pursued to a violent death, brought back to life in a patchwork, crippled body, and put on the sidelines to watch and wait. If they'd left him dead, he could have died knowing he'd tried to help, and died a man, not a ... a ... thing. What was left for him? Sit and watch their death songs? Watch them meditate their way down to zero energy consumption, to total immobility, to death?

"There's something we can do," Markos said, "but you don't care enough to do it. And since you don't care, I don't care." He realized he couldn't speak without consciously breathing. He forced in a breath. "I was wrong in thinking of you as having some human qualities. There are fewer similarities between our races than I thought. I don't think I want to help you." He sighed, but it sounded like air bubbling up in a pot of boiling metal.

"But you have," the young one said.

They pulsed a flash of red in unison. He realized he had no eyelids.

"We, we would not have this any other way," the old one said.

They sat in silence. Markos tasted the air, felt the life and decay in the soil beneath him. The Habers drifted off into meditation, their breathing spaced by minutes. Markos watched with aching eyes, trying to understand.

He pushed himself up, turned his back on the quiescent aliens, and plunged into the field of high, wild grass. He had taken just two steps when the stalks and blades of grass around him dully reflected light from an intricate light-speech that was going on in the settlement just a few meters behind. Markos watched the colors; with new, heightened capacities, even in their dulled, reflected hues, they were beautiful and hypnotic. He realized they had to be arguing, discussing some important point; he had no idea how he knew that, or what the discussion was about.

The grass around him suddenly changed, showing reflected red light.

The Habers had reached a decision.

He walked slowly, aimlessly over the plain, following snaking paths, stumbling across old, abandoned Haber settlements. He tried to adjust to his new form both physically and mentally. He found he lacked two familiar, human drives: hunger and sex.

In his altered body eating was unnecessary. Gandji's native life was similar to most Terran-based life in that eating was required. The Habers, though, ingested food only while in their first cycle, converting it to a complex storage molecule, a molecule that made the human fat molecule seem like a simple, small, volatile storage system prone to flash burning. After the first cycle a Haber never ate. Eating would prolong his life. His final cycle was spent in quiet atonement for ever having eaten living things.

By comparing his size and general shape to individual Habers, Markos figured he was just out of the first cycle and could go without eating for about twenty-five years. Any food he chose to eat would increase his physical size and add years onto his lifespan. He had no idea how the prior geltank treatments would affect his aging, and he had no desire, physically or mentally, to eat.

Sex as he had known it was impossible in this form.

He had walked about twenty-five or thirty kilometers and was exhausted. He found a smooth, flat stone to use as a seat. As soon as he sat, his breathing shifted to regular, deep breaths, providing his body with the necessary oxygen for metabolizing its stored food.

The body was disconcerting and uncomfortable, not at all designed for physical exercise, stress, or abuse. He silently cursed the Habers; if they'd used half a brain, they would have given him a better body. Or left him dead.

A glint of sunlight off polished metal near the horizon caught his eye. A screamer, making its low, swift passage. Van Pelt was up to something. Maybe Straka had already come up with the key to the flow-bridge problem.

He tried to ignore his rising curiosity, telling himself that the Habers knew and didn't care, Van Pelt knew and didn't care, so he shouldn't care either. Neither civilization wanted his interference—the Terrans had taught him the price of caring, and the Habers had taught him its futility.

The screamer disappeared in the distance, its howl finally fading from his ears. Markos felt a chill run through him, a bone-jarring spasm that sent him into paroxysms of pain. He fought to stand, not yet fully recovered from the expenditure of energy spent on the long, rambling walk, and instantly realized his mistake. His body went suddenly rigid, then relaxed. A series of prickly waves rushed over him right below his skin. He felt ill and confused, worse than ever before, and his mind went blank.

He felt weaker—too weak to stand, and pitched forward, falling to his hands and knees. He lacked the strength to support himself and collapsed facedown on the ground. Thought returned, his mind racing with thousands of thought fragments, skeletons of ideas, glimmerings of new concepts, none of which would slow enough to gel, to coalesce into a unified whole, a complete system of thought.

Finally, three hours later, his strength returned as suddenly as it had fled. He glanced upward, scanning the light-blue sky for another screamer, and saw only clouds. Clouds in a blue sky, he thought. So much like Terra, so teeming with life. And yet the natives were far removed from their Terran counterparts. He hadn't truly realized that before; each time he felt he'd had a grip on the Habers' culture, he'd been wrong. He'd understood only in Terran terms, drawing over-simplified analogies, not taking the culture as a truly alien system.

But it hadn't been so with Van Pelt or Straka. They'd both known, had been quick to see the potential of Gandji and the differences of the Habers. And they were all bothered by the same point —if the artifact, flashing that green beacon, had been put into space by these creatures, then where was their technology? And what had happened to the manned pod? Why hadn't it sent a second signal? Why hadn't it returned to Earth?

With the way NASA 2's charter was worded, even with its altruistic, egalitarian ideals, Van Pelt was well within his rights to wipe Gandji clean of all life that threatened Mankind's existence.

Markos figured that Van Pelt had snapped before the *Paladin* had landed. He'd been beside Markos when they met the Habers for the first time and acted extremely jittery around them. Van Pelt had seen what their eyes could do, the way they entranced and enraptured with their eyes.

Markos realized he'd started walking again, but this time without the slow, aimless steps that had led him here. The Habers didn't want his help. They didn't deserve his help.

But they were going to get it.

4.

One step at a time, Markos told himself. Ignore the pain and just keep walking.

Every time his right foot made contact with the ground, the back of his leg spasmed. When he put weight on it, completing his step, his hip felt as if its ball-and-socket joint was lined with thousands of shards of broken glass. His left leg provided a different experience. With weight on it the sole of his left foot felt as if it were being punctured by tiny nails, similar to the way it had when his foot had fallen asleep in his old body. His left knee seemed to lack any lubricating fluid or bursa, and each time it bent, slivers of pain shot through the joint.

Still he walked. At least he had somewhere to go. He didn't

know what he would do when he got there, what he would say to his old crewmates or to Van Pelt, but he knew he had to go back to the *Paladin*, back to where it had all started.

He had to stop every few minutes to let the pain abate. The constant irritation of the pain and fatigue never fell into the background while he walked, and that made it difficult for him to think about anything beyond the immediate goal of reaching the ship. There was something else wrong with his body. It didn't seem to be metabolizing stored food properly and as a result he was tired all the time, and his body felt as if it were in constant need of repair. It reminded him of how he'd felt after a long run—a few hours rest and his muscles would be as good as new—only the run never stopped and his muscles weren't recovering.

When he tried to rest, he kept focused on why he was heading for the ship, what he wanted to accomplish once he got there, but with the Habers out of sight, their plight was less immediate. He really wanted to run, to hide in some cave and wait for Van Pelt and the crew to go away. He wanted to find some comfortable safe place where he could deal with the horrible reality of his body. He wanted to let the Habers fight their own battles and to stay well out of the way.

But he knew, deep down, that if he ignored what was going on, it wouldn't go away, and it wouldn't get any better. He had no choice but to go back and confront Van Pelt. Not to help the Habers, as he'd originally thought, but rather to show Van Pelt what had happened, to make him realize what he had become.

He'd been blaming the aliens for his condition, while it was really Van Pelt's fault. The aliens had given him a new life and had asked for nothing in return. It was Van Pelt he'd originally opposed —not the Habers. All they wanted was to be left alone.

Yeah, he realized, it was all Van Pelt's fault. Take care of Van Pelt and the problems disappear with him too.

He gritted his teeth and set off once again.

The ship glittered in the midday sun, less than a kilometer away, resting at the top of a lone hill. It was like a giant silver egg sitting on top of spindly spider legs. Fearing the worst, Markos used whatever cover he could as he approached: trees; shrubs; the shorter, wild grass. The trick, he thought, was to avoid being shot on sight. He would have to make the last half of the climb, the most dangerous half, in the open.

As he made his slow, cautious way up the hill, Markos realized just how dangerous this was. There was no way to sneak up there —with both the detection screens and the *Paladin*'s high ground, he would be spotted very soon. If he hadn't already been spotted. The observation post was unmanned, though.

Van Pelt had put the ship on defense alert before Markos had fled, treating Gandji and its native life as hostile. NASA 2 would examine the Captain's log and record of actions, and enough would appear in order. The Habers would be described as Mankind's first real outside threat. And Markos had little doubt that Van Pelt had already convinced at least part of the crew that Markos had been senselessly slaughtered by the "warlike" alien race.

It was almost amusing.

He shook his head, staring at the ship, upset with himself. Here he was, ready to confront Van Pelt, familiar with the *Paladin*'s layout and its position and unable to figure out how to make a safe approach.

He stared at the ship, then slowly traced the lay of the ground before it, the slope of the hill, and waited for an idea to come. A breeze rustled the grass, bent the thin, top branches of the oaklike trees, felt cool against his leathery skin. A mendil screeched in the distance. His eyes burned as he focused on the soaring creature, now a distant cousin. He ignored the urge to rub his eyes with his fists— without eyelids, it would do little good.

Sneak up on them and you'll get yourself killed, he thought.

But if Van Pelt spotted him calmly strolling up the hill, out in the open, he'd probably do the same thing he'd done to that harmless group. Either way it was death.

A twig snapped to his left.

Markos froze. Then slowly, a centimeter at a time, he pivoted around. One of the crew? he wondered. If it was, he might be inclined to shoot first and save his questions for the autopsy table.

"Hello?" Markos called tentatively, immediately regretting having said anything. His voice—he'd forgotten what it sounded like.

There was no response from the brush.

"It's me—Markos. Don't shoot. Hello?"

"Markos," a human voice said softly. "Markos?"

"Yes, dammit."

The grass and bushy undergrowth parted and Kominski stepped out. He took a long, slow look at Markos, not bothering to hide the terror on his face, then raised his weapon and pointed it squarely at Markos's head.

"You're not Markos."

"Hold it! I don't expect you to recognize me, 'Minski. Not the way I look. But it's me." His eyes stung with each word he spoke, and fatigue was catching up with him.

Kominski was trembling slightly, his weapon tracing tight, jumpy circles around Markos's face. His eyes darted to the ship, then back to Markos. He was unsure—the best Markos could hope for— and that meant he might not shoot.

"The Habers did this to me," Markos said. Kominski flinched at the sounds. "Please, 'Minski, take me to the Captain."

"My God," Kominski said, lowering his weapon, naked terror in his wide eyes. "My God. Is it really you?"

Because he was still unsure, and for the safety of the ship, Kominski had Markos wait outside while he went in to get Van Pelt. Markos sat on the ground, using the time to his best advantage by letting his body recover and rebuild itself after the walk. He wondered how the Captain was taking the news and smiled inwardly, imagining the tall, lanky man's reaction. Rage? Fear? Or perhaps simple annoyance—another minor problem to deal with? He'd definitely be surprised, though.

Van Pelt appeared at the airlock, looking down at Markos, not saying anything. He stayed that way for several minutes, then finally broke the silence. "Arrest him. Or it. Whatever. Take him up to Markos's cabin and lock him up."

Wilhelm and Kominski came out of the ship to escort Markos. As they led him through familiar corridors and passageways, Van Pelt was nowhere to be seen. They went up to the crew's quarters, and Wilhelm opened the door to the cabin. Markos's head came up to the middle of Wilhelm's chest; once, a long time ago, Markos had been five centimeters taller than he.

"We thought you were dead," Wilhelm said. His tall frame was muscular, healthy, powerful, full of parts which worked right, that knew what to do, that had the ability to back up his libido.

"I *am* dead." Markos walked into his cabin. He made directly for the mirror. When he saw his reflection, he knew it was worse than he'd feared.

Surrounding his eyes were little clusters of crystalline spheres, capable of generating cold light. He stared at them, concentrating on trying to detect any sensation but the stinging pain in them, trying to bring them to life, but nothing happened.

"You're not dead," Wilhelm said awkwardly.

"No? What am I, then?" Markos demanded, wheeling around to face Wilhelm.

"Does that really matter? You're alive, and that's what counts, man. Don't forget it. Christ, you should have seen what it looked like from above—the boulder, I mean. Man." He shook his head. "What a mess."

"*I'm* the mess!"

"Hey, come on! Calm down, will you? V.P.'s edgy enough already. He hasn't been getting any better, you know. He hears you screaming and it'll be over for good. You'll be okay. The medical people will fix you up okay. Just stay cool and it'll work out."

Markos nodded and sat on the edge of his bunk. What was he doing here? What was the sense? he wondered. He got up and started for the door. Wilhelm moved to block his exit.

"Don't, Markos. I told you to stay cool. The Captain's getting weirder all the time. Step outside and someone will burn you. And then you *will* be dead. For keeps. Wait for V.P., man. Please wait."

Markos looked him in the eyes. He didn't flinch or try to look away. At least that was something.

The cabin was too confining and uncomfortable; it was as alien to him as Gandji had been when they'd first landed. No one had gone out of his way to welcome Markos back. Coming to the ship had definitely been a mistake. He knew that now. He hadn't been accepted, much less welcomed, and he was being kept in his cabin under arrest.

He nodded his agreement to Wilhelm and waited for Van Pelt.

Lying down, doing nothing but listening and watching the ceiling, he rarely breathed. Handling Van Pelt was going to be a problem, he thought. Especially in this altered form. Van Pelt will probably keep his distance and be armed, so a physical assault was out of the question.

As he lay there, he tried to figure out just why he had come back. He ground it over and over in his mind. It had made so much sense back on the plain, away from the cold, hard reality of it.

He decided not to breathe when Van Pelt made his appearance, not that Van Pelt would notice.

The cabin door finally slid open. Markos continued to stare at the ceiling. Bare feet slapped the deck, then stopped near Markos's bunk. Markos took a breath and smelled Van Pelt.

"Jesus. You're uglier than I thought."

The sound of Van Pelt's voice almost set him off. Markos got up slowly, trying to keep his mind and body relaxed, trying to keep his anger and frustration in check, trying to maintain control. He faced the Captain and stared at his face, searching the lines of stress and worry etched there. He'd gotten worse, all right. The Captain. The cool, calm, dissociated human being, always in control, always taking control. Just a few more lines on his face, a little more sagging under his eyes.

It was then Markos noticed the gun Van Pelt had pointed at his chest.

"I am," Markos said, reveling in the flash of horror that lit Van Pelt's eyes the moment Markos had spoken.

"You've come back. You went out to help those 'harmless' creatures and they've repaid your good deed. Have you looked at yourself? Have you seen what your harmless little friends have done to you?" he asked, waving the gun wildly.

"I have."

Van Pelt shook his head, scowling. "Don't talk. Just nod or something."

"Don't you like my voice?" Markos asked.

Van Pelt laughed. His eyes opened wide. "You're pitiful, you know that? Pitiful. Don't like your voice? Your voice is your best feature. And now you've come back. Come back to share yourself with us. Come back for help, for consolation. Thrown out by those Habers? Well, what makes you think *we* want you?"

Van Pelt laughed again and started pacing. Markos said nothing. He was afraid to speak, afraid to move for fear of exploding in rage.

"What do you expect, Markos? Pity? You've got it. Disgust? You've got it. Horror? You've got that, too. Or maybe you'd like your old job back, huh? Is that it? Your old job? You'd make one hell of a xenobiologist. Or maybe your old body, eh? How would that be? No, no, couldn't help you there. All our bodies are being used." Van Pelt threw back his head and laughed hysterically.

Markos got to his feet.

The metallic taste in his mouth was back, stronger this time.

"Or your old friends, Markos. How about it? Want to go back with us when our relief arrives? Get sent back home to a woman's loving arms?" He laughed again.

Markos stared at Van Pelt's gleaming eyes, the desire to leap, to tear out his lungs barely suppressed.

"Well, well, Markos. I made a slight mistake there. Sorry. You'd better forget about women. And the rest of the crew. And your little, slimy, alien friends. 'Cause when relief arrives, it's going to be all over for you. You mutinied, and then you deserted. Understand? Mutinied! I'm keeping you right here! And when relief arrives, it's going to be all over. All over, I tell you. I'll send you back, all right—back for court-martialing. And then, after they've put you to death, I'll see you're dissected." The gun pointed at the deck.

Markos shook with rage, but he still couldn't advance. The rage had awakened something—a new, compelling, overpowering emotion, now just a spark, but a spark that glowed with enough intensity to blot out everything else. It took him by surprise. It warmed him from deep inside, a raging fire spreading warmth and energy. The needlelike pains vanished, the hot and cold spots on his skin were gone. His mind was clear—clearer than he could remember it ever having been. He saw what he would become if he stayed with the Terrans.

He felt taller, larger, deeper, more massive with each passing second as if his feet had roots capable of tapping the power of Gandji. He knew what he was, what the Haber had done. His eyes no longer burned.

They glowed.

"Look at me," he said.

Van Pelt looked.

The room had been bathed in a glittering, almost blinding display of colored light when Markos had spoken.

"You may not care, but when I woke up after being changed, I was angry." Reflected beads of light danced on Van Pelt's corneas. "I resented what the Habers had done. And then, much later, I blamed you. I wasn't sure what I wanted to do, what I'd become, but that's over now."

Van Pelt was swaying back and forth, his eyes glassy, his gun by his side.

"Do you understand? I know what to do now."

He stopped to look at Van Pelt, to consider the best way of phrasing what he was about to say, when he realized he'd taken too much time. Van Pelt had stopped swaying, and his eyes were clearing.

Momentarily free of his control, Van Pelt immediately leveled his gun at Markos's chest. Markos saw his finger tighten on the trigger as if in slow motion.

"Stop!" he shouted.

There was a blinding, intense pulse of light.

And Van Pelt stopped. He went rigid, frozen in position as if dipped into liquid nitrogen, and then went limp in the next instant. He collapsed to the deck.

One flash of an intensity Markos had never dreamed possible had stopped Van Pelt, all right—right down to his autonomic nervous system. The pulse of light must have triggered all of Van Pelt's neurons to discharge simultaneously, and his neural network probably overloaded. Fried his medulla. The pulse remained with Markos, a visual echo etched into his own neural pathways.

Markos's body jerked and spasmed for a second. The metallic taste slowly faded, his head and eyes pounded with pain. All he'd wanted to do was to get Van Pelt to slow down, to consider the Habers as sentient creatures—as friends instead of enemies. But with Van Pelt's body on the deck before him, he realized the idea had been doomed from the start.

Only one path was open to him now. He gathered himself, fought back the still-fresh memory, and opened the cabin door. He found Wilhelm leaning against a bulkhead looking confused and apprehensive. He used his eyes to calm Wilhelm, being careful to control their intensity. Wilhelm escorted him out of the ship.

At the bottom of the hill, safe within a grove of trees, Markos was prepared to face himself, to let remorse and guilt overcome him. He was prepared to face the fact that he'd committed murder. But he only felt good. Complete.

And very much in control.

He walked alone, enjoying the sights and sounds and smells of the planet of his birth, a permanent tourist, a visitor in exile, a newborn child thrust into a world that seemed to be made just for him.

He walked and touched and smelled and experienced things his crewmates could never have fathomed.

Haber settlements were spread across the plains, the mountains, and the forests but he made no effort to find one. Even though he was ready this time for what they expected, he wanted them to ask him directly. And he knew, sooner or later, that they would seek him out.

Eating still presented a problem—he wasn't sure he wanted to extend his life. He hadn't yet come to grips with eating on those terms. It was taboo for an adult Haber, and he needed to know what they thought of him before deciding anything else. They would tell him.

A flash of sparkling emerald caught his eyes. The standard Haber greeting. There were two of them, side by side.

"Hello, Markos," the larger, younger one said.

Markos returned the greeting with his eyes, adding a little orange to the edges of his.

"Are you ready to help us, us now?"

"Yes," Markos said.

"Please, Markos, have some food," the older of the two said, holding out what looked like an edible tuber.

"Thanks," Markos said.

And in return, he held his hands out to them for the thing they wanted. They approached, touching him lightly at first, then more firmly as the physical bond occurred, as the chemicals started to flow into his body.

He needed to shout his joy but knew better.

It was the first time he'd felt pleasure coursing through his new body. He'd never even thought that possible. He soared, his spirit lifting, blanketing the whole planet. And as their genetic material flowed into and through him, Markos realized how constant his pleasure could be. He could walk across the plains, greeting countless pairs of Habers.

He would be a different kind of flow-bridge for them, the flow-bridge for which they had been waiting.

His first generation would be strange. He shaped them in his mind's eye before returning the genetic materials. And if these mutations weren't the right ones, there would be others. And there might even be enough time, Markos thought. Enough time to create new ones, others more suitably equipped to deal with the change.

5.

He sat in a small village, surrounded by Habers. The huts were simple, one-room dwellings, formed out of the native grass. His children were newly born, more Haber than Terran in appearance. The two sets of Habers who had birthed them had found the children were more like Markos than themselves and had left them in his charge. He was proud of them and the role he'd played in their births, in the changes he'd made to them as the flow-bridge.

The children had more human musculature, though the muscles themselves didn't resemble their Terran counterparts beyond function. They were a little larger at this stage of their development than a normal Haber child would have been—about ten centimeters taller than Markos.

Their coloring was odd. They had the normal furlike skin that all Habers had, but there were streaks of color that shone through the brown-gray covering. They were beautiful to watch as they moved, expending energy, getting to know their world and their people.

They played noisily, pushing and pulling each other, knocking each other down, playing as though they were normal, Terran children.

The Habers took this aberrant behavior the best they could.

One old Haber seemed genuinely pleased, as if watching this group of young, changed Habers fulfilled a lifelong dream. He stayed by Markos's side everywhere he went, and Markos took to calling him the Old One.

The Old One was different from the other Habers he had met. His eyes were denser, more crystalline spheres within them, and his skin was a little browner than the others. Markos felt at home, comfortable and accepted, his human past no more than a thin memory recalled with a pleasant feeling of pain, a dull throb, a melancholy reminder of what he had been. The Habers never brought up his past, and he felt no need to either.

Adult Habers, those who wanted to mate, arrived daily in small groups. They waited with inhuman patience, watching the sunset with rapt attention, staring at the colors as if the meaning of life were contained in them. When there was nothing else to divert them, they watched Markos's offspring, communicated with the Old One, or meditated in silence.

Markos was glad he had taken the Old One's advice. He had originally planned to walk over the face of Gandji, spending the rest of his life acting as a flow-bridge. The Old One had explained that that was unnecessary; he'd said the mature Habers would come to the village and seek him out.

His children were born with a Terran's understanding of conflict and competition, something they exhibited in play, though it was as alien to the Habers in the village as to Markos himself.

"Are you ready for the next two?" the Old One asked, sitting by Markos's side.

Markos turned away from the child he had named Alpha, the

most aggressive of the children. Alpha had just made a discovery: a stick can be used as a weapon to hit someone.

Markos stood and held out his hands, offering them to the two slowly advancing Habers. It struck him as strange that they would be so shy and hesitant, as if Markos might change his mind any moment and refuse the contact.

They gripped his hands firmly, melted their flesh into his flesh, changed their hands into his hands, creating the link through which their genetic material would flow. He accepted the pleasure that brought, the intense physical sensations and excitement, embraced it and tried to hold it close to his mind, but the feelings were too intense, too glorious to try to hold. He let his mind relax and take control of the genetic materials entering his body. He pictured the children he would produce, an image of stronger, taller, more solidly built Habers than anything he'd imagined before.

Then something happened in his mind that he couldn't stop. The images of the stronger and taller children exploded in size until Markos could detect vast spaces between what must have been molecules. It was as if he were shrinking, falling deep through the images and into some representation of the genetic material that made up the images. He somehow knew that molecules needed changing, and he could see the molecular structures change as he thought about altering them. With each change he made he felt a peculiar but pleasant sensation in his brain.

When the genetic materials had been molded and manipulated, he pushed them out through his hands and into the two Habers. Contact was broken.

The whole experience couldn't have lasted more than a minute or two, but he was left feeling hollow, washed out. The Old One stood and offered him a root, which Markos gladly accepted. As he ate, he remembered what the Old One had said about his eating: "We, we demand this of you. That we, we don't eat out of choice is our birthright."

He rested, giving his mind and body the time needed to recover fully. It was a simple life, one he was enjoying. He was doing something his crewmates could never do, in a way they could never imagine—being a xenobiologist firsthand.

A Haber approached quickly, something odd for a Haber, until it stood before him. Markos flashed green to the Haber, and it returned the greeting.

"The people have destroyed the village nearest their settlement."

Impossible. "Did you see this happen yourself?" Markos asked.

"Yes. I, I saw this happen. I, I was leaving the village on my, my way to see you."

The crew had remained quiet and kept to themselves over the last few months. Markos had walked back to the area in which the ship rested and watched from a distance, curious as to what the Terrans planned. They had been setting up a semipermanent camp around the ship, keeping clear of the natives, being careful not to push too fast or too hard. Markos had been thankful for the time this gave him; his offspring could grow, eat, build themselves up, learn from their father about this strange race of invaders, understand what real conflict was and how to deal with it.

"Did they have a leader?"

The Haber flashed confusion.

"One who directed the others, who told the group what to do."

It flashed red.

"What did he look like?"

The Haber did the best it could describing one of the Terrans. Markos figured it had to be Cathy Straka.

Cathy?

Wilhelm was second in command. Why should Cathy be in charge? What had happened to Wilhelm? A mutiny? Or was Cathy working on Wilhelm's orders? He wheeled around to the Old One.

"What are we going to do? We can't fight them—not yet. The young I've produced are still in their first cycle. They don't really understand what would be expected of them."

The Old One sat quietly, watching the last rays of the sun setting the sky on fire. "This is the change we, we may not survive. I, I do not think it matters what we, we do."

Markos's anger rekindled as he felt old frustrations rise again. The tiring experience of trying to get these creatures to understand the true nature of the Terran threat, something he'd hoped was gone forever with Van Pelt's death, was back, causing him to taste metal. The Haber before him turned his head away, took several steps back.

If Wilhelm were dead, then so were the Habers. He couldn't approach Straka and change her with his eyes as he'd done to Van Pelt. Everyone on the *Paladin* had to know of this ability and would probably shoot him on sight. Wilhelm would have told them all.

Terrific, Markos thought. Death either way.

Their only chance was to fight. But the only beings capable of fighting the Terrans were Markos and his offspring, and they were still too young.

That left only him.

"But we can't just accept it," he said a little too loudly, a little too forcibly in his gravely voice. "They'll kill us all."

"We, we must accept it. It is the way of all things," the Old One said.

"Not where I come from. They can't get away with this. I won't let them."

"Then do what you can."

Yes, Markos thought. He's right. They don't seem to be worried—they don't even care. I'm the one who's afraid. If someone's going to do something about this it's going to have to be me.

But what can I do?

The next two Habers were waiting. The Old One was waiting. The messenger was waiting.

"We'll run," Markos said. He didn't particularly relish the idea of becoming a hunted animal again—once had been enough to make him hate that feeling, but it was run or die. "That cave, that cavern where I was taken after I died. Do you know where it is?" he asked the Old One.

"Yes," he said, flashing red tinged with orange.

"I'm going to take these children there and hide. I'll start teaching them immediately. You can stay here if you want, all of you," he said, turning to face the group encircling him, "but I'm leaving. I'm not going to wait for Straka to grind me under her heels."

"We, we were hoping this would happen," the Old One said. "We, we waited for this change, the change we, we could never understand. Now you can explain it to us, us, and show us, us what it means."

"What?" Markos demanded, totally confused.

"I, I think it is time, then," the Old One said, rising slowly to his feet. The other Habers in the village flashed an emphatic crimson red. "We, we can now go home."

"Home?"

"Yes," the Old One said.

"I don't understand."

"Understanding is not necessary. You understand what we, we could not. Gather your children and I, I will lead you."

Markos stood quickly, his nerves taut. "Children," he shouted, showing pink and yellow, "stop what you're doing and come here."

All ten stopped, turned, then ran to him. While he explained what was required of them—silence, obedience, and self-discipline—the Old One started eating. He started eating everything he could find. Markos was astonished by what the Old One was doing.

"I, I am too close to death to lead you home. I, I do not have the necessary energy for the journey. My, my life must be sacrificed in this manner so that you and your children can see home. This is all important for those, those waiting for us, us. They, they wait for our, our return to understand the change."

Huh? What was that all about? Markos wondered. But there wasn't time to go into it now. The Old One had just nonchalantly turned and walked out of the village. He was heading toward the mountains. Markos quickly ordered the children to follow the Old One, and they all set out through the grassy plain.

The evening was cool, the wind spiked with an icy chill. Mendils shrieked their mating calls in the darkness. The stars were coming out, filling the night sky of Gandji like thin, high clouds. The farther he walked, the worse Markos felt.

Maybe they should have stayed in the village. He was abandoning those left behind to certain death. They would just sit there, waiting for the Terrans to come and kill them. Markos was sure that would happen, and that bothered him deep down. He shouted for the Old One to stop, then walked past the children to talk with him.

"We can't go. I was wrong. We can't leave the others behind in the village. I can't let these outsiders take your planet away from you without giving them a fight."

"They are not outsiders. They belong here just as much as we, we do. You are still of them. You understand them. Do not let your concern over the ones left behind cancel what you have accomplished."

"I still feel the need to stay and get the ones in the village at least well hidden," Markos said.

"And the others? In all the other villages?"

Markos looked at the ground by his feet.

"We, we must leave now and go home. These children are important. They are the answer for the change we, we cannot understand."

Markos knew there was something more here he wasn't grasping, something the Old One wasn't explaining.

"Come," the Old One said. "Or everything here will be wasted."

He turned and walked off through the grass. The children waited by Markos, waiting to be told what to do. He motioned for them to follow the Old One, then followed as well.

They left behind a narrow trail of flattened grass. The children were silent, and Markos checked on them every few kilometers to ensure they were all right. He needn't have worried; they made him proud by their composure and self-control.

They stopped frequently to rest, to let their bodies catch up with them. Markos left the Old One alone. He felt awkward after that exchange they'd had minutes after having set out. He hoped the Haber knew what he was doing.

Just before dawn the Haber stopped. The mountains towered before them, still a half day's walk. They had left the plain and were in rocky ground, with small hills and cliff faces directly before them.

"How much farther?" Markos asked, exhausted.

"We, we are close now."

The old Haber left the small group and walked up to a wall of rock. He touched it with both palms, then he became rigid, immobile; a few seconds later a cave mouth appeared in the rock around the place he was touching. Markos couldn't believe what he'd just seen. It had been a solid wall of rock and then, an instant later, there had been a cave mouth there. He was going to ask what the Old One had done, how he had done it, but he saw how much that had taken out of him. He seemed to have gotten smaller, lost some body mass. The Old One waved them all inside.

Once into the darkness, the Old One bent down and lifted a small rock. He clenched it in his fist and then opened his hand. The rock was glowing, shedding a weak light. He handed the rock to one of the children and repeated it until all held glowing rocks. They each could have generated light from their eyes, but Markos knew that there was a blinding-threshhold: Their eyes' photoreceptors would be blinded by their eyes' cold-light generators if they generated too much. When Markos had flashed light from his eyes, he'd been momentarily blinded, and regulating the intensity of the light was a skill he was still developing.

The light from the rocks was strong enough for them to walk safely into the cave. Markos didn't recognize the cave—this wasn't the place where he'd awakened after his death. He was apprehensive, but only for an instant. They were all in the Old One's hands, and they would have to take their chances.

They were safe. Or as safe as they could be on the planet with Straka in control of the *Paladin*.

The Old One uncovered food stores and they all ate. The cave was large, with walls that gave off a soft, sickly-green light. The floor was dank and cold, but the air was fresh enough. Water dripped down cracks in the walls, slowly but incessantly dropping into little puddles on the floor every few seconds.

They ate tubers and other roots, as well as some vegetation that the Old One needed to modify before they could eat it. Markos watched what the Old One did with his hands this time and was even more confused and amazed. That's what they must have meant by "touch and change," he thought. God, I'm glad they *didn't* do that to the crew.

"How do you do that, Old One?"

"Here. You will understand more once you see this." He handed Markos a large, irregularly shaped crystal.

Markos had never seen anything quite like it before. It had a symmetry that was not immediately apparent. He turned it over in his hands, felt the coolness and solidity of it, and was impressed with its beauty. "It's very nice," Markos said, "but what has this got to do with what I asked?"

The old Haber flashed yellow, and Markos shook his head. What did the Old One want him to do? The crystal was nice, refracting the dim green light in the cave into some beautiful colors, but it was only a crystal.

He handed Markos another one.

Markos turned the crystal over as if searching for a seam or an opening, feeling with his strange hands for something hidden on its surface. It was smooth all over, as though it had been polished or grown artificially. Other than that, he discovered nothing else about it.

"It's very nice," Markos said. "Prettier than the first."

"You do not understand. I, I will have to teach you how to use them."

"Never mind about these," Markos said. "Tell me how you did that to the cave entrance."

The Old One flashed the same lemon-yellow color again, then grabbed Markos's hands, cupping them around the crystal. "Touch and change it, Markos. Penetrate the crystal's surface and find what's been changed inside."

"What are you talking about?"

"The crystal has been changed. There are unnatural dislocations in its structure. They create colors that are very complex. You can detect these changes, understand them, and then understand the colors."

A book?

The more he learned about these creatures, the less sense they made. After having seen that artifact so close to Tau Ceti and finding Gandji circling the star, peopled by these creatures, everyone on board the *Paladin* had been bothered by the inconsistency of their culture.

If this crystal really was a book, then they could have a technology. Still, there was no explanation for where it had gone, or where it was now. And if they did have technology, why did they just sit and wait for Gandji to be destroyed? If they couldn't or wouldn't fight, why didn't they just leave the planet? Or perhaps they had lost the technology enabling them to travel through space? But they had brought him back to life, a task that required an extremely high level of technology.

He turned the crystal over in his hands, and the Haber let go of him. Touch and change it? He wasn't even certain this body had that ability.

Markos couldn't close his eyes to block out the surrounding distractions, so concentrating proved difficult. He looked down, though, staring at his hands and the crystal within them, staring at his mendil skin, at the smooth coolness of the crystal in his hands.

The crystal slowly warmed to his touch. He stared into its depths, clearing his mind of racing thoughts. The more he concentrated on the crystal, the warmer it felt. Suddenly it was warm and alive.

He could feel wild and frenetic movement on its outer surface, as if it were fluid. He shifted into a nonbreathing catabolism. His hands seemed to join the physical structure of the crystal, piercing its top layer.

He panicked for an instant, fearing he would never get his fingers out, fearing a permanent link as they sank deeper and deeper beneath its surface, but he fought it back. One quick glance showed his hands still outside the crystal's surface no matter what it felt like.

He detected the movement of shared electrons on the outer surface and realized that everything there was as it should have been; molecules were correctly aligned and nothing had been altered. He pressed downward with his mind, letting himself sink deeper, trying to become one with the crystal's depths.

Everything was suddenly different as he reached a second level. Atoms were displaced, while others pulsated, giving off light as they expanded and contracted. Groups pulsed together, and Markos recognized the colors, the actions, the complex Haber way of describing concepts and images with color.

He listened to the crystal speak.

And then he stopped listening and became one with the voice. His consciousness was gone, replaced by the mind in the crystal that told the story. He was in the body of a Haber, sharing his thoughts, his deeds.

He stared out over an alien landscape.

6.

Vegetation writhed in animal agony, whipped into motion by circular gusts of wind. The Haber, Yulakna, perceived a strong sense of rightness to the fluid movement, the entwining thin vines wrapping themselves into knotted confusion about each other and huge roots. The vines seemed to have a life of their own, each with a course in life, a series of patterns they had to follow.

Markos felt the crystal held in Yulakna's hand, recording everything that he experienced. He knew Yulakna thought of the planet as "Red tinged with yellow swirled with maroon." Markos thought of it as Red. The homeworld Habers would see this world and decide how many should go to Red, what kind of positive mutations the planet might create in their race, what changes these mutations might create in their physical and mental states.

To Markos, sharing in what Yulakna saw and experienced, the area being scouted was unappealing. The ground was claylike, a grayish ocher. Creatures as small as insects crawled in and out of tunnels and mounds of discolored earth in the few places the vines didn't grow.

Markos noticed the device attached to the crystal. He made a mental note to ask the Old One what it was afterward.

There were trees nearby—huge, massive trees that defined the forceful, erratic gusts of wind that changed direction almost constantly. The upper parts of the trees were devoid of leaves. At the end of each flexible branch hung a small seed pod that dripped a sticky liquid. Their root systems were gnarled and twisted, poking up from beneath the ground only to disappear a few meters along. Vines, whipped in changing directions by the wind, seemed to wrap and unwrap themselves around the roots, causing the overlapping and twisting root system to seem even more complex and beautiful to Yulakna. Markos tried to appreciate Yulakna's point of view, but the oddness of the place kept him detached.

Yulakna walked farther from the ship he and the three other Habers had arrived in, trying to gather as much information about this area of Red as he could. He was already thinking of himself and his fellow Habers as fitting in with the native life-forms.

Off to the right, animals grazed, feeding on the yellow vines. They were the size of small ponies, their six gangly legs supporting barrel-shaped bodies. Their hides were opalescent, reflecting the sunlight in patches of scaly reddish green and silvery white, which shifted as they moved. The natives grazed and did what all Habers understood, what all Habers felt was important. They lived, they bred, and then they died.

Markos realized these creatures were incapable of anything more complex, though he understood now that no Haber looked at it that way.

Yulakna heard something that didn't belong and looked upward toward the source of the noise. High overhead a glint of polished metal appeared, and both Yulakna and Markos knew what it was.

The noise increased; after a few moments its form became visible. Markos knew from Yulakna that the ship was neither Haber nor Terran.

He had seen enough. He had to think.

He let go of the crystal and saw the cave.

"How long have you been on Gandji?" he asked the Old One.

"Not long. Do you understand now?"

"No, but I understand more. When you said you would take us home, you meant to your homeworld, didn't you?"

The old Haber showed crimson.

"And you're not native to this planet. You've had the ability to leave at any time. And I thought you were natives here, that your whole race was going to be wiped out by Van Pelt. Is this right?"

Crimson.

"What was the point to all of this, then?"

"Finish the crystal and you will understand."

"Why let me go through all of this to save a planet that wasn't originally yours?"

"We, we needed Gandji until now, Markos. Finish the crystal and you will understand more."

He picked up the prismatic piece of rock and looked at it. "How old is this? When was this record made?"

"Time is a difficult medium for us, us to use in communication. The crystal you hold is the first of many events that took place long before we, we met the first one of your kind."

"How long before?"

"Generations. They explain about the change we, we will not survive. It is our, our hope to understand how to deal with the change."

Markos showed red. There was little more he could get out of the Old One yet. He gripped the smooth crystal in his hands and let his mind drift down beneath its surface.

Markos thought of the countless complications an alien ship created, but Yulakna did not. Markos was shocked as he realized the true problem the Habers faced as a race. They were totally incapable of conceiving what conflict was. It was beyond them. They lacked the *capacity* to understand. This became patently obvious as Yulakna approached the landing ship with childlike innocence and expectations. How could these creatures have survived at all?

If it had been Markos there, he would have been more cautious and returned to the landing craft. He would have lifted off the planet's surface and observed the aliens from the safety of distance. He would never have put himself in that kind of physical jeopardy.

But not a Haber.

The ship settled to Red's surface, and the winds quickly dispersed the dust and dead vegetation the landing kicked up. The ship was ten meters high, about twenty meters long. From the angle that Yulakna approached it, Markos could see it was shaped like a bunker.

Before the ship's exterior cooled, while the metal skin of the ship pinged, a door opened.

The Haber scouting party showed green and waited.

A row of creatures filled the doorway. They were smaller than Terrans, a little taller than Habers. Either they wore protective armor, suits designed for fighting, or nothing at all. They had shiny black coverings, smooth and polished like an ant's exoskeleton. Their heads were round and a little smaller than what human proportions demanded. White and red markings, bands of color, surrounded their heads. Their torsos were divided in half, much like the thorax and abdomen in an insect. The thorax supported two thin arms that were normally proportioned. Beneath the arms were hundreds of thin, short bristles coming out of their torso. Clamped in each pair of hands was a weapon, pointed directly at the Habers.

Their abdomens were a third larger than their thoraxes. Three legs extended from the abdomen and supported the creatures like a tripod.

The Haber nearest the ship showed green again.

The aliens responded with their greeting: First an overpowering smell, and then heat lasers.

There was no more recorded on the crystal.

He opened his hands and dropped it to the floor. It landed with a dull thunking sound. The children were silent, staring at him with their clusters of tiny eyes. The Old One was silent, too, patiently waiting.

It was all starting to make sense to Markos.

"Give me the other crystal you had," Markos said.

"Do you understand now?"

"I think I understand more than you do, Old One."

He held out his hands and the Haber dropped the other crystal into them. Entering and experiencing what it held was far easier this time and almost instantaneous.

Misty ground fog, the stillness of death.

He stood in line, facing a glowing patch of light about five kilometers away. Habers were linked together, their hands joined, creating a calmness and serenity as they waited, facing the oncoming death. They preferred to die as a group.

The planet's name was Darkness with a Dull Orange Glow. They had been born there, as had those who had given them life. This planet was theirs, settled many generations ago. They had become a part of the soil, part of the planet's food cycle.

The Habers belonged now.

The line of Habers knew what the glow was. There had been a village there. They waited to see if they would survive this change on Darkness.

The aliens would arrive soon, before the swollen red sun rose to burn off the ground fog, before the deep-biting chill in the air was gone.

Markos shared the body of the Haber holding the crystal. Tansak knew they would not, could not survive this change. There was a glimmer of an idea that had spurred him to grab the crystal and its device—the Habers on Homeworld might be able to see this change. They might be able to understand it. They might be able to give birth to Habers capable of surviving the change the aliens forced upon them. And even though he knew they would not understand any better than the Habers on Darkness understood, he did all that he could do.

What else was there?

They stood and waited for the aliens to arrive and show them the change.

They did not have long to wait.

Even in the darkness, through the misty distance, the wave of advancing creatures was easily discernible. They were silent in their approach.

Twenty meters away the advancing black line stopped. One creature, a little taller than the rest, made some noise and the air was suddenly filled with an overpowering odor. The aliens depressed the activating switches on their weapons.

Markos unclenched his hands, dropped the crystal, and tried to stop trembling. His heart raced and his skin prickled with pain. That feeling of standing in line, waiting for death, was strong and haunting. It lingered like a bad aftertaste. He sat there telling himself it was okay, that he was here and not on Darkness with that line of Habers.

He understood a little more now of how the Haber mind worked. His frustration had come from not understanding at all, from thinking that ideas and concepts could be easily communicated from race to race. Well, that obviously wasn't true. His attempts to incite them into fighting for Gandji had been doomed to failure from the start. It was beyond them. They didn't have the vaguest idea what fighting was.

"How many . . ." he started to ask, then stopped as he concentrated on keeping himself calm. His emotions were not suited to this body. He had to do what he could to maintain some level of control.

He stood and walked around the cave, trying not to think of the smell and the noise the aliens created right before the end, trying to let his mind assimilate the things he'd learned about the Habers. He stopped, looking at a glowing wall.

Well, okay then, he thought. Put everything in order. A pod, manned by some poor Terran, is captured by the Habers as it enters the Tau Ceti System. They establish contact and touch the guy and learn about the Terrans. And meanwhile they're suffering attack from some other race, from some other star system—my God!

He turned quickly, facing the Old One. "How many more crystals do you have? And are they all from the same time?"

"We, we have many crystals," the Old One said. "And there are some being made right now, on other planets that are undergoing this same change."

"How long has this war been going on?"

The Haber showed yellow tinged with blue. "War?"

This could get tough. "These unnatural deaths recorded in these crystals."

"There is nothing unnatural about death. There is life, which is change, and the final change, which is death."

"Yes," Markos said, "the act of dying is very natural. It is a natural change. War has little to do with the process of dying or the process of living, though. War is not a *natural* process—it's a process started and maintained by free will.

"This series of changes—each one has some things in common. The change is always the same, you never survive it, and it is not natural. The creatures themselves are the change you don't survive."

"Yes."

"That is war."

The Haber showed lemon yellow tinged with blue.

"Never mind. What are these crystals doing here? How did they get off the planet where they were made?"

The Haber explained about the device. Each scouting party, landing party, and colony had a set of crystals. A matched set remained on the homeworld. The attached device transmitted the changes the Habers made in the crystal, where they were duplicated in the matching one on the homeworld.

"These crystals were given to us, us so that we, we could change on Gandji enough to understand them."

Mutate toward an aggressive Haber? It would sure answer a lot of questions. Gandji as a huge test tube, each Haber a virus capable of mutating toward the answer they need to survive the change. From what Markos had seen, they would never really understand it.

But the children he had with him should understand.

He looked at them, their faces poised, silent, waiting with the patience of a Haber.

They were loyal, aggressive, and only part Haber: A Haber who could deal with the change.

And that was why the Old One had risked everything, including compromising his own views on life by eating. It was to ensure the ten children got back to Homeworld.

"Come on," he told them all. "I understand now. We're going home."

7

The rocks the Old One had changed provided the light they needed as they made their way through the twisty tunnels into the depths of the mountain. They had left the cavern behind and needed to be careful of their footing; the floor of the tunnels left a lot to be desired. Even with the light the rocks provided, the going proved tiresome and slow.

The tunnel suddenly ended, emptying into a large underground cavern. Markos could make out the glint of polished metal a little over ten meters away. He turned to his left, then to his right, then stared up into the blackness trying to judge the size of the cavern. It had to extend at least fifty meters over his head and kept on going into total darkness. He stopped generating light, finding it easier to see without the local interference.

He had a good idea as to where they were, what they stood before, and what they were doing there, so he waited for the Old One to explain. He, for once, was in no rush.

The ten children stood by the Old One, motionless, waiting. One child, a little larger than the others, stood a stride closer to Markos.

The Old One walked forward and stopped before the metallic shape. He touched it with his palms, and the dimensions of the shape became obvious as it began to glow with a soft, dull green light.

It was a large wedge-shaped ship. They were standing before it, looking at it head-on. Its was divided into two identical hulls, joined at the stern by a bridge. The underside of the ship was flat, resting on the cavern floor. Viewed from above, Markos figured, the ship would have looked like a bottom-heavy H the crossbar lowered to join the two hull sections.

Even though he'd figured the ship had to exist and he had been relatively certain of where the Old One was leading them, Markos was still awed by it. This piece of metal was no product of an agrarian, nontechnological civilization, that much was for sure. He knew that the technology needed for the development of space travel, especially for faster-than-light space travel, hadn't been mirrored in the Habers' existence on Gandji. But then their existence on Gandji had never mirrored their civilization.

Gandji was their test tube, a place where the race could regress, leave their advances behind, mutate toward a more aggressive type of creature. He had no idea of how long they'd lived on Gandji, how far a Haber like the Old One had already regressed, but he knew their plan had been doomed to failure. It probably would have failed completely if it weren't for the humans.

As he stared at the glowing Haber ship, he realized that their plan might still fail if the aliens had already reached the Habers' homeworld. But they had to travel the distance, find out what had happened in that sector of space, and do what they could for whatever Haber population remained alive.

The Old One touched the ship again, and a black line appeared on the side of the hull, outlining a large rectangle that became a door, hinged at the top. It opened with smooth, mechanical precision. Markos approached the opening and looked in. It was a large bay area. The Old One stepped up and walked inside, then flashed an orange and blue combination, telling them to follow.

Markos noticed an interesting difference in himself as he walked aboard the ship. Had he still been a Terran, he would have been looking around the ship for machinery that could be used on the *Paladin*, compatible systems, or simply the level of the Habers' technology.

If he'd been a pure Haber, walking aboard the ship would have represented a step toward the safety of home. The Old One was bringing back a solution to a problem no Haber had ever been close to solving.

As the solution itself, Markos felt the alienation from the Old One reinforce itself.

Now his concerns about the ship were practical: How well could the ship maneuver? Were there any systems on board that could be used as weapons? How fast would the ship really go?

He noticed that a portion of the bay deck had been discolored, scarred, as if something had been scraped across its surface. To his left, the top of the bay slanted downward, meeting the forward bulkhead a meter and a half off the deck. He figured there would be forward storage compartments beyond the bulkhead, running up the sharp front edge of the wedge's hull.

To his right a ramp was lit. It glowed with light generated below its surface, making the upward-curving ramp seem like a path studded with glistening gems. Beyond the ramp was a tall, unbroken bulkhead—probably ending at the aft section of the hull.

The bay itself was empty. Markos saw little that indicated the ship was capable of flight, much less fight. But he was learning not to draw conclusions too quickly. After he'd toured the entire ship, he'd have a much clearer idea as to its capabilities.

The Old One was walking up the sloping ramp. When he reached the top, a door slid back and the Old One passed through it.

"Come on," Markos told the children. "Absorb all the information you can about this ship. If anything should happen to him, we may need it. Do you all understand?"

They showed red.

Markos led them up the ramp.

At the top was a passageway, the rectangular section he'd seen from outside that connected the two hull sections. A bridge of any kind would most probably be somewhere off this passageway, he figured. The hallway seemed smaller than it should have been—it was less than two meters high and only a little more than a meter wide. It would have been uncomfortable for a large, muscular Terran.

The old Haber appeared suddenly as he walked from a cabin into the passageway. "Come in here," he said. "This is the area we must stay in for now."

Markos walked into the bridge. The first thing that caught his eye was the startank. What else could he call it? It was a huge cube, three meters on a side. Within the cube was blackness. Thousands of points of light were suspended within.

One point was larger than the others and in the center. It was reddish-orange and distinguished by a tiny, barely visible emerald-green wedge right beside it. He realized the star had to be Tau Ceti, with the green wedge representing the ship. A quick glance at the rest of the cube showed that several stars had green wedges beside them. The stars with the green wedges could be Haber-owned, he thought, and that would make one of them the Habers' home star.

Markos noticed that all the stars with green wedges near them were reddish-orange K-type stars.

If he could locate some more familiar stars, he could get a good idea as to the scale being used and then figure out how far the home-world was from Tau Ceti. He knew there was a binary system nearby, and with that he could sight down an imaginary line to where Sol should be. He moved around the cube until he had the proper angle and had sighted Sol, a yellow dwarf, a little above the level of Tau Ceti.

Yes, he thought, and there's Proxima Centauri, Alpha Centauri A & B, and Barnard's Star.

He knew the distance Sol was from each of the recognized stars, so approximating a scale was possible. He gave himself a rough distance from Tau Ceti to the other K-type stars with green wedges near them and realized they were at least twenty-five to thirty parsecs away. The distance was beyond Markos's imagination.

He took a breath. My God, he thought. One hundred light-years. Even if it's eighty, if I misjudged the distances, we'll never get there in time to be of any help. The *Paladin* would have taken over two years of f-t-l travel to make that journey, and no one knows if the *Paladin* could remain intact while in tau-space for that period of time. Plus the time needed to accelerate to the jump point, then the time needed to decelerate—the trip would have taken the *Paladin* an *absolute minimum* of four and a half years.

A lot could happen in four and a half years. The crew of the *Paladin* would have taken over Gandji and any other habitable planets in the Tau Ceti System, claiming them for Terra.

But if the distance was so immense, and the time it took the Habers to travel it was anywhere close to what Markos felt it had to be, then why did they come all the way across to Tau Ceti? There had to be a closer habitable planet where they could have tried to mutate.

"Why did you pick Gandji?" Markos asked absently.

"It is far enough from our, our home, and from . . ."

He turned to face him. "Your enemies."

"Yes. Our, our enemies."

Well, Markos thought, the Old One is learning new words, even if he doesn't really understand their meanings. Enemies is a good first step. Once they understand that their problems lie with an alien race and not with some "change," there's a chance they can be taught to fight.

They had sought safety in distance, he realized, and that showed a minimal understanding of their plight. But if they understood that, then why didn't they just all get on board their ships and settle in a different sector of space, away from the threat of war?

He walked around the front of the startank and studied the area of space he figured the Habers owned. It was below the galactic ecliptic, further out toward the edge of the spiral arm than Tau Ceti or Sol. Judging by the grouping of green wedges, their home star could have been Alpha Indi, a K-2 star about 25 parsecs from Sol. Add to that the 3.5 parsecs to Tau Ceti from Sol, and that put their home star at about 28.5 parsecs away.

But then where did the Habers' enemies come from? If they had f-t-l drive and their ships were as advanced as the Habers' ships, they could be coming from anywhere.

He shook his head, a throwback to his Terran past, and turned to check out the rest of the machinery on the bridge. None of the controls were labeled or were obvious in function by design, so he touched nothing. What he couldn't surmise through observation he would ask about. He was already learning caution and patience, a quality he would have been thankful for before his flight in the screamer.

The bulkhead behind the startank, directly opposite the entry, seemed to house most of the piloting equipment. There were two chairs that looked anything but comfortable. They appeared to be made of clear, hard plastic or crystalline rock. Knowing what he did about the Habers, he figured it *was* rock. The chairs sat side by side, separated by a console.

Directly before each of the chairs was a thin, clear screen inlaid with a hairline grid. The screens were mounted on thin support pedestals.

The console between the chairs had a tube mounted on it, parallel to the deck, aiming into the startank directly before it. On either side of the chairs were single consoles with what looked like duplicate controls—levers, a few switches, and some touch plates. None of the equipment looked like it could have come from a Terran ship.

The other two bulkheads had storage lockers, each one with a tiny outlined door. Markos had no idea what they might contain. He glanced around the rest of the cabin and felt satisfied—he'd seen enough for now.

"When do we leave?" Markos asked.

"Soon. I, I must finish preparations."

"Anything I can do to help you?"

"There is no need. Most of what I, I will do is routine."

"Fine. I'm going to take the children and explore the rest of the ship."

The Old One showed red, and Markos led his group through the doorway.

The right hull of the ship had two levels. The top one was even with the level of the bridge and was filled with living quarters. Each of the twelve cabins was large, capable of supporting between six and ten Habers in comfort. If comfort were not a concern, he figured the cabins could support fifteen.

The lower level was divided into two major sections. The forward compartment contained row after row of oddly shaped crystals, stacked, linked together by weblike filaments of metal or silicon. He touched one of the crystals, expecting to find a record of events stored inside. The crystal's lattice structure had definitely been altered—he could detect that easily enough—but no image or story appeared in his mind.

The aft section was a storage area, complete with replacement parts for most of the equipment he'd seen on the bridge.

The children followed his example. They touched everything he touched, absorbing what they learned as if the knowledge were food and they were starving. Markos could tell the differences between them—each child was an individual, with enough physical and personality differences to make it unique. If he hadn't been the one responsible for forming them, molding them, mentally creating the mutation in the genetic material, telling them apart might have been more difficult.

When the right hull had been explored, Markos instructed Alpha to lead the others back to the large bay area and wait for him.

When a Haber child was born, his autonomic system let a little color leak from his eyes. The parents who saw this called the child by those colors, naming him based on some genetic uniqueness. Each of the children Markos had created had done the same thing—the Habers around them at birth had been quick to pick up their Haber names and use them. Markos thought in sound-speech, though, and the names were not really translatable. He would have to name them before long.

He walked out of the aft compartment to the other hull and saw three of the children lying on the deck. They weren't moving. He spotted two children with their backs to him, hiding behind an indentation in the bulkhead.

He scanned the bay for Terrans, saw none, and quickly realized they couldn't have found them. And even if they had, they couldn't have infiltrated the ship.

One of the children rushed out of hiding, his eyes flashing a strong, coherent, narrow beam of light toward the two in hiding, temporarily blinding himself in the process. The larger of the two—it looked like Alpha—jumped out and focused his eye-beam on his running brother. The one struck by the eye-beam collapsed instantly to the deck.

"Stop this!" Markos shouted from the top of the ramp.

All the children rose to their feet, gathered around Alpha, who stood in the center of the bay. They were all fine, unhurt, and Markos immediately felt a little foolish and embarrassed, but the metal taste still lingered.

"We were making up a story, like the one you saw in the crystal," Alpha said.

Playing, Markos thought. They were just playing.

He was glad they had been playing—if they'd been pure Habers, they would have been sitting there meditating while waiting for his return instead of playing like that. But there was still something upsetting him. Was it the aggression? No, he thought, it couldn't be that.

The scene continued to nag him, bother him, and he wasn't sure why.

8.

Markos sat in the right seat, the Old One sat on the left. The children, with Alpha as their appointed leader, were safely secured in the cabins. The old Haber had taught them all the trick of hardening their bodies to survive the tremendous force of acceleration.

The ship moved up and out of the mountain through an escape tunnel with the grace and ease Markos had come to expect from anything Haber. They leaped into orbit in one smooth motion that lasted only a few short minutes. The acceleration was tremendous.

He didn't know if their flight had been detected by the crew of the *Paladin*, but detection didn't seem to matter, at least to the Old One. From what the Haber had explained about the wedge-shaped ship, pursuit on the part of the Terrans would have been futile.

The tube mounted on the console between Markos and the Old One was emitting a tight beam of light. It was focused right now on the back plane, piercing right through the tiny globe that represented Tau Ceti. Markos watched as the startank's interior rotated around Tau Ceti. The scene stopped shifting and rotating when the beam of light rested on their target star. Markos recognized it after regaining his orientation to the startank's orientation. The star was Alpha Indi. The Old One explained that as they approached the star, the view within the startank would shift, keeping the center of the startank their location. Alpha Indi would creep toward the center of the startank.

Markos noticed that the Haber touched certain plates and areas on the consoles to activate and deactivate different in-flight systems. The Old One explained that the switches worked by the "touch and change" principle, the switches being flipped by the electron flow between the Haber's hand and the receiving plate.

Markos experienced between two and three Gs, an increased gravity he wouldn't have been able to survive if he hadn't learned the hardening trick from the Old One. As a Terran, there would have been some discomfort, but nothing debilitating. He watched the startank, hoping to see some progress in the changing positions of the stars. Nothing seemed to move—they had yet to achieve light-speed.

When the acceleration increased, Markos was pinned to his seat, unable to move. But he could see directly before him into the startank, and the stars were moving. They must have been traveling well beyond light-speed. Tau Ceti was no longer in the exact center; it was creeping back toward the Old One and Markos.

Tau Ceti began to move, moving to the degree where motion in some surrounding stars could be detected too. Everything within Markos's line of sight on the bridge began to shift color. It was barely discernible at first—the reds seemed a little deeper, while everything else took on a slightly reddish cast. The oppressive acceleration stopped suddenly, then stabilized at one G.

Markos still stared at the startank, this time in disbelief. Within the few hours of takeoff and acceleration, and the hours they'd spent under heavy acceleration, their location had shifted significantly. Tau Ceti was far behind. They had traveled nearly a light-year.

They had been in space just a few days before Markos decided it was time to do something about Alpha and the other children. He saw the need for educating them, making them aware of the differences between play and real, between war games and war.

Markos regretted having left Gandji so early in their life cycle. If they'd had a few more months on the planet, he could have seen the children in action. He would have liked to have seen them kill something, even if it was only a mendil. With their aggressive play they had warrior potential. But that didn't mean they could fight under actual war conditions.

He went into their cabins and gathered them together. He started talking to them, explaining about the horrors and ugliness of battle, but felt his approach lacked something. He'd never been in battle himself.

They took in the information without comment or question. Markos's word was all they needed. He explained what he was, why he had run from the *Paladin*, and then used that as an example of a poor retreat. He granted that it was a necessary maneuver to gain time, but he still stressed the fact that the retreat had been badly executed. He was weaving truth and fiction, trying to manipulate them, make them see what he saw, re-create the reality in their minds, and was doing it fairly well. When he reached the point of killing Van Pelt, their eyes were glowing a dull, deep red.

He made sure they understood the major points of battle. He then gave them the crystals with the insect-alien invasions so that they would know more about who they might be fighting.

Markos used his free time to piece together information from the different crystals and had developed a fairly solid view of how the alien invasions went. While Alpha and the others studied the crystals, looking for details that might help them some time in the future, he went over the general thrust of the aliens' planetary takeovers.

None of the crystals ever showed more than one alien ship landing. That meant the first assault wave was just a single landing craft that served as a base camp and was fortified like a bunker. The ship would land, the hatch would slide open, and an armed group of battle-ready aliens would emerge to mow down anything in their path.

After clearing the immediate area, the first wave left the ship. They set up a small defense perimeter and set up guards. This first wave of soldiers had white markings on their heads/helmets. Markos still couldn't tell if they wore battle gear or if they had chitinous exoskeletons.

Once the immediate area had been secured, the second wave left the craft. While the first wave stood guard, the second wave deposited eggs in the soil. This second group of twenty, most likely female, looked no different from the first assault wave. They had the same physical appearance right down to the white head markings.

Once the egg laying had taken place, the third wave disembarked. This third group of twenty started dismantling sections of the hull only to reattach them in different locations, making the ship a stronghold, capable of withstanding most physical attacks. Primitive weapons would have little effect on those thick metal plates, Markos realized. With the rearrangement of the hull sections, the base camp looked more like a bunker than it had before.

Markos had trouble putting together a coherent sequence of events after that. The crystals had bits of information that made no sense, information that had been recorded well after the initial landing and setup of the aliens had taken place. There were threads of scenes, of slaughter and mayhem, that were recorded well into the aliens' takeover of the planets. Some of these showed smaller aliens, possibly children, without markings at all.

The third wave that left the ship, those who reorganized the structure of their defense, had brightly colored markings. These aliens never seemed to bear weapons, either, and took care of reconnaissance and food gathering.

It was hard to get a feel for the time it took from the initial landing to the second assault, outside the camp area. The scenes were so fragmented and were so short that Markos couldn't develop a strong sense of continuity.

He knew he'd presented more than enough information to the

children for now, and they probably needed time to discuss what they'd learned among themselves before going any farther.

He knew there was more to do, though, before these children could enter into combat. But at least he'd started them on the right path, and the trip to Alpha Indi would give them enough time to follow the path as far as he could lead.

By asking the Old One about the planets that had been assaulted by the aliens, Markos started gathering information that he hoped would indicate what area of space they came from.

Most of their assaults had taken place on planets orbiting K-type stars, though two that he knew of had taken place on planets orbiting G-type stars. All of which only made him more anxious to see this whole thing concluded. Despite his split allegiance, he had been born on a planet that orbited a G-type star. But the aliens did seem to like K-types better than anything else.

That led Markos to believe they came from a K-type star themselves. He studied the startank and tried to see a pattern in the expanding alien wave of ships and captured planets.

The Old One cared little for talking to Markos, even about where the aliens had come from. He stayed uninvolved and detached. Markos feared this might be a result of the Habers' nonacceptance of him, but then realized that even if that were true, something else was bothering the Old One, keeping him silent and distant. While Markos worked on figuring out where the alien threat was coming from, he also worked on getting the Old One to open up about what was bothering him.

As Markos stood before the startank looking for some pattern, some single star from which the expansion took place, he talked to the Old One.

"I know it's here someplace. They've got to be coming from somewhere in this sector," he said, gesturing to take in several hundred stars.

The Old One said nothing.

"Tell me what it is that's bothering you. Please. After what's happened to me, after what you and your race have done to me, I feel I'm owed an explanation."

The Haber flashed red. He then flashed a series of colors that meant nothing to Markos. He'd never seen them generated in a Haber before, but they managed to create a sad feeling, a failure; the feeling of a sentient, caring creature who knows no hope.

Markos asked why he felt that way, flashing yellow tinged with blue.

"I, I have failed. I, I have let down myself and my ancestors by extending my, my life longer than it was meant to be. Your appearance on Gandji made it necessary for me, me to live longer. When we, we get back to the homeworld, to Aurianta, my, my brothers will reject me, me, and I, I will become an outcast. I, I will meditate down in energy until I, I die at last. I, I long to become part of the homeworld's cycle. Even the cycle of Gandji would have been preferable to this life."

Markos nodded. He understood, and he realized there was nothing he could do. The Old One was practically in mourning for himself, and it seemed to be the Haber way.

He expressed his sympathy and tried to take the Old One's mind off his self-pity by getting him involved in locating the source of the alien expansion.

They studied the angles and vectors, tracing them back as best they could without refined instruments, and located a star where five vectors intersected. The star was a K-type star, over thirty parsecs from Alpha Indi. The expansion appeared to be spreading out like a sound wave. From the front of the startank, the K-type star was a little above the relative position of Alpha Indi, but almost the same exact distance from the center of the tank to the front edge.

It was Pi Hydra.

By the time the ship left tau-space and began its deceleration, Markos had named the children and had named the enemy. The children were becoming more verbal as they understood more and more of what they were involved in. He established a chain of command, with Alpha as their leader.

Alpha seemed to have the best grasp of what was expected of them. There were still some weak spots in Alpha's understanding, but there was nothing Markos could do about that. The only way around those spots would have required Alpha to know something about at least three thousand years of Terran history. Markos gave Alpha what little insight he could.

What they knew about their enemy was relatively clear-cut. There would be no negotiating. The crystals had shown quite clearly that the Hydrans were concerned about only one thing—taking over their target planet as quickly and efficiently as possible, with no regard for sentient life.

They knew that at least five planets had suffered the Hydrans' assault—these were probably owned by the Hydrans now. He was willing to ignore them for the time being and concentrate on whatever new invasions had taken place. He had no idea how many planets had been invaded, nor how long these assaults had been going on. For all he knew, they might be decelerating into a solar system held by the Hydrans.

But whatever happened, he was glad he was there and not on Gandji, negotiating with the Terrans. From what he could surmise, the differences between the Hydrans and the Terrans were slight: The Terrans knew how to smile and lie before taking what they wanted; the Hydrans seemed a little more direct. Markos preferred the Hydrans' approach.

Markos wondered what kind of reception they would get when they landed on Aurianta. How many homeworld Habers could still speak? As a onetime xenobiologist, he knew that the Habers had once communicated through sound-speech and that after their culture had advanced to conscious genetic engineering, they had mutated toward light-speech for aesthetic reasons. Most Habers he'd seen on Gandji had had the latent capability to talk, though none really liked using it. And whenever Markos communicated strictly through his eyes, he felt he missed about fifty percent of the informational content while getting about seventy-five percent of the emotional content of the message.

He was sure there wouldn't be any cheering crowds waiting there for them. Even if they had somehow been informed of the ship's arrival time, he couldn't see these creatures piling out of houses (or whatever they lived in) to crowd the streets in excitement. They weren't returning home after having won a war—they were imported talent, a cross between saviors and mercenaries. Cheers? Not very likely.

Now all he had to worry about was whether Aurianta was populated by Habers or by Hydrans.

If it were Hydran, he had a very good idea as to the kind of reception they would receive.

9.

Without a viewscreen Markos had no idea what Aurianta looked like. He sat beside the Old One, squirming in his seat, anxious to get outside and see the planet. If he had been aboard the *Paladin*, he would have already known what awaited them. It would have been easy to see through the logarithmic magnification of the viewscreens. But the *Wedge*, as Markos had named it, had no screens that produced coherent visual pictures. As they landed, the thin, transparent screens before them had lit up supplying landing information to the Haber, but swirling colors through a grid made little sense to Markos.

He was burning to leave the ship, to see where the Old One had brought him and the children. Most of his fears over finding the planet overrun by Hydrans were put to rest; the Old One would know by now if Hydrans were out there.

"Well, Old One, it looks like we've made it," Markos said, smiling inside, bubbling with excitement, eagerness, and anticipation.

The Old One showed a weak, watery, noncommital red.

"You're not glad to be back, then?" Markos asked.

"I, I no longer belong."

"What? That's not true, and you know it," Markos said. "I'm the one who doesn't belong—not you. I don't even have the slightest idea what it's like out there, or what they'll think of me, or how they'll treat me. I'm not even sure they know themselves.

"You're the Haber—not me. You're returning home with the solution you were sent out to find. Doesn't that mean anything? Don't you think your brothers will be grateful?"

"Yes," the Haber said. But the red he generated through his eyes was weak, as though he weren't really convinced himself. "They, they will be grateful, but that does not change the important things. I, I am still taboo."

"Not to me, you're not. Listen to me, Old One. We may not have another opportunity to talk like this for a long time. If you want to spend the rest of your life in mourning, meditating down to zero energy and death, then you go right ahead. But if you do, you'll be failing yourself and your people. You and your brothers have taught me a lot about change. But let me teach *you* something: Your way of life is to accept and deal with change as best you can, right?"

The Old One showed a solid red. "It is time for us, us to go. We, we can leave the ship now."

"Wait a minute. Whatever's out there can wait."

The Old One showed red again.

"If you were on Aurianta and you ate something in your final cycle, then I could understand. But we're at war, and war forces us to change our attitudes. War makes us take a harder look at what we are, where we've been, and where we're going.

"Take a hard look at yourself. You're the closest thing to a friend I have. I need your help. You can't just open the bay door and disappear. I can't fight this war by myself. You change so many things just by touching them. Look at how different I am, and the adjustments I've had to make. But now *you* have to change.

"Changing rock and stone—the wind does that, and the water does too. But it can't change the *inside* of a stone. Inside yourself, Old One—that's where the change has to be.

"Stay with me and help me. Don't mourn something you just couldn't stop. If you hadn't broken your taboo, we would still be on Gandji, most likely dead, and your brothers would lose this war. Do you understand?"

"Yes," the Old One said. "I, I understand."

"Even if it means eating again?"

"Yes."

"Then let's have no more of this. I need your continued help too much to have you sulking."

The Haber flashed red. His eyes stayed red, then the color slowly faded.

"Let's see what it's like out there," Markos said. "I've never been here before, and it's been a long time for you."

"Yes, it has."

They stood in the large bay, positioned by the huge door, tensed, ready to react instantly. If the Hydrans were on the other side of the door, they would have to act quickly to keep their lives.

"You all remember what to do, right?" Markos asked.

The ten children flashed a brilliant crimson.

"All right then, Old One. Start opening the door."

The Old One touched the bulkhead and the door started to swing upward and outward. As soon as it had traveled a few centimeters, the smallest child, Markatens, dropped to the deck and described what he could see through the widening crack. No smoke, no signs of destruction Markos had warned him to look for.

Markos felt trapped in his own body as it reacted to the changing demands. At least when he'd been Terran, years of experience had helped him know what physical feelings he'd have to deal with—adrenaline, hormones, fatigue. But this new body had no in-betweens. Without the immediate threat of battle, it reacted with incredible speed, shutting down his heightened awareness and relaxing muscles that a moment ago were tightly knotted.

He bent down to see Aurianta.

At first glance he thought his body was still playing tricks on him, that the tension of possible battle had created a chemical in his system that changed his perceptions. He felt as though he'd been given a large dose of a hallucinogen. When he glanced up at the Old One and the children, Markos's fears doubled. No one seemed affected by the scene as he'd been.

His mind reeled as he stared, dumbfounded, nearing fright and shock. The ship had landed a few kilometers away from what looked like a city. The tallest building was only three stories high, though needlelike spires pierced the sky ten stories up. Somehow he felt the city was there only as an afterthought, something to add a little sanity to the landscape.

Balloonlike plants floated through the air, drifting on gentle breezes, some high in the prismatic sky while others drifted lazily a meter or two off the ground. Tendrillike roots dangled from the inflated transparent sacs, moved in slow motion, circling, twisting, constantly seeking a place to alight below.

The sky proved impossible to look at for more than a second or two at a time. The sun was either rising or setting, resting on the horizon like a large, diffuse blob of constantly changing colors. The rest of the sky mirrored this effect, though the colors were far less intense and their boundaries less clearly defined. It was like staring up into a huge, deep opal that covered the whole sky, shimmering and changing with each passing moment.

Wherever his eyes rested, they were treated to more of the same, and he flashed again on the idea that he might be hallucinating.

"This place . . ." he started to say, then stopped when he realized he couldn't put the feeling into words.

The ground of Aurianta was reddish-brown where no vegetation grew, almost a maroon, with little shards of dark brown, bright orange, and yellow. Grass grew in abundance, in some areas in tall patches that reached two to three meters, while elsewhere it grew to only a few centimeters. Each clump of grass seemed to have different colored blades, though the taller groups showed many distinctly different shades of green. There were pastel flowers in bloom, each petal a different color, each stem a different shade of green.

There were oddly shaped trees, shaped as if they had been tended by some insane bonsai sculptor. Their long, flat leaves made the memory of autumn in Vermont seem like a black-and-white movie.

He needed to turn away from the overwhelming landscape. "What I don't understand is why anyone would want to leave," he said.

Habers were coming to meet them; they were less than a kilometer away. Markos got the impression that they were just out for a leisurely stroll.

The sun was setting; the diffuse patch of brighter, prismatic color was sinking down, swallowed by a row of distant, faint hills. All the Habers seemed to notice this instantly. The Old One immediately climbed down from the bay door and faced the sun, holding his arms outstretched to either side like a flow-bridge.

All the other Habers had stopped walking and had turned to face the sun. They linked hands and formed lines of at least fifty Habers; the lines stretched row after row back to the city.

Alpha and his brothers climbed down to see what was going on. Markos joined the others on the ground.

A strange noise started building, first like a steady haunting wind; it built quickly to a steady hum like a thousand hydroelectric generators. It came from the Habers.

The Old One's eyes radiated a deep emerald green that touched a sympathetic chord inside Markos. The green was more brilliant than their greeting color. The Old One was making the same sounds, eerily echoing his brothers' calls.

Markos rushed to the Old One's side and grabbed one of his hands. "Come on!" he shouted.

Alpha rushed over and grasped the Old One's free hand and the other children linked up from Alpha. The small group watched Alpha Indi sink below the horizon.

The feelings started immediately. The physical and emotional pleasure was stronger than being a flow-bridge. His whole body vibrated, built up and up, making him lose control. His only conscious thought was to feel grateful.

He started humming too. It helped soothe the raw energy, mellow out the physical feelings. The ecstatic pleasure pulsed within him in rapid bursts of tingling sensation.

Then the sun set, and the sky started to darken into soft twilight. The noise stopped, they all broke contact, and the feeling was gone. The Habers resumed walking.

Markos knew his pleasure had been a shared pleasure. He'd experienced a sense of oneness, of belonging.

"We," the Old One said, "we are home."

The Habers' eyes glistened and sparkled in the soft twilight. As the Old One explained about Markos and the children, the Habers' eyes lit, probing the Old One's color-intensified messages, making him stop for clarification and detail. As long as Markos looked at their eyes, they all looked like Habers.

They were short, tall, thin, and fat, with pear-shaped torsos, barrel torsos, convex and concave—every variation of the basic bipedal anatomy seemed to be represented. Some of their shoulders were lower than Markos figured they should be, and some of their legs seemed only marginally functional. They looked like a great quilt of patches, dolls sewn together by insane tailors with synesthesia.

By the time the explanation was over, the Habers from the city were lined up waiting for something. "What do they want?" Markos asked verbally, afraid he already knew the answer.

The Old One turned and with violet hues in his eyes, colors that passed for a smile, said, "They, they want you to act as a flow-bridge."

"Now?"

"Yes." Flashed with red.

Markos shook his head. "Not yet. We've got to get into the city first, get settled in there, get accustomed to this change. I have to set up some kind of command post. I've got to start training and teaching. We don't have time for this now."

The Old One disappeared into the crowd with a few flashes,

explaining to the Habers milling about that they would have to wait. Silently but with soft, light yellow flecked with a dark blue seeping from their eyes, the crowd ambled back toward the city. Markos's group followed.

The path felt cool and alive beneath his feet. The stars overhead seemed to sparkle in a pattern and harmony, a visual melody, faint and airy, impossible to pin down. The wind rustled the fields and made the grass change shades of gray in the dying light, a faint melody of its own. The flowers swayed, colorful metronomes keeping beat to the visual melody.

It's these eyes, Markos thought. They see things that shouldn't be there.

The city glowed with light, pulling him and the others toward it. The closer he got, the more beautiful it appeared to be. While the sun had been up, the city was bland, a washed-out eggshell white, a sobering, steadying part of the constantly shifting landscape. It had offered a base in reality, an unchanging vision in a world of change.

The closer he came, the less he believed that. The city wasn't actually moving, but he thought it was shifting in and out of phase. It was like watching a mirage dance on the horizon. It shimmered and slid, but the city was no mirage.

But still it danced.

When he was very close, he realized what was happening. The buildings weren't just off-white—their outer shells were plastered with a white covering, but the covering contained tiny pieces of maroon, yellow, and orange, tiny shards of micalike crystal, crumbled bits of blue and green. The colors were embedded in the walls, and from a distance the walls seemed to move. The buildings fluoresced, and each piece of rock and crystal fluoresced in a different, flickering color, like chromatic fire from a jeweled city. When the colored rocks flickered in phase, the color of the building changed to an off-white, tinted by a soft pastel.

He walked the path with awe and pride, overwhelmed by the constant beauty of Aurianta. The only thing he was anxious about was seeing the Habers eagerly lined up, waiting for him to act as a flow-bridge. He wasn't going to tackle the whole city. What did they expect from him?

But as he walked, watching their backs before him, he figured he was overreacting. They had politely accepted his answer. Too many things had to be accomplished before he could think of creating so many changed Habers. He no longer felt that acting as a flow-bridge was a proper thing for him to do. He could end up contaminating an entire race with his mutations, and until it was proven necessary, he would avoid it despite the sensual pleasures involved.

The streets of the city were unpaved, firmly compressed earth, with small patches of weeds and grass poking up in corners and untrodden areas. The buildings themselves were clean and new, as though the whole city had been built weeks ago. There were no signs of erosion, no cracking or crumbling facades or towers; the freshness of color and the age of the streets contradicted each other.

The city swallowed the returning Habers. Singly and in small groups they entered buildings. Other Habers stood in doorways and windows, beneath graceful, pointed arches, in alleys leading to arcades, watching the Old One lead Markos and his offspring through the streets.

There were many Habers who resembled the Old One, though none had the same dull gray-brown covering. He was reassured by their familiar shape and size; he doubted he could feel any real kinship for those Habers whose phenotypes were radically different from the Old One's.

"What's the name of this city?" Markos asked. His gargling, bubbly voice sounded obscene within the city and its beauty. He had grown so accustomed to it that he had almost forgotten how it sounded. Memories of Van Pelt's frozen, horrified face flashed in his mind.

"I, I believe its translation would be 'War.' "

"What?" Markos asked.

"Not now," the old Haber said, stopping before a building. "We, we are here. This is the place we, we will live in. I, I will explain about this city."

Markos looked around. They were centrally located, near the heart of the city. This building had no outstanding characteristics to distinguish it from all the others. "How many entrances does this structure have?" he asked.

"There are no doors," the Old One answered. "There are two entrances; this one and one in the back."

Markos nodded. "Alpha, you stay out here. After we're inside, let no one in or out without my permission. Understand?"

Alpha flashed red and positioned himself outside.

"Markatens, walk around through the house. Take VeePee with you. Make sure no one is in there. When you're done, send VeePee back out here and position yourself by the back entrance, the same as Alpha. Understand?"

Markatens and VeePee flashed red, then entered the building.

"What is all of this for?" the Old One asked.

"It's a test."

"There is nothing in this building that can harm us, us."

"I know that, and you know that, and all the children know that. But let's stop taking chances and going on assumptions."

VeePee appeared at the arch by the front entrance. "It is uninhabited," he said.

That piece of information and VeePee's safe passage through the building were worth more to Markos than anything the Old One might have said. He hadn't thought the building was unsafe, but they needed to be treating their situations as real. They needed the practice. "Let's go in."

They walked through the arch into a honeycomb of passageways. He immediately realized that VeePee couldn't have possibly checked out every passageway in the building in that short length of time. He was right, then, testing them. He would have to talk with them, show them how foolish doing a sloppy job like this was. But later.

The Haber led them through the building, explaining the basic layout of the house. He made it sound as if the building was centuries old. He assigned rooms to the children, then told them to explore the place, learn all they could about everything they saw and touched. He told them to meet him in the common area when they were done and stressed that they were not to leave the grounds. He assigned VeePee as relief for Markatens, and Triand as relief for Alpha.

"Okay, Old One. Tell me about this city."

The Haber flashed red and led him into the common room. It

was large enough to hold fifty or sixty Habers. They seated themselves on chairs of molded rock; Markos did the trick the Old One had taught him while on board the ship, hardening his body so that the chair could be comfortable. His breathing shifted into its rest cycle.

"This house is yours, Markos," the old Haber said. "It was made for you long before you were born, before we, we left for Gandji. This city was made by those Habers who needed to understand the change. It is a refuge, a community for Habers devoted to finding an answer. We, we came here, or our, our ancestors did, from all over Aurianta to find an answer to this . . . this . . . war.

"When we, we realized the answer could not be found here, the Habers of this city built the ship. Most volunteered to sacrifice their lives and leave Aurianta for Gandji. Few were taken. Those Habers who remained behind stayed here to wait for the answer, to help when it arrived. We, we named the city, The Place Where the Answer to the Change Would be Found. In your language the city's name is War."

"No, my friend. Not War. It's closer to Peace."

"Peace?"

Alpha suddenly appeared at the passageway. There was yellow tinged with blue in his eyes. "Markos?"

"What's wrong?"

"You should come out and see for yourself."

Markos rose to his feet.

He reached the front arch in full stride, then froze in his tracks. The streets were filled with thousands of Habers. Their multiple eyes, protected beneath the transparent outer coverings of their faces, were trained on him, flashing green at his appearance.

"What the hell? What's going on?" Markos asked.

"You said later," the Old One said from behind. "It is later. They, they wait to bear the changed ones."

Markos fought the metallic, bitter taste as he stared out over the sea of faces. They stood there like an anxious army, or a group of starving Terrans waiting for their names to be called for the food dole. They waited in streets, overflowed into alleys and doorways of buildings, every face turned to him, every group of eyes radiating tiny pulses of green.

"They, they have waited a long time, Markos. They, they have been ready since our, our original group left for Gandji, and from before that."

Did these creatures have any idea what they were doing? What they were asking? He wasn't ready to accept the responsibility for changing a significant portion of the Haber race.

They thought that linking up with him would stop the war? That by giving birth to a generation of changed ones everything would be okay?

He was willing to fight for them and let the children fight for them. He was willing to teach them all how to fight. And when he'd been on Gandji, he'd been willing to be a flow-bridge for the entire population.

But he couldn't be a flow-bridge for them now. This wasn't Gandji, and he knew about the war and what was really going on. First this city, Peace, Markos thought, and then the others will follow, one by one, spreading the corrupt seed of aggression through a whole race that had conquered this primitive emotion millennia ago.

"Translate for me, Old One. I want to talk to them."

The Haber flashed red and worked his way forward so that many Habers could see his eyes.

"I will not create the changed offspring you desire. Not unless that is the only answer. We are all involved in this change—a change my ancestors knew well. Our word for it is *war*.

"War is fought in strange ways. If you resist the change and fight, or if you give in to the change and die, it is still war. We'll need more than a generation or two of changed offspring to resist this change.

"Fighting, resisting the change, is all-consuming. We would need a great number of changed Habers if war were fought on Gandji alone. Or on any other planet. We could possibly win in these small confrontations by sheer number. But war isn't fought like that. There are no rules to war.

"We can't just fight in the fields, in the streets of a city, on some planet's plains or valleys. We must learn to think in terms of fighting whenever and wherever possible. And in the most efficient way possible. Thinking like this is an all-consuming problem."

He stopped and looked deeply into their glowing eyes, hoping to see some colors of agreement or understanding. If they understood, they showed no signs. They remained in the streets, waiting.

He turned to the Old One. "Forget it. Just tell them to go home. Tell them the answer is not more children."

The Old One stared at Markos with confused colors sparkling beneath his face.

"Just tell them!" he screamed. His pulse rate soared, and his skin felt as if it was pierced by thousands of tiny needles. The metallic taste in his mouth made it difficult to talk anymore. His eyes glowed a pure-white light, the light of anger and frustration. "And you!" he said, shouting at Alpha. "Remain here."

He turned and strode away, back into the depths of the building.

How did they expect to survive? They understand so little. If there had been a Terran anywhere on this planet, Markos would have sought him out for companionship. Even if the only Terran had been Van Pelt. He wanted to get into his cabin, crawl under the sheets, and let the massager bunk do its work on his body. He wanted to climb into the geltank and slip quietly beneath its surface and put his mind on hold for a few hours.

But by the time he reached the common room, he had started to calm down. He knew the Habers in the city weren't people. They were Habers, pure and simple. Markos dropped into a chair, forgetting to make his body hard, and suffered with the pain. He looked up, staring at the ceiling as if hoping to find an answer there.

His children and the Old One stood silently, waiting for Markos to say something, to do something, to give them the guidance and instruction they wanted and needed.

Terrific, Markos. The more involved you get, the worse it becomes.

Part

Two

.

CATHY

.

STRAKA

.

10

The *Paladin* traced a long, slow orbit around Alpha Indi. Cathy Straka sat in the command chair of the control center watching the viewscreens that covered the bulkheads, ceiling, and deck. A bored, tired look was on her thin, pointed face. She looked drawn, haggard, and was aging far too fast for a woman in her thirties.

In every direction she looked, Straka saw black space studded with points of light. Sitting in the captain's chair was like sitting in a chair floating through space, unprotected and unobstructed. Just Straka and the stars.

The ship's exterior cameras supplied the computer with holographic images, and the computer re-created the images to scale, giving anyone sitting in one of the chairs the feeling of being surrounded by the depths of space, as if the bulkheads weren't even there.

"We should have gone to Earth," Jackson said. "This idea of yours is ridiculous. We don't even know he's here."

Straka turned slowly and carefully as if afraid of spooking the skittish man and said, "He's here."

"He is? Where?"

"Be patient, Jack. He'll show."

They were on a platform that had four chairs, each facing a different quadrant of space. Before each chair was a console with controls. At one end of the platform a narrow ramp led back to the door, though with the screens on, the door was invisible.

Jackson shook his head and rose to his feet. He turned around full circle, staring out into the lonely blackness, searching for a sign of motion that didn't belong. He walked up the ramp to the door.

Straka continued to scan the surrounding space, waiting. He would show up, all right. That murderous freak was here, somewhere, hiding in Alpha Indi's system. He would show. It was only a matter of time.

Jackson opened the door, and light streamed in. Straka squinted against the light, glancing at Jackson's outlined figure. "Why don't you check the tau translators?" she said to Jackson's back.

"Check them yourself," Jackson said, disappearing behind the closing door.

Straka was plunged into blackness and the depth of space again. She shrugged, shaking her head. "Suit yourself," she muttered. "I don't care if they don't work. We'll just never see Earth again."

Which was fine with Straka. It was to her advantage to stay as far away from Terra as possible. By now NASA 2 had probably assumed that the mission had been a failure. Since Van Pelt had never radioed their safe transition out of tau-space when they'd arrived at Tau Ceti, NASA 2 had no way of knowing if the ship had been destroyed or if something in the translators had malfunctioned and stranded them.

Sure, Straka thought. The *Paladin* was destroyed, had never even made it to Tau Ceti. Everyone on board had been obliterated. Even me.

She leaned back and let loose a loud, horsey laugh.

Those poor earthbound slobs, she thought. I've got their ship, their crew, and there's no way for them to stop us, even if they knew what we were doing. And there's no way they can. No word from us since we left the Solar System. They haven't the slightest hint of what's happened.

And the crew. Christ. They think we're taking care of Markos so that we can go home. And why shouldn't they? It's a carrot that keeps them in line. Let them think what they want. At least there's some semblance of discipline.

She smiled as she pictured returning from space, years, decades overdue, after having stolen NASA 2's one and only f-t-l ship. Fat chance.

She laughed again.

Following the alien ship had been the easiest part of her plan. Every ship burns fuel, even if it doesn't use a reaction-drive propulsion system. It leaves some waste behind. It leaves a trail. One molecule per cubic meter of space or one atom per cubic kilometer of space—what difference did it make? It was only a matter of quantity. A careful, painstaking scan of local space surrounding Tau Ceti had found the trail. It had been thin, spotty in places, but it had been there.

The difficult part of her plan had been convincing the crew that their lives depended on following it. Once they were relatively certain that Markos was headed in the general direction of Terra, they agreed without argument.

Straka had been certain that Markos was aboard that alien ship. What alien on Gandji had enough sense to run?

Just by the very existence of the alien ship, Straka realized that other planets had to be populated by these soft, amoebalike humanoids, these poor excuses for biological life. Markos had somehow gotten them to take him someplace safe, someplace where he thought Straka wouldn't follow.

But Markos hadn't figured Straka correctly. Straka really wanted to follow. She convinced the crew to share her ambition, but that hadn't been easy.

"We've got to find the little freak," Straka had said.

"Let's just go back," Jackson had said. "I'm willing to take my chances."

"Really? How naive." Straka had paced, adopting one of Van Pelt's command tricks. "They'll be real glad to see us now, won't they? Or at least they'll be glad to see the ship."

"I don't get it," Kominski said. Ever since Kominski had been inside the one geltank that had malfunctioned, he hadn't been right. Kominski's round face glistened with sweat, eyes open wide, mouth hanging open as he tried to decide if there was more to say.

"Okay, comrades, I'll lay it out for you in detail, then," Straka had said. "First, Van Pelt blew our directives by not radioing our safe arrival. Then he took it upon himself to start ripping up the native population. We all went along with him, remember?"

Katawba, a tall, angular man, nodded.

"Everyone except Markos, who deserted. But Markos's desertion was technically the right thing to do. We should have all deserted or mutinied instead of following Van Pelt like we did."

"So then we're in trouble?" Kominski asked, his face showing the depth of his confusion.

Straka laughed. "Trouble? Brother, that's just the tip of it. How do you think those chair-bound officials waiting for us back on Terra are going to feel about this? You think they'll take it in their stride?

"Sure, why not. Can't you see them? It's only normal that they spend years and years and hundreds of billions building an f-t-l ship, only to have it violate their prime directives and never establish radio contact. Sure, they'll be overjoyed to see us. They might even throw us a party before frying our brains."

"Yeah, right," Kominski said.

"And it gets worse. Lots worse."

"How?" Martinez asked. His smooth olive skin was wrinkled with concern and confusion.

"To start with, there's a witness to all that's happened here on Gandji. A traitor."

"Markos Dressler," Katawba said.

Straka nodded. "Markos Dressler."

Kominski swallowed.

Wilhelm stayed on the edges, watching, listening. Wilhelm had handed over the command position to Straka. Command had never interested him, and if Straka had a plan and a desire to take control, it was all right with him.

"What do we do, then?" Martinez asked.

"We grab him. No witness, no problem."

"I don't know . . ." Jackson said.

"Do you want to see home again?"

Jackson nodded.

"Then we've got to get our hands on Dressler. There's no other way. Without him we'd have to blame this whole mess on Van Pelt, and we'll never make that stand without Markos's help. And don't forget, Markos went nuts and killed the Captain. If it comes to it, we can kill Markos and say we tried to stop him, but we were too late and Van Pelt was dead."

"No problem," Maxwell said. "Only, where *is* he?"

Straka shrugged. "We'll find him."

"I'm not sure. Maybe we should just go back and forget this idea," Jackson said.

"What's the *matter* with you, Jackson? Open your eyes! We're free now—the first really free human beings ever. You don't want to lose that yet, do you?" Straka asked. "There's no one to stop us. No one!"

"Well . . ."

"We'll have to find him," Maxwell said.

"Don't worry," Straka said. "He's got to be hiding out in one of these villages. We'll just eliminate places for him to hide. When he makes a run for it, we'll grab him."

And they had tried. They had set out to destroy villages and settlements on Gandji in hopes of flushing out Markos. They had destroyed the second one when the alien ship had fled Gandji.

Straka had cursed bitterly, eyes narrowed to tight slits, mouth drawn into a cruel, thin-lipped frown. She'd stared at the screens for longer than necessary as her mind churned, trying in vain to figure out a way to get the alien vessel to reverse its course.

She had known that Markos presented no threat. The chances of Markos's ever returning to Terra were slim, or none. But she still needed to capture Markos alive. She had assisted Markos on some tests when they'd first landed on Gandji, and if the tests were anything close to what Straka thought, her future life depended on picking Markos's brain for the answer.

Straka didn't look away from the screens when the door to the bridge opened, flooding the place with light. She figured it was Jackson and knew that if she turned, her pupils would contract painfully.

"Anything yet?" Jackson asked.

"No, Jack. Nothing."

"How long are we going to wait here?"

"As long as necessary."

"You really think he's here someplace?"

"Don't you?" Straka asked.

Jackson shrugged and sat in the forward-quadrant control seat. Before him were dials and buttons and a series of small, console-mounted screens displaying the quadrants out of his line of sight. "He could be, or he could be dead already."

"He's not." He'd better not be.

"What makes you so sure?"

"I'm not sure of anything, Jack. I only know that until we see his body, we're not safe."

"So what do we do, then? Just wait?"

Straka nodded. "We have no choice. He'll soon discover the *Paladin*'s here. He'll come out to see us, to find out what we're doing, to make sure we don't start killing all his little alien friends."

"I hope you're right."

So do I, Straka thought. If only I'd known about that ship the Habers had, I could have stopped this before it got out of control, stopped Markos while he was still on Gandji. But who would have thought those humanoid cows would have an f-t-l ship?

She glanced over at Jackson. Jackson was starting to show his anxiety and his frustration. If he was so close to the edge, the rest of the crew couldn't be that far behind. If Markos didn't show soon, Straka knew she was heading for trouble. Sooner or later the real grumbling would start, and then they'd take the ship back to Terra regardless of what she did or said.

The geltanks had made the four-year chase across the spiral arm tolerable—most of the crew had spent six days in the tanks for every one day out. They hadn't aged much biologically over the two-hundred-some-odd days, and they were still in good enough frames of mind to pull this thing off. As long as Markos showed himself soon.

They were all anxious. They needed to feel ground beneath their feet, breathe fresh air, meet someone different, have their sexual desires taken care of by something more than a geltank. They wanted to go home, to try to live with the changes the years had left them with.

They had all agreed to the chase, all right—as Straka had presented it, they really had no choice. Either chase and catch Markos, or remain on Gandji for the rest of their lives. And what was on Gandji? There hadn't been anything worth staying for. When the Haber ship had left Gandji, the crew had been willing to give up and go home. Straka couldn't afford to let that happen. Not while she still needed information from Markos.

"What's that?" Jackson asked, pointing to a sector of space directly before him.

Straka's face changed as a smile emerged. Her eyes hardened and her cheek muscles knotted beneath her skin. "It's him. It has to be."

She immediately slapped the alert button, plunging the ship into emergency status. Sounds of activity filtered into the control center as crew members rose from geltanks or left the lounge and took their emergency positions.

Straka threw a few switches, and the pedestal-mounted viewscreen before her sprang to life. A tiny, moving dot appeared on the screen, then grew as it was logarithmically magnified. If it wasn't the exact ship Markos had used to make his escape from Gandji, it was close enough.

The navigational computer quickly supplied the ship's estimated flight path and time to possible interception. It was headed straight for the *Paladin*.

Straka spoke to the ship's computer. "Prepare for evasive maneuvers."

"Maneuvers laid in," the ship responded.

"Is it him?" Jackson asked.

"We'll see. Now it's only a matter of time."

The alien ship did not respond to their radio transmissions. Straka wasn't surprised by that, knowing what she did about the Habers' method of communication. There had been a certain amount of risk in letting the ship approach the *Paladin*, but she'd had little choice. The *Paladin* had no offensive weapons; none had been outfitted, and the computer refused or was programmatically incapable of helping them design any. If the alien ship was going to destroy them, it was well within range. After a few nervous moments, Straka realized there would be no attack on their ship.

The crew had strict orders not to fire on Markos when he showed himself. They were to trap him in the airlock, subdue him, then take him to the lab. Straka would oversee the questioning. Straka would get her answers. She would learn what Markos had learned from the Habers.

The tests that she and Markos had run had shown that the Habers were, for all intents and purposes, immortal. More immortal than she could ever be through the geltanks. She was sure that Markos knew how the chemical process worked and had somehow worked it on himself. As the alien ship docked, Straka daydreamed of living forever, of having the time and the ship to explore areas where intelligent, helpful life could be found, life that understood the values of commerce, of power, of control. She was free, but only of Terra and its chains. At the end of her freedom lay death, ready to claim her, to end her dreams and hopes and plans.

A backlit figure stood framed in the bridge's doorway, breathing heavily. "Cathy? You'd better come and see." It was Wilhelm.

"What is it?" Straka asked, getting to her feet, adrenaline coursing through her system.

"It looks a lot like him, but we can't be sure."

"Christ. Let's go," Straka said, rushing up the ramp.

They ran through the passageways, Wilhelm dripping sweat, breathing heavily, muttering curses and invectives at Markos and NASA 2. As they approached the airlock, Straka saw that Jackson and Kominski were already there waiting for them. They stopped before the airlock, and Straka peered through the thick, transparent window. The thing on the other side of the glass looked a lot like Markos.

Katawba, De Sola, and Martinez arrived a few seconds behind Straka.

"Open it," Straka said.

Jackson pressed the airlock button. The door slid open, revealing more of the Haber.

"Can you understand me?" the alien asked.

Straka blinked, then swallowed. A lump lay in her throat. "You're not Markos."

"No, I am not Markos. I am Markatens. Are you Straka?"

"Where's Markos?" Straka demanded.

Wilhelm looked at Straka as if she were crazy. "What good will—"

"Shut up, Wilhelm! Which planet, Markatens?"

Markatens's eyes glittered, flickering between violet and yellow. "He told us you might be coming, though he really didn't think you would. Before this goes any farther, I must tell you that my ship is manned and very effectively armed. If I am detained here, the crew has orders to destroy this ship."

Kominski turned his panic-stricken face to Straka, pleading for a sign that everything would be okay. Straka ignored him.

"There won't be any need for that, Markatens. You're not a prisoner. You're free to leave whenever you wish."

"I appreciate that," Markatens said, "but I'm afraid I cannot extend the privilege. Markos taught us a lot since Gandji. Your ship and crew are my prisoners."

11.

The *Paladin* was in a stable orbit around Aurianta, manned by one of the Habers. Straka had had no real choice but to surrender. Markatens had ably demonstrated his ship's weaponry, and the entire crew realized that they had no chance of fighting. The crew had stared at Straka with accusing eyes, muttering their discontent. Their accusations and resentment slowly hardened their expressions. Dealing with Markos and an alien civilization were bad enough—she didn't want to have to deal with the crew too.

The Habers took few precautions transporting Straka and the others to the surface of the planet. Few precautions were needed. Straka and the crew were prisoners as surely as if they'd been chained to the deck. Escape was possible, but there was no place to escape to; leaping out of the alien ship's airlock without a protective suit was suicide, not escape.

There were two Habers aboard. One guarded the crew while they sat in the bay area, while the other one was somewhere in the ship, probably at the controls, piloting them down to Aurianta's surface. The crew glared at Straka, and she glared back, doubly anxious over her position.

"What do you think they'll do with us?" Wilhelm asked Jackson.

The large black man shrugged. "Who knows? Kill us maybe?"

"Kill us?" Kominski asked, wild-eyed.

Jackson nodded. "Probably right after they try us for what we did on Gandji."

"No! It's not fair!" Kominski cried.

"Come on, 'Minski. Take it easy," Straka said calmly.

"Who asked you?" Jackson asked. There was enough bite in his voice to cause Straka some nervousness.

"Jack, there's no need to be—"

"I said who asked you. We wouldn't be here now it it wasn't for your screwy plan."

"But—"

Jackson cut her off. He leaned over and gathered the top of Straka's worksuit in one hand, choking her.

"You just shut up, Cathy. You understand? Shut up. We don't need any more help from you."

"Okay, okay," Straka said, rubbing her throat.

"You really think they'll kill us?" Kominski asked.

Jackson nodded. "I know *I* would."

But you're not them, Straka thought, and that's what counts. Not one slimy creature on Gandji had put up a fight. What makes him think they could kill us in cold blood?

"Why don't you two lay off?" McGowen asked.

Straka was surprised to see McGowen participate. He'd always been a loner by choice, quiet and calm on the outside, but on the inside, capable of clean, efficient violence bordering on the psychotic.

"Why don't *you* just shut up?" Jackson asked.

McGowen smiled without humor. "That's funny, Jackson. I'll tell you what—put me on report and when we get back to Terra, you can have me court-martialed."

"You really think they'll kill us, Jack?" Kominski pleaded.

Jackson slapped him across the face with the back of his hand. Kominski yelped in pain and surprise. Everyone froze for a moment, startled by the noise. McGowen was on Jackson almost instantly. They rolled on the deck of the alien ship, McGowen pummeling Jackson's face and head with quick, powerful blows. De Sola and Martinez pried them apart before Jackson got on the offensive.

Kominski, crunched against a bulkhead as if trying to melt into it, mumbled incoherently, gibbering. Katawba moved over to Kominski's side, trying to see if he'd been hurt. Straka remained seated, watching as if she had a front-row seat to some incredibly cruel sporting event. This is no time to jump in and get involved, she thought. Not if you like breathing.

"Stay the hell away from me, man!" Jackson screamed, half-crazed. He spat blood and rubbed his split lip with the back of his hand. A thin red gash on his left cheek trickled blood. He shrugged himself free of Wilhelm's grip. "You stay away from me if you know what's good for you."

McGowen was breathing calmly. Except for the manic gleam in his eyes and his scraped, bloodied knuckles, he seemed the same calm person he had been moments earlier.

"You leave *him* alone," McGowen said, nodding toward Kominski, "and I leave *you* alone."

Jackson looked away.

"Did you hear me?" McGowen asked.

"I heard you, all right. Just stay out of my way."

McGowen smiled, and Straka thought there might be humor there this time. "Gladly," McGowen said.

Kominski scrabbled his way to Jackson's side, eyes wild. "You think they'll kill us, don't you. We're all dead now."

Straka watched a thin trail of saliva slowly run down Kominski's chin. Jackson's cheek was swelling, and one of his eyes was starting to close. Jackson glared at Kominski, and Straka could see it was about to happen again. Against her better judgment she decided to say something.

"'Minski?" she asked.

Jackson pointed a warning finger at Straka, but before he had a chance to say anything, McGowen interceded. "That goes for her, too, Jackson."

Jackson leaped to his feet, hands balled into fists. "Just who the hell do you think you are?"

McGowen showed his bright, white teeth.

"They're going to kill us," Kominski wailed. "I can tell!"

McGowen stood slowly, with controlled power. Katawba and De Sola leaped to their feet and stood between Jackson and McGowen.

"Sit!" came a shout from the ramp behind them. They turned and looked at the Haber, his presence completely forgotten in the heat of the moment. He held a weapon and it was aimed at the group.

They sat.

Straka used the opportunity. "Listen, 'Minski. No one's going to kill us."

"No?" Kominski asked.

"No," Straka said.

"If you're as sure about that as you were about finding Markos, then we're as good as dead right now," Jackson said.

"I'm right, Jackson."

"Then they're not going to kill us?" Kominski asked, his face a tortured mask of confusion.

"No, they won't," Straka said.

"How the hell do *you* know? You've been wrong about everything else," Jackson said, lightly touching his puffy cheek.

"I know."

"Then they're not going to kill us?" Kominski asked with the fervor of a begging dog.

"No, 'Minski. They won't kill us," Straka said with a gentle smile, hoping to coax Kominski out of it.

"Oh," Kominski said.

Jackson shook his head in disbelief. "You know something, Straka? You couldn't have handled this thing any worse. Where the hell did these Habers get weapons, huh? Where's their peace-loving spirit gone to now?"

"I don't know where they got their weapons from," Straka said, "but I'd guess that has something to do with what happened on Gandji and the fact that Markos is here."

"And that's just the point, you idiot!" Jackson shouted at Straka. "What makes you think they won't try us for what we did?"

Straka shrugged. "That's a long way off, and 'Minski is here right now. The guy can't handle it."

"A long way off, huh? All of an hour or so," Jackson said.

Straka sighed. "What the hell do you want from me, Jackson? I tried. I came up with a plan. All you can do is slap around Kominski here and get into fights." She saw the burning anger in Jackson's eyes and resolved never to turn her back on the man. "Why don't we take it easy on each other? Torturing 'Minski won't do anything but tear us apart. If we're going to survive, we're going to have to stick together."

"I agree with her," Wilhelm said.

"You would," Jackson said. "Well, not me. Don't try to give *me* any orders."

Straka shrugged and smiled weakly. "That's fine with me, Jack."

"And don't call me Jack!"

McGowen smiled.

What orders *could* she give? Straka wondered. Try to take over the aliens' ship? And then what? Even if they could pilot it, where could they go? Back to the *Paladin*, with an alien aboard? No, they were stuck right where they were for now. At this point the fewer orders given, the better, she figured.

Just as long as they didn't tear out each other's throats before she got a chance to speak to Markos. Alone, and very soon, Straka thought, touching the spidery lines of age around her eyes.

"They're going to kill us," Kominski whined. "I know we're dead."

The other Haber appeared at the top of the ramp and flashed prismatic displays of light to the alien who'd been guarding them. The guard flashed back a series of odd colors, then flashed solid red.

"What's going on?" Maxwell asked.

Straka glanced at Maxwell. He was short, a little over five feet, wiry, and tough. His face was thin and angular, almost too large for the rest of his body. "I'd say we've landed," Straka said.

"No kidding," Jackson said. "What gave it away?"

"Take it easy, Jackson," Wilhelm said.

She gritted her teeth. It's okay, she told herself. They're not all on his side yet, and if I play it smart and safe, there's a chance I can maintain control.

The huge bay door began to swing open, and light from the planet's surface began to flood the bay.

"Jesus Christ! Will you look at that!" Maxwell exclaimed, pointing outside.

"Good God. What is this place?" Straka mumbled as she stared out over Aurianta's beauty. The planet's surface was like nothing she'd imagined possible. She'd known that variation from planet to planet could be extreme or subtle, but nothing like this! So much difference in the vegetation's coloring, the sky's iridescence. . . .

Entranced, the crew rose to their feet and moved slowly toward the bay door. Kominski babbled something while the rest, dumbstruck, stared in silence.

"Everyone outside," the Haber with the weapon ordered.

Kominski was the first to touch the planet's surface. Wilhelm followed, then the rest leaped down. Straka remained, watching the Haber behind her, trying to see what it would do if she refused to move. The Haber raised its weapon and pointed it at her. Straka jumped down.

They were on a plain, standing in a field of wild grass the likes of which hurt the eyes. It reminded Straka of a cross between impressionistic, surrealistic, and psychedelic painting, except that everything was in motion. It made no sense—the whole landscape looked aesthetically planned, like a work of art. There was no way the vegetation could have been so varied in hues under normal conditions.

Kominski was rolling on the ground, facedown, making pleasant sounds that bordered on the sexual. He was rubbing his nose in the dirt, reveling in the scents of natural life. The others milled around as if waiting for something to happen.

Straka was disappointed. She'd been frustrated at every turn.

When the alien ship had approached them in space, she'd been sure Markos was aboard. When he hadn't come to the airlock, she'd been sure Markos would be waiting for them aboard the alien ship, having sent someone else out to take the risks. But he hadn't been aboard the alien ship at all.

And Straka had felt certain that Markos would be here, on the planet's surface, waiting for the alien ship to land. He should have been there, waiting, ready to meet Straka and the crew.

But still no Markos.

There was a small, primitive building not far from the ship. Less than fifty meters away Straka could see a post set into the ground. She turned around in a circle, saw the three other posts, and realized the ship had put down inside some kind of compound. There was no question in her mind—there would be a barrier, a fence of some kind, designed to hold them here.

Kominski rolled over and stared into the changing sky. "You really think they're going to kill us?" he asked softly, quietly, a litany that had lost all meaning.

Straka walked slowly toward the building, hoping she'd find Markos inside waiting for them. The smells of the planet were sweet, fresh and uplifting. After four years in space, it was good to feel real ground beneath her feet again, feel the wind on her face, listen to a place live and breathe.

She entered the building, glanced around, and saw instantly that it was empty. There was no furniture, and the windows were no more than holes in the walls. There were no doors—only doorways. A shaped, hollow shell. They can't expect us to stay here, Straka thought. There's no food, no running water, no facilities.

Unless they really do plan on killing us, she realized.

The sound of the bay door closing caused her to wheel around. The Habers had stayed aboard their ship and were probably getting ready to take off. Not yet! Where was Markos? If they left now, they'd be stranding them without hope of surviving.

But that Haber Markatens—he had told her that Markos had thought they might arrive. If they'd been prepared, then why weren't there accommodations?

There was no way they were going to let them live. They

weren't even prisoners—they were fenced-in animals. What did the Habers think, they could graze on the grass and survive?

"Well, we've got Markos right where we want him now," Jackson said, laughing.

No one shared his amusement. Wilhelm joined Straka in the doorway, and the others started moving toward them.

"How's it look?" Wilhelm asked.

"See for yourself," she said, waving her hand for Wilhelm to pass. Maxwell stood in the doorway, peering around the edge. "You too, Maxwell. Have a look around."

Maxwell shook his head. "No need. I've seen more than enough."

Straka walked back toward the ship, leaving the crew to mill about the building area, to mutter and complain. Her lips were salty, and she needed to get into her geltank.

Her mortality hung in her mind.

Far off in the distance was a city. If they could get through the barrier, assuming the posts really were some kind of barrier, they could make it to that city. But what could they do in the city that they couldn't do here?

Well, we could get killed, she realized.

We stay where we are, she decided. And if they all want to leave, I still stay.

The ship started to hum, and Straka stopped walking. The ship rose off the ground, hovering a meter or so over the wildly colored grass in the compound, then shot away with incredible speed. Straka clapped her hands over her ears to protect them from the thunderclap as air rushed in to fill the vacuum where the ship had just been. The crew rushed out of the building to see what had happened, fear and excitement in their eyes.

"What—" Jackson started to ask, then stopped as he saw the area where the ship had been.

"Oh, God. They left us here to die," Wilhelm said softly.

"Where'd they go? Which direction?" Maxwell asked Straka.

"We're stranded," De Sola said.

A bloodcurdling scream came from Kominski.

Jackson let loose a roar, then flung himself on the round, babbling Kominski. Kominski was incapable of defending himself against the huge man. Jackson easily managed to get onto Kominski's chest, hands clamped around Kominski's windpipe. Kominski emitted terrifying choking, gurgling sounds.

McGowen's flying tackle knocked Jackson off of Kominski, and Wilhelm immediately rushed to Kominski's side to try to help. No one bothered to separate McGowen and Jackson this time.

They rolled over in the grass, arms and legs flailing. Jackson managed to break free and leap to his feet. He kicked McGowen's head like a football, and the sound of contact made Straka's stomach turn. McGowen groaned and covered his head, rolling onto his side.

Katawba, Martinez, and De Sola shouted for Jackson to stop but made no move to intervene. Maxwell took a few hesitant steps, then backed away when he caught the look in Jackson's eyes.

McGowen rolled, and Jackson kicked him a few times in the ribs. McGowen managed to get to his knees only to be kneed in the head by Jackson. He fell back to the ground, clutching his head.

Maxwell, small though he was, leaped at Jackson. His attack did little more than distract the large man for a moment or two, but that was all McGowen needed. He rose to his feet, and by the time Jackson had flung Maxwell a few meters, McGowen was waiting. McGowen swayed a little and bled a lot, but Straka could see he was not about to stop until this thing had been settled. Permanently.

McGowen wore a maniacal grin, waiting for Jackson to advance. He didn't have long to wait. When Jackson was in range, McGowen tackled him about the chest and they both went down in a churning heap.

With a bloodcurdling scream Jackson flung McGowen off, then overpowered him, sitting on his chest. He hit him in the head again and again, pounding McGowen's face with his huge fists until McGowen lay still.

"Jack!" Straka shouted.

Jackson continued his onslaught.

"Jack! You're killing him!" Straka shouted.

Jackson continued. Straka could hold back no longer—if they were ever going to get out of this mess, she would need all of them. She ran around behind Jackson, then struck him in the back of the head with both fists as hard as she could. Jackson groaned softly, then fell over on top of McGowen.

Katawba came over with Martinez and helped Straka roll Jackson away. The two men were a mass of blood, lying beside each other in the alien grass.

Straka checked that McGowen still breathed. She could see there was no way he would survive without medical treatment. His jaw had been broken, his cheeks had been broken, his neck was bleeding, one of his eyes was in sorry shape. His pulse was weak and his breathing was ragged and shallow.

"See if you can find something to tie up Jackson with," she ordered Katawba and Martinez.

"Right," Katawba said.

Straka rose to her feet and looked around the area once again. Without water there was no way McGowen's wounds could be cleaned. There was no good way of determining just how serious they were. My God, she thought, these Habers are little better than animals. How could they leave us here like this?

Jackson groaned and rolled over onto his side. Katawba returned, hands open, showing he'd found nothing they could use for rope.

"How is he?" Wilhelm asked.

"Not good," Straka said. "And Kominski?"

"He'll recover."

Straka nodded. "That's good. I wish I could say the same for him," she said, indicating McGowen with a nod of her head.

"What is it with these guys?" Wilhelm asked.

Straka shrugged. "I don't know. I'm not sure it matters anymore."

"Look!" Maxwell shouted.

Straka looked at Maxwell, saw he was pointing into the sky, and followed the path to a ship. It was heading out of the city. A smile lit her weary face.

At last. Markos. The Habers had gone to get him.

The ship hovered over the compound, then slowly settled onto the grass a safe distance from the group of Terrans. The bay door opened, and an armed group of Habers stood in the doorway, weapons poised and ready.

"You will remain where you are," one of the Habers said. "We have food and water for you. We will unload it and then leave."

"You can't just leave us here!"

"Wait!"

"Take us with you!"

The Habers unloaded containers, and the bay door started to close. "Wait!" Straka shouted. "We need help! One of our men has been seriously injured. Without help, he'll die."

The bay door stopped its downward motion, and a Haber put down his weapon and jumped to the ground. The bay door reopened. He stood before Straka, staring up at her with his fragmented, crystalline eyes.

"Which one?"

Straka led him to McGowen's side. The Haber bent over and touched McGowen's face with his hands. After several minutes the blood stopped flowing and the lacerations closed. McGowen's breathing improved. The Haber stood and looked up at Straka again.

"He will recover, though I don't know why he would want to."

"What's going to happen to us?"

"What is happening is what will happen. Do not concern yourselves over the future. Concern yourself with the present. At this time it is all you have."

12

Straka took charge of rationing the food and water and tried to keep the men from each other's throats. It looked like the food was made from dried vegetables tightly packed into little cakes and dried meat cut into thin strips. From its color, smell, and taste she was sure it wasn't native grasses they were eating. The meat strips were pink, the color of a newborn baby's skin, and they chewed it like dried beef. She was uncertain of its nutritional content—it certainly wasn't very filling.

After the first day she realized that no matter how well rationed they were, their food would run out quickly. She divided up the water so that it would run out at about the same time as the food.

No one was satisfied with the way this worked out. They

wanted more food, more water, and managed to blame the shortages on her.

After nine days they were even less pleased. The Haber ship had not returned to restock their supplies. Everyone went hungry as the food and water ran out. The only things they had left were hope and a deep, abiding distrust for each other.

It was night, and Jackson, De Sola, Wilhelm, and Martinez were outside standing watch. Each man stood at a corner of the compound where the posts were driven into the ground. Nothing could come in, nothing could go out, but still they stood watch. All except McGowen. He had refused the duty.

She would have liked for McGowen to stand a watch, too, but what was Straka supposed to do, court-martial him? Put him on report? They had all seen the need to stand watches without having it discussed, and they all went along with it as if it were the normal thing to do. McGowen's refusal to play along with the fiction made them all uncomfortable.

After nine days the alien landscape still looked alien. She couldn't believe that the strange sky and the startling colors would ever appear normal to her. She didn't want to get used to this place, used to being kept alive like an animal in a stockpen.

She knew she couldn't live much longer like this—conditions were unsanitary and primitive. With the food and water gone, she was starting to lose hope. She no longer cared to figure out why the sun never appeared as anything more than a diffuse blob, why the grass was so variegated, why the Habers hadn't come back with more food and water. They were dying, and that was all she could really think about.

If only they had access to the geltanks. If only they could get in touch with Markos. If only she could somehow get aboard the ship, the Habers would never hear from them again. If only, she thought.

Sure, I chase some biological freak across the galaxy to find immortality and look what I end up with. I'd settle for what's left of my life and my freedom.

She sat on the floor listening to the crew breathe. The building smelled like any building that was peopled by humans who hadn't bathed in days. The crew's smell had ripened over the days like rotting fruit.

They were all dying, and they knew it. No one talked about it.

At least they still managed to keep standing those watches. The action kept them sane, anchored in a past to which they could relate. It was something to do, something to keep their minds off what was happening to them, something to help combat the feeling of total helplessness that awaited anyone who truly gave up hope.

Discipline was nonexistent and unnecessary. They all did as they wanted. And what could they do?

She felt some responsibility toward her crewmates, since chasing Markos had been her idea. She felt some guilt—though she had deceived them into chasing Markos for her own purpose, they had agreed to follow her. And since they had followed her, they had accepted her leadership. She felt she owed them all something.

Maybe it was some kind of strange effect of being in command, but she felt a lot more responsibility toward the others than she ever had before. When they were still on Gandji, she couldn't have cared less about any one of them. At that time it was her against Markos —find the freak and get him to talk. Maybe she felt more responsibility toward the others because the others expected that of her, treating her as their leader, looking to her for answers, for suggestions, for guidance.

She felt a bond she had never felt before, a concern for their well-being. Had someone told her she would feel this way just a few months ago, she would have laughed in his face.

She looked around the smelly building, the single, bare room, then rose to her feet. McGowen and Kominski were asleep, side by side, the innocent and the protector. Maxwell was still awake, probably kept up by hunger and discomfort, back propped against the wall, vacantly staring straight ahead. Katawba snored noisily on the other side of the room.

Straka walked to the doorway and stood there, leaning against the doorframe, breathing in the cool, sweet night air. She glanced overhead and immediately regretted it as she was overcome by a deep pang of isolation.

"Can't sleep?" Maxwell asked. He got up and made his way to Straka's side.

"No. You?"

Maxwell shook his head. "Too hungry. And thirsty. It's getting bad."

"It's going to get worse," she said.

"It can't get worse."

"It can, and it probably will, unless another ship arrives." She looked out over the landscape at the distant city on the horizon. "You know, it just doesn't make sense to me. But then, I'm not a Haber. If they're trying to keep us alive, you'd think they would've given us enough food and water. Nothing special, mind you—no cots, blankets, or medical attention—just the things we really need to survive."

"That's *if* they want to keep us alive," Maxwell said. "We're not sure of that. I think it's probably a simple thing, a simple explanation we've overlooked, something either really alien or really absurd."

"What?"

"Well, I'm not a Haber, either. I don't know how they think. But from what I've seen, I don't think they can just kill us. It's beyond them. They couldn't just march into the compound and shoot us, no matter how much they might want to. So they give us some food to soothe their consciences—enough to keep us alive for a week or two. And then they let us kill each other, or they let entropy take its course."

Straka nodded, still staring off at the horizon. "Unless they . . . no, forget it."

"What?"

"Well, I was just thinking. If they even want us dead, then why did they fix McGowen?"

"Good point," Maxwell said, a little hope creeping into his voice.

"Maybe something's happened to them—maybe they just can't get back here. Maybe they want to, but they're busy with something else."

"Like?"

"Like a fight, a war. Yeah, that could be it. You remember what Markatens said when we were on the *Paladin*, don't you? He ordered us to surrender and called us his prisoners. Not exactly peacetime terminology."

"Okay, then, who are they at war with? Us?"

Straka shrugged. "If it's us, this is one hell of a way to fight."

"Then maybe it's not with us."

Straka laughed through her nose, a short exhalation. "Who else is there?"

She stood outside, waiting.

There's only one thing that doesn't change with time or space, Straka thought, and that's being a prisoner. You quickly learn the basics of survival—hoarding food scraps, stealing from weaker prisoners, sneaking an extra swallow of water. If there had been guards, there would have been informants. You watch the others watch you, and then you watch the sky grow dark as another day passes. You wait for the sun to come up and pray your hope rises with the sun. In the still night, when there's nothing but the sounds living creatures make, or the sound the wind makes whipping through the vegetation, you lie there with half-closed eyes, blurred vision, feigning sleep. You wait for everyone else to sleep so that you can creep toward the food stores. Or you stay up and watch and wait and pray no one tries it before you.

None of this would be happening if the Habers had only given them an idea that they would return. The crew could probably survive a few more days without looking at the plump little Kominski with atavistic longing, saliva freely flowing. That was weeks away yet. By then the Haber ship would have to have returned with more food and water. Water was the real concern.

If we're prisoners like Markatens said, then why the hell don't they treat us like prisoners? Straka wondered. What kind of battle is this? An entire planet against nine human beings? We attacked first, but that was on Gandji, and things were different there. And that had been Van Pelt's doing. It was his fight—not ours. Why should we have to pay for his insanity?

She was struck with a numbing thought: The Habers might truly never return; the food and water they'd dropped off was all they'd receive. She may have had those thoughts before, and she may have always feared it was true, but she'd never really believed it, understood it deep down inside until now.

She shivered. Starved to death. And some of us will live longer than others, she thought. That much is for sure. Kominski will be the first to go—the plumpest, the least capable of defending himself, the least capable of functioning. Her stomach churned, and she worked hard to stifle the urge to vomit. Just thinking of butchering Kominski was enough to push her over the edge. Yank an arm out of a socket, like a leg on a roasted chicken. Nothing to it.

But she was panicking, letting her imagination get carried away. It hadn't gotten that bad yet. This was only their first day without food, and there was enough water for tomorrow. They had some time before they degenerated to cannibalism.

She rubbed her gritty eyes and went back into the building.

Had Aurianta's sky been normal, or even close to Terran, sunrise would have been a welcome sight. But the blob of shimmering color that crept slowly off the horizon and into the strange sky only reminded them of where they were.

There were beautiful things to look at, strange vegetation and life-forms to wonder about, to marvel at. There were small animals outside the compound's protected perimeter, grazing animals, food on the hoof waiting to be rounded up and herded into the compound to serve a more noble purpose than simply eating, sleeping, and procreating.

The crew sat on the grass outside the building, too weary with depression to do much more than gaze longingly at the grazing animals. McGowen was chewing on something, and everyone noticed this at about the same time.

Jackson was on him in a second, and Straka braced herself for the worst. McGowen put up no resistance, though, as Jackson worked his way to sitting on McGowen's chest. McGowen opened his mouth and gladly let Jackson remove whatever morsel of food he'd been chewing.

It was grass, in all shades of green.

Bitterly disappointed, feeling cheated, Jackson dug his knee into

McGowen's midsection as he rose. McGowen said nothing, and did nothing to protect himself.

McGowen sat upright and yanked another handful of grass out of the ground and started chewing off the tips. Jackson reached down, picked up a few blades, and stuffed them into his own mouth. He spat it out immediately.

"Christ! How can you eat this?" he screamed.

McGowen smiled. "It's good."

"It's what?" Straka asked, incredulous.

"It's good."

"How long have you been eating that stuff?" she asked.

"A few days."

"What?" Maxwell shouted.

"A few days," Straka muttered. She reached down into the grass growing before her and plucked a few blades. She put them into her mouth and tried to chew. As soon as her teeth broke the outer membrane of the blades, she gagged. She spat the blades out as she collapsed to her side, feeling the dry heaves coming on in a powerful wave.

Maxwell had tried the same thing but had swallowed a mouthful and was retching with such force, his body was out of control. He convulsed with huge spasms.

The others had been smart enough to wait.

McGowen continued to chew and swallow complacently. Straka slowly stopped heaving and managed to sit up. She felt weaker than ever. Maxwell was still convulsing.

"You okay?" Wilhelm asked by her side.

Straka nodded. "Barely. The grass is toxic."

"That's putting it mildly," Wilhelm said. He left her to check on Maxwell. He bent over and looked at him, determined there was nothing that could be done, then sat down to wait for the convulsions to subside.

Straka glanced hungrily at the animals. They could be as toxic as the grass, she thought. And then she caught sight of Kominski, waddling up to the barrier.

"Come back here, 'Minski!" Straka shouted with as much strength as she could muster.

Kominski showed no signs of having heard. He stood fifty meters away from the grazing animals. They looked a little like Terran pigs in general shape. Their hides were creamy yellow, their hindquarters covered with a brown, downy fur.

Kominski walked straight into the barrier, attempting to close the distance, then jumped back in surprise. The barrier had given him a small shock—nothing debilitating—just a warning of what would come if he pressed too hard against it. He tried again and recoiled from the shock.

"'Minski!" Straka shouted.

Kominski pressed forward again, this time letting out a little yelp of pain. The crew watched, amused.

"Leave the poor slob alone," Jackson said. "Let him fry himself. That way we won't have to cook him when the time comes." He laughed a sick laugh, slightly over the edge.

Straka shook her head, swallowing the bile taste that lingered in her mouth. Kominski was beating against the barrier with his fists, emitting a short cry of pain with each blow. His hands seemed to penetrate the barrier's inner surface, but didn't go all the way through. Perhaps with a concerted effort—

"Wilhelm? Go on out there and give Kominski some help," Straka said. "It looks like it's giving a little. Maybe with the two of you it might collapse."

Wilhelm was on his feet and moving toward Kominski before she had finished talking.

"You really don't think that'll work, do you?" Jackson asked. "We tried that four nights ago, while you were sleeping."

Straka glared at Jackson. "Thanks for telling me, Jack. You're a real sweetheart."

"Don't mention it."

Kominski and Wilhelm were working together, trying to break down the barrier. They were getting nowhere with it. "Come on back, Wilhelm. And bring Kominski with you," Straka shouted.

"Spoilsport," Jackson said. "It was just getting to be fun."

Straka didn't let the man get to her. She'd had enough run-ins with him to know when she was being baited. If she lost her temper and Jackson felt justified, there would be a fight, and Straka knew who would be the loser. And dinner for the crew.

Maxwell had stopped convulsing and was breathing shallowly, panting, staring into the sky with glassy eyes. De Sola approached and sat beside Straka.

"You think they'll be back today?" De Sola asked.

"The Habers?" she asked, stalling.

De Sola nodded.

"Of course she does," Jackson said. "Don't you, Cathy?"

Straka shrugged.

"Why don't they come back?" De Sola asked.

"Tell him, Cathy. Go on," Jackson said.

"I don't know, De Sola. I really don't. I'd like to think they're coming back today. If they don't—"

"If they don't, Cathy, guess who's going to be the first to go?" Jackson asked.

"Shut up, Jackson!" De Sola shouted.

McGowen lay on his back, chewing on the native grass.

Wilhelm and Kominski returned from the edge of the compound.

"You think they will come, though, don't you?" De Sola asked.

Straka nodded. "Let's finish off this water now."

"But what will we do if they don't?" De Sola asked.

Straka sighed. What *could* they do? It was up to her to come up with some kind of answer that could appease them enough so that they'd restrain themselves from killing and eating each other.

They were taking her advice, looking to her for leadership. Van Pelt had been the real captain, the person no one but Markos had questioned, the one who had been trained to be a leader.

Straka's desire for command may have been self-serving, but she had given the crew a goal, something to live for, a direction in which to move. It had been different then; her taking command had been symbiotic. She helped the crew by taking on responsibility, and they unknowingly helped her by going to Alpha Indi so that she could find Markos and the answer to death.

She had found the wrong answer, though—death by starvation.

And now, when command meant nothing more than responsibility, De Sola continued to force it on her, like the others. Command through default, command through convenience. Command without a ship.

"Cathy?" De Sola asked.

"Huh?"

"What are we going to do if they don't come back?"

"Give me that!" Katawba shouted, leaping on Martinez.

Martinez struggled, trying to fight off the heavier and larger Katawba. Straka saw it for what it was—a fight for survival. Martinez had probably hoarded a small strip of the dried meat and had been caught trying to slip a tiny piece of it into his mouth unnoticed.

Straka, De Sola, and Wilhelm moved as quickly as they could to break up the fight, but it was over by the time they got there. The men were tired and weak, in no condition to wrestle with each other.

Martinez finished chewing, flat on his back, Katawba's tears of frustration and anger slowly making their way down his cheeks.

"I'm sorry," Katawba sobbed. "I didn't mean it."

Straka bent over and put a comforting hand on his shoulder. "We know you didn't. Don't worry about it."

"Cathy?" De Sola asked again.

"Oh, yeah. What to do, what to do. Let's see, De Sola. About all I can say is that we've got to keep our heads. We need to keep from killing each other." Jackson leered at that. "There's a real chance they'll come back today with food and water. And if not today, to-morrow."

De Sola nodded, then dropped to the ground, shaking his head.

The answer seemed good enough for him, Straka thought. For now, anyway.

13

"I know what I'm doing, Old One," Markos said. The Old One looked at him, eyes yellow tinged with blue. "I don't want you to worry about this anymore."

The common room in Markos's house was their command center. One whole wall was lined with crystals; each contained a life-and-death experience of some encounter with the Hydrans. Markos had studied them all and had learned a lot about his enemies.

The Old One rose slowly from his chair and walked to the window. He looked out onto the street, watching young Habers play in their strange, nonaggressive way, listening to the wind whip through the alleys. "I, I have faith in your judgment, Markos."

"But?"

"Yes, there is a but. These actions are hard to condone," the Haber said.

Markos flashed red. "I understand. I appreciate your point of view. If we were dealing with any other life-form, I might agree. But they're Terrans, and I know how they think. They're not like Habers at all.

"If these creatures could flash green, they would. You would approach them in friendship, and they would do the same. You would turn around and flash something to another Haber with you. And then they might kill you, while your back was turned. It has happened before. I've learned through experience the best way to deal with them, and trust has its place. But trust is not enough."

"Very well. I, I only wanted to voice my, my feelings. You do what you must do, as always. I, I understand this. But you must tell me, me how long this will continue."

Markos looked at the Old One's back. He shook his head slowly, empathizing with his friend's cultural and biological bias, with the Old One's attempts to pick up the way Markos thought, with his frustration and anguish over the senseless deaths that had occurred, that would occur. If only there were some way to make him understand.

"I'll let this situation continue until it's too late. Until they all die. Or kill each other. Until trust is no longer a consideration. Until it's just the right time." As he spoke these words, he thought of the imprisoned Terrans in the abstract. They weren't the people he'd trained with, traveled to Tau Ceti with, shared the geltanks with. They were simply Terrans, components in some total system, gears within a war machine.

If he had thought of the filth, the hunger, the fear these creatures felt while struggling to survive, he might have said something different, something sympathetic. He might have done something he knew he shouldn't do.

"I know what they're like," Markos said. "I've seen what they're capable of. You have, too, or don't you remember what they did on Gandji? It wasn't that long ago for you to forget."

"I, I remember."

"This is the same group of creatures."

The Haber turned to Markos, flashing a weak red. "Yes, but creatures change, as do all things."

Markos shook his head. "Even if there were a chance we wouldn't need them, I couldn't let them go."

Alpha walked into the room and stood a meter away from Markos. He said nothing, did nothing to disturb him, waiting to be recognized.

"We can't afford to take chances," Markos said. "If there's a chance, no matter how slight, of winning this war without their help, we'll do without it, and then feed them to Aurianta."

If the Old One could have shrugged, Markos figured he would have then.

"What is it, Alpha?" Markos asked.

"The crystal is complete."

"Did he ... survive?"

Alpha handed Markos a small, smooth crystal structure. "No."

Markos said nothing. Triand, the first of his children to meet the enemy, was dead. He didn't want to know what was stored inside. He didn't want to see Triand die. He tasted metal, felt his breathing shift, saw particles of dust swirl through the room with incredible detail and resolution, heard his bodily fluids oozing through his veins.

The Old One approached and laid a hand on Markos's shoulder. Markos looked up into his eyes. The Old One started to speak to him in patterns, in graceful displays of scintillating colors and shapes that sparkled in his mind. He became aware of the fear he'd been suppressing, the grief he was afraid to deal with. It may have been war, but Triand had been his child.

The pain surged and peaked, then was suddenly gone as the Old One did something with his eyes. He felt washed out and tired. The old Haber took his hand away.

"Thank you," Markos said in a raspy whisper.

"We, we will leave you alone with your thoughts and the crystal. Call if you need us, us."

"Thank you," Markos said.

Some of his strength was returning. He turned the crystal over and over in his hands. It was cold and hard, and all that remained of Triand. He watched the old Haber and Alpha leave the common room and disappear around the corner of a tubular hallway.

He glanced at the wall of crystals opposite him. *All of those encounters, and I still had to send Triand to Theta Alnon. Alone, as a test—a test that didn't work.*

He was starting to shake, and he realized he was gripping the crystal with all his strength. He relaxed his hold on it and dropped it into his lap, shaking his head.

I have to get control of myself, he thought. *I can't go on like this. I've got to put my personal feelings aside and find out what happened. That's why I sent him there in the first place. I hoped with all my heart he could survive, but I knew all along. . . .*

He breathed a few deep breaths to prepare his body for the experience.

I've got to face it. It has to be done.

He let his eyes wander and picked up the crystal. He forced himself to touch and change its surface, delve into the depths of its lattice structure. When he saw something move, he was looking through the eyes of his child, Triand.

The ship descended in an unpopulated area. Triand watched the grid on the thin screen before him swirl with colors. The patterns showed him a safe place to land and he guided the wedge-shaped ship down to Theta Alnon's surface.

According to the information Markos had put together from the crystals, this area of the planet should be experiencing the Hydrans' advance. Small splinter groups from the original settlement should have set up distant outposts. These outposts would themselves grow until their population could justify sending a further party out into the planet's wilderness. The Hydrans colonized in leapfrog steps, and this should be as far as they'd settled.

At least he wasn't setting down in the middle of an established encampment, a small city filled with Hydrans. Here, he stood a small chance. If he couldn't win this skirmish, then there was little hope of taking on the larger, more organized encampments.

When the ship's flight systems had been cycled off, Triand rose to his feet and began inspecting his weapons. He had killed living things before. For long months Markos had drilled him and his brothers in the arts of combat. Some of the things Markos taught made little sense, and those things confused him. He remembered the long and tiring discussions in the common room, with Markos patiently going over and over the reasons behind these confusing actions, the ideology behind hand-to-hand combat. He understood as much as he could, but even with that, he was sure he'd missed the major thrust.

Triand was constantly aware of what was expected of him, what his responsibilities were. All he had to do was kill sentient creatures and return home. He hoped he would be strong enough to meet those expectations. He hoped Markos would be proud of him.

He reached down and picked up the crystal and its tiny transmitting device. It was of a different design than those the Habers had used over the generations. Markos had told the Old One what he wanted this crystal to do—transmit a constant record of what happened to Triand while on Theta Alnon without Triand's having to touch and change it—and the Old One made the necessary modifications. It had to be in Triand's immediate vicinity and, since there was no way of telling if he'd be able to hold onto it, he swallowed it.

He grabbed his protective belt and strapped it around his chest. Once it came into contact with his body, it was activated. Within the belt was a photon-deflection unit, which would protect him against laser fire by bending the beam around him. With the unit nullifying the Hydrans' primary weapon, he figured he would have few problems.

He paused from looking over his lasetube. If he did manage to accomplish this task, what would his brothers think when he returned home? And what would the stolid, pacific Habers think? Would they accept him or shun him?

But this was no time for introspection—not with what lay ahead. He remembered Markos's instructions and tried to clear his mind of distracting thoughts.

The bay door opened, and night crept into the wedge-shaped ship. Triand stood on the edge of the deck, looking out over the surface of the planet. It reminded him of Gandji, the planet of his birth. He felt strange, almost as if he were returning home.

He could make out the lights of the aliens' camp almost a kilometer away. It was a sleeping tumor on the landscape, the small metal huts like boils ready to erupt, to spread the Hydran pus over Triand's helpless, slaughtered, innocent ancestors.

He leaped to the ground and tried to become one with the scents, the sounds, the gentle, constantly changing night. The Hydrans must have detected his landing and had probably sent out a scouting party. If they wandered across his ship before he wandered across them, he would be stranded. He set out for the alien camp.

The photon-deflection unit had to be tested under real battle conditions. Markos had assumed the Hydrans used lasers, but he'd only been guessing—all the data had to be deduced from the crystals. The Hydrans appeared to have a military organization, but Markos needed to see them on the defensive, see how they fought when someone fought back. Triand was proud of the role he served: the first real Haber to go into battle.

He had traveled half the distance to their camp when he saw the changes around him. The smell was the first warning and helped him see the subtle changes in the wind, in the vegetation a short distance away. He had found the scouting party.

He lowered himself to the ground, gripping the lasetube tightly in his hand, his eye clusters at peak receptivity, tuned to the planet's rhythm and flow. The group would appear within scant moments, and he braced himself for the confrontation.

There!

He froze for an instant, then changed the handle on his lasetube, activating it by sending a steady stream of electrons through his hand into the unit. The thin, tight beam cut the advancing line of Hydrans down like a giant scythe, separating their bodies in two sections. They toppled in a heap, exuding a powerful stench.

He had killed, and it had been easy.

But there was chattering activity coming from the camp now. He could hear it, like the screeching of metal against metal, like the smashing of thousands of panes of glass. He rushed to his feet and advanced.

There was a small group of trees on the fringe of the camp's perimeter and he ran for their cover. He made swift progress; before his body had exhausted its reserve energy, he was by the trees, watching the flurry of activity in the camp. The stench was incredible, an instinctive odor emitted by the Hydrans as they went onto battle, a call to arms. But he had expected the smell.

The metal huts spewed out Hydran after Hydran, their black, three-legged bodies a churning mass of motion. Some were larger than others, some moved more quickly than others, but they were all armed.

They still hadn't discovered Triand there, close by, waiting to mow them down like inanimate targets. They were organizing into small groups. If he put off his attack much longer, his chances of surviving would decrease drastically. The less organized they were, the better.

He got down on one knee, pointed his weapon into the camp, and activated it.

He managed to lase down twenty or so before they could return his fire. The tree beside him burst into flames as beam after beam struck it and the surrounding grass. For an instant Triand wondered if the beams had struck him and had been deflected by the belt, or if the Hydrans were just bad at aiming their weapons.

He fired back, burning a few more, then sought safety behind another tree. So this is killing, he thought. What's so difficult about it?

The Hydrans scattered. Two of the groups started to run toward him. He lased down the first wave easily, and the second wave of Hydrans stopped, falling to the ground for cover.

One of them got off a good shot as Triand left the sheltering tree for a better position. The beam had been deflected. The unit worked. He thought of testing the belt further, offering himself as a target.

He recognized the need for immediate retreat, before all the trees around him burst into flames. He knew he was protected from their lasers, but burning trees presented a different problem. As did falling trees, or the flames leaping up from the grass around him.

He fired a few quick blasts to keep the Hydrans' heads down, then sprinted out of concealment, heading back toward the ship. The group of Hydrans rose to their three legs and started pursuit.

Triand ran as fast as he could, pumping his legs up and down with all his strength, but his body had limitations. It hadn't been designed for running, and the Hydrans were catching up. He scanned the immediate area as he ran, searching for some cover.

Another grove of trees lay ahead about thirty or forty meters away. He tried to remember what Markos had taught him, going over and over bits of information, searching for the answer to this wrong situation, but nothing came to him.

He glanced behind as he ran and saw they were closer yet, less than twenty meters and closing. He thought he saw about ten of them.

He would never make it to the woods. He angled off to his left, running through the tangled undergrowth, away from the woods and his ship.

The Hydrans followed.

A burst of laser fire surrounded him, split and rejoined in front of him, charring the grass in his path. He altered direction again.

Another burst of fire.

He realized he would have to make a stand. He flung himself to the ground, making his body hard as he hit the ground, and came up firing. He burned half of them away before they could stop their headlong rush.

But the other five continued to advance, now less than ten meters away. He could smell them, smell their battle frenzy, hear them chittering and clacking. They split up before he could get off a well-aimed shot, two Hydrans to the right, two to the left, while one continued its straight-on advance.

Triand immediately lased the single, oncoming Hydran. The beam neatly sliced off its head, and momentum caused the head to roll within a meter of Triand.

Where were the other four?

Two to the right, two to the left, probably going to try to encircle me, take me from the flanks. If I stay here and wait for them, I'll be caught in a crossfire. I can't watch both groups at the same time.

He rolled onto his back, sprang to his feet, and ran between the enclosing groups.

He might have gotten away if he hadn't assumed they were trying to surround him. He was running full speed into a waiting Hydran. The Hydran fired. The beam split around Triand. Triand fired back and burned a gaping hole through the Hydran's thorax. The smell of charred flesh mingled with the evil odors of the battle.

He was tiring too quickly. He realized he wasn't thinking clearly and had lost his edge.

Something caught him around the foot, and he went down hard, like an animal caught in a snare. His lasetube fell from his hand, rolling out of reach. He kept his body hardened, draining precious energy away from his senses, and turned over onto his back. It was a Hydran, holding him by the ankle. It must have hidden in the undergrowth instead of coming around his flank.

Its other hand held a blade poised above Triand's midsection. The blade plunged downward and snapped in half as it made contact.

He brought his hardened hand down with all his might, aiming for the alien's head. The blow glanced off. He tried again while the alien clawed at his chest and tried to pierce his skin with its clawlike fingers.

He put all his energy into one eye-beam hoping to at least blind the Hydran for a moment. The white light pierced the night, and the alien let go of Triand to shield its head. Triand took this moment to roll for his lasetube. He grabbed it and wheeled around, activating it and shooting the Hydran at close range.

The Hydran let out a horrifying shriek that echoed in Triand's mind.

He saw that his protective belt had come loose, that it dangled from his chest. He sat there and tried to decide whether to strap the belt back on when he smelled the other three Hydrans right on top of him.

Markos released his death grip on the crystal. It dropped to the floor. He knew what had happened next, even though the act itself hadn't been recorded. Triand had been lased by one of the remaining Hydrans before he could adjust the deflection belt.

Seeing the battle Triand had fought made him face what he had to face, but with great reluctance. The realization was inescapable. The farther he ran from it, the worse things would get.

The children were soldiers, could be warriors of consummate skill, though they would require many runs through training courses, mock battles, and real skirmishes. But they could never win this war by themselves.

They lacked too much in cultural experience or aggression. Even their lives on Aurianta did more harm than good. And worse, they didn't understand the meaning of death the way a Terran understands, and understanding was the thing that made good fighters.

The Old One had reentered the room at some point while Markos had been involved with the crystal. He sat across from Markos, waiting.

"It's no good, Old One," Markos rasped painfully. "It's not going to work the way I'd hoped. If we send any of the others out, they'll die too."

"I, I understand. Alpha and I, I have discussed it."

"Good. I only wish that Triand had killed less and survived more."

"He did what he could."

"Yes, Old One, you're right. Now we must do what *we* can. We must let the Terrans die."

"Die?"

"Yes. Dead humans don't argue."

14

Dawn. The morning light was feeble, creeping through the building's windows. Straka stirred, shifted position on the hard floor, and blinked her eyes open. In the faint light everything looked gray.

Her hips hurt, bruised from the long nights she'd spent sleeping on the bare floor. She rolled onto her back and stared at the ceiling. Her stomach was empty, a bottomless pit harboring a restless, tiny monster growling furiously with the first light of day. It had kept her awake long into the night as it searched for something to digest other than itself. Her eyes were gritty, her mouth tasted foul, and she stank. She was coated with caked-on dirt and grime; it covered her like a second layer of skin, trapping her body heat, sealing her pores, smothering her beneath its sealed surface.

McGowen wasn't in the building; he was probably up and around, walking the camp's perimeter or sitting on the grass watching the sky come to life. She could hear the large man's humming filter in through the doorway while the rest of the crew slept on fitfully.

As Straka moved back to prop herself up against the wall, her ribs hurt. The edges of bone felt tender, as if they were disintegrating. She winced in pain as she touched them.

She rubbed her face with her hands, trying to remove the mask of sleep and dirt, only making matters worse. She ran her tongue over her chapped, cracked lips. They hurt, and when she touched them with her fingertips, they felt hot and swollen.

There's no reason we should be this far along, she thought. We've been here for nine or ten days. I can't remember exactly. But we've been without food for only two days now, and this will be our second full day without water. It doesn't make sense.

But then, what does on this planet?

Her eyes burned and she was forced to close them. It felt like there was a thin layer of fine sandpaper on the insides of her eyelids. She rubbed them gently with her fingers, trying to get her tear ducts to give them a little bath. It helped a little and she was thankful her body still had some fluid to spare.

She opened her eyes to find it had grown lighter, and the dingy, overcast feeling had lifted from the room. Maxwell was sprawled on his back, an arm thrown over his eyes, groaning softly. He hadn't been right since he'd swallowed that native grass yesterday. Had it only been yesterday? Straka wondered. How could she have gotten so much worse overnight? She doubted Maxwell would make it to sundown.

Kominski was less round than ever before. His cheeks were deep hollows in his face, his eyes sunken, rimmed with dark circles. But we all look like that, Straka thought. Even McGowen.

Straka tried to stand. She pushed with her arms and legs, using the wall as a brace, a third point of leverage, but she wasn't strong enough. She got onto her hands and knees easily enough, then put her right foot flat on the ground, forward of her left leg as if ready to break from a sprinter's starting blocks. She could manage to stand this way, and she rose unsteadily to her feet. The room spun for a moment and she had to lean against the wall to keep from falling. She was all right after a few seconds.

Sure, we're all right, she thought. All we need is a few steaks, some potatoes, and maybe a nice salad to hold us over until the ship gets here.

Her stomach churned and she regretted her sarcasm. Just thinking about that kind of food sent her digestive system into overdrive.

She moved toward the door like a tired old woman, shuffling one foot forward, scuffing and sliding it over the ground, placing her weight on it as if afraid to trust its ability to support her. Her hips shrieked with pain. She shifted her weight and slid the other foot forward like an ancient woman. Waiting for the end, she thought. A woman in her thirties, waiting for death.

She stood in the doorway looking out over Aurianta's magical beauty. The alienness of the world was inescapable, far too obvious to allow self-deceit. She felt cheated, betrayed by fate, by her own desires and greed. The planet was draining her of life, soaking up her remaining will to survive.

McGowen was sitting a few meters away, back to the building, staring at the grazing animals in the distance.

"Morning, McGowen," Straka said. She couldn't bring herself to say "good."

McGowen turned and got up easily, fluidly. He walked to Straka's side and slipped an arm around her waist. He walked her over to where he'd been sitting.

"Doesn't it ever rain here?" Straka asked.

McGowen smiled but said nothing.

"Not much strength left," she said, settling onto the grass. "I'm glad one of us has some."

McGowen continued to smile.

Straka took a closer look at his face. He looked almost as bad as the rest of the men. His cheeks were as sunken as his eyes, and he had the same unhealthy pallor. But at least he has some reserve strength, she thought. He must have been in better shape than the rest of us. With the geltanks, we were all in pretty close to perfect health. But then, how could he have eaten that grass yesterday without any ill effects?

145

She knew her mind was working slowly, was missing points that should have been obvious, but she was thirsty and hungry. Weak, tired, thirsty, and hungry.

It must have something to do with what the Haber did to him —his healing, she realized.

The realization came to her suddenly, and she was shocked she hadn't seen it immediately, yesterday, when she'd spotted McGowen chewing on the native grass. That had to be it. The Haber had somehow changed McGowen's body chemistry.

As the adrenaline surge subsided, her weakness returned. The feeling of helplessness and confusion had left her, though, and this new understanding, so simple and obvious, buoyed her and rekindled her thirst for life.

She reexamined the last nine days, recalling things she'd observed but had been too tired or weak to consider at the time. Things like the huge man not having been involved in a fight or even a loud discussion with Jackson since he'd healed. And McGowen had always been volatile. Especially when Jackson was around. Here conditions were perfect for them to be at each other's throats all the time.

"Do you find the fact that you're still strong while the rest of us are weak a little strange, McGowen?" she asked.

"I hadn't given it much thought," McGowen answered calmly.

But Straka could see the man was lying. She'd spent too much time with him to be fooled. She turned back and glanced at the building; none of the others were up and around yet. "You feel any different from how you used to? Notice any change in yourself?" she asked.

McGowen eyed Straka with raised eyebrows, giving her the once-over. He picked up a blade of mint-green grass and played with it, spinning it between his fingers. "No," he said.

"No change at all?"

McGowen shook his head. "None to speak of."

"Okay, McGowen. You've got the ball. I won't pressure you anymore."

McGowen sighed heavily. "Let's just drop it, Cathy, okay? It's not going to help all of us. So I'm a little better off than the rest of you. So I can eat the grass. So I'm not starving. What's the difference? We'll all be dead, sooner or later. So my death takes place a little later. It's all the same thing, just a few days this way or that."

Straka said nothing. She'd heard enough to have her suspicions confirmed. McGowen was different from the way he had been, and was different from the crew. He had the potential to outlive them all.

"Okay, McGowen. I said I wouldn't pressure you." For now, anyway, Straka thought. I won't bring it up again unless I have to. But when I do, you'll tell me, and you'll tell us all. Or we'll make sure you're the first to go instead of the last.

Straka's spirits were still high, despite McGowen. Just having been able to spot the important points, to see that McGowen had lied, gave her the lift she so desperately needed. It didn't help her decaying physical state, but it did help her ignore some of the pain and discomfort.

Katawba came out of the building, and Straka watched his approach. The man had never seemed so lanky, and his tall, once-healthy and straight form looked hunched, as if his spine were curving, collapsing under its own weight. His shoulders were hunched forward, and he moved slowly, idly, but without the shuffling gait Straka had had to use. The lack of strength, confidence, and authority in his steps was painfully evident.

"Come on over and join us," Straka said.

Katawba nodded as he walked to their sides and sat. "You look great, Cathy. You, too, George," Katawba lied.

"So do you," McGowen said.

Straka nodded her agreement.

"I only wish I felt as good as you say I look," Katawba said.

Straka thought of bringing up McGowen's strange strength again, this time in front of Katawba just to see how McGowen reacted, how defensive he would get. All she had to say was, "McGowen feels fine," and let them take it from there. But she decided against it. McGowen knew something he wasn't going to tell. If he wouldn't tell Straka alone, there was no chance of his opening up in front of Katawba.

"How are the others?" Straka asked.

Katawba shook his head slowly. "Maxwell may not make it through the morning. De Sola has a fever. You know how Kominski was?" Straka nodded. "Well, he's worse. He woke me up in the middle of the night to tell me he'd missed his turn in the geltank and wanted to trade with me. Jackson's not up yet. Martinez woke up hallucinating."

"Things just keep getting better and better," Straka said through tight lips. "What about Wilhelm?"

Katawba shrugged. "He seemed all right last night. But that was last night. There's no telling if he'll be sane this morning, or what he'll be like."

Straka nodded. "Well, if he's sane, I want to talk with him, and I want you two there when I do. There are a few things we have to discuss, and the rest of the crew isn't going to be much in the way of help."

Katawba's eyebrows seemed permanently arched. "Oh, really? Okay. I'll check to see if he's up yet."

McGowen was on his feet before Katawba could make a move. He was smiling. "Save your strength. I'll check for you."

Katawba returned the smile. When McGowen had disappeared into the building, Katawba motioned with a slight nod. "What's up?"

"Something's wrong. We missed something yesterday that we shouldn't have missed. All of which leads me to believe we're missing more than we're spotting. Watch him when he comes out."

"Who?"

"McGowen. Watch the way he moves."

"Right," Katawba said.

Slowly, painfully, they shifted positions so they faced the building a little more. McGowen appeared a few moments later, half-carrying Wilhelm by putting an arm around his waist. Wilhelm's arm was draped over McGowen's shoulder. Wilhelm's feet touched the ground, and he moved his legs, but it was clear he was contributing little to their progress.

"He's sane, but weak," McGowen said, a meter away.

"I see what you mean," Katawba said softly.

"Put him down, will you?" Straka asked.

"Yeah, man. Put me down."

McGowen lowered his crewmate to the grass as if he were made of leaded crystal.

"Hey there, cuties," Wilhelm said.

"How're you feeling?" Katawba asked.

"About as good as you look," Wilhelm said. "But this big goon didn't really have to help me. He was just showing off."

Wilhelm smiled.

"But I did appreciate the help," Wilhelm added.

"Listen. McGowen went inside to get you so that we could talk before the others are up. I need some opinions," Straka said.

"Fire away," Wilhelm said.

"First off, we're starving when we shouldn't be."

"Huh?" Katawba said.

"I don't get it, man," Wilhelm said.

McGowen said nothing. He played idly with another blade of grass.

"How long have we been without food?" Straka asked.

Katawba shrugged. "A few days. And I don't miss it."

"We all do, Katawba. We all do. But two days isn't nearly long enough for us to be starving like this. We shouldn't be so weak. We haven't been exercising, so our muscle tone is bound to be pretty bad, but it's not like we're stranded in the middle of a desert or something."

"Yeah," Wilhelm said. "Good point."

"Then tell me where all those calories have gone. Tell me what we ate for . . . how long was it? A week? Eight days? Whatever. Tell me why our bodies have been going downhill from the moment we stepped onto this planet.

"The only thing that makes sense is that we haven't been eating since we got here. Sure, we've put something that looked and smelled and tasted like food into our mouths, but there was no nutritional value to it."

"Or it was like celery—eating it costs you calories," Wilhelm offered.

"Possibly. Or it could have been so thin in nutrition it barely kept us alive. For all we know, the Habers could have assumed the food would last us for months. They may have thought it was a concentrate. Who knows? The important thing is that we've been starving since we got here."

"No way. I can't buy that," Wilhelm said. "If that's true, then that would mean that Markos is doing this on purpose."

"Markos?" Straka said. "I don't think so. I don't think he's even here. Or if he is here, they're probably keeping him in a pen like this one, somewhere else."

"What?" Katawba asked incredulously. "What are you saying? We know he's here. He's got to be here."

"Who told you that?"

Katawba looked at her. "You . . . yeah, okay. You told us."

"And I was wrong."

"Not necessarily."

"Okay, then, let's just forget about Markos," Wilhelm said. "He's not important right now. If we've been dying like this, slowly from starvation, then how come McGowen's still so strong?"

Straka looked into McGowen's eyes. "Well? How about it?"

"You said no pressure, Cathy."

"That was before. Well?"

"Well what?" Wilhelm asked, confused by their conversation.

"I want to know why we're weak and he's not. I want to know why yesterday, of all of us who tasted the grass, he was the only one who could eat it. I want to know why Maxwell is in there dying while he's out here strong as ever," Straka said.

Katawba was already looking at McGowen suspiciously, and Wilhelm soon turned his gaze in McGowen's direction too. "Yes, McGowen. Why?" Wilhelm asked.

McGowen rose to his feet in a swift, fluid motion. "I don't want to discuss it. I didn't want to discuss it before." He turned away and walked toward the barrier.

Katawba moved as if to go after him, but Straka put a hand on his arm. "Wait, Katawba. Let him go. There's no way you could stop him, and there's nothing we can do to make him talk."

Katawba looked unconvinced.

"Chase him, then. Go ahead and waste what little strength you've got. All he has to do is keep walking and stay out of arm's reach."

"I bet he could run if he had to," Wilhelm observed.

"So, then what do we do?" Katawba asked.

"Right now, nothing. I just wanted to make sure that you saw what I saw, that I wasn't so far gone I was dreaming the whole thing. On this planet I haven't been sure of anything."

"But there's more," Katawba said. "I can tell. There's something you're not telling us."

Straka gave him a look of surprise. "There is?"

Katawba rubbed his lower lip, unsure of whether or not to press her. "I think there is."

Wilhelm touched Straka on the arm. "Are you holding something back?"

"No, not really. It's nothing definite."

"Well, tell us anyway. We have a right to know."

"Okay. Since you put it that way. I think we're suffering from something other than, or in addition to, starvation. Look at Kominski. No, never mind. He's a bad example. But look at De Sola. He's feverish, isn't he? And Maxwell—he's dying for sure. And not from starvation."

"I see what you mean. Then what is it?" Wilhelm asked.

"This place. Bacteria. A virus. Something like that. Maybe the planet itself is poisonous to us."

"Beautiful," Wilhelm said. "Just what we need. I mean, what more could we ask for?"

"How about a little alien ship floating down out of the sky with some real food and water?" Katawba asked.

"Dream on," Wilhelm said.

But Straka wasn't listening. She was staring at the horizon, at the approaching ship. "Gentlemen? What's that look like to you?" she asked, pointing.

They looked to where she pointed. "Oh my good God," Katawba said.

"Baby Jesus," Wilhelm said.

McGowen ran over to the group. "Do you see it?" he asked like a little boy at a three-ring circus.

"We see it all right," Straka said. "Go in and get the rest of the crew out here. Carry them if you have to."

15

The Haber ship landed in an open area twenty meters from the building. The whole crew with the exception of Maxwell waited for the bay door to open. Straka, McGowen, Katawba, and Wilhelm stood in a tight little group. McGowen was helping Straka stand. De Sola swayed back and forth unsteadily, a few meters away. Kominski was closest to the ship, standing motionless like a hunting dog pointing out a quail. Jackson stood nearby, eyeing the ship hungrily.

But the ship just sat there, humming quietly, a neutral gray in the early-morning light.

"What the hell are they waiting for?" Wilhelm asked.

Jackson wheeled around and glared at him.

Jackson turned back to the ship, and Straka caught Wilhelm before he had a chance to respond. "Cool out," she said softly to Wilhelm. "This is not the time to react to him."

After what felt like hours, the bay door slowly rose. Kominski started to whimper like a little child, making mewling sounds. He was drooling, wild-eyed, waving his hands as if communicating with an invisible being.

The Terrans faced the same unfriendly scene they had faced once before; an armed group of ten Habers in the doorway, small weapons by their sides. Straka recognized one of the Habers, the one who stood a step closer to the deck's edge than the others. His name was Alpha, and his eyes sparkled with color and life. She swallowed air as she waited for them to do what they must have come there for—to unload the stores.

Kominski was crying. He threw himself on the ground in the direction of the ship and started crawling on his stomach, rooting in the dirt like a wild hog. He made strange grunting sounds, muffled by the grass, once in a while letting out a short squeal of excitement.

A chill ran up Straka's spine. "Get him to his feet!" she said to McGowen.

McGowen walked over and lifted Kominski as if he were a doll. He sat Kominski on the grass and had to slap him across the face several times before he was silent. McGowen returned to Straka's side, frowning.

Alpha jumped to the ground. He stayed by the ship, out of the line of fire. "Get into the ship, Straka," Alpha said.

"Where are you taking us?" she asked.

"Not all of you. Just you, Straka. Get into the ship."

An icy flash ran down her spine, pinning her to the spot. Her hands started to tremble. Her eyes darted from man to man, looking for support. She touched her lips with her tongue; both were too parched to give each other any moisture. But still she sweated; beads of moisture ran down her sides, her face.

"I'm not going anywhere. Not until my crew is fed," she said with as much conviction as she could muster.

"You must come with us," Alpha repeated.

"Not until we get some water," she said.

The crew murmured their agreement. "And some food," she added.

"We have no food with us," Alpha said.

"What about water?" she demanded.

"We have no water," Alpha said. "Get in the ship."

"A one-track mind," Wilhelm commented.

The crew laughed, easing the tension for a moment.

"My men are starving. We need food and water and medical supplies."

"We understand. But you must come with us now."

"What for?" Straka demanded, losing patience.

"That is unimportant," Alpha said.

"How'd you like your face flattened?" Jackson asked.

"Take it easy," she said. "Take a deep breath, Jack." She looked at Alpha through burning eyes. "Why should I go with you? Why don't you feed us? What's going on?"

"Nothing is going on until you get into the ship. We will take you away for a short time, and then we will return you. It is that simple. When you are returned, there will be food and water."

"No way," Wilhelm said. "You're not taking her that easily. Not without a fight."

"Take it easy, Wilhelm," she said. "There's no need for that." Not yet, she thought. Maybe in a second or two ... "What you say may be true," she said to Alpha, "but it is not good enough. I'm afraid you'll have to show us some good faith, like leaving one of *your* men here in exchange."

"No."

"Don't you people know what good faith is?" Straka asked.

"We know," Alpha said. "But you are not in a position to de-mand or negotiate." He pointed to the ship with a gray, fur-covered hand. "Will you get in now?"

She didn't move. She barely breathed.

"Ready!" Alpha shouted.

The armed contingent in the bay raised their weapons and pointed them in the direction of the Terrans. There was no mistaking the intent of that action, or its Terran origin. Well, she thought, it was worth a try.

"Stay cool, Cathy," Wilhelm said. "Don't blow it now." Wilhelm took two extremely painful steps, positioning himself directly before Straka, shielding her from possible laser fire.

She knew the action would prove ineffective if the Habers fired, but that only increased her amazement.

McGowen instantly moved to her left, sharing the most forward, vulnerable spot with Wilhelm. A split second later Katawba, Martinez, and, strangely enough, Jackson had moved to the front. They formed a semicircle of protection between her and the ship.

Straka's shock increased. She was totally taken by surprise by the crew's actions. If she lived to see the end of this day, she would never forget this. Never. She swore to set things right with them for having deceived them, for having used them. A dull ache throbbed in her chest, warming her, reminding her of her ties to these men, her brothers on an alien world.

"Step aside, men," she said in a hoarse whisper. They all turned to face her as if unsure of what she'd said.

"Step aside," she repeated, this time with the force and conviction of a captain. The crew looked at her with a respect and camaraderie she'd never before seen in their eyes. Not even when Van Pelt had been alive, sane, and on top of things. There was hope there, too, and a little surprise of their own. But her tone had demanded obedience, and they parted, opening a path between her and the Habers.

"Where do you plan to take me?" Straka demanded.

"That is unimportant," Alpha said.

"To you, maybe, but not to me, and not to these men. They're not going to sit by and let you take me away like this, unchallenged."

"None of you is in any condition to challenge anything," Alpha said.

Straka threw back her long, narrow face and laughed.

Everyone froze. The planet seemed to stop spinning for an instant as everyone in the encampment turned to look at Straka.

"You know nothing about us. You haven't the slightest idea about humans. Saying something like that shows your total ignorance." She lowered her gaze and stared hard at Alpha. "Don't make me teach you about Terrans the hard way," she threatened.

"We have no need to learn more. We know what you did on Gandji."

"And you still haven't learned anything from that, I see. Well, well, well. Interesting, isn't it, men?" she asked.

The crew made grumbling noises that voiced their agreement, nodding their heads, smiling evilly, shifting their positions.

"Humans enjoy fighting," she said, watching Alpha, hoping to see some kind of reaction in that strange, alien face. "They'll fight under extreme conditions. They'll fight when they're unarmed against an armed enemy. They'll fight when hopelessly outnumbered. They'll fight when death is inevitable, just to take someone with them. Some continue to fight while dying."

"Get in the ship, Straka," Alpha said.

"The Captain stays with us!" Wilhelm shouted at Alpha. Alpha turned his head slightly so that he stared directly into Wilhelm's eyes.

"Yeah," Jackson yelled. "You're not going to take her!"

Alpha's head whipped around so that he looked directly at Jackson. The rest of the crew voiced their agreement.

"Aim!" Alpha said, looking straight at Straka again.

The Terrans stared down the barrels of ten lasetubes. Straka thought quickly: They won't fire. They can't. They're Habers. They're pacific.

But I can't afford to take that chance for all of us.

"Wait!" she said, voice cracking.

Everyone waited. The Habers were like statues sculpted by some psychotic inmate. The Terrans were like attentive puppies waiting for their master's voice.

"At least give us some assurance that we'll be fed if I comply with your request," she said.

"Unlike humans, we do not live to deceive, Straka. I already told you that you will be returned here as soon as possible. We will not harm you. And when you are returned, we will bring food and water."

That seems to end negotiations, she thought. But I can't just walk out of the compound like this—I've got to set up some chain of command.

"I need a few moments with my men before I board your ship."

"Fine," Alpha said.

Straka wasted no time. "McGowen—you're in charge. Wilhelm is second in command. And Jackson, so help me, if you make trouble while I'm gone, you'll pay dearly. I want all of you to watch Kominski. Make sure he doesn't do anything too stupid." She looked directly at McGowen. "Like eating the grass."

"What about Maxwell?" McGowen asked.

"Good point." She looked across the compound to Alpha. She broke away from the tight group and took a few painful steps toward the Habers. "Listen," she said, "one of my men is dying. He's seriously ill. Could you do for him what you did for that one?" she asked, pointing out McGowen.

"Yes," Alpha said. "When we return."

"But he may not be alive then!"

"Come quickly, then, Straka. We waste time. Get in the ship now. Each moment you delay brings that man closer to death."

Straka knew she couldn't change Alpha's mind. She turned to glance back at the building, then walked slowly, painfully, in shuffling steps to the alien ship. When she reached its side, Alpha picked her up as if she weighed nothing and placed her on the deck.

"She will be returned," Alpha said to the group of staring men. He climbed up to the bay deck.

As the doors started to close on the outside world, she heard Kominski wail. Then she heard a sharp crack, someone being slapped across the face, immediately followed by, "Shut up, 'Minski!" in Jackson's voice. "Cool out!" Wilhelm shouted. "Don't give *me* orders," Jackson shouted back.

The bay door closed and shut off the noise from the compound. Straka shook her head, weary, tired, parched, hungry, and filthy, afraid of what she would find if and when the Habers returned her to the pen.

Their weapons made her nervous. Being without her crew made her nervous. Not knowing where the Habers were taking her, or why, made her nervous. Their eyes made her nervous. She remembered far too well what Markos had done to Van Pelt.

Two Habers communicated silently while the others rested. It looked as if they had dropped into a deep meditation, but instead of their breathing slowing down, it sped up in ragged gasps. She looked around at some of the quiescent Habers and saw that not all of them were breathing.

By the time she had settled in and made herself as comfortable as possible on the deck, the ship had landed. There were no distinct physical sensations that cued her to this, but the reappearance of Alpha at the top of the ramp and the meditative Habers' stirrings were enough signs. They held their weapons trained on her. Alpha walked down the ramp and motioned Straka to her feet. She tried to stand but lacked the strength.

"Get up," Alpha said.

"I can't," she said bitterly.

Alpha bent down and lifted the woman to her feet. Straka swayed uncertainly, then started to crumple to the deck as her legs gave out. Alpha caught her before she hit.

"You are close to death?" Alpha said.

Straka eyed him warily. "Yes," she said. "Thanks to you."

Alpha turned to his fellow Habers and communicated with them through his eyes. Straka watched the display with rapt attention, fascinated and enchanted by the beauty and grace of those crystalline eyes, fearful of their potential power.

"They will carry you," Alpha said.

The bay door opened and she watched the outside world appear before her. They were on the edge of the city, the glittering buildings she'd seen on the distant horizon from the compound. Up close, the buildings were magnificent.

She knew now where they were taking her. After all she and the crew had been through, she was going to see Markos. Only now she was in no rush. She would have to talk to the mutated Terran on his own terms, and she didn't relish that.

One of the Habers picked her up in his arms and leaped down from the ship. They waited for the rest of them to join up, then started off for the inner city.

Habers lined the streets, silently watching Straka being carried.

Straka watched back, amazed at how different they all looked. All of their eyes radiated the same soft green, though. There were some the size of midgets, some the size of Jackson. Not one of them had the same colored outer covering that Alpha and his crew had, though. Some of them, a few scattered along the side of the road, had rainbow-hued coverings, while some were covered with swirls of pastels running over their bodies in gentle designs.

She observed what she could, but drew no conclusions about them or their way of life. She couldn't possibly divine enough information just by observing, so she stopped trying to figure them out. She saw things she didn't understand and took them in stride.

They stopped before a building. "Can you stand?" Alpha asked. "I'll try."

The Haber holding Straka gently lowered her to the ground. Straka leaned against the creature to steady herself and test her legs. Her knees buckled and she felt herself falling. The Haber caught her before she reached the ground.

"Give her to me," Alpha said.

The Haber moved to one side to let Alpha slip his arm around Straka's waist. Alpha gripped her tightly and started through the arch into the building. Straka glanced behind and saw that no one was following.

"Is this where he is?" she asked.

"You will see," Alpha said.

He helped her through the tubular corridors. The one they took emptied into a large room. One wall was lined with row after row of rock crystals, each one about the size of her fist. One wall had two windows. The other two had doorways cut into them. There were translucent pieces of furniture, and by their size and placement she assumed they were chairs. Alpha set her down on one of them. It was hard and uncomfortable beneath her. A small, old gray Haber stood in a corner of the room where the windows and the crystals met, silently watching. It was not Markos.

"Hi," she said as calmly as she could. Her heart pounded against her chest.

The alien flashed green, and she threw her arm across her eyes as if shielding them from a laser blast. She immediately felt foolish for having done that. The alien had probably been saying hello, trying to be friendly. This was no way to open negotiations.

"Would you happen to have any water?" she asked.

The old Haber pushed himself away from the wall and walked out of the room. Straka sat quietly, waiting for Markos to appear. The chair was hard on her hips. She wondered how the crew was doing without her there to keep them off each other's backs. She wondered if the old Haber would bring her some water.

She caught a flash of orange out of the corner of her eye and turned to see what it was.

Markos stood in the doorway. There was no mistaking that freakish skin coloring, the orange and greens, the reds and blues, the spotting and coloring of a mendil, the parody of the human form, the ugly reminder of seeing a being who had once been human. His face, unlike all other Haber faces, had the distinct symmetry of a human face. The eyes were spread out over a much larger area, and the nose was just a small, irregular bump on his face, but the structure was close enough to be recognizable.

Straka could see into Markos's body, beneath a layer of skin, see fluids oozing through his system, see the perversion of muscles that lay there.

Markos.

At last. She was within reach of what she'd risked everything for, what she'd traveled across the Galaxy for. But those things she wanted no longer seemed as important as they once had, and she found herself thinking of the men's welfare, concerned about getting them out of the death trap she'd walked them into, about getting the *Paladin* back.

"You don't look well," Markos said.

Straka recoiled at the sound of his voice. She'd forgotten how ugly it was. Even the Habers had nicer, more mellifluous voices than Markos, though they never really sounded human. It sounded like it had been dredged up from the deep, hidden corner of a twisted soul, from the bottom of a murky ocean. She wanted to tell him to clear his throat.

"I'm not well," she said. "Nor are the rest of your crewmates."

"*Your* crewmates," Markos corrected. "My ex-crewmates. Yes, I knew you would bring that up. Just remember, Cathy—they're *not* my crewmates, my brothers, or even of my race anymore. I feel no kinship toward them. Or to you.

"You should never have come here. You weren't invited. You inadvertently walked into something you know nothing about." Markos stopped as the Old One returned.

The Old One walked directly to Straka's side holding a clear container that held a few sips of clear liquid. Straka sniffed it, detected no scent, and tasted it carefully. It was water. She nodded her thanks and took a swallow of it greedily, letting it cut through the layer of parched tissue lining her mouth and throat. Her stomach hurt.

She breathed raggedly a few times, overwhelmed by the refreshing drink, staring into the container as if searching for an answer to her problems in its bottom.

The subject had to be broached, and she decided it would be best to tackle the most difficult aspect of it first.

"You've got to help us," she said.

"I do? Why?"

She looked at Markos, wiping her parched lips with the back of a dirt-encrusted hand. "If you don't, we'll die."

Markos shook his head, then said, "I'm sorry about that. I truly am. But there's nothing I can do."

"There's nothing you *can* do, or there's nothing you *will* do?" she asked.

"Either way."

"Then I take it you're not a prisoner here?"

Markos's mouth changed shape, and she thought she saw the remnant of a Terran facial expression—a smile. "No, I'm not a prisoner."

"Then why won't you help us?"

"A good question, Cathy. Unfortunately the answer is quite complex."

"Too complex for a simple Terran like me to understand, huh?" she said.

"Don't push it, Cathy. I'll explain what has to be explained. Nothing more, nothing less."

She suppressed her rising anger and frustration. She knew that if she let her emotions get the better of her, so would Markos. She needed to remain in control as much as possible. "Are you going to let me go back to the men?"

"Eventually."

Straka nodded. "All right. What do you want from me? Why did you send for me?"

"I need to know why you're here."

Straka shrugged, then slowly finished off the water. It was good, like a razor-sharp, ice-cold blade cutting through her body, slicing its way down her throat. She held up the container to the old Haber. "Could I have some more?"

A violent burst of nearly pure-white light pulsed from Markos's face and filled Straka with instant fear.

"The Haber you just addressed is not a house servant nor a messenger. Don't treat him like one. If you want something, ask me for it. Understand?"

Straka nodded, still stunned by Markos's outburst.

"You don't need any more water to talk."

She glared at him. "All right. No more water. What do you want to talk about?"

"I've asked you once. What are you doing in this solar system?"

"Looking for you."

"You found me. Why were you looking?"

"We were afraid for you. You were one of us, or don't you remember?" Straka asked, trying to put some bitterness into her voice. "With Van Pelt dead we thought you might join up with us. We thought you might have been a prisoner."

"I remember, all right. But I don't buy it. Give me some credit. That sounds like something Van Pelt would have said. What's the real reason you came here? What did you expect to find? Riches? Power? What?"

Straka shrugged. "Whatever the reason, it's not important anymore. What's important is that we're here, and we're going to die unless you do something to help us."

"You'll get no help from me until I find out what you're doing here."

"Listen, Markos, Maxwell is as close to death as you can get. Kominski is off the deep end. Jackson and McGowen have been—"

"The reason, Cathy! The reason!"

"Tell me what you plan to do with us first. Are you just going to let us die?"

Markos leaned forward in his chair, and she looked at him long and hard, wishing she could read something in that face, see some sign of concern, of worry, or pleasure or pain. Anything would have helped.

"I've been thinking about that. It all depends on what happens here today. How much you choose to cooperate. But you haven't been so inclined."

"Then there is something I can say or do to persuade you to help us?"

Markos moved his mouth into a perverted smile again. "There may be."

"What is it?"

"Just tell me why you and the crew chased me from Tau Ceti to Alpha Indi. That's an awfully long distance for the cavalry to come to my rescue, Cathy. Why make the trip? Did NASA 2 send you? Are you acting on their orders?"

Straka stared at the floor and gnashed her teeth. How could she tell him now? It all seemed so foolish.

"Straka? You're going to tell me sooner or later."

"Is that a threat?"

"Only if it has to be."

What to tell him? she thought. I'm going to have to tell him *something*. But what? The truth?

Markos's eyes pulsed in time to Straka's heartbeat.

"There are methods I can use for getting at the truth, Cathy. A few flashes from my eyes will do it. Like it did to Van Pelt. You can see that I'm not too good at controlling Terrans with my eyes, but the choice is yours. I'm willing to take the chance."

With my life, she thought. Of course he'd be willing. "Your own truth serum," she said bitterly.

"Would you prefer bamboo shoots under your fingernails? Oh, sorry, no bamboo on Aurianta. I'm sure we could find a suitable substitute."

"Humor, Markos? At a time like this?"

"Like what?" Markos demanded. "You're stalling. I'll give you one minute to decide."

Straka knew now that no amount of lying would stop Markos from getting what he wanted. Her existence on Aurianta was precarious, with one foot in the grave. But she clung to the life she had, in no rush to spend her last few hours as a brain-wipe courtesy of Markos's eyes.

"All right," she said. "No need for that kind of pressure. I'll tell you what you want to know. I suppose once I've done that, you'll kill us all."

"Perhaps," Markos said. "After I hear the reason for your coming here, we'll talk about your future. If you have one."

Straka started at the beginning, at the time when she'd assisted Markos on the preliminary physiological tests and examinations on the Habers. She voiced her belief that the Habers were immortal and then explained why she had lied to the crew and had talked them into chasing Markos to Alpha Indi.

"Incredible, Cathy. All this way, all this trouble, just for a few extra years of life. I never thought you'd deceive the crew like that. Have they figured any of it out yet?"

Straka shook her head.

"What about NASA 2?"

"No. They don't know anything at all."

"Nothing? You didn't contact them after what happened to Van Pelt?"

"No. For all they know, we're just so many atoms floating in tau-space."

"So. Van Pelt never contacted them either."

"No. They were never contacted. Ever."

Markos rose from his chair and looked at the old Haber standing in the corner. Straka had completely forgotten about him.

"Did you hear that, Old One? They know nothing!" Markos said.

The old Haber flashed red through his eyes.

"What's going on?" she asked.

"Straka, you've given me the *Paladin* and more."

"The *Paladin*?"

"Spoils of war."

"But you're not—oh my God! You can't be at war with Earth?"

"No, I'm not. Nor is the Haber race, despite your aggressive actions on Gandji. We just attribute that to the insanity of a race. Despite what I say, they refuse to hold those actions against you."

"Then you won't kill us?"

"I didn't say that. All I said was that we're not at war with the Terrans. And we plan to keep it that way. The less NASA 2 knows, the better."

Straka sighed, shaking her head. "Now that I've told you what you wanted to know, let us go. Help us. Or are you going to let us die?"

"Take heart—life is very fluid if you let it be. As circumstances change, lives change."

She knew then that Markos would not let the crew die. She watched as he advanced on her slowly, exuding power and control, letting it seep out of his eyes.

"I don't want to die," Straka said softly.

Markos stopped right before her, his skin glistening with clashing colors.

"You're going to kill me," she whispered.

"No," Markos said, "but I should."

16

The old Haber in the corner of the room started flashing colors at Markos. Straka watched the colors reflected off of Markos's face and neck. She had to look away. She was too drained to follow much more. Her body was weak—weakened more by the short but emotionally charged confrontation. Markos remained standing before her and she could see into his freakish body, see the alien colors and horrors too closely for her taste.

She closed her eyes and rubbed her forehead with her fingertips. A headache had started after drinking that water and it wasn't letting up. It started at the top of her scalp and extended down the sides of her head and into her neck. It felt as if some invisible hand rested there, squeezing tighter and tighter with incredible strength. Her stomach churned, and the gurgling sounds it made seemed overly loud in the quiet room. Her lips were sore and her mouth felt as if it were coated with cotton.

"We've reached a decision," Markos said, looking down at Straka.

She looked into Markos's face. "What is it?" Her voice was getting hoarse.

"We have a proposition for you and any crew member who doesn't want to die in that compound."

Straka knew better than to hope, and yet she couldn't help feeling a little optimistic. Clearly whatever Markos offered had to be better than dying out there.

"What's the proposition?" she asked warily.

"We're at war, and we need fighters. We want to hire you and your crew as mercenaries."

"You can't be serious. Fight? Us? Have you any idea what the men are like now? Half of them can't even get to their feet. Maxwell's probably dead. Kominski's little more than a gibbering idiot. McGowen's too strange to really trust for long. And Jackson —God, Jackson! And you want to hire them as fighters?" She laughed once, a short exhalation through her nose. "You're crazier than I thought."

"Maybe I am," Markos said, "but the proposition still stands. We want to hire all of you."

Straka nodded. Sure, she thought. Hire us. Why not?

Whatever conditions were tacked on could be dealt with. Now that she saw that Markos needed them, there would be a chance to negotiate, to make a few demands of her own. All she had to do was hold out until just the right time and she'd probably get the two things that mattered most—her life and the ship.

"I'm interested, but only interested."

"Good. That's all I ask for now. If you agree to fight for us, we'll give you back the *Paladin*. It will be yours to command. Any of the crew who qualifies can have one of our ships to command. I'll supply any additional crew you may need."

"To fight this war you've mentioned?"

"Yes. To fight the war."

"Against who?"

"Not Earth, if that's what you're worried about. We can talk about the Hydrans later. If you agree."

"Hydrans?"

Markos nodded.

"And you need us to fight them?"

"Yes. After what you did on Gandji, I think you should jump at the chance to set things right with the Habers. This is your opportunity."

"Fight or be killed? Is that it?"

"Yes. I'm offering you a position in my . . . forces."

"What do you need *us* for? You've got Habers who can fight, don't you? Or was that armed contingent you kept sending into the compound incapable of fighting?"

"They're capable of fighting, all right. And killing."

"Then what do you need us for?"

"I told you before, the answer is complex. I'm willing to explain it now. Are you willing to listen?"

Straka nodded. "Sure. If I fall out of the chair, though, I'll probably be unconscious. Or dead."

"I'll run it by you as quickly as possible. I'll fill in the details later if necessary."

Markos began explaining about the ten children and how he'd mutated them, and about Triand's battle on Theta Alnon.

"I thought he was strong and cunning enough to win, but as soon as he arrived on the planet, I realized my mistake," Markos said. "I could tell by what he was thinking that he really didn't understand what war and fighting are all about. He approached his little push into the enemy's camp as a different kind of experience."

Straka rubbed her forehead to try to ease the pain, but it didn't help. "I don't understand what you mean by 'a different kind of experience.'"

"He primed himself for the battle," Markos said, "like any creature would. But the things that worried him should not have been a concern, and the way he approached the skirmish was all wrong. And when it came to his life or some alien's life, he lost. It was *life* he was dealing with, and he never really understood that.

"The whole thing stems from this attitude. He was immortal, Cathy, just as you suspected."

Hearing her suspicions confirmed gave Straka a jolt of adrenaline, clearing her mind for the moment.

"You see, Triand died when he wanted to die, or so he believed."

"What are you talking about?" Straka asked. "If he was killed in battle, how could he have died when he wanted to die? Unless he never wanted to live through the battle in the first place."

"That's close to the truth, but not quite there. Look at it this way: He was at least fifty percent pure Haber, and probably closer to eighty or ninety percent—the exact proportion makes little difference. Ever since his birth, Triand believed he was immortal. He knew it on a biological level. And like all Habers, he *was* immortal. If nothing external happened, he could have lived forever."

"Forever," Straka muttered absently.

"But they don't live forever," Markos said. "They can, but they don't. They don't *want* to, and they don't have to. Just knowing they *can* is enough. They eventually commit suicide by meditating their way down to the point where they've used all their stored food. Taking in additional food is taboo. But that's what passes for their religion. They also have an intellectual, philosophical approach to immortality. They understand that immortality is the most important aspect of life. It's what brings everything else into focus for them. Without it they fear they would live millennia unable to appreciate the things they appreciate most."

Straka swayed in the chair and she felt herself slipping. "Markos . . ."

Markos reached down and grabbed Straka by the shoulders to steady her. He let his hands reach down and penetrate Straka's shoulders, doing some probing and fixing.

Some of Straka's strength returned in a rush, a flush of well-being.

"Better?" Markos asked.

Straka nodded. "A little. Go on and finish."

"This religious attitude was a part of Triand, and I'm afraid it's a part of all the other mutated children. It seems to go with the genetic territory. No sane creature, or sane by Terran standards, would throw himself into battle the way Triand did. He lacked caution, guile, and the one thing I've yet to see in this Haber race or in any mutation."

"What?"

"A killer instinct. They lack the ability to perceive cruelty. To them this war is some kind of game they have to play. They move to the right, the enemy moves too. So they use maneuver three. But if that maneuver doesn't work, what do they do then? They try other things, such as trying to understand the rules of the game, and by the time they're approaching some level of dealing with rules, they're dead. They lack an understanding of conflict."

"They just need better training."

"Don't think I didn't already think of and try that. There's just no way those things can be trained. The potential isn't there."

Straka nodded. She felt herself falling toward the floor again and felt Markos catch her before she hit. She closed her eyes for a moment and when she reopened them, found herself lying on the floor. The ceiling sparkled with bits of brilliant color. Or was that Markos's eyes?

She could feel Markos's hand on her chest, could feel the glittering eyes calming her. Some of her pain and exhaustion disappeared. She tried to sit up, but Markos put his other hand on her chest, preventing her rising.

"Stay where you are a little longer. Let your body heal a little."

"Right," Straka said weakly. "Continue talking, though. I can listen better now."

"Fine. Do you see where the problem is?"

"I see some of it. Your children don't have a refined survival instinct."

Markos thought for a moment. "Interesting. Do you think that's it?"

"Well, it's part of it, anyway."

"Yes. It would have to be. Good, Cathy. Very good. Will you help us?"

She was feeling better. Her head was clear, and her stomach wasn't knotted in pain. She could concentrate on something other than food and water. "Sure I'll help. You said you'd give me the *Paladin* back?"

"Yes."

"And you'll save the crew?"

"Yes."

But it made no sense, and Straka knew it. There had to be something Markos wasn't telling her. Why would he let them aboard their own ship? He had to know they would set out for Earth immediately after gaining their freedom. Markos couldn't think that Straka would feel that indebted or obligated just because he'd saved them from a death he himself had planned.

"What's the catch?" Straka asked.

"Are you feeling better now? Try to sit up," Markos said.

Straka found she could sit up easily and her hips didn't bother her as much. Her head throbbed and spun for a moment, and then the pain vanished. "I feel pretty good," she said, amazed at the sudden change.

"Don't get carried away," Markos warned. "The well-being is temporary."

"Oh. What do I have to do to make it permanent?"

"Permanent. Now there's an alien concept," Markos said in a liquid, bubbly voice.

"I'm not laughing."

"So I see," Markos said.

Straka tried to stand. She pushed herself up and was able to maintain her balance. She tried a few steps, found that with some pain she could walk, then returned to the chair where she'd been sitting. Markos returned to his chair.

"All right. I understand why you need us—"

"Want. Not need."

"Fine, then. I understand why you want us to help. You said you were willing to hire me and the crew. What are you willing to pay?"

"I've already made my offer. You get the *Paladin*, I'll supply any extra ships if you want them, and you and your crew are returned to health."

Straka smiled, nodding her head once. "That sounds very good, for openers. But let's talk price."

"What price? A reward? Precious metals? Jewels? Sure. Why not? You can have all you want. But I know that as soon as you get aboard that ship, you and your crew will be long gone. You'll run right back to Terra and take your chances there, right? So why talk about money yet? I'll have to have some assurance from you that you'll fight and not run."

"The thought had crossed my mind."

"Like a railroad track," Markos said. "I'll have to explain something about the Hydrans. We're not fighting for the fun of it. We're fighting for our lives. They're planet stealers. They're a textbook case of expansionists. I don't know why, but they're spreading throughout this entire sector of space. They swallow and destroy everything in their path. And their assaults are so deceptively simple—it all starts with just one small ship.

"They're spreading out like a sound wave," Markos said. "And Sol, as well as other stars, is in their path. Which means that sooner or later, they'll get around to Terra. Unless we stop them now. Before they're unstoppable."

"I have only your word to go on, Markos. Do you have any proof?"

"None that you would be able to understand or see yet," he said, motioning toward the wall filled with crystals.

"Well, if you're right, if what you say is true, Terra could be in trouble."

"Then you'll help?"

"I didn't say I would. I just said that Terra could be in trouble, and that's too bad for Humanity."

"Loyal to the end, eh, Straka? Well, that really doesn't surprise me. If you can steal their one and only f-t-l ship and use it for personal ends, I should have known you wouldn't know the meaning of loyalty."

Straka froze, her system struck by a sudden release of emotion, her pent-up anger and frustration finally finding a release. She leaned forward in her chair and looked at Markos's grotesque face. "Don't talk to me about loyalty, Markos." She spat the words, almost choking on them, through her long-unreleased feelings. "I remember when you were a human being. A human who betrayed his ship, his crewmates, his captain, his whole race."

Straka knew she was pushing Markos, perhaps a little too far, but there had been no need for him to question her loyalty. Straka felt justified in returning the favor. She watched Markos's eyes glow and subside.

"I am not the same person I was then," he said. "Let's leave it at that."

"Fine," Straka said. "I'm not either. I've got a sense of loyalty and a sense of responsibility. It just so happens it doesn't apply to Terra."

"Well, you should think of this. If you run back to Terra, you may eventually have to face the Hydrans there. If NASA 2 lets you live that long."

"Let's stop dancing, Markos. We seem to have hit the unanswerable problem. Nothing you've offered so far would be ample payment to ensure our loyalty. You've appealed to my sense of justice, to my feelings of guilt, to my natural desire to protect my home planet. But it's not good enough, Markos. It's not even close."

She didn't want to push him too far, but Straka knew that they had yet to reach the kernel of the real offer. She might lose everything by pressing forward, demanding more, but it was a chance she would have to take. Negotiating from the weakest position imaginable made it far more important to get everything possible.

"I don't know what else to say, Cathy." Markos looked across to the old Haber and flashed something through his eyes. The Haber flashed something back, and then Markos turned to Straka. "Of course, there is one last thing."

She'd hoped so. "What is it?"

"Immortality."

Straka wasn't sure she'd heard that properly. "What was that you said?"

"Immortality."

Straka's heart raced, pounded against her weakened ribs. She couldn't believe it. Markos had the answer.

"That's what I thought you said. Markos, you just hired yourself a Terran. I can't speak for the rest of the crew, but once I explain, I'm sure they'll agree."

"Perhaps they will," Markos said, "but there are some conditions you should know about first."

"What?"

"I won't exactly be hiring Terrans. In order to make you immortal, I'll have to change you—like the way the Habers changed me."

"What?"

"That's the deal. It's the only thing we've said that really makes sense. To be immortal, you'll have to be changed."

"Changed? Changed into what?"

"A different creature than what you are now. Something more than what you are in most ways, less in some other ways."

"What ways?" Straka asked, panic creeping into her voice.

"The details are unimportant. Your present physical form is incompatible with immortality. It's unable to provide the necessary genetic and chemical base. Your basic physical makeup will have to be altered. I'll have to change what you are. It's that simple."

"Nothing's that simple! I don't want to be changed. Not like you. The only thing I want to change about me is my mind. I reject your offer."

"Then have a good life, Cathy. And enjoy it while you can. You've chosen to die as surely as you're sitting there, trembling."

Straka buried her face in her hands. Her stomach was tight, and she felt an emptiness in her lungs. Her whole body was collapsing, losing strength, caving in on itself. She looked up to Markos, avoiding the mockery of his facial features, and was entranced by those pulsing eyes.

"I don't want to die!"

The Old One flashed red.

17.

Straka sat on the deck of the silent ship watching Markos's eyes glow softly with throbs of untapped power, waiting for him to say something. When Straka had calmed down enough to accept that she could never be immortal until her form was changed, she'd started asking Markos questions. But Markos had remained silent, had deliberately not gone into the details, letting her think the worst.

Straka had told Markos that she was willing to accept the necessary physical alterations right then and there. Deep inside, Straka was anything but sure—her commitment was for the moment, and she told herself she would back out if things got too threatening.

Markos had touched her with his hands, suffusing her body with well-being as he had done earlier. But as they walked through the bizarre city to the waiting wedge ship, Straka knew it was too late to back out. She knew she was only fooling herself into believing there was an alternative.

What kind of an alternative was death?

They had boarded the ship, sat on the deck facing each other, waiting in silence for the bay door to close. Markos's breathing had shifted, dropped to a few short breaths per minute.

Straka stared at Markos's body. A chill ran down her spine and she shivered at the thought of looking like that. Was that the price of immortality? she wondered. To look and sound like a freak, a monstrous, chaotic mosaic—bits and pieces of alien creatures?

Her mind would remain unchanged—Markos had said nothing about altering her personality. He'd only talked about physical change. He'd said that the Habers needed Terrans to fight, mercenaries who thought with human minds. She would still be that thing that was Cathy Straka inside, where it counted. But there was no telling what she'd be like on the outside.

The bay door closed and Markos stirred.

"I'm ready to answer some questions now," Markos said in his liquid voice.

To be like that . . . "Just how changed am I going to be?"

"Enough so that you won't look human. You'll be something between human and Haber. As your genetic structure is altered, I'll change your phenotype to accommodate the necessary adaptations. But what difference does this make? You either want to die or you don't. I'm offering you the chance to live until you choose to stop living. If you want that, you must be willing to make certain sacrifices. It's that simple."

"Nothing is that simple."

"At least you have a choice, Straka. The Habers gave me none."

Straka's stomach turned. "I'm sorry for you."

"Don't be. I don't want your pity—only your answer. You told me yes in the city, and I see you vacillating. Decide once and for all. Once I change you, there's no turning back."

"But what if the crew doesn't go along? What if I'm the only one?"

"Yes or no, Straka."

"Yes, yes, yes," she said bitterly, spitting the words.

"Even if they call you a traitor?"

"Yes!"

"Even if we have to turn around and leave them to die in the compound?"

"What are you talking about?"

"Leave them to die. What would you like me to do with them? Let a violent race wander over the planet? Give them the *Paladin* back? Keep them penned up? If they don't throw in with us, what good are they?"

Her men! Markos was talking like that about her men, her crew. They were human beings—not some group of unrelated objects. "You can't just let them starve, Markos."

"I can't? All right. Then *you* decide what to do with them."

"What are you doing this to me for? Why are you torturing me?" Straka whined.

"I'm not torturing you. I'm just letting you decide the fate of your men. That's what you wanted, isn't it?"

"I don't know, I don't know."

"It's all part of the price, Straka. New loyalties demand new dividing lines."

Straka was silent for a moment. She breathed deeply a few times, trying to get her mind clear enough to tackle the problem.

"We'll have to explain it to them," Straka said. "They'll have to understand. They'll want to help. They're good men. I'll explain it to them and they'll understand."

"I hope so," Markos said. "I prefer having them with us, but you know I'll go either way."

"McGowen should be easy to convince. He's already different from the others."

Markos smiled. On him the smile was lopsided, a tight grimace. "I know. When Alpha touched him, he had to change him a little. His metabolism slowed down. He's about one one-hundredth along the way to total change."

"He eats the grass."

Markos nodded his misshapen head. "I know."

"And he's still strong."

"He should be. You can feel part of that same change within yourself. You should realize deep down that I'm capable of fulfilling my part of the bargain."

"I've always believed you. That was never the problem."

Straka felt a slight thump through the deck and assumed the ship had landed in the compound. "Are we there already?"

Markos nodded. "There are a few things I need to tell you, to make sure you really understand before you go out to talk to them."

Straka braced herself by thinking of her pending immortality.

"As I promised, you'll be changed, but only physically. Assure the crew of this and you stand a much better chance of convincing them. After the first process—"

"First?"

"Yes. I'm breaking the conversion into two stages. The first stage will let you live for around a thousand years. This should give you and the crew plenty of time to deal with your aspect of the Hydran War. When you return—"

"If."

"Right. *If* you return, successful or not, I'll make the final genetic alterations to give you immortality."

"What's to stop us from figuring out what to change and doing that to each other? Aren't you afraid we'll do it ourselves?"

"Not at all," Markos said. "I'm counting on your being too busy."

The bay door started to open.

"That's about all for now. Are you ready?"

Straka shook her head. "No, I'm not, but I don't suppose that matters."

She got to her feet and stood in the widening opening, flexing her fingers, listening to the joints pop, gritting her teeth, preparing herself for the worst. Before the bay door had stopped opening, she could see their gaunt, filthy faces. They stood in a ragged line, heads tilted back, eyes wild with desperation. One of them lay on the ground, rolled onto his side, curled into a fetal position. It was Maxwell.

Straka stared at the little man's back and sides, hoping for some sign of life, of breathing, but there was no motion there at all. He was either breathing very shallowly or he had already died.

She felt a hand on her shoulder and wheeled around. She'd forgotten Markos for a moment, surveying the pitiful sight of the crew.

"Go on," Markos said. "I'll be here until you're ready to come back or until you need me down there."

Straka turned back to her men. They looked dead on their feet, like prisoners did in the old films of war—unwashed, unfed, improperly clothed, waiting for death to creep up behind them. They all needed a long immersion in the geltanks. They stood defiantly as if waiting to be mowed down. She felt separated from them by more than physical distance. Her decision had made her future real, concrete, endless, while they still fought to remain in the present. Straka realized she no longer related to them as she had before. The camaraderie was gone as their situations changed.

She climbed down from the ship to the ground as if lowering herself into a leper colony.

They were on her in a second.

"The food, Cathy! Where's the food?"

They swarmed over and around her, leaning on her for support. They were so weak and fragile, she could have swept them away with a wave of her hand. Stick figures. Mockeries of what they had once been. The smell was overpowering, intensely human.

De Sola was knocked to the ground by the jostling and seemed unable to rise again. Kominski was gibbering, hanging onto McGowen's back. Wilhelm was smiling, warmth in his eyes, glad for Straka's safe return if nothing else.

They were injuring themselves in their desperation and excitement, and Straka realized she would have to get control of them and the situation immediately.

"Back off! All of you!"

They stopped the weak but frenzied clamoring and seemed to sag like marionettes with their strings loosened.

"Sit down. I have to talk to you."

"We never thought you'd return," Wilhelm said.

"We're glad you're back," McGowen said, lowering Kominski to the ground. The others settled to the ground, wincing in pain.

"Did you bring food?" Jackson asked.

Food. Straka had completely forgotten the food. Food and water. My God, what was she going to say? When they found out she'd returned with a promise instead of what they craved most, they wouldn't listen at all.

"Food, food, food," Kominski babbled. "Food, food, food."

"Shut up, 'Minski," Jackson growled. He hardly seemed strong enough to force him.

"I didn't bring food," Straka said, lowering herself to sit before the crew.

"What?" Katawba wailed. "What?"

"Food," Kominski said, playing in the ground, pushing blades of grass aside with his fingers, looking for tiny insects.

"They returned me, as they promised, and I've been unharmed. If you listen to what I have to say, you'll see they kept their promise to you too."

"How? You brought no food with you," Martinez said.

"Take it easy and I'll explain."

Straka waited a moment to see if they were too intent on complaining to listen. They were angry and bitter—that much was obvious—not the best attitude to face under these circumstances, but it was what she had to work with. There was no other choice.

"Where is the food?" Kominski asked like a three-year-old. Straka saw that his lips were swollen and split and his cheeks were freshly bruised.

"Help?" De Sola asked. "How?"

"Are they going to let us go?" Wilhelm asked. "Did you straighten this mess out? Do they understand we mean them no harm?"

"Give me a second, both of you. What about Maxwell? Is he dead?"

"Very," McGowen said.

"When?"

"About an hour after you left."

She sighed. "I'm sorry. Really sorry. But there's nothing we can do for him now. I'm more concerned about all of you. We've got some decisions to make."

"Another great Master Plan, Straka?" Jackson asked.

"Slow down, Jack."

"Give her a chance," Wilhelm said.

Kominski was lying on his back, staring up at the ever-changing sky. "They're going to kill us," he said in a singsong.

"Give it a break, Kominski," Jackson said.

"Let me lay this out for you quickly. They took me to see Markos. He offered to give us all back our health, our freedom, and our ship, and something very intriguing if we agree to help him."

"Help him what?" Jackson asked.

"Fight a war. The Habers are being innocently slaughtered by a race called the Hydrans. These creatures are expansionists. No one seems to know why they're doing what they're doing, but Markos doesn't really care. He needs fighters."

"The pay?" Jackson asked.

"All I've told you, plus immortality. Immortality at a price, that is."

The crew remained silent for a long, tense moment.

"Food, food, food," Kominski said.

"Are you going for the deal?" Katawba asked.

Straka nodded.

"I'm not sure I understand. We fight for Markos and the Habers? And in payment we get to live forever?" De Sola asked.

"Basically," Straka said. "He will have to make some alterations to our bodies, but he assures me that our minds won't be affected."

"And you *believe* this cretin?" Jackson asked.

"Yes. I believe him. He needs our minds more than anything else. We offer him the fighting edge he can't get with his Habers or his mutant offspring."

"Where do I sign up?" De Sola asked.

"You're serious?" Straka asked.

"Goddamned right I'm serious. I'm not crazy. I don't want to sit here and die slowly like this. I don't want to die at all. If you're not putting me on, I'm with you all the way."

Thank God, Straka thought. "What about the rest of you?"

The others remained silent.

"Katawba?" Straka asked.

"I don't know," Katawba said. "I'm not up for fighting a war, if you know what I mean. Especially for some furry creatures who can't fight for themselves. What are these Hydrans like?"

Straka shrugged. "I didn't even think to ask. It doesn't matter to me if they're four meters tall and built out of permaplast. I'd rather go like that than sitting in this pen."

"I take it, then, that this is the real choice?" Wilhelm asked. "Remain here or join up with him?"

Straka nodded.

"Count me in," Katawba said.

"Me too," Wilhelm said. "Whatever awaits us out there can't be worse than this."

"Don't bet on it," Jackson said. "Especially if Cathy had something to do with it. She got us into this in the first place."

"Count me in, too," McGowen said.

"They're going to kill us, aren't they?" Kominski asked, sounding very sane and rational for a moment.

"No! But if you keep that up, I will!" Jackson shouted.

"Markos can fix Kominski, too. He'll straighten out his head and give him a good, strong, healthy body," Straka said.

"Well, Martinez? What about it, kid?" De Sola asked.

Martinez shrugged. "Sure. Why not. What the hell do I have to lose?"

"Jackson?" Straka asked.

"What?"

"You're the last one."

"So?"

"Are you joining us?"

"I guess I have to. No way I'm staying in this place by myself."

Straka smiled. "All right, then. There's no time to lose. Markos is waiting in the ship for us. He'll take us out of here to the city and fix us up."

"You mean change us around," Jackson said.

"Yes. Change us."

Straka rose to her feet. She felt a great burden lift from her shoulders. She bent over to help them to their feet, one at a time.

They made a ragged procession to the nearby ship. Straka turned around and noticed that McGowen was still seated on the grass.

"What's wrong?" she asked.

"Maxwell," McGowen said. "I don't know what Markos is planning on changing us into, but right now we're still human beings. We ought at least to bury the poor bastard."

Straka looked over at Maxwell's form.

Markos appeared in the doorway.

"Fine. Let's bury him," Straka said.

18

After Maxwell had been buried, Markos helped the crew onto the ship. As he touched each one, lifting them up, guiding them to the deck, he healed them a little, taking away some of their hunger and pain, giving them a little better outlook on the future. They commented on their newfound strength to each other noisily while Markos sat on the deck and waited for their takeoff.

Jackson broke away from the group of chattering men and approached Markos, standing defiantly before him, hands clenched into fists. "Just what do you intend to change?" he asked.

"Your entire body. I promise you won't be disappointed, Jackson. You'll be stronger, live longer—far longer than you'd previously imagined possible."

"What will I look like, though?"

"Like nothing you've ever seen before."

"Just make sure I don't look like you."

The bay fell silent.

"You won't," Markos said.

"I had better not."

Markos's eyes glowed stronger, throbbed in time with some unseen heart. "Just sit down and don't make trouble. We need each other. Don't let your feelings of strength and health go to your head. I can reverse it without even touching you."

Jackson bit off his reply, shifted his weight, then returned to the group.

"What were you trying to prove?" Wilhelm asked him.

"Forget it, Wilhelm. You'd never understand," Jackson said. "You'd do anything he said, wouldn't you? You let him get away on Gandji."

"Keep quiet!" Markos shouted. "I don't want to hear your petty arguments! Sit down on the deck. The ride will be over soon. Those of you who are having second thoughts can be returned to the compound as soon as the rest of us have left the ship."

They looked to Straka. Straka nodded. They sat. The ride was over in a few moments.

The bay door opened, revealing the city streets thirty meters away.

"I want you men to understand something," Markos said. "These creatures think you're the answer to the problem they've been having for hundreds and hundreds of years. That's the way I've been presented to them, and that's the way I want to present you. They don't understand what human beings are capable of. They don't know what you are. All they know is they're incapable of helping themselves, and you're here to save them."

He rose to his feet and left the ship.

"What's with him?" Jackson asked.

"I don't think you understand," Straka said. "This entire race has given Markos the problem of fighting and winning a war."

"Yeah, well, let's get out of here. The faster this is over with, the better."

They murmured their agreement and followed Straka from the ship. Markos was waiting a few meters away, standing on the road that led into the city. The Terrans took a few moments to stare at the city, the city they had seen only on the horizon.

It was almost sundown, and the streets were filling with Habers.

The setting sun bounced crazy hues off the white city buildings, setting the walls into glittering fires of light, and turned the sky around it into a huge blob of kaleidoscopic light. It was sundown. The Habers linked hands and stood motionless, facing the setting sun. They started to hum.

Markos sprinted a few meters to link up with a group of nearby Habers.

"What the hell?" Jackson said.

"That sound—we heard it in the compound," Straka said. She looked over at McGowen.

McGowen was smiling like a Buddha, humming very softly.

They all felt a slight tingling around their navels and then a warm feeling washed through them. They were left feeling strangely secure and unthreatened.

The feeling stayed with them a few seconds, until the sun had set and the Habers broke their linkup. A large number of Habers remained in the streets, turned now to face Markos and the Terrans, waiting for them to walk by.

"This isn't what I expected," Straka said. "They seem friendly."

"They are," McGowen said. "I can feel it."

They walked forward until they stood beside Markos. Markos looked at each man with his pulsating eyes, then said, "These are good creatures. They're just curious. They find a strange symmetry in your forms. Don't be offended by their stares."

"No problem. As long as I can stare back," Jackson said.

They moved through the streets, commenting and laughing at the differences they saw between Habers. Markos tried to put a stop to the laughter by explaining that they were creatures who liked change, and changing themselves was one of their genetic abilities.

By the time they reached Markos's building, the Terrans were unsure of just what a Haber was. There were some similarities between them all, and some differences too. The phenotypical Haber they had come to know from Gandji seemed to be far outnumbered by stranger, more exotic mutations.

As they entered the house, Markos explained that the largest Habers were usually the youngest ones. He briefly explained their metabolism and life cycle, preparing them for the change they were about to undergo.

He showed them through the corridors and rooms, explaining the use of each piece of furniture and the spaces within the rooms. He led them through a long hallway that emptied into a circular room with a lot of hard rock chairs. Straka recognized the room immediately. There was a corridor leading off that dead-ended. Off this corridor were twelve small rooms. He assigned a room to each of them, told them to relax, to put their thoughts in order, and make their final decision. Markos told them he would reenter the room later to touch and change them. After that it would be too late to turn back.

Straka settled onto the hard, uncomfortable floor. The room had no windows. She was impatient to undergo the change. She wished Markos would come back in already; the longer she waited, the more nervous she became. She didn't want to have to deal with the nagging self-doubts and fears. She wanted to be immortal, and that was all there was to it.

The room offered no distractions. The walls were plain white, the floor an off-white. The chair in the room was rock crystal. There was nothing of interest to look at. She closed her eyes and wondered what it would be like to have a new body. Would there be pain? Would she be like a newborn, unable to care for herself until she got used to the way her new body worked?

A small Haber stood in the doorway, the same one Straka had talked to a few hours before.

"I'm sorry I offended you by asking for water," Straka said.

"I, I was glad to help," the Old One said. "Markos does not present me, me accurately. No offense was taken."

"Are you their leader?" Straka asked.

"No. Markos leads us, us in the thing that matters, the change we, we will not survive, the change he calls war."

"Oh. Were you on Gandji with him?"

The Old One took several moments to answer. "Yes. I, I was. Are you ready? Markos is about to begin, and he wishes to start with you."

Straka nodded. "I'm ready."

"Let me, me counsel you. When Markos touches you, do not fight the strange feelings and changes you feel happening to your body. Let your body float and pay it no attention. Think of who and what you are inside your mind and you will remain the same creature you are now, only physically different. Grasp that and ignore all else."

"Thank you," Straka said.

The Old One flashed red.

Markos walked through the doorway. "Ready?" he asked Straka.

Straka nodded.

"Second thoughts?"

"None. Let's get it over with."

"Lie back."

Straka lay back and stared at the white ceiling, trying to do exactly what the Haber had instructed her to do. If they were deceiving her, taking their advice would make no difference—she would end up no worse than if she'd stayed in the compound. But if they were truly trying to help, she would be that much ahead of the game by doing as she was told.

She remembered her youth, her parents, her past loves as Markos bent over and obscured her view of the ceiling.

Markos's eyes came alive, glittering and dancing in swirling patterns of intricate beauty, pulling her into their whirlpool. Straka was entranced, locked onto one thought—the totality of being Cathy Straka. The colors flashed to their opposites, then began to mix like paint being slowly stirred.

"Close your eyes," Markos said softly and gently in his sandpaper voice.

Straka smiled and closed her eyes.

She felt her body float away.

Straka regained consciousness with a rush of vision, her senses turned on full. She felt absolutely terrific—no pain, no discomfort, stronger than ever, more in tune with her body than she'd ever considered possible.

The ceiling above her head looked different, and it took her an instant to realize it sparkled with color, as if it were shot through with tiny chips of mica and shards of jewels. Had they moved her? What the hell was going on?

She sat up in a rush, saw the walls with their intricate and subtle colors, saw the air move in beautiful patterns before her, saw the floor with its rich textures, and knew for certain she'd been moved. But why? What could Markos hope to accomplish?

Her mind was the same—whatever had happened, Markos and the old Haber had kept their promise about that. She was still Cathy Straka.

The air before her billowed for a meter as her body's movements acted on the still air. She was struck by a numbing thought: She could see through the air, transparent as it always was, and yet she could *see* it at the same time.

She looked down at her hands and realized then that she hadn't been moved to a different room. She'd been changed. She was no longer human.

Her hands were off-white, covered with a thin layer of soft fur or hair. It was pleasant to touch as she rubbed her palm over the back of her hand. Her palms were soft skin, opaque, a few shades deeper than the fur. Her arms, chest, and legs were covered with the same thing.

She felt her face. That, too, had been changed.

She took a breath of air into her lungs, watched the air currents close in to fill the vacuum her breath had created, and realized she hadn't breathed until then.

She felt her body tingle, then flush hot and cold as her mind went into shock. She needed to cry, to run, to figure out what they'd done to her. She leaped to her feet with a surge of power, clenched her hands into fists. Her body grew more and more powerful as her anger and frustration mounted. Her body became more massive, her skin tougher, her vision more acute. She needed to unleash herself on something, someone, break a chair or a wall, smash her fist through something hard to release the emotions running out of control. They were trapped inside, working strange tricks of change on her new body.

"Markos!" she shouted, then turned on her heels and strode determinedly down the hallway to the large, circular room.

Markos was sitting there calmly, waiting, facing the hall and Straka's approach.

Straka rushed into the room, stood before Markos, her mind fluctuating wildly. In an instant she was overcome by a tidal wave of glee, of manic elation, of gratitude and power so strong she could find no words to express herself. In the next instant she was filled with rage, anger, hatred so strong she could feel it seeping out, radiating from her mind in waves of pure power.

She stood there, vacillating at stroboscopic speed, with laser intensity, unable to say anything but "Markos, help me."

Markos's eyes reached out and enveloped her in colors, wrapping her in a muted blanket of calm, tinting the very air between them. Like a warm bed on a chilly morning, the colors from Markos's eyes surrounded and comforted her. The fluctuations of Straka's emotions continued, but their intensity was lessening slowly but surely. Finally, after long and tense minutes, her mind calmed to the point where the emotions blended into a homogenous mixture of rational and emotional thought.

"Sit down, Cathy," Markos said calmly, softly, issuing it not as an order but as an invitation.

Straka sat in the seat beside Markos. The seat was, for the first time, comfortable.

"The change is a lot to deal with at first. Take your time. Try to remain as calm as possible. Don't upset yourself with needless worry. Everything is fine—you went through the change like a true Haber would. I'm very proud of you. Of all of you. The Old One was immensely impressed."

"The Old One?" Straka asked. "The old Haber who came in to talk with me?"

"Yes."

Straka realized that even in her changed form, Markos's voice was still difficult to listen to. At least her own voice was the same, or it sounded the same in her ears. Ears? Straka reached up, touched the side of her head—she had no ears.

"You don't need them," Markos said, watching Straka's reactions. "They'd only get in the way."

Another creature appeared in the doorway from the dead-end hall. He was covered with the same color fur as Straka was, and as Straka looked up at his face, she recognized him.

McGowen.

Enough of the human features had been preserved to act as a reminder of what McGowen had once looked like. The nose was an irregular bump on his face, and the eyes—the eyes! "Are my eyes like ... that?" Straka asked.

"Yes," Markos said.

Straka turned back to stare at McGowen. He seemed to be smiling, and his eyes were radiating a faint reddish light. Straka glanced at Markos.

Markos was tense, rock hard, waiting for McGowen to undergo the emotional turmoil that Straka had experienced. But McGowen seemed to have a better grip on himself and he approached them slowly, calmly.

"Hello," McGowen said, his eyes leaking a minute amount of green light.

Markos flashed green.

McGowen smiled.

Markos smiled.

Straka watched.

"I ... I don't know the proper custom now that you've made me into this," McGowen said, "so I'll have to settle for something simple and Terran." He approached the few steps until he stood by Markos's chair, then held out his hand.

Markos rose to his feet and grasped McGowen's hand.

"Thank you," McGowen said. "It doesn't express the depth of my gratitude, but it will have to do for now."

They shook hands.

"How are you feeling?" Markos asked.

"Like never before. When Alpha touched me, I knew there was something more waiting for me, and now I know what it is."

"And there's more to come," Markos said. "But there'll be time for that later. Right now another crewmate is about to come out of the sleep I placed him in. I timed the changes pretty closely. Sit and wait with us."

"Without doubt," McGowen said. He sat gracefully as if he'd been born to this body.

The next crew member came into the room a few minutes later. It was Kominski. There was no mistaking the facial structure. Kominski looked totally bewildered.

"Where am I? What's going on?" he asked, panic in his voice. "What is this?"

Markos's eyes leaped to life, soothing and calming Kominski, drawing him closer until he stood directly before Markos. He touched Kominski and explained things to him with his eyes and with words. Kominski absorbed the information the way a hungry child eats food.

"I was crazy," he said at last.

"Yes," Markos said.

"It's true, Straka?"

"Very true, 'Minski. It happened when a geltank malfunctioned. It was no fault of your own."

"But no one asked me if I wanted to be changed into something like this!"

"You were in no condition to be asked. It was either change you or leave you insane, dying in your human form."

Kominski sat beside Straka, silent, staring at the floor.

The others drifted in over the next hour.

"The hardest thing you face in your new bodies is your emotions. They used to serve an important purpose—now they're a vestige you'll have to learn how to overcome. When you were human and you got angry, hormones prepared your body for fighting or fleeing," Markos said.

"Adrenaline increased your strength, your heart rate, sharpened your senses, made everything around you appear to move more slowly. But you don't have adrenaline anymore. You don't need it either. Your emotions expect certain physical reactions—it's a learned response, one you're going to have to unlearn.

"Do you all understand?"

The group of changed Terrans nodded their heads and murmured their understanding.

"This is the hardest time for you. You're being overwhelmed by the sensory inputs your bodies are providing, and you have to sort it all out. Your emotions are acting as they did when you inhabited human bodies. You can control the arms and legs you were given, but not the entire body. There are tricks—ways of altering what information your eyes pick up, what your tactile senses tell you. You don't have to hear all the time. You can shut off some parts of your body and turn others on that you don't even know about yet," Markos said.

"But there's time. I want you all to follow me outside, into the afternoon light, onto the surface of Aurianta. You can get hypnotized by the beauty you'll see. You have to learn how to dampen your vision before we go out."

"I think I know how to do it," McGowen said.

"Sure you do," Jackson said. "Care to explain it?"

"I focus my attention on a spot right behind my eyes. I imagine I still have eyelids, and I'm squinting. That cuts down some of the light and images that get through."

"Hey!" Kominski shouted. "I can do it too! It works!"

Markos was surprised. They were learning fast.

Straka learned the trick instantly, too, and found she was proud of herself and her fellow . . . fellow . . . fellow what? What the hell were they, anyway? What had they been changed into?

"Markos," Straka said.

"Yes?"

"What are we? I mean, we're not crossbreeds, we're not Terrans, and we're not Habers. So then what the hell do we call ourselves?"

"You can call yourself whatever you like, but you are all Habers, like it or not. Genetically speaking, that is."

Haber? That race must cover a lot of genetic territory, a lot of phenotypical variations, Straka thought.

"Shall we go?" Markos asked. "You seem ready, but please be careful. These are not idle warnings. Don't get carried away by what you see, and don't wander off too far, and don't fight your emotions. Study them, analyze them, and learn how your bodies respond.

"I'm going out with you, and I'll teach you some things you didn't know Habers could do. You'll be pleasantly surprised."

Markos led the group through the circular passageways and out into the street. Straka was in the lead, and as she saw what the light in the sky did to the buildings, she felt like crying.

She felt that the years she'd spent as a human being had been wasted, spent in a sensory-deprivation tank. Nothing she'd seen as a human being was the same now. Everything was alive. And everything was constantly changing.

Markos brought them to a small area in the city that was not developed, where no houses or streets existed. The crew stood in their new bodies as if standing in a new set of clothes, craning their necks to see their backs, turning their hands over and over, searching for new functions for their anatomies.

Kominski was on his hands and knees, staring at the ground. Every few minutes he would mutter, "Oh, wow," then fall silent again. Wilhelm took his change stoically, wandering around, wondering at the strange sights, smells, sounds like the others.

Markos kept a close watch, supervising as a nursery school teacher would during recess, concerned for the safety of his charges.

Straka knew what Markos was doing and was grateful for his stabilizing presence. She knew the transformation and the adaptation necessary would have been a knife-edged experience, too painful and emotionally charged to have to undergo without his supervision.

Jackson, Katawba, and—who was that?—Martinez? Yes, Martinez. They played like children, running and leaping into the air, shouting in glee, chasing each other around. Straka understood what they felt and wanted to join them. They weren't reverting back to a second childhood; they were simply enjoying themselves for the first time in a decade, totally free of the autocratic control of NASA 2, of its geltank imprinting, of the Terran feelings of loyalty, duty, and responsibility. They were reveling in the simple joys of motion, of being in healthy, strong bodies, elated with the prospect of immortality in bodies that saw, felt, and could do things they never could before.

Yes, Straka thought, immortality. We're more than halfway there.

She was in no rush to join the frolicking crewmembers. She didn't need the physical release yet, the expression of pure joy in physical form. For now, she was content to watch, to think, to wonder what immortality was like.

"Something wrong?" Markos asked in his rough voice.

Straka turned. For a moment she felt surprised to find she was no longer repulsed by Markos's physical form. The violently clashing reds, greens, and oranges of his translucent skin, his lack of Haber fur, all added up to a strange totality, some awesome beauty. Even the fluids detectable beneath the surface of Markos's skin. Straka had been blind to it all until now.

"Straka?"

"Oh, sorry. No, nothing's wrong. Everything's right for a change. I was just enjoying it."

"It's good to see you indulging, but remember that everything is far from being right. We're at war."

"The war. I know. But I was talking about now, right here, inside my head. Being thankful for life."

Markos nodded and flashed red. Straka noticed her own eyes tingle. "It's almost sundown," Markos said. "Gather up the crew with me and we'll link up."

"Link?"

"You'll see."

Straka tried to smile but had no idea as to what it looked like. She called out, and the crew slowly stopped what they were doing. They drifted over to where Markos and Straka stood and listened while Markos explained the techniques required for linking up.

"It's the easiest way to learn about touch and change. It should also introduce you to the little power source we have inside."

"Power source?" De Sola asked.

"It's simpler to show you than to explain it. Here," he said.

De Sola and the others reached forward and touched Markos's proffered arm. It became incredibly hard, the skin inpenetrable. "I add mesons to the atoms of my outer skin. It increases my outer density," Markos commented.

"I like that," Jackson said.

Straka was about to say something, but she felt the need to be silent. The others had fallen silent too. It was time to link up. Straka had no idea how she knew that, yet she knew. An emotional change had occurred, one she could detect on an almost tangible level. A huge gaping void had opened inside as though someone she had once loved deeply had died. But that wasn't quite it; there was no pain or grief there—just the void.

Someone touched her hand and she did as Markos instructed, grabbing hold, groping for Markos's hand with her right. Her eyes were drawn to the sky, to the blob of shifting light on the horizon. Markos grabbed her right hand, and the link up was complete.

As she felt her skin dissolve, the barrier between her and the others dropped away. She understood the strange feeling for a split second—gates had swung open in her mind and soul, creating that void. And then she lost the grasp she had of the abstract concept as the physical reality overwhelmed her. The others were surging through her body, entering through her hands, buoying her, comforting her, giving her immense company within her singular body, sharing themselves on a soul-baring level far deeper, far richer than love. In a split second all distinctions between their personalities were gone as they blended into a whole, a gestalt that swept her away deep into Aurianta's core, high into its insanely refractive sky.

The colors she stared at, created by the setting sun, said something, composed some inscrutable visible message. She was sure of that, and yet she couldn't understand it. She could gather some of the emotional content as her body surged and fell with the rapid changes in the sky. She wanted to tell it she understood. All she was capable of doing was opening her mouth to thank the sun, the sky, the planet, and all the Habers for their existence, to be a part of such an awesome whole. It was more than she'd ever dreamed of accomplishing.

The words came out as a steady hum.

The feeling of belonging, of being truly accepted, was intense. And then the sun fell below the horizon, the colors faded in intensity from the sky, and it was over. She was Cathy Straka again.

But she was no longer human.

Some subtle change had been worked inside through the linkup. Now she belonged. She felt at peace with herself and the others. She was home.

"Come," Markos said. "We'll go back to the building. We should rest for a while and eat. Then we work. There's a lot yet to learn."

Part Three

AFTER
THE
CHANGE

19
.

He stood on the bridge, a place he thought he'd never see again. It felt strange being back on board—especially with Van Pelt dead, with the crew waiting to transfer from the Haber ship. Old memories drifted by, reminding him of who and what he'd once been.

His hand rested on the back of the command chair, surrounded on all sides by bulkheads lined with screens. Markos could remember too many watches when he'd sat at the west-quadrant control seat, staring at the screen before him, his psyche easily absorbed into the awesome view he faced, only to be snapped back by Van Pelt's half-insane exclamations of how nothing made sense. Van Pelt had occupied this chair, had earned the privilege and the responsibility.

And Markos had taken that and everything else away from him

with an uncontrolled burst from his newly found Haber eyes. It's ironic, he thought. Van Pelt was always afraid of an alien threat, and look where his destruction came from.

Van Pelt's essence lingered in the control center, permeated the screens, the chairs, the control panels mounted on the pedestals. Markos tried to ignore the strange feeling of someone looking over his shoulder.

He edged around to the small panel before the command chair and touched a sensor switch. The walls melted away as the screens came to life, and Markos realized he'd made his body hard without thinking. Surrounded by the unobstructed view of space, his mind had jumped back to when he'd been floating between the two ships.

He felt someone there, wheeled around to fight, and saw no one.

Calm down, cool out, he told himself. There's no one there. Van Pelt is dead.

And yet he couldn't shake the eerie feeling of someone watching, someone disapproving of his very presence on the bridge.

Too jumpy, he thought. Like waiting for the owner of the ship to wander in and catch me trying to steal it. I've got to calm down.

He edged around the control seat, eased into Van Pelt's chair, and gazed at the screens. The Haber ship hung in space several hundred meters away off the port side, while Aurianta rotated slowly, majestically, beneath him. It would have been so simple to throw a few of the familiar switches, plot a course, and lay it into the navigational computer. A few switches are what separate me from getting the hell out of here, letting the whole mess resolve itself in its own natural way, or sticking around, waiting for the Terrans to transfer aboard, seeing this situation through to the end.

A small section of the Haber ship started changing color—the bay door must have been opening. That meant that Markatens had given them the ready signal and they would be starting the transfer procedure. If he was going to do something about taking the ship and going somewhere else, he would have to do it now.

Tiny specks of light appeared outside the bay, and Markos pressed one of the switches on the console. The view off the port side was magnified. He increased magnification until he could see the specks of light as forms, the crew making their way across the dangerous distance. Leave them? he thought. Before they're too far away from the wedge?

They all liked Aurianta well enough. And they've been changed, so they could survive there. And the wedges were capable of f-t-l travel. I wouldn't really be abandoning them.

The Habers don't really need me. They just need someone. It could be Straka. Or Wilhelm.

But Markatens was on board. What would he do with him? Come on, son, we're off to see the galaxy? Let me show you some of my favorite night spots? Let's find some life-forms and get weird?

Not likely.

And he couldn't very well throw him off the ship, point him toward the wedge, and hope he made it to safety.

He sighed, something very strange to do while in a body that had no physical excuse for sighing. He figured he'd better get down to the airlock and help on this end, in case any of Straka's people had trouble with the transfer. He switched off the screens, his window into space, and walked up the ramp to the door.

They sat around the rec lounge, an old, familiar place for the crew, oddly different for each of them in thousands of minute ways. Nothing looked the same, felt or sounded the same, yet they knew that nothing had changed but them.

They had all lived on board the ship for a long time, and a lot had happened there. Each cabin, each passageway held some reminder of the past. Markos remembered arguments over geltank time, over standing watches, over what they should do if and when they encountered an alien race.

"Everything looks so different," Straka said.

"I'll say," Jackson said.

But no matter how much they each insisted things were different, that *they* were different, Markos knew better. Deep down inside, nothing of them had been changed. They were still the same people, still the same chauvinistic Terrans, the same opinionated, prejudiced beings. They were still the people who had sided with Van Pelt. The people who had chased him across the Galaxy.

"Just look at the bulkheads," Wilhelm said. "You can see the structural defects there. And look—stress marks here," he said, pointing to a ripple in the metal they would never have been able to see before.

Markatens stood by, trying to melt into a corner of the room, trying to make sense out of what everyone was talking about. He clutched the recorded crystals in his hands, waiting patiently for them to be needed. The crew had carried them across with them, though they hadn't really known what they were.

"These chairs aren't that comfortable anymore," Martinez said.

"Did you see the swirl in this table?" De Sola asked, pointing to the top of the plastic table mounted in the deck. "Probably appears naturally from vacumolding."

"You'll get used to it this way," Markos said, slightly amused at their discoveries. It was something he had gone through on Gandji, though for him it had been a painful experience, each difference spotted a revelation of horror.

"I doubt it," McGowen said. "We must not be seeing the same things."

"We are. I've just been seeing the differences longer, and I don't notice them as differences. It's just the way I see now. My mind's adapted."

"That figures," Jackson said.

Everyone ignored him.

"I never thought I'd survive that trip," Kominski said.

"I know what you mean," Katawba said. "I've never felt more alone, more vulnerable."

Martinez laughed. "What a high! Watching Aurianta below, huge and swollen, Alpha Indi a small disk—"

"I wasn't worried," Jackson said. "If *he* could make it, I knew I would," he said, motioning toward Markos with his head.

"Well, what's next?" Straka asked Markos.

Markos shrugged. "There's a lot we have to do before we can leave. We should probably start with the crystals." He held out his hand toward Markatens. Markatens handed over one of the crystals. "Put the others on the table," Markos said.

"Does he have to come along?" Jackson asked.

"No," Markos said. "And neither do you."

That seemed to do the trick. Markos could read the colors that seeped from Jackson's eyes, slight though they were, and knew he had dealt with him properly.

"One of problems is that all of our information is either dated or secondhand. We've never captured a Hydran, so all we know about them is here," he said, holding out his hand, "and in those," he said, pointing to the crystals on the table. "They're about all we have. None of you have seen what's inside them, but I want you to try to now."

Markos described how to enter the crystals' structures and what to look for inside. Straka was the first to pick up one of the crystals. The other crewmembers looked on as she gripped it in her hands. She had little trouble figuring out how to use it properly. Markos was pleasantly surprised at how quickly they were adjusting to their new capacities and capabilities. One by one the crew followed her example. All but Jackson.

"What's the matter," Markos asked him.

"What makes you think something's the matter?"

"Well, you haven't picked up one of them yet."

"I will. Just tell me something," Jackson said.

"What?"

"If you can change things so easily, why the hell don't you change your voice? Have you got any idea what it sounds like?"

"My hearing hasn't been altered that much."

"That's not what I asked. Why not change it?"

"Does it bother you that much?" Markos asked, his patience wearing thin.

"Yes."

"Good. It bothers me too. That's why I never changed it. It helps remind me of something I never want to forget. Now, pick up the crystal."

Jackson's eyes leaked a dark blue, the Haber way of saying no, and said, "Sure. Why not?"

He reached over and grabbed the nearest crystal. Markos was amused by Jackson's inability to lie. Jackson's innermost emotions would leak through his eyes until he learned how to control them better. Until that time Markos had a real window into Jackson's mind.

Markos looked over the crew. Straka's eyes were mirroring the colors she read within the crystal's structure, flashing by at incredible speed. Like reading with her lips, Markos thought. He hoped they could understand the way the images were coded in those colors. It was a lot like asking a human to plug himself directly into a computer and understand its binary language without an interface, he thought. Only we Habers have a small advantage there.

Straka dropped the crystal as if it had suddenly been electrified and had shocked her. She looked over at Markos. Yellow tinged with blue seeped from her eyes—just enough of it for Markos to recognize her confusion and disbelief. "These are the creatures the Habers are at war with? These are the Hydrans?"

Markos nodded.

Straka took another crystal, placing the one she'd just finished to one side.

Wilhelm dropped his crystal. "My God," he said. "Just like that. Burned them all. Nothing else. Just burned them away!"

"Just like Van Pelt did," Markos said.

"What? Van Pelt? Get serious!"

"It's true," Markos said. "I was standing watch at the time. That was what made me run, seeing him do that."

"I don't believe you! He said you'd done it!"

"It's true, Wilhelm. They were young Habers. Unarmed, totally incapable of understanding aggression."

"I can't believe it. I know Van Pelt was over the edge, but he wasn't that far gone."

"Then don't believe it. It doesn't matter anymore."

Wilhelm picked up another crystal, the one Straka had placed aside. Straka was well into her second one. De Sola and Martinez were going through their crystals silently, without showing anything in their eyes. Markos was sure they were being moved by the experiences stored inside; they just weren't the types to show it. Kominski seemed sane enough, capable of delving into the record of destruction in his crystal. Jackson placed his on the table and turned to face Markos.

"Is this your idea of a joke?" he demanded.

"What?" Markos asked.

"Fighting these things? How many of them are there?"

Markos shrugged. "I don't know."

"Oh Christ." Jackson shook his head. "You know, Markos, I never really liked you. You never gave me much reason to. But recruiting me to help fight these insects—"

"We're not sure they're insects."

"They're insects, all right. Can't you even tell that? I refuse. I flatly refuse to fight them. It would be suicide. If we had an army, then I'd consider helping. But just the nine of us—"

"But you've only read one crystal."

"One was more than enough."

"Look at another, Jackson. You may see they're not all that powerful an enemy. There's one crystal in particular—one with Triand fighting them on Theta Alnon. That one should show you more—"

"Forget it. I've seen enough," Jackson said.

"Let him be, Markos," Straka said. "If he doesn't want to help, we'll just leave him behind."

Markos looked at Straka, a questioning yellow tinged with blue in his eyes.

"Just make sure you alter his physical structure so that he'll be incapable of causing any trouble on Aurianta's surface," Straka said.

Jackson reached for another crystal. "All right. I got your message."

Markos was starting to appreciate Straka's presence. There was an art to handling Jackson, he realized, and confrontation was not part of the art.

Jackson was the same as he always had been. They'd never really gotten along. But then, no one ever really got along well with Jackson. He can mutter and mumble, complain and bitch, get into a fight now and then, but none of that matters, Markos thought. Just as long as he doesn't make serious trouble. He was just what the Habers needed on their side: a true killer with a fine sense of survival. With Straka helping to keep him in line, there was a chance their mission could succeed.

McGowen, on the other hand, didn't seem right. He'd been a lot more volatile, active, similar to Jackson in some ways. He used to supply Jackson with the sparring he needed. That could be why Jackson's been lashing out at everyone, Markos thought. To try to find a new counterpart.

McGowen must have undergone some personality change when Alpha had touched him. Alpha had little firsthand knowledge of human anatomy and psychology. Markos remembered how heavy-handed the Habers had been when bringing him back to life on Gandji. They approached the human condition as if it were an integrated circuit in need of repair. Except that the Habers' tools were hammers.

When they were finished with the crystals, he would take the time to discuss what they'd observed, making sure the similarities and differences from his own conclusions were noted. He would turn on the on-board computer and let it listen to the discussion. Maybe then, when it was over, the computer could draw a logical, consistent view of what the Hydrans were like, where they had truly come from, and what they were attacking.

Perhaps someone would come up with a decent plan of attack.

Then again, maybe not.

Markos was the one responsible for figuring out how to win the war. None of them had any experience in that. None of them was really a soldier. In either case, they were not going to move the *Paladin* until Markos was sure where they were headed, why they were headed there, and what they would do when they arrived.

20.

The ship no longer resembled the *Paladin*. Its once-smooth, globular shape was broken up by a ring of Haber ships attached to its hull, surrounding it like a belt at midships. The Haber ships alternately faced forward and aft to give the *Paladin* added versatility in acceleration in both directions. The computer had pointed out the need as the parameters of their mission became clearer; they would need landing boats, escape boats, fighters, and reconnaissance ships, all of which had to be added to the *Paladin*'s basic structure. The Haber ships were the right size and were powerful enough individually to out-accelerate the *Paladin*.

The added acceleration alone would have made the delay caused by modifying the *Paladin*'s hull worthwhile. They knew nothing about the Hydrans' ships, so the *Paladin*'s improved maneuverability could possibly swing any battle in space their way. Markos looked at it this way: every added advantage was a necessary precaution for survival.

The Old One was extremely helpful when it came time to attach the smaller ships to the hull of the *Paladin*. His native ability to touch and change made the hull's atomic structure seem obvious. He taught the crew which electrons to move and which ones to absorb to make the attachment sturdy enough to withstand the tremendous stress and yet be reversible in an instant if they needed to free one of the ships as a fighter. They improvised nonpressurized airlocks between each ship and the *Paladin* to maintain the big ship's integrity.

The most difficult part of the modification proved to be the process of tying in the controls from each wedge-shaped ship to the *Paladin*'s bridge. They tried running the control circuits directly through the hull but found they were spending far too much time insulating one molecular layer from another. Without the insulation the system would have grounded out and been worthless.

De Sola hit upon a workable solution—using existing wiring, that of the life-support systems. He rerouted and doubled the wiring's function, then created a switching device on the bridge. Once on the bridge, the circuits were divided so that life support and systems analysis went to one control panel, while the engine controls and monitors went to a different control panel.

Initially only one wedge-shaped ship had any armament. They duplicated lasers and field nullifiers in each of the remaining seven ships and added a full complement of weapons to the *Paladin* just to be safe. The weapons controls were tied into another control panel on the *Paladin*'s bridge.

The weapons controls had an override switch and duplicate controls in the command chair.

With the *Paladin* as the mother ship, and the eight wedge-shaped Haber ships as its scouts, Markos thought they had enough of a chance to justify risking everyone's life.

"We're ready to head out," Straka said.

Markos nodded, barely listening. He stood on the bridge, eyes fixed on the slowly turning Aurianta. The planet's beauty made him long for its surface, for home. He hated the role he was stuck in, the responsibility thrust onto his shoulders. He would have given anything to be able to return to Peace, to his house there, to spend the rest of his days in quiet meditation. Seeing the planet from this distance only made the feelings and desires stronger.

"Markos? We're ready," Straka repeated.

Markos shook his head and forced himself to look away from Aurianta. "Fine," he said.

"Not quite. The Old One wants to come," Straka said. "And so does Markatens."

"I was afraid of that."

"They don't want to go back to the surface. The Old One says that you owe him, that his life should have been over long ago. He says he's broken so many taboos, nothing matters anymore except seeing this through to the end."

Markos knew there'd be no convincing the Old One to stay behind, and he lost a little more enthusiasm for his position. He sank into the command chair and stared into the black area of space directly before him.

"I'm sure he knows the risks," Markos said, thinking aloud, "though they mean nothing to him. I wish he'd be content to . . ." But no, the Old One had been changed by his continuous contact with Markos, by Markos's constant talk of reponsibility and action. There was no way the Old One would go home and meditate his way to death. Not anymore.

"Content to what?" Straka asked.

"Huh? Oh, sorry. Forget it." He sat silently for a few moments, then looked at Straka. "Markatens is as committed to going, I suppose?"

"No question," Straka said, her eyes leaking a little red. "They're both in the rec room, in a meditative state. Jackson got a little angry at their lack of cooperation and tried to pick up Markatens. Seems they've bonded themselves to the deck."

Markos laughed, struck by the absurdity of the scene he imagined. Straka's eyes betrayed the shock she felt on hearing Markos's twisted voice laughing.

"All right. If they're so set on coming along, I see no point in forcing them to stay. They might actually be able to help," Markos said. "Tell everyone to prepare for acceleration. We're ready, and the longer we hang around here, the worse I feel. Get the first watch in here."

"Right," Straka said. She walked up the ramp and out of the bridge.

Markos turned to gaze at the planet one last time. It filled most of the lower screens, one of its major continents clearly visible beneath a little scattering of clouds.

It's better that you all sit down there, going through your life cycles as though nothing were happening, he thought. There's been enough senseless Haber deaths. Let us teach the Hydrans something for a change. It's our turn.

McGowen, Martinez, Jackson, and De Sola walked down the ramp and stood near Markos. They looked at Aurianta suspended below their feet, then took their seats, each before a control panel, each facing a different quadrant of space.

Silently they manipulated the dials and controls set into their panels, double-checking all shipboard systems. McGowen sat before the weapons controls, bringing the weapons up to full power for a sustained test. Jackson was busy getting feedback from the engineering systems, checking the *Paladin*'s ability to get her engines back into operation before applying any order to fire. Martinez played with the navigational computer, punching in different courses, testing it to see if the plotted course would fling them into a star. De Sola checked the life-support systems, ensuring the integrity of the hull, seeing that all systems were in proper working order.

"Gentlemen," Markos said, "before we leave this sector of space—"

"One minute," Martinez interrupted.

Markos waited until Martinez was ready, until his last test was done. When Martinez turned and nodded toward Markos, he continued. "As I was saying, I wanted to thank each of you for giving the Habers a chance at survival. And for helping Terra."

"Yeah, right," Jackson said. "But we're not doing it as a favor to you, so don't thank us."

"Jackson's right," McGowen said. "We're not doing it for you, or for the reward of immortality."

"Oh, yeah?" Jackson said, his old sparring partner once again come to life. "Then why the hell *are* we doing this?"

"Because, Jackson, we're Habers now, too."

"I'm no Haber," Jackson said, flashing dark blue and violet. "I just don't like insects."

"I share your feelings, Jackson," Markos said.

"I'm just glad to be able to do something for my brothers," McGowen said.

"Can we go?" De Sola asked.

"You're sick, McGowen," Jackson said. "I'm here against my better judgment."

"Yeah," Martinez said, "but you do everything against your better judgment."

"Funny, Martinez. I see you kept your sense of humor for this suicide mission," Jackson said. "You're going to need it."

"Just like old times," Markos said. "Are we ready?"

They each flashed red.

"Plot a course for Epsilon Scorpio," Markos told Martinez. "If it isn't already occupied by Hydrans, it should be next in line."

"Epsilon Scorpio," Martinez said, entering it into the navigational computer. "K-2, planetary bodies unknown," he said, reading the output. "You sure it has a planet?"

Markos flashed red. "Last we looked, it was Haber owned and occupied."

Martinez updated the data on Epsilon Scorpio. "Distance: 17 parsecs in tau, 2 light-years in real. Time of journey: approximately four years objective."

"You didn't reset that?" Markos asked.

"No. Until we find out just how fast this ball of metal will go, I didn't see the sense."

"You should have entered it as an optional program," Jackson said. "No way it's going to take four years with four wedges adding acceleration through tau."

"I know that," Martinez said.

"Then why didn't you enter the optional program?"

"What's the difference, Jackson?" Markos asked.

Jackson sat silently for a moment. "I guess there isn't any real difference."

De Sola shook his head. "Don't worry about him. You know Jackson. He hasn't changed that much since the old days. We're used to him like this," he said.

"Jackson? Want to get us out of here?" Markos asked.

"If it'll move," Jackson said jokingly.

Markos bit back the retort. It would take some time to get used to working alongside Jackson again. The others were easy enough to work with, mellowed enough to accept their fates and have some hope for their futures.

"Let's start off slow and easy," Markos said. "If there's some problem, I want to know about it before the stress of acceleration gets too much for the ship to handle."

"You and me both," Jackson said.

He punched in quarter speed and the ship began to accelerate. Markos wanted to watch Aurianta shrink in size as they moved away from it, but he needed to monitor the four crewmen as well as his own controls. They all seemed to be doing a competent job, checking and rechecking systems to ensure they had control of the ship, that the wedge-shaped drones were still attached.

"How's it look, De Sola?"

"Fine. No problems yet."

"McGowen?"

"I've powered down the weapons just in case we need the reserve power. They held up fine. They should work as long as the circuits aren't damaged."

"What's our course?"

"We're right on a straight line to our target star," Martinez said: "0.17 R by 6.21 L. We should be able to translate into tau and come out a few billion miles from Epsilon Scorpio."

"If the coordinates are accurate," Markos said.

"They should be accurate. This area wasn't extensively mapped," Martinez said, "but NASA 2 did a pretty good job."

"Let's just hope it's good enough."

The G forces started to push them back into their seats. Combined with the artificial gravity, it was tolerable but not comfortable. Markos knew that under full acceleration they would have to make their bodies hard. Once the Haber ships' engines kicked in, no one on board would be able to survive unless they were encased in their thickened outer shells.

"De Sola, check with the rec room and see how the others are doing," Markos said.

"Right," De Sola said.

De Sola pressed the paging device and said, "Rec room." The screen in the rec room was activated and showed the rest of the crew, the Old One, and Markatens seated around the cabin, watching the screens.

"Everything all right there?" Markos asked.

"Yes," Straka reported. "Are we up to full speed?"

"No. Quarter power. We'll let you know when we're going to translate."

"How does it handle?" Straka asked.

Markos shrugged. "Stable enough, though there won't be any way of knowing until we pour on the power."

Straka's eyes seeped red as she nodded.

"We're going to bring it up to half speed," Markos said. "Prepare yourselves."

"Right," Straka said.

"Okay, De Sola." De Sola broke the communication link. "Want to give us half power?" Markos asked Jackson.

"Sure," Jackson said. As soon as he started to enter the speed change, Markos started to make his body hard. "Ready?"

"Ready," Markos said.

Jackson pressed the panel and Markos felt the minor weight increase, the pushing force making him want to become one with the seat. Compared with what it would have felt like for a human, the G forces were barely noticeable. They would have had to have been in the geltanks by now, surrounded and protected by the life-sustaining liquid.

"Everyone all right?" Markos asked.

The bridge was tinted with red light from their eyes.

"Get the rec room again and tell them to prepare for translation.

We'll power up to three-quarter speed, and if the ship holds together, we'll go right for full power. Then we'll effect the translation."

"Right," De Sola said. He established contact with Straka and relayed the information.

"Martinez? Jackson? McGowen? Status reports?" Markos asked.

They each reported that everything was holding together and everything looked fine.

"All right, then, Jackson. Let's get out of here."

Jackson entered three-quarter speed. They noticed another change in weight and the ship remained in good shape. Markos knew that being overly cautious at this point in their journey was necessary—if something happened to them, the Habers would be little more than a memory, a dead civilization, ground under by the Hydrans expansionist drive. For that matter, Terra would probably end up a casualty too. Or at least a battleground.

"De Sola?" he asked.

"No changes. Everything's stable."

"Do it, Jackson," Markos said.

"Wait! I'm getting a warning signal from the hull," De Sola said.

Markos slapped his armrest, immediately opening communications throughout the ship. "Straka—there's a hull problem. You and Markatens get over to—where, De Sola?"

"Haber ship two," he said.

"Haber ship two, and make sure you're protected, in case we've lost integrity."

"Right," Straka said.

"Power down?" Jackson asked.

Markos took a deep breath, raising his energy level. "No. It might just be a monitor malfunction."

"I'm checking on that through the backups," De Sola said.

"We ought to power down," Jackson said. "Just in case."

Markos said nothing.

"I'm going to power down," Jackson said.

"Don't," Markos said. Jackson froze, and Markos realized he'd ordered Jackson with enough force to kill a human. As he'd done to Van Pelt. "Wait until we hear from Cathy. What about the systems, De Sola?"

"The backups show everything as being normal. I don't understand."

"I'm waiting," Jackson said. "Let me know when. I've entered the change."

"Good."

Where the hell was Straka? It wasn't that far from the rec room to Haber ship two's junction. If there'd been a hull breach, they would have known about it by now.

"Markos?" Straka's voice said over the shipboard communication channel.

"Yes, Straka. What's going on there?"

"Nothing. We can't see a thing wrong."

"Lock yourselves onto the hull and open the hatch. The Haber ship might not be there anymore, so be careful."

"Right," Straka said.

"Jackson, get ready to kick in the translators," Markos ordered.

"What?"

"Not now. I didn't ask you to kick them in yet. Just get ready."

"All right," Jackson said.

"Markos? Straka again."

"Where are you?"

"On the bridge of the Haber ship. There's nothing wrong. Anymore."

"De Sola?" Markos asked.

De Sola flashed red. "Everything shows clear on systems one and two. Backup confirms."

"What was it, Straka?" Markos asked.

"Just a loose connection at the interface. Nothing to worry about."

That didn't sound quite right to him. Something was wrong, and he could tell from Straka's voice. He could tell Straka didn't want to talk about it over the intercom, and that could mean only one thing. "Okay, Straka. Close up and meet me in my cabin immediately."

"Right."

"Markatens, post yourself at the hatch to Haber ship two."

"Right," Markatens said.

Markos slapped the button that closed off the communications channel.

"Before we do anything rash, like entering tau or powering down, I want to let the ship continue on under full power. Let it shake out some bugs. We'll just keep up this speed. Have we reached full real velocity?"

"Yes," Jackson said.

"Fine. Keep the engines on for another few minutes, then cut them off. Let's see how the *Paladin* does at point 99 light."

Markos rose from his chair. Moving around was a little difficult, but manageable. "McGowen, take over. I'll be back in a few minutes."

"Anything I can help with?" Martinez asked.

"No. Just make sure your equipment is working properly. That goes for all of you."

"Right."

"Either someone made a big mistake or someone wants to have his own personal escape boat," Straka said.

"What?"

"Who was working on ship two, tying in the interface for command control?" Straka asked.

"I really don't remember," Markos said. "Is that what happened? The interface fail?"

"No. The interface has to exist in order for it to fail."

Markos was shocked.

"Someone was planning on boarding the Haber ship and taking off by himself. He'd rigged the circuitry so that it would have been undetectable. I figure whoever did it wanted to get as close to Earth as possible before detaching himself from the mother ship."

"Pretty serious charges, Straka."

"I know that."

"Are you sure?"

Straka flashed red. "Unfortunately."

"Couldn't someone have forgotten to make the proper circuitry connections?" Markos asked.

Straka flashed dark blue. "I only wish that could be the case."

Terrific, Markos thought. Just what we need.

"I'm just guessing that it's Earth he wanted to get close to. But I don't think that really matters."

"I agree. Well, we ought to try to figure out who it is," Markos said.

"Get serious," Straka said. "Who else could it be?"

"It doesn't *have* to be Jackson."

"No? Who was it, then?" Straka asked. "The Old One? You? Me?"

Markos nodded grudgingly. "Okay, so it was Jackson. What do you suggest we do about it?"

"I don't know. Just keep an eye on him, I suppose. I fixed it so that the ship can't be freed from the *Paladin* without a command from central control. He's not going anywhere, now or later."

"You seem to feel that's all we have to concern ourselves with —his leaving with one of the Haber ships."

"For now," Straka said.

"But anyone with that attitude . . . we won't be able to count on him if and when we need him," Markos said.

"Perhaps."

"Then we're better off spacing the slime."

"Whoa," Straka said. "Take it easy, here. We're not *sure* it's him."

Markos made a face at Straka he was sure didn't communicate his disbelief. "You know him better than I do," Markos said. "Of course it's him. And you still think we don't have to do anything else about it?"

"No," Straka said. "Whoever did this isn't suicidal. He'd have gone up with the ship if he was. We're as safe as possible."

"For now," Markos said.

Straka flashed red. "For now."

Markos shook his head and sighed. "I've got to get back to the bridge. We're about to translate into tau and then run some more tests."

"Fine," Straka said. "I'll get back to the rest of them. I'll be in the rec room if you need me. Should we leave Markatens stationed outside Haber two?"

"Not if you assure me you've taken care of the problem."

"I have."

"Then take him back to the rec room with you."

"Fine," Straka said, getting to her feet.

Markos watched Straka approach the door, walking under the stress of a hardened body and tremendous G forces. "Oh, and Straka?"

She stopped and turned. "Yeah?"

"Thanks."

Straka smiled. On her it looked natural. "None necessary."

"Thanks anyway."

"Sure."

Markos waited until Straka had left before dropping into a meditative state. He needed to work out why Jackson would want to take off for Earth like that. The being who had once been Jackson was capable of violence, anger, and a certain amount of rebelliousness. But that didn't make him a deserter. He was always a necessary ingredient, a necessary abrasiveness in any situation. If there weren't that friction or animosity, everyone could fall asleep at the controls. NASA 2 had known what it was doing in selecting him as one of the crew, all right. He served an important function. And Markos didn't want to lose him.

Jackson knew that he was no longer a Terran. Still, he viewed himself as being more Terran than Haber. This served another important function for the crew, serving as a reminder of what they had been, what they were now, and what they were going to become.

But none of that helped him better to understand why Jackson would want to desert. Granted, he did everything under duress, but that was only his verbal personality. If he ever truly objected to something, he would stand firm in his commitment and not give in unless directly ordered. He just bitched about everything. That was his nature. Still, he did what he had to, what his responsibilities demanded, what he'd been ordered to do.

Straka felt fairly certain it was Jackson, and she was a lot closer to Jackson than Markos had ever been. That experience on Aurianta must have shown the naked sides of their personalities, from humane to atavistic, and that was something Markos had thankfully missed. But Straka hadn't.

He would have to keep an eye on Jackson, see what he did, how he reacted to orders, to stress, see whether or not he was truly that disgruntled or just making his standard noises.

If only he could remember who did the work on Haber two's interface. The crew had moved around so much and had worked on so many different areas, it was impossible to separate it out. Almost all of the work had been done without any supervision. Who would have thought they needed supervision?

Markos took a deep breath to bring up his energy level and pushed himself up to his feet. No matter what Straka thought, there was no way he could be sure of any crewmember again. Someone wanted to desert. He knew of one way to find out just who it was, but there would be time for that.

As he left his cabin, he resolved to be certain of one thing: When the time came to put Jackson into one of the Haber ships, he would not be alone.

The tau translation was flawless. The mother ship was holding up under its apparent unstable configuration and its added mass. The crew on board had all made their bodies hard and were well protected from the crushing G forces translation had created.

Markos sat in the command chair, the second watch occupying the quadrant seats. Katawba relieved McGowen at the weapons control post; Wilhelm took over for Jackson at engineering; Kominski replaced Martinez at navigation, while Markatens replaced De Sola at the systems monitor. Straka stood by Markos's side, ready to relieve him of his watch.

"Are you all ready?" Markos asked.

Everyone flashed red.

"Cathy, would you sit on the deck and attach yourself there, just in case?"

"Fine," Straka said.

"All right, then, Wilhelm. Cut in H-one."

Wilhelm punched in the Haber ship's engine, and they immediately felt the crushing G forces. They let up after a few moments.

"Markatens?" Markos asked.

"No system malfunctions."

"Velocity?"

"Two c," Wilhelm said.

"Cut in H-three," Markos said.

"Brace yourselves, brothers," Wilhelm said.

They felt the jolt of pressure. None of it was nearly as bad as Markos had anticipated. Not with their hardened bodies.

"Velocity?"

"Four c."

"Cut in H-five."

"Right."

The jolt of G forces seemed less this time.

"Velocity?"

"Sixteen c."

"Cut in the last one," Markos said.

"Right." Wilhelm pressed the button.

No one felt any difference in acceleration or G forces.

"That should be two hundred fifty-six c," Wilhelm said, his voice filled with awe.

"Now we're getting somewhere," Markos said.

"At two hundred fifty-six times the speed of light, I should hope so," Straka said.

They were drifting through tau-space, watching the stars move by in the viewscreens.

"It's all yours, Cathy. I'm going to get some rest. I'm exhausted."

"Fine. Don't worry. Everything up here looks great."

He relinquished the command chair to Straka and stood for a few moments, watching the ship's progress through tau-space. The beauty of the scene was hypnotic, and he listened to the colors the stars in the screens sang to his eyes. The Habers belonged in space just as surely as they belonged on Aurianta, Markos realized.

Each sunset, each linkup, they listen to the sun speak to them through the atmosphere, telling them the Tao of Space, teaching them the order of the Universe, he thought.

Until it taught them about the Hydrans.

21

Epsilon Scorpio appeared as a disk under logarithmic magnification through the screens. The *Paladin* was undergoing deceleration, braking into a distant orbit in the Epsilon Scorpio System. The time in tau had passed quickly and quietly for the crew—there were enough diversions on the ship to keep them pleasantly occupied for centuries if need be. Without the need for geltanks, space travel took on a new meaning for the changed crew.

They had agreed on the first piece of offensive action, and there were several volunteers for the mission. The entire second watch volunteered as a group under the leadership of Straka. Markos's watch had volunteered too.

Markos wanted to go down to the planet's surface and confront some Hydrans face-to-face, so he was more inclined to go with his watch—Jackson, McGowen, Martinez, and De Sola. Straka had quickly pointed out that if anything should happen to him, they wouldn't stand much of a chance in saving the Habers. Markos could see her point.

"Besides which," Straka said, "if we get into bad trouble, we'll need a backup party."

"Like the cavalry," Markos said.

"Sure," Straka said, smiling. "Whatever they are."

"All right, Cathy. You've got first crack at them. But don't forget—they're ruthless, and possibly not even sentient. Don't spare the weapon power."

"Look, Markos, if you're that worried, why don't we just slice up the planet from up here?"

"No, no. Sorry. I just don't want to lose you. Any of you."

"I don't want to lose me, either," Straka said. "Just don't worry until it's necessary. How close are you planning on getting us?"

"I figure midway between our jump point and the planet. We'll leave the mother ship in command of the Old One. You take Markatens, Katawba, Kominski, and Wilhelm in H-Two. I'll follow in H-three with my shift. We'll both keep our transmitters open so that the Old One can keep up to date and decide whether or not to go on without us. He can continue on to Pi Hydra with our last effort if we don't make it."

"Right. Let's get ready."

Everyone in the rec room looked calm and relaxed, though a Haber always looked calm and relaxed. They were ready to leave the ship, to fight, to take out the frustrations of what being changed had done to them, of those long days pent up in the compound on Aurianta. Jackson whined and bitched and grumbled about not getting to go along in the first wave and begged Markatens to trade places. Markatens was the wrong Haber to ask. He flashed every color through his eyes but red, and Jackson finally had to give up.

Markos passed around the crystal the exploratory team had made of the planet a millennium ago, when the first Habers were about to settle the planet. Each crewman melted into the crystal to acquaint himself with the planet's terrain and vegetation, to get a better idea of what he'd be facing. They discussed what they had seen in the crystal and decided on a course of action.

The planning session lasted less than an hour. Markos quickly saw what had been missing for those long years on Aurianta, what he'd been missing in trying to figure out how to deal with the Hydrans. Human minds. How quickly they pick up the necessary points for battle, Markos thought. How quickly they formulate plans based on unknowns.

Their highly refined instinct for survival added significance to each detail of the plan, to each step in planning, to each stage of execution. Leave little to chance, Markos thought, and the odds for survival increase dramatically.

The thought of having to face the Hydrans with just his children made Markos realize how grateful he was to have the changed crew alongside him, ready to fight. Even the Old One seemed to make a positive difference. He had always figured, deep down inside, that when it came to the fighting, it would be just him, Markos, against the entire Hydran civilization.

It was time for the final preparations.

"Come on," he said, standing, holding out his hands.

The Old One approached and stood on Markos's left, linking hands. Markos motioned to Straka with his right, and Straka linked up too. Wilhelm, Katawba, and Markatens added to the chain on Straka's side, while Markos's watch shift joined in the circle. Kominski hung back, approaching the almost completed circle warily. His eyes leaked no color, and his body showed only a little uncertainty, a little hesitation.

"Don't worry, Kominski," Jackson said. "No one's going to kill you."

Kominski didn't find it funny. He stared directly into Jackson's eyes, his own eyes mingling blue with pure white.

"I'm sorry, 'Minski. I didn't mean anything by it," Jackson said.

"Yeah, right." Kominski linked hands, completing the circle.

There he is, Markos thought. I feel him. The traitor, the deserter. He's crying out—

Others swept through his consciousness until the circle of minds became one gestalt. Markos kept a strong hold on his consciousness, not letting it slip as much as he usually did. He had found the person who had fixed the Haber ship so that it could be quickly and easily detached.

When the linkup was over, they all turned to face Kominski.

"So it *wasn't* Jackson," Markos said.

"I owe you an apology," Straka said to Jackson.

"Later. Right now, what do we do about him?" Jackson asked.

"Leave him to me," Markos said.

The Old One flashed light yellow flecked with dark blue, and Markos turned to watch what the Old One had to say. The Old One wanted nothing to be done to Kominski, though his arguments weren't strong. He no longer pleaded for Kominski's rights, as he would have a few months ago. Perhaps, Markos thought, these Habers are really capable of understanding what the hell is going on.

"Well, Kominski, you saw what the Old One said. I won't bother translating it all, but what it came down to was that your life should be spared."

"What *are* you going to do?" Straka asked.

"Leave him to me," Jackson said.

"No, much as I'd like to."

"Why don't we just space him?" Martinez asked.

"Yeah," McGowen said.

"No, that's not the answer either. Despite what I feel about him, I can't just waste him like that. Didn't you all feel what he feels when we linked up?"

"What?" Kominski demanded, vocal at last. "That I detest you? All of you? That I want to be human again? That I don't like being a freak?"

The room fell silent.

"What's wrong with that?" Kominski demanded. "Well? I never asked to be changed into this creature I am! I never asked for some freak to mold me in his image! One day I go into the geltank. Sure. And the next I wake up in this body, off to war. Well, not me! I'm going home. Maybe they can change me back!"

"You're dreaming, Kominski," Jackson said.

"We'll see about that," Kominski said.

"The best thing for you to do is accept it, try to live with it," Markos said. "I know these people had a choice. You and I didn't. I was angry at the Habers for a long time. And I was angry at you, too. All of you. It cost Van Pelt his life. And Maxwell his."

Kominski was shaking his head back and forth.

"Enough of us have died, Kominski. Don't make me kill you too."

Kominski backed up a step, but behind him was the bulkhead, and the crew blocked off any other possible exit. Markos knew that Kominski wasn't listening, couldn't be listening, wasn't interested in changing what he thought or the way he felt about being changed. Markos wasn't sure what to do, but whatever he decided, he would have to do it soon. They were well within the Hydran sphere of influence, and every wasted moment increased their chance of discovery.

Kominski tried to backpedal through the bulkhead, and Markos channeled most of his energy into his eyes.

He thought calming, relaxing thoughts, focused them into his eyes, speaking a language of light with no words, a language of pure emotion. He spoke words with his raspy voice, words that spoke of a saner, calmer time, when things were right with Kominski and the Universe. His eyes swirled with hypnotic colors, his bubbly voice talked to some inner resource that was the essence of Kominski. Kominski resisted, but had stopped trying to get through the bulkhead, had stopped trying to escape. Markos knew then that he had him.

He reached out to touch Kominski's skin, switching all of his calming and relaxing thoughts to his hands.

The instant contact was made, Markos's mind floated beneath Kominski's skin, traveled up his arms to his mind.

He found what he was looking for. It was like a little ball of clay, a moldable piece of Kominski, his ego, the root of his Terran soul.

Markos removed it.

In its place he created a desire, a drive, and a strong feeling of loyalty. Whether Kominski liked it or not, whether he understood what had happened or not, he was a changed being. He was now a Haber.

* * *

H-2 was anything but crowded. It was large for a fighter, for a reconnaissance ship, for an escape pod, but it was the Haber mold. They were fast—faster and more maneuverable than the *Paladin* would ever be—and capable of withstanding more stress. They could never have been considered one-man ships, but they were the best thing available.

The Haber controls had been modified slightly as the need for weaponry and visibility had increased. Straka sat in the pilot's seat, and Wilhelm sat beside her. The large startank before them showed the stars of surrounding space, the odd guidance system that worked so well for the Habers. The screens directly before them had been modified, though, by duplicating the engineering of the *Paladin*'s screens. When they'd test-flown the Haber ships, the Old One had backed them up. They'd had a difficult time understanding the swirls of color that appeared on the screens during the landing sequence. Their first test flight had been a near-fatal crash, with the Old One interceding just in time to save them.

By changing the swirling colors to visual output, the crew found they could handle the rest of the strange instrumentation well enough. Watching those screens had been like trying to watch thirty Habers in a heated debate.

The intercom clicked on. "Ready to launch?"

"No. Give us a few seconds to check out the systems," Straka said.

She would let Wilhelm do the actual piloting from the seat beside her. She would handle the weapon systems.

Kominski stood by, armed, deflection belt strapped around his chest, lasetube by his side. He would be the first one out of the ship when it landed. He had demanded the honor. Straka feared that Markos may have gone a little too far in altering Kominski. It was spooky the way he'd changed instantly.

Markatens sat on the deck, calmly relaxed, dropping in and out of his meditative cycle.

"Everyone ready to go?" Straka asked.

They all flashed red.

"Good. If there's a way to get out of this thing alive, we'll find it. No heroes, please. We'll be outnumbered a few billion to one, if what the *Paladin*'s sensors say is true."

"We're too far away to give them much credence," Wilhelm said.

"So much the better. But even if there are only two Hydrans on the surface, don't be a hero. Understand?"

Kominski nodded. Markatens flashed red. "We'll be cool," Wilhelm said.

Straka pressed the intercom button. "We're ready to go, Markos. How about you?"

"We're ready."

Markos's voice was even more distorted over the intercom. Each time Straka would start getting used to the way it sounded, something would happen to point it out to her again. And that would bring back the memories of her half-insane chase across four and a half years of space. Her lying to the crew. Her desire for everlasting life. How she had used and abused the trust the crew had given her.

"Old One? Can you hear us?"

"Yes," the Old One said.

"Release the ships for launch," Straka said.

"They are released," the old Haber said.

"Okay, Wilhelm, this is it. I sure hope you know how to fly this thing as well as you say you do."

"No sweat," Wilhelm said. "If it moves, I can fly it."

Wilhelm settled his hands over the strangely shaped armrests and touched the control plates to his left. By leaking electrons and capturing them, he activated the necessary switches to put the ship into motion.

"We'll be in a stable orbit in about thirty minutes," Wilhelm said.

"What'll you bet the place is crawling with Hydrans?" Kominski asked.

"Let's hope they're not even there," Straka said.

"I hope they are," Kominski said.

"I think I liked you better before you became so enthusiastic," he said to Kominski. He turned to Straka. "Spacey, isn't he?"

"The more Hydrans I kill, the better I'll like it," Kominski said. "Haven't you got any idea what they've done to our people?"

"Our people," Wilhelm said softly.

"The thing is, Kominski, that if we don't find any down there, then there's a chance the Habers living on this planet are safe," Straka said.

"Oh, yeah. Never thought of that."

"Swift," Wilhelm said.

"Pay attention to the controls," Straka said.

"Sure," Wilhelm said, knowing full well there was nothing to do for quite a while.

This was no time to be arguing, picking on each other, getting on each other's nerves. Things were going to get hot and heavy, and very soon. Straka had to keep these two cooled out. Markatens wasn't a problem. He looked like he didn't even know what was going to happen. Well, Straka realized, he probably didn't. The less he knew, the better.

Straka sat back and watched the planet grow in size on the screen. There was little else to do until they arrived. She patted the belt around her waist and prayed it worked properly. She touched her lasetube by her side, brushing it with her fingertips just to make sure it was still there. She decided it wouldn't be such a bad idea to pray a little, to offer her atonement for some of her past ill deeds.

But as she thought about it, she realized she had no idea who she should be praying to. Or what. When she'd been a Terran, there was always God. And now God didn't seem to be the same thing. God wasn't like what Straka had learned about in school, or from her parents. God seemed to be something entirely different.

To her, God looked like the primary rule in the Universe, a physical law or set of laws, a spiritual path for life. That was what the Habers understood.

Change.

But how in all hell could you pray to Change?

22.

Wilhelm piloted the ship through the atmosphere as if it were a screamer—small, tight, and maneuverable. Without the fear of G forces crushing them, blacking them out, he could whip the ship around like an appendage of his body. He flew over the equitorial region, the area where the Habers had originally settled.

Straka watched the planet through the screens, trying to pick up signs of civilization—buildings, machinery, small villages. If the Hydrans had landed on this planet, she should have been able to spot some signs of Hydran life. There should have been some small villages at least.

A few hundred kilometers in from the western coastline, Straka spotted a settlement. She had Wilhelm return to the site and hover a kilometer overhead while they examined the structures below through the screens.

"What do you think?" Straka asked.

"It's definitely not Haber," Wilhelm said. "At least not like those we saw on Gandji or Aurianta."

"Let me see," Markatens said. Straka made room for Markatens, and he peered into the screen. "No," Markatens said. "It's definitely not a Haber settlement."

The settlement appeared as a series of concentric rings. The innermost one looked like a domed structure. The other rings showed no distinct internal structures from that altitude.

"I wish we had a bomb," Kominski said. "We could drop one right on the center of the inner dome, and then we could move on to the next one."

"Sure, Kominski. That would take us only about a hundred thousand years to do, too. After all, the Hydran Empire couldn't be that big, right?" Wilhelm asked.

Kominski moved his head away from the screen and walked away.

"What *is* it with him?" Wilhelm asked. "A little gung ho?"

"Why, Wilhelm," Straka said. "I never knew you were such a master of understatement."

Wilhelm laughed.

"I no longer understand him," Markatens said. "And I am concerned over his welfare."

"Don't be," Straka said. "He knows how to take care of himself."

Straka looked into the screen and tried to figure out the best course of action. Their task could be relatively simple if the Hydrans acted anything at all like Terrans. They would have to land—that much was for certain. And all they had to do was capture one or two live, uninjured Hydrans. Sure, Straka thought. Nothing to it. Just swoop down on them and steal one out of its crib.

If a Hydran ever left that settlement, alone and unarmed, then there's a good chance we can pull this off without any extreme danger. If the Habers were already wiped off the face of this planet, and if the planet was definitely Hydran-owned, as it appeared to be, then there was no reason for the Hydrans to remain armed and in large groups.

Sure. That's all well and good, Straka thought. That's *if* they think like Terrans. Which I doubt. All we know for sure is that they kill Habers like there's no tomorrow.

"You see anyplace you like a lot?" Straka asked Wilhelm.

"There's a place about a kilometer to the north," he said, pointing to a spot on the screen. "We could try that."

"All right. Kominski? Markatens? This is it. We're going down there. Now remember what our directives are. And please—no heroics."

They all flashed red.

"Weapons ready," she ordered.

They flashed red again.

"Let's go, Wilhelm."

The ship dropped downward like a stone. Straka activated the ship-to-ship radio and told Markos they were going down. They had landed by the time Markos replied.

"We've got you," Markos said. "We're five miles straight up. Holler if you even *think* you need help."

"Right," Straka said, then broke off communications. "Let's move."

They ran for the bay. The door was half open by the time they got there. From the top of the ramp Straka felt the chill of the planet's atmosphere creeping in, smelled the rotting heaviness in the air. She made her body hard and activated her belt.

They leaped from the ship to the ground, and the bay door closed behind them. This area of the planet was rocky, with huge boulders and strange-looking broken hills surrounding them. The ground was muddy—thick and difficult for walking. There was little vegetation in the immediate area, and what little there was seemed to be dying. It was near midday, with Epsilon Scorpio high in the sky, offering little warmth. They were chilled to the bone.

Straka looked around, carefully searching for signs of life—Hydran, Haber, or native.

The air was still, and a thin ground fog hovered half a kilometer away to the south, just a meter or so off the ground. "Key yourselves for the smell," Straka reminded. "When you catch that, get ready."

They spread out into an expanding square for ten meters, trying to spot a lone Hydran or two, hoping against hope their job would be easy. Within a few minutes of scouting they had determined that either no Hydrans still occupied the nearby settlement or they all occupied it, with none of them straying from its safety. In either case, none were around the immediate area.

"Which way?" Straka asked Wilhelm.

Wilhelm pointed to the south, into the ground fog. "Single file?"

"Yes."

They started out toward the settlement. They had to get a prisoner. If her group failed, Markos's group would land and try to finish the job. They were up against far too many unknowns for Straka to feel anything but anxious about the whole encounter. Too damned many unknowns. And if they failed, failure would be permanent.

"There," Markatens whispered. "Look."

He pointed to a spot east of the settlement, off to the left. A small group of Hydrans were walking away from the settlement. "Let's circle around," Straka said.

"I don't see why," Kominski said. "Let's just charge them and get this over with. These belts work, and that alone should be enough of a surprise for us to—"

"No," Straka ordered. "No direct confrontations unless absolutely necessary. We'll circle around and try to head them off." She sighted a course down the path the Hydrans were taking. "All right, follow me."

She set off through the muck.

Nothing in life is ever as simple as it seems, Straka thought. Markos says he wants our help to fight a war, we agree, and look at us now. The Hydrans were bad enough in the crystals, but we had some distance from them then. There's a feeling of safety in the back of your mind when you're reading one of those, no matter how real they may seem. All that's in the back of my mind now is fear.

From their intersecting path Straka couldn't see much detail of the Hydrans' bodies. She could see their three body sections and their black, shiny exoskeleton, if that was what it was, and their strange three-legged gait. She couldn't tell if they were carrying weapons yet. Three legs, she thought. A horror in hand-to-hand combat.

They were making good progress through the swampy ground, leaving the rocky, boulder-strewn terrain behind, moving into a wetter area. This was a place Straka would be glad to leave. There was nothing about the area to make her feel comfortable, and she would have found it hard to ever consider herself at home here. The Habers who had lived here must have done some severe adapting.

They reached the spot where they wanted to be without detection and settled in for the short wait. The Hydrans would be along in a matter of seconds. Straka turned and checked each of her crew, making sure their bodies were hard, that their lasetubes were still in their hands.

If Straka had adrenaline, it would have been pumping. As it was, her mind was tense and uneasy over the upcoming confrontation. Her body was relaxed, ready to go into overdrive as soon as needed.

When she turned back to face the Hydrans, she saw them clearly. The six creatures were practically identical, and none of them had the white markings Straka had been cued to look for. Those with the white markings had mowed down anything in their paths that moved.

They might not be armed, Straka thought.

The Hydrans were fifteen meters away, approaching slowly.

"As soon as they walk past, we'll move," she whispered.

The Hydrans continued their approach.

When the first two had walked past Kominski, he leaped up from the brush and lased them down. The smell was incredible. All hell broke loose.

The two farthest away started to run at an incredible speed through the wet ground, the three legs working like a horse's at full gallop. They exuded an overpowering stench that Straka recognized from the crystals. Markatens and Wilhelm had thrown themselves at the other two aliens, the ones trapped in the middle.

Straka's laser blast caught one of the fleeing Hydrans in the back, and it crumpled to the ground. The other one kept running, and Straka realized she would have to set off after him or run the risk of the entire encampment being alerted to their presence. She hoped Kominski would help Markatens and Wilhelm if she didn't get back immediately.

The ground pulled at her feet like suction cups. Running was a difficult task, though a necessary one. The alien had a healthy lead. Straka just hoped she could get off a good shot. Overtaking and capturing him was out of the question. The Hydran seemed to be gaining more and more ground—she made a mental note to report their speed to Markos. If she ever saw Markos again.

They were rapidly approaching the Hydran settlement. Straka realized she would have to lase the creature now or run for her life. If the Hydran made it inside those walls, the rest of them would probably pour out of the place armed and angry.

She stopped and aimed the tube, making her entire body as rigid as possible. She activated the tube and swung it in a tight arc. The Hydran's body toppled.

She then did something distinctly human. She breathed a sigh of relief.

She hurried back to the others, to see how they had done. Between the three of them they should have been able to capture both of the creatures.

The smell and cold and murky scenery were no longer noticed as she made her way back. The way her feet made sucking noises, the way her vision was sweeping over the electromagnetic spectrum, the way she felt after killing those two Hydrans—none of it mattered. She would have time to think about those things later in the safety of the mother ship. The important thing now, the *only* important thing, was finding the others and making sure they were alive.

She felt like she'd been walking a long time—too long a time —and realized she might have missed the others. She was afraid of shouting to attract their attention; she might end up attracting the Hydrans too. How far had she run? It couldn't have been this far.

Nothing around her looked familiar. As she stood there, she realized there were no real landmarks, that the swampy vegetation looked pretty much the same, that it was just one, big, overgrown area. Panic started to creep into her mind, and she tried to stop it. If it got the better of her, she'd be finished.

I'll just walk straight ahead, like I was doing, she thought. Maybe it was farther than I thought.

She kept her lasetube in her hand, ready to raise it to the firing position at a moment's notice. She walked, trying not to think about where she was, what she was doing there, while still keeping her mind painfully attuned to her surroundings and the changes in them.

She walked another twenty meters when she saw them, sitting on the trail. She felt a smile emerge as she saw the group, glad to see them alive, glad to find them at all. Her eyes leaked green.

"Did you get them?" Kominski asked.

Straka flashed red. "I had to chase one for a while. I was afraid he was going to get away. These bastards can really move."

"How fast?" Wilhelm asked.

"About a half again as fast as we can. What happened here while I was gone?"

No one said a word.

"Where are the Hydrans? You didn't let them get away, did you?"

"No," Wilhelm said.

"Well? Where are they? What happened?"

No one answered.

"I lased one of them," Kominski said.

That figures, Straka thought. "What about the other?"

"He's back in the swamp," Wilhelm said, motioning with his hand to an area off the trail.

"Alive?" Straka asked.

"We think so. Through no help of Kominski, though."

"Can't we kill it? We could stay and find some more of them to fight," Kominski said.

Straka shook her head. "I'm going to take a look at it. It had better be alive, Kominski."

"God, 'Minski, I thought you'd killed enough for one day," Wilhelm said.

"Killing Hydrans isn't really killing," Kominski said.

Straka took a few steps off the trail in the direction Wilhelm had pointed. When she saw the first corpse, she understood why Wilhelm was upset. Right beside the corpse, lying flat on its back, was the second Hydran. Little hairs around its neck moved as air rushed in and out of its body.

The dead Hydran had been lased four times—once longitudinally, once laterally, and twice on the diagonal. Like slicing a pie, Straka thought. Kominski is sicker than ever.

The Hydran had to have been lying right there, helpless, the two of them side by side, when Kominski sliced up the first. It must have seen and understood what Kominski had done and had remained totally motionless. It was certainly capable of feeling fear, or else it was exercising caution. Either way it recognized the value of remaining motionless. In any case, it was smart enough not to panic.

"Can you understand me?" Straka asked the Hydran.

It didn't move.

It didn't make a sound.

"Don't waste your breath," Wilhelm said. "We already tried, verbally, with signs, and with our eyes."

"Well, it seems alive enough to me," Straka said. "Let's see about getting it on its feet and back to the ship. We got what we came for."

"Not me," Kominski said.

"Fine," Straka said. "Then we'll leave you here. We'll be back to pick you up in a few thousand years objective."

Wilhelm laughed.

"Let's get it back to the ship," Straka said.

"Right," Wilhelm said, rising to his feet. "Give us a hand?" he asked Markatens.

Markatens, Wilhelm, and Straka managed to get the Hydran to its feet. Kominski remained seated.

"He was only kidding, Kominski," Wilhelm said. "You can't stay here."

"But I *want* to."

"Forget it," Straka said. "I was only joking. Come on. We've got to get moving, and that's an order."

"Oh, all right. I was getting to like this place. So many Hydrans," Kominski said.

"Sure you were," Wilhelm said.

Straka motioned for the Hydran to start walking. The Hydran remained immobile. "Give him a little push, Markatens."

Markatens pushed, and the Hydran started off.

"He's giving off some odor, some kind of chemical," Markatens said as they walked. "It's faint but detectable."

"You figure that's normal?" Straka asked.

"He wasn't doing it while lying by the path," Wilhelm said.

"It's similar to the smell they give off in combat," Markatens said.

"Perhaps it's just from physical exertion," Straka said.

No one said anything.

"Well, it was just an idea."

Wilhelm took the point position, walking four meters ahead of Kominski, Straka, Markatens, and their Hydran prisoner. When the group approached the end of the vegetated area, Wilhelm stopped and held his hand up for the others to stop. He motioned them down, and they crouched low, waiting for him to motion them forward. Straka figured it was another patrol of Hydrans, like the one they had ambushed.

Wilhelm ran back to the group. "You're not going to believe this, man, but we're surrounded."

"What?" Straka said. "How the hell can we be surrounded?"

"The ship. They've encircled the ship. I can see it from here."

"Kominski and Markatens, stay with the Hydran. I'm going up there with Wilhelm to check this out. Don't let the Hydran get away."

"Right," Kominski said.

Straka hoped Kominski wouldn't just kill it and say it tried to escape. Without the prisoner they had nothing. Straka followed Wilhelm, slowly and silently making her way through the muck and the mire. They came to the edge of the swampy area; a rocky plain stretched out before them, a large clearing dotted with clumps of boulders and large rocks, dying vegetation. Their ship was about two hundred meters away, surrounded, just as Wilhelm had said, by a ring of Hydrans.

"What are they doing?" Wilhelm asked.

"It looks like they're waiting. Waiting for us to return, or waiting for us to open the bay door and leave the ship."

"I don't get it."

"They may not know we've already left the ship. They may think we're still on board."

"Then what do we do?" Wilhelm asked.

"I'm not sure. They look armed." She surveyed the scene carefully, trying to take in as much information as possible. "Let's get back to the others."

They retreated cautiously, unsure if the Hydrans could detect their presence over that distance, but feeling safety and caution were definitely in order. If there had been Habers surrounding the ship, Straka was sure they would have been spotted. Habers could detect visual change easily. They had no idea about the Hydrans' ability to see, though.

When they returned to Kominski and Markatens, the Hydran was the same as he'd been when they left. At least it hadn't detected the large group ahead.

"How many are there?" Markatens asked.

Straka leaked a canary yellow from her eyes. "I'm not really sure, though it may not matter."

"How's that?" Kominski asked.

"We're not going to be able to do any fighting. Not with him," Straka said, motioning toward the alien.

"I'd be glad to take care of him," Kominski said, raising his lasetube so that it pointed squarely at the Hydran's chest.

"Don't!" Straka ordered. "This isn't over yet. We need him alive, Kominski. Not freshly dissected."

"Then what do we do with him?" Kominski asked.

Straka looked away. It was a question whose answer she knew too well. In a fight to regain their ship, their belts would protect them from the Hydrans' laser fire—but nothing would protect the Hydran if they carried it along with them. Once the Hydrans saw their laser fire being deflected by the crew's belts, they'd be swarming all over Straka and her men in a moment, a horde of ruthless killers, soldiers, destroyers.

I can't afford to leave anyone behind to guard the Hydran,

Straka thought. What *do* you do with a prisoner when you go into battle? I mean, what do you do with it besides kill it beforehand?

"I have a suggestion," Markatens said.

Straka looked over at the young Haber. "What is it?"

"Why don't we immobilize the Hydran, attempt to make our way back to the ship, and return for it if possible."

"How?"

"It should be a simple matter to probe its physical being, a far easier task than trying to alter its mental state. We could alter its joints so that they no longer bend."

"Good, Markatens. Good idea. Can you do it?"

Markatens eyes flashed red as he reached over to touch the Hydran. Straka watched, fascinated, as Markatens' eyes began to dance with colors. She was glad Markatens was part of their little assault team—his mind worked differently, came from a different cultural perspective, from a different race, and his approach to problems was unique, a positive addition.

The Hydran remained passive and after a few seconds Markatens broke contact with it.

"It is done," he said.

"Good," Straka said.

"Insect statue," Wilhelm said.

Kominski laughed.

"What do you plan, Straka?" Markatens asked.

Straka shook her head. She wasn't really sure. She knew she was starting to tire, that the strain of keeping her body hard, of activating her lasetube, of running through the muck after the fleeing Hydran, was wearing her down more than she actually felt. She wasn't sure they were capable of facing fifty to seventy-five Hydrans. She wasn't sure they would have enough energy to power their lasetubes for an extended confrontation. She wasn't sure their belts would work that long either. They were continually drawing on their stored energy, their own bodies, and they would need to rest and rebuild for a long time.

"I know this, Markatens: Whatever we do, we must do it quickly. We aren't strong enough to enter a long, drawn-out battle. We're all tired and we're constantly draining ourselves."

"This is true," Markatens said.

"Our best chance is to walk at a rapid pace toward the ship. We may get ten or twenty meters before they actually do something. When they start firing on us, we run straight for them. We can lase them down at close range, getting as many as possible."

"And if something happens?"

"Then something happens, Wilhelm. We know we can't sit here, and Markos isn't going to drop out of the sky to save us. Our radio's in the ship, which doesn't do us a lot of good here. Markos doesn't even know what's happened. We could wait, and he'd come eventually, just as we prearranged. But we've got our prisoner, and we run the risk of being discovered just waiting here. The one thing the Hydrans don't expect from a Haber is offense."

"True," Kominski said. "And I like that thought. Taking them by surprise."

Straka wished that Kominski hadn't agreed. She was starting to distrust everything the newly changed Kominski thought.

"Well, if we're going to do it, let's get it over with," Wilhelm said. "Just sitting around like this is draining me more than fighting would."

They left the swampy vegetation behind, walking in single file, stretching their legs out and moving as quickly as they could without running. They headed directly for the ship, for the mass of Hydrans. As they walked, Straka flashed on the thought that this plan was almost suicidal, that it probably would have been smarter and safer to just wait for Markos to come to their aid. But deep down she knew why she was risking herself and the others—some atavistic urge, some drive that made her become more than just Cathy Straka, surfaced when she was faced with death. She felt the larger-than-life quality to her being, the unreality in facing down so many Hydrans.

She was surprised they hadn't been spotted yet. They had covered more than thirty meters.

And then the real reason why she was doing this struck her. She was flirting with death in a way she'd never been able to before. She was risking more than her life—she was risking immortality. It would have been far safer to sit and wait, but she'd somehow known, she'd somehow understood what Markos had once told her about the way Habers lived. They chose to die. Immortality would be nothing if she was afraid to live, to take chances, to get the most out of every waking moment.

Even if those moments were numbered.

Fifty meters, and still no sign from the Hydrans.

That in itself confirmed her suspicions that the Hydrans assumed they were still on board the ship. They were all facing H-1, waiting for the creatures inside to make their appearance.

Still, those Hydrans facing away from them would spot them soon enough.

Sixty meters.

"Let's run," Straka said.

They ran. They made another ten meters before the Hydrans spotted their approach. Straka expected an immediate laser attack and was surprised to see them moving around instead of firing.

Those on the far side of the ship were emerging from around the ship's sides, grouping up with those Hydrans whose backs were to the advancing crew. The Hydrans were forming up in a single, wide line.

Straka couldn't believe their luck. She saw an opportunity and grabbed it.

"Pour it on," she shouted.

They ran at full speed, closing as much distance as possible. They were fifty meters away from H-1 when the line of Hydrans opened fire.

The beams were deflected by their belts.

They continued to run.

The Hydrans continued to fire.

The ground around them popped and crackled as the lasers cooked what little moisture was there, sealed it over in a fused shell.

"Hold up!" Straka shouted.

They stopped running, aimed their lasetubes at the line of Hydrans, and just sliced them down, from left to right. It was over in two seconds. They stood there, staring at the toppling bodies.

Kominski was laughing softly, almost chuckling.

All they had done was point their weapons, activated them, and moved down the line, slicing Hydran after Hydran in half.

It had been too easy. Too fast.

Straka went numb with the shock.

"Cathy?" Wilhelm asked. "You okay?"

"Yeah," Straka said. "Fine. I just didn't expect it to go like this."

"I'll go back for the Hydran," Markatens said.

"I mean, it was over in a second. They didn't have a chance."

"Cut it out, Straka. You saw the crystals. You saw what they did to the Habers. Unarmed Habers."

Straka seeped red from her eyes. "I saw, but I'm not sure I really believe."

23

202

Markos docked H-3 first. He wanted to be on board the mother
ship when Straka and her crew unloaded the Hydran. He wanted to
see the Hydran close up, give it the benefit of his past training and
recent firsthand experience in xenobiology.

Up until now, all knowledge of the Hydrans had been gleaned
through the information contained in the crystals—nothing solid
enough to help plan a campaign against them. Soon, though, it would
be different. Questioning the creature would be enlightening, if not a
little repulsive. He remembered the problems he'd faced breaking
through the language barrier with the Habers. Markos hadn't been
sure they could communicate verbally. With the tools NASA 2 had
provided, with the rudimentary translation techniques, finding a way

to communicate with the Habers had been slow and painful, a hit-or-miss process until one Haber pointed to itself and said, "Haber." It had touched Markos and had learned his language.

Now, with his ability to penetrate the Hydran's mind, snake his way through whatever thoughts the Hydran had, translation would be unnecessary. All he would have to do would be to touch it, let his electrons flow along its neural pathways, or its equivalents. Once he'd accomplished that, he would have the answers to the Hydrans.

He stood beneath the docking bay, waiting for the hatch to open. It opened slowly. He saw the face and upper body of Markatens framed in the opening. "Have you got it?" Markos asked.

Markatens flashed red, then eased himself down through the hatch. He turned to receive the prisoner. Someone's hands were passing the Hydran out through the hatch, and Markos was puzzled. The Hydran was as stiff as a piece of the bulkhead.

"Did it give you trouble?" Markos asked. "Is it dead?"

"No. This one is alive," Markatens said. "We had to make sure that it was incapable of motion, though. I touched and changed its joints. After it is properly guarded, I can change it back."

Markatens propped the alien against the bulkhead. Its three legs formed a tripod, though the legs were not spread apart far enough to support it. From the way it was arranged, Markos surmised that it had been lying down when Markatens had frozen it.

Kominski and then Wilhelm exited H-1. They both greeted Markos, and neither looked any worse for their mission. Kominski seemed to be highly animated, enjoying himself, while Wilhelm tried to ignore Kominski. Wilhelm immediately put a little distance between himself and Kominski. Straka was the last one out of H-1, and she eased herself onto the deck of the mother ship silently. She looked once at Markos, then turned and walked away. Something had happened.

"What's the matter with her?" he asked.

"She is deeply troubled by what occurred on the surface," Markatens said.

"She'll be okay," Kominski said.

"Maybe," Wilhelm said.

"What the hell happened?" Markos asked.

"It was an unpleasant experience," Markatens said. "I am not sure that Straka fully understood about war."

"Keep an eye on her, will you?" Markos asked Markatens. "See if you can do anything for her."

"I will try, but she remained within herself throughout the return trip."

"Do what you can. Wilhelm, will you give me a hand with the Hydran?"

"Sure."

"Let's get him to the lab."

Markos picked up the legs and Wilhelm held it by its head. "Is it still alive?" Markos asked.

"Seems to be," Wilhelm said.

They carried the Hydran through the passageways toward the lab. They walked in silence for a few moments, then Markos asked, "What happened?"

"What do you mean?"

"On the planet. What happened?"

Wilhelm said nothing.

"Wilhelm?"

"Kominski went over the edge again. We had two prisoners, but he sliced one up. Then we ran into a rather large suicide squad of Hydrans, hell-bent on being lased down."

"Explain it to me," Markos said, coaxing with his eyes.

Wilhelm told him what had happened in detail. By the time they had placed the Hydran on a lab table, he had related most of the experience.

"What about you, Wilhelm? Are you upset?"

"Upset? Most definitely. But *upset* isn't the right word, man. I'm disgusted—disgusted by the role I played in the little battle, by the way we had to slice them down like trees. I'll live with it, though. They were armed."

Markos flashed red.

"But then there's Kominski. I don't like him anymore. I want you to know that, man. He's sick. Really sick. Whatever you did to him, he's worse now. You should have heard him laugh when we sliced them down. He may not be the same kind of sick he was before, but he's just as sick as ever."

"That's probably what's bothering Straka," Markos said.

"Ask Straka, man. That's what's bothering me. I'm going to eat something and then get some rest. I'll be in my cabin." He turned to leave, walked a few steps, then stopped. He faced Markos again. "Oh, yeah. If you don't change Kominski, I will."

Wilhelm still clutched the lasetube in his hand. Markos understood.

As soon as Wilhelm left, Markos turned his attention to the Hydran. The problems with the crew dissolved as he looked at the shiny black creature. It was a little smaller than what it should have been, compared with those he'd seen in the crystals. Its shiny black covering was not artificial, like a spacesuit or battle armor. It was most probably an exoskeleton, which supported the insect analogy that much more. There were small holes in the shell covering the head. There were slitted holes along the neck, with tiny hairs rimming the insides of the slits. The hairs moved in and out as the Hydran breathed. On closer visual examination Markos found these hair-rimmed holes at the point where the torso met the legs and also at various spots along the arms and legs.

The Hydran was emitting a constant odor, similar in scent to the odor Markos was familiar with through the crystals. Perhaps their primary method of communication was through pheromones, he thought.

He was fascinated by the creature, reveling in the process of deduction and speculation about its biological makeup. That was what he'd been trained to do as a Terran, using methods that were primitive in comparison to those he now had available. It had been so long since he'd done this—so many years, so many miles traveled, so many changes seen. Doing this was like putting on a comfortable old shirt, something familiar, something he knew how to do well.

But there was an added depth to his abilities now, an added tool for measuring, for deducing correct answers. He looked at his hands, at his palms, their red and green and orange translucent skin, and placed them on the Hydran's chest. He let his mind relax.

The interaction started almost instantly as he felt his hands and its chest mingled. There was little to be learned from its exoskeleton—the shell was made up of a proteinlike molecule and a combination of common minerals. It was not yet fully formed, though. He could tell that the growth process was still taking place as he reached the inner level of the shell.

He delved deeper, finding the internal organs of the creature. They had strange functions and an interdependence that would take him a long time to unravel. But one point was painfully obvious: None of the organs was fully formed, either. The growth rate seemed abnormally fast. Either the Hydran's metabolism was extremely high in certain areas of its body, or else it was still growing.

He pressed deeper, trying to gain more substantial information. He found what passed for neural pathways, connecting fibers that linked one organ with the others. He touched it, allowed himself to be there, to travel down its layers, peeling them back one at a time.

He touched its conscious mind.

It was truly chaotic. Seeing through its eyes, seeing through his own eyes, thinking an alien's thoughts, proved too much for him. He broke contact.

As he stood there staring at the creature, he knew it could never supply all the answers he needed. But it was the only example of Hydran biology and psychology he had, and he was determined to make the best of it.

He wondered how Straka would take the news, though. They had captured a child.

By the time Markos had completed his examination, he knew the following things:

1. They communicated through sounds and through smells.
2. They had sensitive hearing, ranging from about 20 to 80,000 hz.
3. There were two distinct sexes, and this one was male.
4. Their prisoner was a child.
5. The markings on the heads indicated adults. Males had iridescent markings, while females had white markings. From this he deduced that the females were the warriors.

6. They had several independent hearts placed throughout their circulatory systems. Each heart pumped autonomously. There was no central heart or pump.

7. Their social structure combined militarism and a caste structure, as near as he could tell. Children had to complete a rite of passage that involved killing any form of intelligent life.

8. They were egg layers.

9. They ate protein exclusively. The child held a scene of adult Hydrans eating their dead enemies.

10. They ate their own dead for the protein and to perpetuate their ancestors' memories.

11. Their basic life-molecule was simpler, less complex, than DNA and trivial compared with the Haber molecule.

This last piece of information was unmistakably the most important. After taking a few moments to put the individual pieces of information about the race into a whole picture, Markos realized he would have to analyze the molecule carefully. He needed to know how much social interaction and instructions were passed from generation to generation as a function of instinct and how much was taught. If everything these creatures did was a direct result of instinct, or even closely related to instinct, he would have a far better understanding of why they lased down the Habers on planet after planet.

He touched the Hydran again and delved down, singling out one molecule to unravel. He took his time, making mental notes about the chemicals, the way they would interact with one another, what effect they might have on a race, on a culture. When he was done, his original view of the Hydrans collapsed. He didn't like that.

And he didn't like what he found.

Nothing like a little cultural chauvinism, he thought. Nothing like drawing stupid conclusions from observation. The Earth is flat. The stars? Oh, simple. Points of light shining through a velvet curtain. The Hydrans? Hey, everyone knows they're insects, nasty dirty insects hell-bent on taking over the Universe.

The Hydran equivalent of DNA taught him some interesting

things, especially about differences in cultural perspectives. The Hydrans were little more than complex breeding machines, designed with one purpose only—spread the complex molecule as far and as fast as possible. The molecule wanted to replicate itself, its own survival instinct honed and perfected over years of mutation. If it didn't need to be carried around in a Hydran body, it would have covered its native planet like a fungus or like algae, leaving no room for other kinds of life.

The Hydrans would breed and reproduce in one area until there was either no more room or no more food. Markos realized that on a planet with a limited food chain, this would create constant, natural wars. It was the only reasonable result. They couldn't cut back and limit their population—the driving force of their beings wouldn't allow it.

He figured that civil wars must have been common among the Hydrans. They must have fought over their native planet time and time again, wars that spanned centuries, reducing the population to a point where rebuilding could begin again. They would overpopulate and then the procedure would start all over again.

Genetic expansionists, he realized. They won't stop breeding until every piece of habitable rock in the Universe has been claimed and colonized to the point of overpopulation.

Sometime in this growth curve, when peace reigned for a few centuries, they must have developed space travel. An awareness of more rocks out there, just waiting to be filled up with more Hydrans. It must have appeared as a solution to their own planet's mess, so they directed their efforts outward, to seeding the stars.

Markos was grateful they had limited life spans. As a result of this there was only so far they could have traveled through space during their first wave of colonization. But still—once they'd settled their outer planets, establishing strong population centers and outposts, the second wave of expansion would have begun.

All of which caught up to Markos, shook him to the core of his being. He had made a glaring error in jumping to a conclusion. The Hydrans were not at war.

They, like the Habers, probably didn't even know the meaning of the word.

The Hydrans were doing something far simpler than making war. They were living life.

The Habers on Aurianta and Gandji had had a better grip on what was occurring than he had.

The Hydrans were an aggressive race, wiping out everything in their path like a plague of swarming locusts. There's no thought behind what a locust does. There was no right or wrong to what the Hydrans were doing. There were no moral questions, no higher principles, no concepts of peace. There would be no way of talking to the Hydrans, of negotiating with them to keep their expansion limited. There was no way of stopping them from wiping out every last Haber in existence.

It wasn't even close to war.

It was the change the Habers would never survive.

Markos needed rest. It took all his strength to walk to his cabin, open the door, and collapse on the bunk. He lay on his back and watched the air currents drift between himself and the ceiling, listened to the air-support systems' dull throb, felt his body ache more and more with each passing moment. Explaining what he'd discovered to Straka, the crew, the Old One, and Markatens seemed an impossible task right now. It would have to wait.

The Hydran still lived, and Markos knew he should have killed it. Keeping the creature alive made little sense; it had served its purpose and deserved better than being immobilized, paralyzed, frightened beyond understanding. He had seen its soul, its hopes and desires, and they had scared him. Its thoughts were too alien for him to grasp. He knew he should have killed it earlier, when he had been in the lab, right after he'd found out what he needed from it. But after the contact he had trouble reaching the necessary level of clinical detachment he needed to kill it without thought.

He flashed on Kominski, his ability to kill Hydrans without any thought, and wondered if that might be why he hadn't changed Kominski before examining the Hydran. Leave the messy murders to Kominski? Keep him around to take care of the distasteful cleanup details?

No, Markos thought, it wasn't like that at all. Examination of the alien had rightly come first. I'll get to Kominski soon enough.

And, if necessary, I'll find the strength to kill the Hydran myself.

He knew what had to be done. He knew about their aggression, now, their social structures, their psychology, and most importantly, their inherited attitudes. He remembered the disappointment he'd felt on finding out it was only a child. He had figured then that Straka would have to return to the surface to get an adult for examination. He could imagine the confrontation all too well.

"You want us to go down there again?" Straka would say. "What are you planning on doing, starting a family?"

Well, don't worry, Straka. That was before I examined the genetic molecule. There's no need for another specimen. I've learned all I have to know from the child. From one molecule.

I've learned that we're finished—finished before we've really started. How the hell can you fight something like this? If it was war, if it was something even *like* war, we could do something positive about it. We could make a dent in their population, make them realize that someone out here is fighting back, get their attention and negotiate for a peaceful settlement. But how do you negotiate with a laser speeding straight toward your chest? That's what the Hydrans are like: single-minded, determined, unaware of the ramifications of what they're doing. Talking to these creatures about peace would be like talking to the Habers about war.

Even if we wiped out a few planets, which could be quite a mess, or even if we had the means to reduce their population by ninety percent, it wouldn't solve a thing. It would only be a temporary fix, forestalling the inevitable. It would be like cutting out most of a cancerous tumor but leaving behind enough cancerous cells to start the process all over again. And knowing how weird these creatures are, they might even be grateful to us for reducing their population so that they could breed faster.

Just thinking about it made him feel heavy, dense, as though his body was hardening from the inside out, turning from liquid to solid. He took a shallow breath, then tried to relax, to stop resisting his body's need to process some food, his body's strange way of reacting to emotional stress. His metabolism finally shifted.

Energy trickled into his system slowly, like ice water melting in a spring thaw. He didn't feel revitalized, though—not with the decision still facing him.

Markos knew what he would have to decide. Still, he didn't want to think it, to make it something real. He wasn't a god, capable of deciding the fate of an entire race. And yet he knew he must, and he knew equally as well that he could never live with the decision.

It all came down to this: It was either the Hydrans or every other sentient life-form.

He would have to see it through to the end. He would have to wait for his ultimate peace of mind. And then, on some deserted section of Aurianta, he would meditate his way down to death.

Van Pelt had had the right idea on how to deal with an alien race. Only he had elected to kill the wrong race.

24.

Markos heard the Old One approaching the cabin. There was no mistaking the way he walked. He heard the Haber stop in the doorway, waiting to be asked in. Markos remained on his bunk, faceup, watching the air.

He didn't care what the Old One wanted. He needed some privacy. He needed to get back in touch with himself, with the core that gave him his sense of rightness. He'd done too many things recently out of guesswork, out of wishful thinking. The war wasn't much of a war anymore, and he needed time to think about that.

Time to accept the decision he had made to wipe the Universe clean of Hydrans.

Let him stand there, Markos thought. He's not bothering me,

waiting in the passageway like some silent Buddha. He doesn't know anything more about life or death than I do.

"Markos?"

Markos ignored him, calmly watching the changes in the air circulating, the patterns created by the Old One's spoken words. There was a delicacy in the way the air moved that he was thankful for. Perhaps if Terrans were as aware of their surroundings as the Habers were, there'd be more meaning to their lives, he thought. But in his state of mind he managed to doubt even that.

"Markos?" the Old One said again.

Markos continued to ignore him. It was for the best, he thought. If they got into a discussion now, Markos was sure he'd say things he might end up regretting. Perhaps sometime in the future, when he had a better grasp of the decision, when he better understood its full scope, he would talk. The fact that every Hydran was a sentient creature, involved in doing the only thing their genes could command them to do—not something their social structure had devised—was still something he couldn't deal with. They weren't expanding through greed, through hatred, through a desire for racial extinction, through any misunderstanding—they were expanding because that was all they knew, because it was right, because it was the way it was intended to be.

And that meant only one thing to Markos: They *had* to be destroyed.

Not one planet could be overlooked.

There was no other way.

After a few more silent moments the Old One left, walking back in the direction from which he had come. Markos was glad that the Old One respected his need to be alone. He would be able to work out his feelings and face the massive lump in his throat, the tremendous cancer in his mind, the spreading emotion that blocked out everything else. He recognized the emotion once the Old One had left. He had felt it before, but only on a trivial level.

He could barely deal with the guilt the decision itself brought. How could he possibly deal with the guilt once the real killing began? And then later, when the Hydrans were little more than a memory, a nightmare to scare children, a barrier between himself and every other living creature—how could he deal with the guilt then? How could he ever live with himself?

He was beginning to understand what the Old One must have gone through on returning to Aurianta after having eaten, thus breaking their prime taboo.

Well, the only way Markos could see out of it was to stick to his resolve, to return to Aurianta and do what every sane Haber does: meditate his way down to zero energy. A peaceful death. If there were an afterlife, he hoped he would be spared the memories of what this life had forced him to do.

He wished he could shut his eyes and see nothing but blackness. He wished he had eyelids. He did the next best thing: He rolled over onto his front side and put his face down, into the bunk, blocking out all the light.

He tried to relax.

"Markos?"

It was Straka, at the doorway. Several hours had passed since the Old One had come to his cabin, and Markos had done no thinking in that time. He had just remained facedown on the bunk, breathing every few minutes, letting his body metabolize a few molecules of food at a time.

He could hear Straka walking into the cabin.

"Markos? What's going on?"

He remained silent, wishing Straka would just leave.

Straka touched his back, right where his shoulders had been before he'd been changed. He felt Straka's fingers probe his skin for signs of life.

"What is it, Markos? What's wrong?" Straka asked.

Markos rolled his head so that he could talk. "Leave me alone," he said.

"What's bothering you?"

"Just leave me alone."

"Not until you tell me what it is."

"Leave," Markos asked.

Straka took a step back. "What is it? Is it something you learned from the Hydran? Is that it?"

"Please, Cathy, I don't want to talk. Do you understand?"

"Frankly, no. We don't have the time or the manpower for you to indulge yourself. If you want to hide in a corner and lick your wounds, let me know and we'll drop you off someplace of your very own.

"This is supposed to be an offensive move on our part. We're supposed to be figuring out what to do about the Hydrans. Play your games when this is over. Not now, when we need you."

"Get out, Straka."

"Markos, please!"

"Get out!"

Straka stormed out of the room. Markos turned his head back down into the bunk. He could hear Straka's muttered curses bounce off the bulkheads through the passageway.

Straka really hadn't understood, Markos thought. She'd been wrong. This wasn't a case of self-indulgence, he thought. There are too many creatures, too many planets involved. How the hell were they going to wipe out the Hydrans, anyway?

The others on board the ship would just have to leave him alone until he managed to accept what had to be done and had some clear idea as to how to do it. This wasn't like planning a battle skirmish, or even like getting the Terrans to fight for him. This was something else entirely.

He figured he'd never be considered some kind of hero or savior. He knew history would view him as a mass murderer. That's probably how the Habers would see him.

When he was ready to face them all, he got up. There was a shift in the underlying feeling on board the ship, an undercurrent of anxiety. Markos could feel it in his cabin, isolated from the others, separated by passageways and bulkheads. The crew knew something was wrong, and they knew better than to verbalize their fears. But he could almost smell the upset.

He walked deliberately through the wide passageways, heading for the bridge.

He passed Wilhelm along the way.

"Hey," Wilhelm said. "You all right?"

"No," Markos said, and he kept walking. He listened for Wilhelm's footsteps, but he didn't hear him move. He walked down the ramp onto the bridge and saw the planet as a disk, Epsilon Scorpio a larger disk in the distance. His men were sitting at their controls, checking the ship's status every few moments.

"Are we ready to go?" Markos asked.

De Sola wheeled around, surprised by Markos's appearance. "We can be in a few minutes."

"Good. We're leaving."

"For where?" Jackson asked.

"I'll let you know, Jackson. Give me a few seconds."

"Sure," Jackson said. "Sure. Whatever you say."

McGowen sat in the weapons chair.

"Make sure all your weapons are ready to fire. Understand?"

McGowen flashed red.

"Engines are powered," Jackson said.

Straka appeared in the doorway and walked down the ramp. "What's going on?"

No one responded.

"Lay in a course for Pi Hydra."

"Why?" Straka asked.

"Later. McGowen, train your heavy weapons on this planet's surface."

McGowen's half-Haber face registered the shock as he realized what Markos had in mind. Markos saw it, acknowledged it, and felt sorry for him. "Locked in?"

McGowen flashed red.

"Jackson, get ready to get us out of here. No need to risk being hit by exploding debris."

Jackson looked at him, dumbfounded.

"You heard me," Markos said.

Jackson entered the power requirements to the interface. "Ready."

"You can't do this, Markos," Straka said.

"Why not? It's the only solution."

"What the hell are you talking about?" she demanded.

"I'll explain later. Fire, McGowen."

"With all due respect, Markos, I can't. Not until you explain."

"I'll throw the switches myself," Markos said, moving toward the command chair.

"Wait." It was the Old One.

"Wilhelm told me, me something was wrong. What is going on?"

"Stay out of this, Old One. You wouldn't understand," Markos said.

"I, I would understand, Markos, and I, I will," he said with force. His eyes emitted blinding light, and Markos's grip on the arms of the command chair loosened.

"Shut down the systems," the Old One said to the crew. "And then meet me, me in the rec area. There is much to discuss."

They followed the Old One willingly enough—as soon as Markos had moved away from the switches that could activate the weapon systems. No one questioned the control the Old One had exhibited, and no one questioned Markos's obedience.

They were silent, some sitting on the deck, some sitting in chairs. Straka's watch, those who had heard Kominski's laughter on lasing down the line of Hydrans, had talked little since then. There was a strangeness in the air, as if Markos were on trial, and the crew were the jurors, deliberating on a verdict without knowing the crime or hearing the evidence. Each felt that something was required of him, and yet none knew what it was.

Markos knew that this feeling had been created by the Old One.

"Is it really necessary to destroy the planet, Markos?" the Old One asked.

Markos said nothing.

"Are there no alternatives?"

Markos stared at the stress patterns in the metal plates of the deck.

"You owe us all an explanation. We cannot be party to such mass destruction," the Old One said. "We have not lost the ability to reason. Please explain it to us so that we, too, can understand what must be done."

"Please, Markos," Straka said.

There was no pleading in her tone, no whining, no demand. Just a little more of a request, strengthening the Old One's request. Markos looked at Straka; he expected her to look away for some reason, as if she shared in his guilt. She continued to look at him.

"I'll tell you," Markos said, "and you'll want to give up. You won't like what you hear."

He waited then, giving each of them time to decide, but their expressions remained neutral. They were waiting for him to get it out in the open.

"Okay," he said. "The problem is genetic. We're not really at war," he said. "There is no war."

"What?" Jackson asked.

"They expand by instinct. They don't think of it in terms of conflict. Which means there's no way of communicating with them, much less negotiating. So we have to wipe them out. All of them. They don't understand what it is they're doing. To them this expansionism is life."

"But it's wrong," Straka said.

"No," Markos said. "I only wish it were. It's not wrong because there's no morality there. To them what they're doing is morally correct. It's just living life."

The Old One seemed to shrink a little under that piece of information. He sat down on the deck and stared at a spot directly before him.

"So what are we supposed to do? Run around the Galaxy and blast every Hydran we run into?" Jackson asked.

Markos said nothing.

"You can't be serious," McGowen said.

"You're nuts," Jackson said. But Markos could tell from his voice, from the colors in his eyes that Jackson didn't think he was at all insane. Jackson was just trying to negate the awful truth.

"There has to be another answer," Straka said.

Markos looked at him incredulously. Of all people, Straka should have known better. "Why?" he asked. "There doesn't have to be another answer."

"There does."

"Why?" Markos asked.

"Because this one is totally unacceptable," Straka said.

The crew mumbled their agreement.

"Fine," Markos said. "I'm all for another answer. You think I like this? You think I have the stomach for mass murder?"

No one said anything for a few long moments.

"We have to face this," Markos said. "If we don't, they'll find us. We can run—we can run for a long time, but understand this: Sooner or later it's going to be them or us. There's no peace making, no negotiation."

Straka shook her head violently. "I can't believe that. There's got to be another way out of this. If we all talk it through, we're bound to come up with something better. We can't just go around slaughtering them."

"I don't like it any more than you do," he said. "But you've all got to realize that until they're dead, every last one of them, no other race will be safe. Once their second wave of expansion starts, they'll spread like a cancer and take over every planet worth inhabiting."

"That'll take millennia," Straka said.

"Sure. Let's say it takes billions of years. What's the difference? You still don't get it. It's a *genetic* problem."

Straka froze, her eyes suddenly lit with green, scintillating, dancing.

"What, Cathy? What is it?" Markos asked.

"You said it yourself—it's a genetic problem. We have to find a genetic solution," she said.

His body went into shock as he realized the truth of what he'd almost done to a planet, almost done to an entire civilization, twisted though it was.

He opened his mouth to tell Straka that she was right, that he'd been wrong, that if a genetic solution could be found, the answer could be lived with by all. He sat there, though, the thoughts of what he'd almost done paralyzing him.

The crew looked at Markos and saw the answer in his face.

They had found an alternative.

* * *

It had taken two days, with the Old One helping, Straka searching alongside Markos as they had done in the old days aboard the *Paladin* before the change. They found the molecule that, when properly introduced into the Hydran genetic molecule, would block their expansionist instinct. Then they developed a tiny virus whose waste products were this blocking molecule. The virus had a unique behavior pattern: In all but the reproductive cells, the virus replicated itself quickly enough to make it highly contagious, but within the reproductive system, it united with the genetic molecule. This meant that the first generation born after infection would be less expansionist.

Markos was withdrawn and moody throughout their search. He went through the motions of Haber life, but he had lost some spark and drive. Straka figured he'd lost it on the bridge, giving McGowen the order to fire. She worked hard at trying to draw Markos out of his shell as they worked side by side, but she knew there were limits. Markos had withdrawn to some little island of safety inside his mind.

"Maybe this isn't the answer," Markos said, watching the chemical interactions take place through Terran instruments with his changed eyes.

"It's the answer, all right," Straka said.

"How can you be sure?"

"Desperation," she said.

Markos looked at her, and she couldn't even begin to unravel the emotions that played through Markos's eyes.

They brought the answer to the crew. They showed the group the vial that contained the virus they had made and explained how it worked. "It multiplies at an enormous rate. It should spread itself across a planet in a year or two. It attacks the Hydrans on a genetic level. The waste products it produces are the chemicals needed for blocking the 'overbreeding' instincts." Markos said the words without emotion in his gravelly voice.

"We'll try it out on our prisoner to see if there are any side effects. I doubt there will be," Markos added.

The Old One stood by, the silent observer once again.

Straka had never been able to get a grip on what went on inside the Old One's mind. She wondered what he was doing there with a half-Terran crew. Markos had told her about how they'd met in the Gandji village, how the Old One had arranged for Markos's flight from Gandji, how he'd befriended him, but none of that really helped her understand that strange Haber way of thinking.

"Markatens, we'll need your help," Straka said.

Markatens rose to his feet.

Markos said, "Release the Hydran from the paralysis. The rest of you line the bulkheads with your lasetubes drawn, ready to fire should the Hydran try anything stupid."

They followed Markos, Straka, and the Old One from the rec room to the lab. With lasetubes in hands they formed a large circle. Markatens approached the creature, touched its body, and slowly released its joints. He stepped back quickly, joining the others in the circle.

The Hydran emitted a strong odor.

"Fear," Markos said. "Be careful."

But Straka knew the creature had intelligence enough to recognize the futility in trying to escape or overpower them. She watched as it slowly rose from the table, awkwardly getting its three legs over the side, placing its feet on the deck. It moved with a grace that was both beautiful and horrifying. With each motion it made, Straka flashed back to the chase, to lasing those two Hydrans in the back, seeing those alien bodies topple to the ground as if in slow motion. She saw the neatly sliced-up Hydran lying on the ground beside this one, the line of unknowing Hydrans being lased down one after the other, presenting themselves in a mockery of many friendly Habers.

The Hydran stood on its own, exuding a different scent, radiating a quiet composure that was unsettling.

"Don't worry," Markos said. "It's curious, but not afraid anymore."

"That makes one of us," Straka mumbled.

Markos approached it with the vial.

The scent changed as Markos approached. He immediately took a step back. The scent shifted slightly.

"Just throw the vial on him," Straka said. "Unstop it and let it fly."

"Yes," the Old One said. "There is no reason to approach it and risk yourself. We still need you."

Markos looked at the Old One, and Straka caught his expression. It was similar to the one she'd seen a few moments before, just as inscrutable, just as distressing.

Markos took a step forward. The smell returned.

"Markos?" Straka said.

"What?" Markos said, his eyes on the Hydran.

"Don't bother. If you want to commit suicide, there are cleaner ways to do it. Besides, I won't let that creature take one step toward you. I'll lase it down before it gets close. Now, just throw the vial."

"I hear you, Straka." He removed the top of the vial, aimed it for the creature's torso, and then flung it at him. Markos retreated quickly. The Hydran's body immediately defended itself by closing its breathing holes and all the other controllable pores.

Straka knew the Hydran's actions were in vain. It might take the virus a second longer to work its way into the Hydran's system, but it would find its way nonetheless. The smell of fear returned, the one she'd grown to recognize on the planet when she'd towered over the supine Hydran lying beside its dead companion.

Its eyes were dull like pieces of black coal. The Hydran swept its head from side to side, waiting for the Habers to engage in a life-or-death struggle. Straka was sure it felt it could beat them all, one by one. It was waiting for them to make the first move.

After a few silent moments the airholes opened on its body and Straka knew the virus would soon be doing its work.

"Be careful now," she said to the others. "It might do anything at this point. There's no telling if there'll be violent reactions."

They waited.

Straka was on edge, knowing from firsthand experience how quickly they could move. Markos stood by her side, taking a ragged breath every few minutes. No one in the circle seemed to be bored or to let his attention fade. They all understood the importance of what they were doing, and Straka was glad for that. She knew the crew members of her watch were being extra careful after their run-ins on the planet. They knew what tenacious fighters the Hydrans were. At least their children.

"How much time has passed?" Straka asked.

"Enough," Markos said. "The virus should be in its system, doing its damage."

"It works that quickly?" Wilhelm asked.

"Yes," Markos said. "We made the virus. It's the way we planned it."

Straka sat in the command chair watching the Hydran-occupied planet suspended in the viewscreens. She wished Markos were here in the chair instead of her. But Markos had insisted on being allowed to return the young Hydran to the planet's surface.

They had eased themselves out of the lab, leaving two crew members behind to guard the Hydran. After an hour they had flushed the lab's air, pumped fresh air in, and waited a few minutes before testing the new air. Once they'd run a quick analysis on the air, they found it had been adequately contaminated with the virus. The virus would thrive on any organism, one of a million such viruses in every organism, invisible, benign to its host—as long as its host wasn't Hydran.

"Ready to disengage," Markos's voice came over the intercom.

Straka touched the communication button. "Fine. Have a safe trip, and keep communications open."

"Right."

Straka's watch sat in their chairs. "Do you think we should follow in H-three? Just in case?" Wilhelm asked.

"There's no need," Straka said. "They're not going to fight. Just to deliver a little present."

"The Hydran," Wilhelm said.

"The very contaminated Hydran," Straka said.

H-1, the ship Markos was piloting, appeared in the screens as it hurtled toward the planet. It should only take a few hours, Straka thought, to change every living Hydran on the face of the planet. It sure beats the hell out of dosing their sun with heavy radiation or dosing their atmosphere. Or even blowing up the ball of rock they're existing and breeding on.

* * *

H-1 came back on schedule, with the crew safe. They had deposited the Hydran on the planet in the same general area where it had been captured. Even if the Hydrans killed the infected one, they would all be infected. Even if the infected one never found its way back to its settlement, the Hydrans would be infected.

The Habers had found a path to peace.

25

Markos had docked H-1 and immediately called a meeting in the rec room. He knew their best shot was to dose the atmosphere of the oldest Hydran outposts and colonies with the virus. But he'd be damned if he'd make that decision on his own.

He remembered all too well what had happened when he'd tried it the last time a big decision needed to be made.

They needed to stop the second wave of expansion. And yet he knew that sooner or later they would also have to travel directly to Pi Hydra and meet the Hydrans on their own ground, to stop the root of the expansionist waves. If they didn't, they'd be fighting a losing battle. For every outpost Markos and the crew nullified, the Hydrans would start up two more.

Markos explained this to the crew, waited while they talked among themselves, and listened to all the positive and negative points. Making a decision like this might take longer, but points would be brought up that he never would have seen on his own. He figured that for once he had done the right thing by not shouldering the entire responsibility himself. And the crew seemed to appreciate the chance to decide their own fate.

They talked and argued, discussed and gestured wildly, and at last came to an agreement. The plan was unanimous. They would travel directly to the home base in the Pi Hydra system and stop them at their point of origin. At maximum speed, attainable only in tau, the trip would take a little more than two months.

Markos's watch, under his leadership, started the *Paladin* into motion once again, heading deeper into the Hydrans' territory. Straka was in the command chair when the relative-motion detector went off.

"What's that?" Straka asked.

There was a flurry of activity as the watch came to life. The crew turned their full attention on the instruments. As systems officer, Markatens was the first to speak.

"It's one of your detection systems," Markatens said. "There's an object traveling at near light, small enough to be a ship, too small to be a planetary body."

"Oh God," Straka sighed.

"Orders?" Markatens asked.

Straka hit the control panel on the command chair. "Markos, report to the bridge immediately. And bring the Old One." She turned back to Markatens. "Just shut off the warning system, please. Kominski, get a fix on this ship. Katawba, power up the weapons, and Wilhelm, get ready to decelerate at maximum speed and translate."

Now all she had to do was wait for Markos. She tried to find a little moving blip on the screens that surrounded them, in the vastness of space into which she stared, but there were far too many points of light in motion. At the speed they were traveling there was no way of distinguishing the relative motion of the stars from the constant motion of the ship.

"What is it?" Markos demanded from the top of the ramp. He was followed by the Old One.

Straka got out of the command chair and pointed to it. "It's all yours. One of NASA 2's systems went off, and Markatens tells me we've spotted a ship."

Markos's eyes flashed canary yellow with surprise and questions. He sat in the command chair.

"You want my watch here?"

"How long till they're relieved?" Markos asked.

"A few hours."

"Sure. Kominski, have you got its course yet?"

"Yes," Kominski said. "But if it's a Hydran ship, it makes no sense. The ship is heading in the general direction of the Epsilon Scorpio System, but with a distinct downward angle relative to the galactic ecliptic."

"What's down there?"

"I don't know," Kominski said, "and the navigational computer doesn't know either. There's nothing within the first-wave radius—no K-type stars—they could possibly be heading for."

Markos slapped the command chair's console, opening shipwide communications. "Prepare for maximum deceleration," he said. "Immediately. Get ready, Wilhelm."

"Ready."

"Are there *any* K-type stars in its path, Kominski?"

"Yes, but none that aren't already colonized."

"It doesn't make any sense. You're right, Kominski." He turned to Straka. "We have to intercept it."

"I figured," Straka said. "That's fine."

"Deceleration in ten seconds," Markos said into the communications network. "Attach yourselves."

Straka needed no further reminder. She sat on the decking beside the Old One and altered her outer covering to merge with the deck, then made her whole body hard. The others on the bridge were doing the same thing in their seats. Wilhelm provided a calm countdown, then hit the engine controls, starting the engines on the four Haber ships that pointed backward. The tremendous force blocked out everything else in Straka's mind as she felt every molecule in her body shift forward to try to keep up with the speed they'd been traveling, try to escape through her skin. The deceleration surge lasted almost half a minute and then was gone.

"Translate," Markos said.

Wilhelm switched in the translation equipment, transferring them from tau to real.

"Have you projected an interception course?" Markos asked Kominski.

"Working on it. Should have it in a moment."

"When you've got it, lay it in."

"Okay."

Kominski entered the course a few seconds later.

"Entered," Kominski said.

"Time to interception?"

"One hour," Kominski said.

"We should try to establish radio contact," Straka said.

"What for?" Markos asked.

"Well, what are you going to do, blow it out of space?"

"No. But we can't let it continue on its present course without at least contaminating it with the virus."

"I agree. Let's try to establish contact," Straka said. "We might be able to intimidate the crew of their ship. The *Paladin* does look pretty imposing."

Markos shrugged. "I suppose it's worth a try."

Markos had Markatens channel a radio beacon into one of Katawba's aimed lasers. Katawba took three minutes to reprogram one of the tight beams, then aimed it at the distant ship.

"Are you hitting it?" Markos asked.

"Yes," Katawba said.

"We'll wait a few minutes to let them respond by radio. Then we'll dump the signal and try that light-intensity laser. Use single pulses and see what happens."

"Right," Katawba said.

Straka had never expected the Hydran ship to respond to either the radio waves or the light beacon. There was something about the Hydrans, perhaps their single-mindedness, that precluded interruption on their flights. Why else would you have two-way radio communication on board? No one on their home planet was going to send a message for them to turn around and come back. She figured that even if something went wrong, the Hydrans would let their colonizing ship drift endlessly—the bodies on board could be happily replaced by the home population.

"Try the light beam," Markos said.

"Right," Katawba said.

Even if there were some other reason for communication between the ship and its home, the Hydrans didn't seem to be the type of creatures who would use it. They were far too driven, far too obsessed with expansion to bother with ship-to-ship communication. Their colonizing ships were little more than projectiles hurled into other star systems, exploding the Hydran seed on whatever planet they happened to land. Still, they had to make the effort.

"Nothing," Markos said to Straka.

Straka flashed red.

"Do we know it's a Hydran vessel?" Wilhelm asked.

"No," Markos said. "Though we will soon enough. Markatens, put the screen in the unknown ship's sector on maximum magnification."

Markatens did as ordered.

"Kominski, plot in a nearly parallel course. I want to stay about this distance, closing in on them slowly, heading in the same direction as they are."

"That will take a few," Kominski said.

"Take your time."

"What are you planning?" Straka asked.

"I'm not going to risk everything, especially now that we have a solution. I can't bring the *Paladin* in too close. But we could send out H-one. It's fully armed. We could send a crew of two, carrying the virus. They could move in a lot closer than we could."

"You want them to dock?"

Markos flashed a strong red. "What a great opportunity this is, Straka. We've never known how the Hydrans travel through space, how they pilot their ships, how many Hydrans are actually on board their first-wave ships. There's so much we don't know about them.

We don't even have a clear idea as to where they are technologically."

"Sounds like a suicide mission to me," Straka said. And it did. If the Hydrans had any weapons on board, which they had to, they would use them as soon as H-1 got within their range. And it was highly doubtful the Hydran vessel itself was unarmed. Just because they didn't have ship-to-ship radio or light-beacon communications didn't mean they weren't armed. And they still didn't *know* that the Hydrans were without communication—they just knew that the Hydrans hadn't responded to the hailing.

"I'm not asking you to go," Markos said.

"I didn't offer my services," Straka said.

"Course is prepared," Kominski said.

"Lay it in, Kominski."

"You want to go with me, Wilhelm?" Straka asked.

"Sure," Wilhelm said. "Sounds like tons of fun."

"No," Markos said. "I'm going."

"No way, man," Wilhelm said. "Every time some lousy job comes up, you volunteer for it, and you get all the fun. You've got to learn to let others enjoy themselves too."

Markos flashed red. "All right. You two can take H-one. And don't forget the virus."

"I wouldn't go anywhere without my virus," Wilhelm said.

Straka sat in the control seat of H-1 studying the startank before her. It was studded with stars; the one closest to the center had to be Pi Hydra. She saw the dot that represented H-1 and the small moving dot that represented the Hydran ship. It wouldn't be too hard to match its course and run parallel to it, catch up to it, then slowly close the distance between them. After a systems check they broke off from the mother ship and angled in toward the Hydran ship.

Straka watched the screens with Wilhelm. They could see the Hydran ship clearly now, though it was still a tiny speck of light.

"What do you think?" she asked Wilhelm.

"About what?"

"About what we're doing."

"What's to think? We take our chances. We get in close enough so that their weapons can be effective and then we pray a lot."

"Really," Straka commented.

"You take care of the weapons, and I'll pilot the ship. At the first sign of trouble, blow the suckers right out of existence. Show them everything they ever wanted to know about the afterlife."

Straka continued to stare at the screens.

"Look," Wilhelm said, "Markos can get pretty heavy sometimes. He gets a little carried away. You should know that about him by now. He wants us to dock with the ship, do all that viral infection, take care of things. Sure. I'm all for it. Only if things look bad, I'm not about to get fried. You take your best shots, and I'll get us the hell out of range."

"You're right," Straka said. "Let's stop at a point where their weapons should still be ineffective."

"I don't know where that point is. I don't even know what they've got for weapons."

"True. I don't either." She turned and smiled at Wilhelm. "No one does."

"Okay, then, make yourself hard and we'll do a little dance going in. I'll zigzag a random course, alter speed, do everything I can to present our cute little friends a terrible target."

"Now *that* I like."

"See? Everything's cool, amigo. Stick with me. We'll make it."

They closed in on the ship in an insane course no computer or sentient creature could predict. There was no possible way any weapons system could be aimed and fired before Wilhelm made another zag. Wilhelm had the skill and was piloting a ship capable of responding to his masterful piloting.

"We're getting to the point where maneuvers won't make much difference," Wilhelm said.

"How big you think their ship is?"

"From what I can tell, it looks like it's about twice our size."

So much for that idea, Straka thought. She'd hoped they could open the bay door and swallow the ship. But now they had no other choice but to dock with it. "It is Hydran, isn't it?"

"Without doubt," Wilhelm said. "I've seen these babies in the crystals. This is the same type of landing craft they use to colonize. No question about it."

Straka glanced at the screen before her. Indeed it was the exact same configuration.

"Funny, it's not armed," Straka said.

"Yeah, I know."

"Let's dock."

"Okay. Hold on."

Wilhelm maneuvered H-1 to within a few meters of the larger Hydran ship. It was a slow operation and demanded his intense concentration. Straka was curious as to how they were doing but didn't ask for fear of breaking Wilhelm's concentration. They would know soon enough.

At last Straka heard a dull clang as the ships touched. Wilhelm kept a minute amount of pressure to the starboard side of H-1 to keep the two ships locked side by side.

"Let's move," Straka said.

"Be sure you attach the hulls before you slice through," Wilhelm said. "The engine pressure should hold us, but I don't want to rely on it totally."

"Right," Straka said. She barely heard what Wilhelm had told her. She was in a daze, removed from the insanity and fear by a defense mechanism she had developed years ago: detachment. As she walked to the section of the hull where they would create a semipermanent docking and breach the hulls, she walked in slow motion, through water, her mind floating, her eyes taking in everything and nothing.

"You okay?" Wilhelm asked.

"Huh?"

"Snap out of it! Come on."

Straka shook her head, trying to clear it. She covered her multiple eyes with her hands and took several deep breaths. "I'm okay now. Where's my lasetube?"

"It's attached to your waist! For God's sake, if you don't shape up I'm going to get us the hell out of here. We don't know what's on the other side of their hull, and I'm not opening up any holes with you like this."

"Give me a few seconds and I'll be okay."

But she could see the line of Hydrans waiting there, lasers pointed at her chest, the two of them running through the muddy ground, the ship sitting in the distance, Kominski's insane laugh....

"Straka!"

"Huh?"

"Jesus. I'm getting us gone. That's it."

"No, wait! Give me a few more seconds."

What's wrong with me? she wondered. She rubbed her hands on the bulkhead, seeking the reassuring touch of something she knew was real, was solid. It felt as it should have felt; she took a few more deep breaths, then turned to Wilhelm.

"I'm okay, now. Sorry. Let's attach the hulls, okay?"

Wilhelm was half a meter away, looking at her with grave concern. "It'll wait another minute or two. You back in control? I mean really in control?"

"Pretty much so. It just came on like a wave. It's leaving, though. I'll be okay in another minute."

Wilhelm flashed red and waited. A few minutes passed before Straka felt the dissociation dissolve in her mind as she returned to full awareness and control.

"Okay. I'm fine," Straka said.

"You sure?"

She flashed a deep red.

"Okay," Wilhelm said.

They touched the bulkhead together, sending their probes through to the Hydran hull. The Hydran hull was made of a three-metal alloy, nothing extremely complex, and they bonded the two hulls together over several meters. When they were done, they removed their hands, looked at each other for a moment, then drew their lasetubes.

"Let's make ourselves hard, then start with a small hole," Straka said.

"You got it."

279

They began burning their way through the hulls.

They activated their defense belts once they were about to pierce the Hydran ship's hull. "If they're standing there with weapons, don't waste any time," Straka ordered. "Just lase them."

"Right," Wilhelm said.

But when their lasers burned through the Hydran hull, there were no screaming Hydrans on the other side. A small amount of air from the Hydran ship leaked in, bringing with it a strange odor, faintly recognizable. With their bodies hard, recognizing strange odors was difficult at best.

"What *is* that smell?" Wilhelm asked.

"I can't place it; but I know I've smelled it before," Straka said.

"It's really familiar," Wilhelm said.

"It's probably from lasing through the metal. Let's open up a larger hole," she said.

"Right."

It took them just a few more minutes, and after they had removed the charred hull sections, they peered into the Hydran ship.

It was dark and murky inside the cabin. Straka and Wilhelm could barely see a thing. A chill ran up Straka's spine. She poked her head through the hole, then quickly withdrew it. The smell, the one she couldn't recognize, was stronger than ever.

"What is it?" she asked. "What's that smell? It reminds me of NASA 2."

She had seen vague shapes through the hole, like large cases or crates, probably filled with supplies or weapons, spread out over the deck of the cabin. Each case was several meters long, a meter high and a meter wide.

She absorbed some of the electrons from her outer covering, making her nostrils permeable and her ear openings fully receptive. The scent was stronger. All she could hear was her own and Wilhelm's bodily functions—nothing stirred within the Hydran ship. Her skin was still slightly toughened, though not rock hard.

"I'm going in there," she said.

"Not without me, you're not," Wilhelm said.

She peered through the opening again, then looked into Wilhelm's multiple eyes. They were throbbing with dull light, showing his tension and excitement. "Wait here for me. If I run into trouble, I'll yell. Don't hesitate to jump through and don't spare the fire power."

Wilhelm flashed a weak red.

She climbed through the opening.

As her feet touched the Hydran deck, her lasetube was in her hand, ready, and her skin was once again rock hard. She listened with all her attention and heard only the dull humming of the ship's automatic systems. She was afraid to move, afraid of setting off some chain reaction. She braced herself and took a single step forward, silent and cautious, hoping that movement wouldn't unleash a screaming wave of violent Hydrans.

Nothing happened.

She took another step.

Still nothing.

But she felt anything but safe. She bent down and placed a palm on the deck for stability. The deck vibrated with steadiness, with the ship's life-support systems. She glanced back at the opening, at Wilhelm, and as she turned her head back, caught the glint of something shiny. A surge of fear raced through her body, freezing her for a moment, until she realized that her own eyes were glowing, had probably been reflected off some shiny surface

She stood up. She felt a need to stabilize herself, calm herself down, and placed her free hand on top of one of the shiny crates. Her hand plunged through its top, touched liquid, and she yanked back her hand.

"What?" she whispered.

Her voice was shaky. She leaned over the top of the crate and stared at its surface. It shimmered in the light reflected from her eyes and her fear returned, doubled in intensity as she recognized the medicinal smell. She wanted to run back and get Wilhelm.

She reached down again, deliberately this time, and let a finger break the surface of the liquid, then added another finger. She rubbed the liquid between her fingers.

The reflection of her face was distorted by the ripples of the surface. She was sure she knew what it was. Her knees felt weak. She forced herself to calm down and touch the liquid again. She plunged her hand down deep and felt the cold hard exoskeleton of a Hydran.

She withdrew her hand as if the liquid burned. She turned to the opening, to Wilhelm, to what little sanity was left. She looked toward her friend, and opened her mouth to tell him what she had found. No words came out at first.

"What?" Wilhelm asked. "What is it? What's wrong?" He stepped through the opening and walked quickly to Straka's side. He looked down, saw the shimmering surface, and pierced it with a hand.

"Gel?"

Straka flashed red.

"Geltanks?" Wilhelm said.

26

The *Paladin* continued to parallel the Hydran ship's course. Markatens was left alone on the bridge to monitor the systems and instruments from the command chair, to make sure the Hydran ship did
nothing unexpected. Markos had promised to send someone up to
relieve him as soon as the debriefing was over. Straka and Wilhelm
had returned in H-1 and said nothing about what they found.

Markos had asked what had happened once and they'd refused
to answer. He hadn't pushed the issue. They had offered to link up
with everyone, open their minds to the entire crew, and let them live
the experience as if they had all been there themselves. Both Straka
and Wilhelm felt it was important for the crew to experience what
they had experienced and that a verbal debriefing just wouldn't ac-

complish that. Markos hadn't objected to the idea. In fact he appreciated it.

He did have some trouble restraining himself. He wanted to ask questions, to find out what had happened as soon as possible. His curiosity was overpowering, and though he knew that he would have all the information soon enough, he found it hard to wait.

As Markos accompanied Straka and Wilhelm to the rec room, some of the noise subsided. The rest of the crew were there, busily speculating on what might have been found on the Hydran ship. Their moods were transparent as each set of eyes radiated a dull yellow around their outer edges. Even when McGowen flashed a welcoming green, the outer edges of his eyes stayed yellow.

Straka and Wilhelm flashed green to the crew.

The few crewmembers who had been sitting rose to their feet.

"Well? What did you find?" Katawba asked.

"You'll see for yourself soon enough," Straka said. There was an edge to her voice that spoke a warning, that altered the mood in the room.

She and Wilhelm held out their hands to start the linkup. One by one the crew joined hands until the circle of ten was complete. Markos stared at the deck and waited for the scene to unfold in his mind, for Straka and Wilhelm's experience to become accessible. His lower back tightened and he tasted metal.

In a sudden rush he was aboard H-1, the docking completed, looking at Straka through Wilhelm's eyes. He immediately switched into Straka's mind, felt the strange dissociation, experienced the slaughter on the planet around Epsilon Scorpio, heard Kominski's insane laughter ring through his ears.

The shock and horror of finding the geltanks was Straka's, and then Markos felt Wilhelm's reaction. He lived their numbing terror as Wilhelm climbed through the opening and plunged his hand into the nearest geltank. The smooth, cold exoskeleton of the Hydran beneath the surface was unmistakable.

Experiencing it through both of them made it difficult for Markos to detach himself emotionally. Numbed by their discovery, Straka and Wilhelm had explored the rest of the ship. Cabin after cabin was filled with geltanks. They poured the vial containing the serum into the gel's recirculating system. They found the ship's bridge at last, unattended, running on automatic. Wilhelm glanced at the small unit mounted in a bulkhead and Markos shared his shock of recognition. Wilhelm immediately recognized it as a NASA 2 navigational computer. He walked toward it slowly, as if afraid it might leap off the bulkhead and make for his throat. He touched it with his hand and probed beneath its surface to investigate its circuits, just to be sure.

Straka found the autopilot, a direct copy of the autopilot developed by NASA 2.

They turned to each other and saw the shock of their discoveries mirrored in each other's eyes.

With a sudden jolt of disorientation, Markos found himself back on the *Paladin*, standing in the rec room, the linkup broken by Straka and Wilhelm.

The metallic taste was overpowering, making him gag, weakening his knees with the shock of understanding and realization.

The others were shouting; blinding colors whipped through the rec room; arms waved and someone grabbed him. He felt himself being lowered to the cool, hard deck, heard someone shouting, "Earth! It's Earth!" over and over. He looked up and saw the calming eyes of the Old One staring down at him, pulsating with colors and patterns that soothed.

Self-control returned a few moments later and he sat up. The panicky argument continued.

"What else could it be?" Jackson screamed.

"It doesn't make any sense," McGowen shouted. "It doesn't."

"Earth!" Kominski screamed.

"We were fools! We're finished!" De Sola said.

"It just doesn't make any sense," McGowen repeated.

They shouted at each other, wanting and needing to express their fears, too wrapped up in yelling and shouting to listen. Markos understood now why Straka and Wilhelm had demanded a linkup.

Dammit! McGowen was right. It didn't make any sense. Earth wouldn't side with the Hydrans. Even if given the opportunity, which is something the Hydrans would never do.

He struggled to his feet and surveyed the room. Martinez was sitting in a chair, hands covering his face, head shaking from side to side as he tried to deal with the truth.

"I was there! It really happened, idiot!" Wilhelm was shouting at McGowen.

This is insane, Markos thought.

"I'm not fighting anymore. That's it. No more," De Sola said. "No way. We're finished!"

He had to stop them. There had to be another answer. "Quiet!" Markos shouted, unleashing a blast of powerful white light from his eyes.

The crew was silent.

"Earth," Kominski whimpered.

"Quiet!"

Kominski was silent and took a step away from Markos.

"We don't know that Earth is involved," Markos said.

"What? You're crazy," Jackson said.

"Are you serious?" Wilhelm asked.

All at once, Markos thought. They all have to talk at once.

"Will you listen? For once?"

"I've listened to enough of your lies," Jackson said.

"Jackson!" Markos shouted in warning.

"You know all the answers, don't you?" Jackson said.

Markos swallowed the strong metallic taste.

"Earth," Kominski said.

Markos wheeled around and emitted a powerful blast of multicolored light from his eyes, which froze Kominski to the spot. All signs of awareness and intelligence vanished from his face.

Everyone froze in fear.

"He'll be all right in a while," Markos said.

"I'm not fighting Terra," Martinez said. "I don't care *what* you do to me."

"No one's asking you to!" Markos shouted. "McGowen's right. It doesn't make any sense. That should be easy enough for all of you to see. Earth would never side with the Hydrans, no matter what. They're not blind. They'd be signing their own death warrant."

"Then where'd they get the geltanks? And the navigational computer?" Wilhelm asked.

"Not from Earth," Markos said with some certainty. And with the statement came a sudden realization. "But they could have gotten them from an Earth-based ship. . . ."

"The missing pod," Straka said.

"What?" Jackson asked.

"That's it!" Markos said. "That has to be it. It's the only thing that makes any sense."

"That's crazy," Katawba said. "The only pod that wasn't accounted for was the one near Tau Ceti. Tau *Ceti*!"

"Yeah. That's way across from this sector of space! It might as well be on the other side of the Galaxy," Wilhelm said. "No way could it have traveled—what, fifty? Maybe sixty light-years?"

"What was its velocity?" Katawba asked.

"Don't buy this!" Jackson shouted. "What's the matter with you fools? Can't you see what he's trying to do? Those pods had a maximum speed of maybe a quarter light. Wilhelm, am I right?"

Wilhelm nodded.

"There's no way *any* pod could have made it to this sector of space by now."

"Yeah," Wilhelm said.

"All right, it may not be exact," Markos said, "but it makes a lot more sense than Earth being involved, doesn't it? We still don't know what happened to the pod after it telemetered information from Tau Ceti. It found the Habers, and we were sent out to investigate. . . ." And then Markos had another realization as everything fell into place. He turned to the Old One.

"Well? What about it, old friend? What did you do with NASA 2's pod?"

"We, we sent the pod to Pi Hydra," the old Haber said.

"Pi Hydra?" Straka asked. "Why?"

"I, I will explain." The Old One explained how they had sent the wedge up to intercept the pod, how they had captured it in their bay, and how damaged the Terran inside it had been.

"It had been a long and lonely flight for him," the Old One said.

"At first we, we thought he was a Hydran, a different mutation, but we, we quickly realized he was from another place. He was so badly damaged in his thought processes, it was difficult to make much sense out of what was real and what was not.

"He talked to others who did not exist. When we, we probed his mind we, we found that the people existed inside himself only. It was from him that we, we learned something about Terrans and Terra. There was no question in our, our minds that this Terran was not a Hydran. And yet there were similarities that could not be ignored—aggression, an understanding of the change we, we could not survive—and so we, we decided it would be best to increase his life span, repair what damage we, we could to him and his pod, and send him to the Hydrans.

"We, we hoped his appearance near the Hydrans' home planet would confuse them. We, we hoped they might have concentrated their efforts and expanded in another sector of space. They might have thought that this Terran was a Haber. They might have seen his aggression and thought better of taking our, our planets.

"We, we needed time to develop the mutant strain and we, we hoped that by sending this pod to Pi Hydra we, we could gain valuable time."

"That's it?" Markos asked. "An attempt to gain time?"

"No," the Old One said. "There is something else. We, we feared the Terrans too. Aggression is such a strange concept. It was so totally beyond our, our comprehension then. We, we feared what might happen if we, we returned him to his home planet. There were so many confusing and violent images in his mind of that place. We, we just could not afford to let him go back, and we, we could not just leave him there to die."

Markos was shocked. How could they have been so naive? But even as he thought that question, he realized they were Habers, without any understanding of the change in which they were involved.

Straka shook her head slowly from side to side. "You didn't help, Old One. Your interference has only made it more difficult for us now."

Increased his life span? Markos thought.

"I, I am sorry for that, but you must understand that we, we were alone against these creatures—"

"Even so," Jackson said. "Sending him out there in hopes he could lure the Hydrans to Earth." There was no mistaking the disgust in his voice.

"No," the Old One said. "That is not what we, we meant to do. And that is not what I, I said."

"This man you examined," Markos said. "You mentioned something about increasing his lifespan?"

The Old One flashed red.

"By how many years?"

"What's the difference?" Straka asked.

"Two thousand," the Old One said.

The shock showed on Markos's face as a chill ran up his spine. Two thousand meant that there was a chance, no matter how slim it seemed, that the man on board NASA 2's first-wave exploratory pod was still alive.

Still alive.

"We at least have to look for the poor son of a bitch," Straka said, saying it for all of them.

27
.

Translation from tau to real occurred one billion kilometers from Pi Hydra, close enough to be well inside the star's gravitational field, far enough out to be safe from detection by any inhabited planets closer in. The drop in speed was undetectable, and as they sat at their battle stations, all systems on board were fully operational.

McGowen sat in the weapons chair, its converted headpiece covering his multifaceted multiple eyes. Jackson was keyed up, ready to accelerate the mother ship at a moment's notice. Martinez had five alternate courses laid into the navigational computer in case they were needed for offensive or defensive maneuvers. De Sola stared intently at the panel of lights before him as he monitored the ship's operating and detection systems. Markos sat in the command chair, tuned to each of his crew, to the ship's status, to the space they had just translated into.

Straka and Wilhelm occupied H-1, ready to launch. Kominski and Markatens occupied H-2, facing the other direction, ready to serve as rear guard or backup. Katawba sat alone in H-3, serving as second backup should anything happen to H-1.

The Old One was attached to the deck on the bridge by Markos's side, prepared for possible acceleration in case maneuvering was required. They had known what to expect immediately after translation to real—their sensors showed they would enter unoccupied space, with no solid bodies within 100,000 kilometers, the range of their intermediate sensors.

A good enough safety margin, Markos thought as he stared into the space that filled the screens around him.

Pi Hydra was visible as a bright, tiny disk directly before them.

"Let's start the planet search," Markos said.

"Right," De Sola said.

De Sola pressed a touchplate on his panel and three computer-generated circles appeared on the screen.

"Magnify the one on the left," Markos said.

The circle expanded until it filled the forward screen. Within it was a disk, a planet covered in clouds.

"Doesn't look like much. Try the one closer in."

De Sola returned the screens to their original mode, then zeroed in on the next planet. Under full magnification it didn't seem to have an atmosphere—no clouds, no bodies of water. It was distinctly smaller than the first one they'd observed.

"Where's the third?" Markos asked.

De Sola shook his head. "Too close to Pi Hydra. Even with a K-type star, odds are against it supporting life."

"Then what about the first one we viewed? Any orbital data on it?"

"Some. It's about one hundred and twenty million kilometers from Pi Hydra."

"Pretty far," Markos said.

"Right on the borderline for a biosphere," De Sola said.

"Period of rotation?"

"Not enough data for an extrapolation yet."

"Anything more at this point?"

"Not really," De Sola said. "Bring us in closer and I'll see what I can do."

"Course?" Markos asked Martinez.

"Laid in."

"Okay, Jackson. Bring us within short-range sensor probes."

"Right," Jackson said.

They felt the slight push of acceleration.

Markos glanced back at his monitor panel and saw that everything was fine. "Screens back to normal mode," he said.

The screens returned to normal. They watched as the small speck of light slowly increased in size until it became a disk.

"Starting deceleration now," Jackson said. "Unless you want us in closer."

"We within range?" Markos asked.

"Yes," De Sola said.

"All right, Jackson. Decelerate."

Jackson touched the control plate, and the mother ship came to a relative stop.

"Well, De Sola? Anything yet?"

"Yes. Sidereal period, estimated at two hundred and twenty-seven days. Diameter estimated at eleven thousand two hundred kilometers. No visible satellites. Need more?"

"No. It sounds close enough for a habitable planet circling a K-type star."

Markos was certain they'd found the Hydrans' home. "Bring us into a close orbit, De Sola and Jackson."

They both acknowledged Markos's command and after De Sola calculated the proper approach with the navigational computer and laid in the course, Jackson activated the engines. Markos sat calmly, watching the planet grow in the screens as they made their approach.

"Keep a close watch, McGowen," Markos said.

"No problem."

They entered a synchronous orbit, hovering above what looked like a major continent far below.

"Let's have some magnification," Markos said.

De Sola increased magnification on the screens and they got their first glimpse of the Hydrans' home planet. Magnification was low, and clouds covered parts of the upper atmosphere, but they could still see the surface clearly enough to realize that the planet was no place they wanted to live.

Overpopulation had created nightmarish landscapes below. There were some grayish open areas where there were no buildings, but these were few and far between. The rest of the planet's surface seemed to be covered in buildings and craters. Markos assumed the craters were not naturally formed and were a result of some past war. It was hard to spot any vegetation, but he couldn't tell whether that was because of their distance from the surface or because there just wasn't much.

"They did a complete job on their home," Markos said.

"That poor guy," De Sola said.

"Who?"

"The one in Pod Three. If he landed on that piece of rock, there's not a chance he's still alive."

Markos said nothing. He preferred that alternative. If the Terran in Pod 3 was still alive, or if there were a significant chance of his still being alive, the crew would insist on landing, on finding him, on getting him out of there. One look at the planet was enough for Markos. He might have considered setting down and doing some exploration and reconnaissance in hopes of finding something out about the Terran, but that had been before, when they'd been in deep space, when they weren't orbiting a ball of rock crammed full of Hydrans.

All he wanted to do now was dump the virus and take off. They had too many planets to visit, too many settlements to contaminate to risk everything for a man who might be dead.

"We don't know that," McGowen said. "He could still be alive, and we're not leaving until we find out."

Markos said nothing. Now was not the time for an argument or a discussion. If it looked like their mission would not be jeopardized, no lives lost, then he might consent to sending down a search party.

"Straka? You ready to launch?"

"Ready, Markos."

"All right. Just dump the virus into the atmosphere and return to the ship."

"Fine," Straka said.

"I'm launching, too," Katawba's voice said over the intercom.

"What for?" Markos asked.

"Backup. We still don't know if they have any defense."

"Forget it, Katawba. You stay where you are."

"What? I can't hear you, Markos. There must be something wrong with the intercom."

"I said don't launch!"

"Can't hear you."

Markos felt the tiny jolt of Straka's launch followed by a second launch, obviously Katawba's.

Wilhelm handled the controls with ease, dropping H-1 into the Hydran atmosphere at the maximum safe speed. "You want to dump the virus first or head right for the surface?"

"The virus first," Straka said.

We owe the Habers at least that much. Just in case we don't make it back, Straka thought.

"Are you going to inform Markos?" Wilhelm asked.

"Yes. After the virus is dumped."

"Fine with me. Let's get it over with, then. We're low enough now."

Straka took the vial and walked down the passageway to the top of the ramp. The bay door was still shut; she walked down the ramp and stood directly before it, making her body hard, attaching her feet to the deck. She waited a few minutes for Wilhelm to hit the switch opening the bay door. The door opened slowly, stopping about a meter up. Air rushed in, foul with heavy smells of decay, strong enough to permeate the hardened skin over her nose. Straka opened the vial and threw it to the wind. Within a few days the virus would be an integral part of the Hydran metabolism. There would be no more first-wave ships launched from this planet. There would be no more territorial wars. There would be no more genetic drive making these creatures insatiable expansionists.

The bay door closed, Wilhelm assuming that the seeding had been accomplished, and Straka released her foothold on the deck. She walked slowly back to the bridge.

Straka was a Haber. And Straka was a Terran. Her loyalties were divided, and she knew it. Markos had renounced his past, expatriated himself beyond anything Straka could understand. She knew that Markos would never let anything stand in the way of the mission's success and would have put a stop to what she, Wilhelm, and Katawba were about to do.

There was a human being down there, a fellow guinea pig of NASA 2, a first-wave explorer, who had had his life horribly changed beyond human comprehension. It had been changed by the Habers. The Habers had sent him there, and now the Habers were going to help him, make him whole, return his life, make amends. Whether Markos liked it or not.

Straka remembered too well the time she had spent on Aurianta locked in the pen, being treated worse than any animal would have been treated. No food. No water. And worst of all, no hope.

"Done?" Wilhelm asked.

Straka flashed red and settled into the other control seat.

"Katawba?" Straka asked into the microphone.

"Here," Katawba said.

"Good. We're going down. Follow us by a kilometer. We're going to skim the surface and find a prisoner. Some smart Hydran who knows about the pod."

"Right," Katawba said.

"Get back up here," Markos said.

"Forget it, Markos. We have to do this."

"Don't be ridiculous! The three of you will get killed. What good will that do?"

"Don't make me disconnect the radio," Straka said. "We're not returning until we know whether he's dead or alive. And if we find out where he is, we're going to investigate."

"But the mission, Straka. The mission—"

"There are enough of you left aboard to complete the mission. We talked the whole thing over and we all decided on this course of action. We owe him this much, and we owe it to ourselves. The matter is settled."

Markos said nothing.

"You told him," Wilhelm said.

"I said I would. As soon as the virus was dumped."

Straka would have wanted the others to do as much for her. If H-1 were shot down, she would want Markos to send out a search party for her. If he were still alive, the man in Pod 3 was waiting, but who or what was he waiting for? NASA 2? Not a chance. NASA 2 had no idea as to where he was or what had happened. They had sent the *Paladin* out to investigate and establish contact with the alien race he had discovered at Tau Ceti. And part of their mission was to find out what had happened to the missing pod.

Straka wondered if the remnants of the geltank training had something to do with their drive to rescue this man.

"Five kilometers up," Wilhelm said.

"Good. Start circling at the equator."

Straka watched the ground rush by in the screen mounted before her. At this rate, she thought, we should be able to get around the planet in a few hours. But we're really going too fast to see much of anything ... "Wilhelm? You want to cut back a little so I can see what we're flying over?"

Within a few seconds H-1 had slowed to a more reasonable speed. The screens showed the same basic scene, over and over again. It reminded Straka of a treadmill; she started to think that H-1 was hovering over a piece of moving ground connected to some continuous loop. Craters and buildings and buildings and more buildings, then a few craters, then the buildings again. No fields. No farmlands. No parks. None of the area seemed capable of industrial manufacturing either. As far as Straka could figure, they were passing over a continuous city that had seen better days.

"See anything?" Katawba asked.

"Tell him not yet," Straka said, flashing a deep blue.

"Not yet," Wilhelm said into the radio.

"Have you found a place to land yet?" Markos asked.

"No," Wilhelm said. "We're not even sure there is such a thing on this planet."

"How long do you want us to wait?" Markos asked.

"For what?" Wilhelm asked.

"For you."

Wilhelm's eyes blazed white. "Hey, man, I really couldn't care less. These ships have their own tau drives and navigational systems, so whenever you're tired, just take off without us. Let me know where you're going and we'll catch up. Sooner or later."

"Funny," Markos said.

"Well? What the hell do you want from us? You want to get out of here faster, get your ass down here and help us out!"

Straka looked at Wilhelm with a tinge of yellow in her eyes. She motioned with her head for Wilhelm to kill the transmitter for a moment.

"You think he'll come down here?"

"Who knows? He's been so weird, there's no way of telling."

"Turn on the radio," Straka said. She spoke into the transmitter. "If you send some more help down here, we might just make it back alive."

"I understand, Straka. I just don't like being blackmailed."

"Join the club. Just send some help."

"I'll do what I can."

With four ships they had enough for a real landing party. If they could find a place to land. Straka started to feel hope growing inside.

28

Markos was starting to think Straka would never find a safe landing spot. From the command chair on the *Paladin*, Markos had been unable to spot a large enough clearing far enough away from a populated area. There should have been some farmlands if the Hydrans ate cultivated food, animal or vegetable. There were seas, large enough to hold other kinds of life-forms, but there was no indication that the Hydrans fished or farmed the oceans. The more Markos saw of the planet, the less he liked it. It made no sense at all.

But then, he was getting used to the idea of things not making sense. Getting into H-4 with Jackson made little sense. Trying to rescue the Terran without even knowing where he was or if he were still alive made even less sense.

"You think he's still alive?" Jackson asked.

"No. Not really."

"I don't either."

"Then what the hell are we doing here, Jackson?"

"We're here because we're not sure. And that's reason enough."

Markos looked at him with a tinge of humor seeping through his eyes.

"Is it really? If he's still alive, how sane do you think he'll be?"

"I don't know. And you don't know either. And until we see him, if he's here, it's useless to talk about it."

Markos turned away and stared into the screen. Straka's ship was only a few minutes away. Jackson's attitude was slightly disturbing. Markos tried his best to see it their way, but he couldn't divorce himself from what had to be done. There was the seeding. Without that there would be more and more Hydrans to deal with. How could the crew consider one human life more important than the seeding of those Hydran-occupied worlds?

"One more thing, Jackson. I'm trying to understand just why we're doing this, but I can't. Explain it to me."

"I don't expect you to understand, Markos. None of the crew really understands. When you come across something important, you do it no matter what. Like the way you ran from Van Pelt. Once you'd done that, the matter was settled—no room for argument or discussion.

"Well, we're the same way about this. Once our minds are made up, nothing can change them. We just happen to feel that going after this person is as important as seeding the rest of the planets. We need to do this. We feel for each other. We stick together. We have our differences, but we learned a lot in that compound you kept us in."

Loyalty? Is that what Jackson's talking about? Markos wondered. Some antiquated feeling? What was the name for it, fraternity? Racial unity? What's the difference? Markos wondered. Whatever it was, whatever its name was, they were willing to risk their lives for it, for a man who might no longer exist.

"Here we are," Jackson said.

"Let's get this over with."

* * *

It sounded simple enough when they'd all been discussing it over the radio, but Markos knew that Straka was courting disaster. Straka was going to the surface to get a prisoner. That alone looked like suicide.

This was no outpost, recently colonized. This was a heavily populated planet, a Hydran stronghold. But Markos knew better than to try to talk them out of the plan.

Kominski and Markatens were in H-2, hovering beside Markos and Jackson, ready to act as a secondary backup should anything happen to Katawba. Markos glanced at Jackson and then turned back to the screen. There were no answers in that face, he thought. Not anymore. He had learned to control his eyes. These changed humans were becoming aliens to him—as alien as the Habers had once been.

He watched H-1 settle to the ground right beside a crater in the middle of a populated area. There didn't seem to be anything they could do about where they landed—one place was as bad as the next. H-3 settled to the ground right beside H-1. There was a lot of activity in the surrounding streets as Hydrans scurried about in a panic. But there was no way Markos could tell whether or not there was some goal behind the movement, whether or not the Hydrans knew what was happening at all.

The bay door on H-1 opened, and the movement of the Hydrans ceased. They froze in their tracks.

Straka held the lasetube tightly in her hand. Wilhelm stood beside her. They stared out at a scene that made them both wish they were back aboard the *Paladin*.

Hydrans were all around, standing motionless, turned toward their ship. One Hydran, just a few meters away, had been eating. Neither Straka nor Wilhelm had ever seen a Hydran eat before. Now they wished they hadn't. It was holding a piece of meat, and there was a small black shell on the ground by its feet. There was no mistaking the origin of the shell. It had come from another Hydran.

The frozen moment passed, and the Hydrans burst into a flurry of motion. Straka and Wilhelm didn't wait to see what the Hydrans would do. They leaped to the ground and ran for the closest Hydran. They ran with a vengeance that sprang from revulsion and disgust.

The Hydrans seemed to be confused, disorganized. Some of them were gathering in a tight little group, while others ran for the sanctuary of the nearby buildings. Straka knew how much faster the Hydrans were than she was. If it came to a footrace, she would have to lase their legs off.

She and Wilhelm managed to overtake the one who'd been eating, who was frozen in shock. They had just a few seconds left before all hell broke loose. Wilhelm wrapped his arms around the Hydran before it could react and sealed its joints with his palms. A simple but effective technique. They ran back to the ship with it.

Wilhelm threw it up into the bay and wheeled around in time to see the group of unarmed Hydrans mounting an attack. Straka had made it back to the ship, and Wilhelm could tell they'd be on him before he could hoist himself up into the bay.

He saw no choice. He turned to make his stand.

A thin, slicing beam shot from over his head, lasing the approaching group. Wilhelm took the opportunity and put his hands on the bay's deck.

Straka hoped Wilhelm had enough time to get on board. She kept careful watch of the crowd of Hydrans, ready to slap the bulkhead to start the bay door's closing mechanism.

And then Wilhelm disappeared from sight, dragged downward as if by some tremendous undertow in a sea of Hydrans. Straka leaned over the edge and peered downward. Three Hydrans had Wilhelm down on the ground. They were pounding away at his hardened skin, biting at his eyes and face with their slicing mouths. Straka took careful aim and sliced one of them in half. But that did not deter the other two. She glanced up and saw another group of Hydrans advancing from the left. She realized they were trying to flank her. She had to get Wilhelm aboard, and fast!

She leaped to the ground right beside the churning bodies. She kicked at one of the Hydrans' heads and landed a good blow. The Hydran fell away. Wilhelm had another Hydran left on top of him, but Straka had to let him handle it on his own. She had to deal with the advancing left flank. In another moment or two they would be on her. She activated her laser and swept it back and forth for all she was worth.

Another group started advancing from her right. Where the hell was Wilhelm? What was keeping him? She wheeled to her right and started lasing down the other advancing group. Wilhelm was still on the ground. Another group was mounting an attack from the left. One group directly before her was still coming on, and her right flank was being surrounded too. This was no time for trying to be nice, no time for heroics, Straka realized. She had to get that last Hydran off of Wilhelm, and she had to do it now!

Let them come, she thought. All I need is a second or two.

She ran a step to her right, then looked at Wilhelm. The Hydran was all over him. She stomped down hard on the Hydran's back to get its attention. When it turned, Straka kicked it squarely in the head. Then she lased it. Wilhelm remained on the ground. He wasn't moving. Straka started to get panicky. They were all around her now, advancing at top speed.

And then she saw Wilhelm's chest, bathed in red. She wheeled to face the Hydrans.

She started lasing them, turning 180 degrees, slicing and toppling bodies as if they were targets in a shooting gallery. A few moments of that slowed them enough to give her a few seconds. She reached down for Wilhelm, lifted him under the arms, and flung him into the bay. The advancing group of Hydrans was only a meter away now, coming on fast. She had only an instant to activate her lasetube.

She sliced down body after body as they toppled at her feet. And still they came.

Straka had no idea how much longer she could keep this up. Activating the lasetube drained huge amounts of energy, and she knew she would tire far too quickly to keep it powered.

Where the hell was Katawba? Couldn't he see that they needed help?

Maybe Katawba's in worse shape than us, Straka thought.

Maybe this wasn't such a great idea.

The advancing Hydrans were climbing over the bodies of their fallen ranks, coming on strong, not letting a few hundred dead stop them. But it was taking them longer to get within attack range. If her energy held out, Straka figured she had a chance. Slim, but real. While they were climbing over bodies, she lased them down, adding to the barrier of dead Hydrans between herself and the ever-advancing wave.

She decided they were slowed down enough for her to take a chance. She turned, reached for the deck, and pulled herself up. No time to close the door yet. Keep firing. Christ. How many of them are there? A few Hydrans managed to get close enough to touch the deck, to try to scramble up. Straka lased their hands off. And then she looked up, out over the immediate threat, and saw something that made her blood run cold.

A whole new wave, reaching back as far as she could see, was advancing. They walked over the bodies of their dead cousins, knocked each other down in their frenzied attempts to get to the ship. Straka touched the wall, activating the closing mechanism at last. The door started its slow descent, cutting off her view of the distant advancing wave. That was fine with her.

After lasing through the narrowing opening, after the eternity of the closing sequence, the bay door closed, mangling several sets of Hydran hands in the process.

She slumped to the deck, exhausted.

And then she looked at Wilhelm.

Wilhelm wasn't moving.

Markos knew this rescue attempt would cost them something in time and energy. There were some cutoff points—realistic limits—and they were quickly approaching them. He watched through the small screen and tried to make sense out of what he saw. It was impossible to make out any details or get a true feel for the flow of the battle.

He started to think that something was going wrong. Still, if it were, Katawba was down there, ready to help, as were Kominski and Markatens in H-2. But it didn't look right. It shouldn't be taking Straka this long.

"What's going on?" Jackson asked.

"I can't tell," Markos said. "Not through this screen. All I know is they're still fighting."

"Let's get down there. Now. If they're still fighting, they need help."

"They've got help if they need it. There's no need to move."

"We're going down," Jackson said.

"Don't even think of it," Markos warned. "Or I'll do to you what I did to Kominski."

Straka knelt on the deck, arms wrapped around Wilhelm's bloody torso. The skin around his neck had been severed by the Hydran's attack. Straka needed to cry, to feel the tears roll down her cheeks, but the tears wouldn't come. They couldn't.

This wasn't supposed to happen, Wilhelm. This wasn't the way it was supposed to be, she thought.

Straka rocked on her knees, swaying to some unheard heartbeat, a pounding throb in her own chest. She looked at Wilhelm's quiet face, his clear, crystalline eyes. She wished she could go back and make things right, do things differently.

"Give me another chance," she said softly.

But no one heard her plea. She turned to the Hydran, her immobilized prisoner, and eased Wilhelm to the deck. She stood, rushed to its side, eyes blazing with strong clashing colors, light reflecting off the Hydran's shiny black body. Straka made her fist rock hard and in the same instant brought a crushing blow down on its chest.

Something cracked.

"I'm going to kill you," she told it, knowing full well it couldn't understand. "Slowly. In stages."

Hand still clenched, still rock hard, she turned back to Wilhelm. Dead Wilhelm. Somewhere in the background, Straka could hear voices filtering through, calling her, calling Wilhelm.

I'm sorry, she thought. Sorry it was you. Sorry it happened.

It isn't fair.

She could hear the voices again. They were coming from up in the control room. She looked up the long ramp and remembered the radio. It had to be someone calling. She didn't want to answer it, to talk to anyone, to face anyone even over the radio. She would have to tell them what had happened to Wilhelm.

Still, she knew she had to.

She turned away from the motionless Hydran and walked up the ramp. She felt tired and old. She recognized the voice as she approached.

"Are you all right? Straka? Wilhelm? Answer!"

Straka sat in the control seat, the seat Wilhelm used to sit in, and buried her face in her hands. Her hardened right hand took her by surprise.

"Straka? Are you there? Wilhelm? What's going on?"

Straka softened her hand and flexed it, staring at it as if it weren't a part of her body. "I'm here, Katawba," she said. "I'm here."

"Straka? Wilhelm? Are you there?"

Straka realized she hadn't activated the transmitter. She touched the plate and activated it, then said, "I'm here. Wilhelm is dead."

"Is that you, Straka? What did you say?"

"I said that Wilhelm is dead. The Hydrans got him."

"Listen to me, Straka. Get the ship up. There are Hydrans crawling all over it. And there are groups of them forming in the streets with some strange-looking weapons."

"Right," Straka said.

She started activating H-1, thinking about Wilhelm. They had never been truly close until their imprisonment on Aurianta. And it had been Wilhelm, the best pilot, who had chased Markos on Gandji, when Markos had slammed into the boulder.

... Slammed into the boulder?

Everything around her came back into clear focus. Wilhelm may be dead, she thought, but with the Habers death can be a temporary thing. Just like it was with Markos.

Her hands flew over the activating plates as she brought the ship up. She realized the sooner she got Wilhelm back to the mother ship, the better his chances of being brought back to life.

Markos had changed him, and now Markos could resurrect him. It was the least he could do.

29

Markos knew what was coming and he didn't like it. Though he knew there was nothing he could do, Straka and the others would never believe him. His wedge docked with the *Paladin*, and Jackson touched the bulkhead, making the docking permanent.

Markos didn't even want to get out of his chair. He sat staring at nothing in particular, in no great rush to enter the mother ship. He felt weary from the constant impossible battle with the Hydrans, from the hundreds of little confrontations with the crew. His supposed allies.

And now Wilhelm, their best pilot, was dead for no good reason. He was dead for trying to help some Terran he never met, who might not even be alive.

"You coming?" Jackson asked.

"I'll be there in a minute."

"I'll see you on board."

He was certain they wouldn't believe him. They were like that—sure of things they knew nothing about. He wondered how far they would push him. Well, they can demand all they want, Markos thought, but there's nothing that can be done.

When he finally mustered the strength and entered the mother ship, he could feel a difference in the air. The mood on board was intense. The crew had gathered in the rec room, with Wilhelm's torn body stretched out on a table. Markos glanced at Wilhelm, then swept his gaze over the crew.

He had been right. It was obvious in their eyes, in the way they held themselves, in the way they had laid out Wilhelm.

"Where's the prisoner?" Markos asked.

"In the lab," Straka said.

Markos turned to leave.

"Wait," she said. "I want to talk to you."

"Can't it wait?"

"No."

Markos glanced once more at the crew. They looked hostile. He realized he shouldn't have stayed aboard H-4 for so long. They had obviously set up some unified plan of action.

"Then come with me," he said, "and we'll talk."

"Talk here."

"I've got a lot to do, Straka. Unless you've given up the rescue attempt. If you haven't, the Hydran has got to be questioned."

"He'll keep. Wilhelm won't."

"Every moment we delay could prove costly. I don't look forward to spending an additional hundred years finding new Hydran colonies that wouldn't have been there if we'd acted now. The longer we wait to complete the seeding, the more Hydran outposts we're going to have to seed."

"Wilhelm's life is worth it."

"Wilhelm is dead."

Straka locked eyes with Markos. Markos knew what was coming. "So were you," she said.

"True. And sometimes I wish the Habers had left me dead."

"Just bring Wilhelm back," she said.

"Let's talk about this alone, Cathy. Please."

"Talk here—now, in front of everyone."

"I can't do a thing for Wilhelm. I know nothing about reviving him."

"Just bring him back, Markos," she said with a little more force in her voice.

"Believe me. I would if I could. But you forget—I was on the receiving end of it. Being brought back didn't make me capable of doing it for someone else."

Straka rose to her feet. Markos didn't like the way her facial muscles were tensed, the way the power throbbed in her eyes. The rest of the crew was tensing up, and he saw that she was leading them. The Old One was nowhere to be seen, and Markatens was probably in the control room, monitoring the systems and keeping an eye on the planet.

Straka pointed to Wilhelm. "Are you going to bring him back or not?"

"For the last time, Straka, I can't. I would, but I don't have the knowledge."

Straka wheeled around to face the crew. "Get the Hydran," she said. Jackson flashed red. "The rest of you know what to do."

They all seemed to hesitate for a moment, grudgingly getting to their feet. Straka turned back to face Markos. "Last chance. Are you going to bring him back?"

Markos flashed a pure dark blue. He had no idea as to what she had in mind, but he knew there was nothing he could do. He would just have to let it play out. He was telling them the truth. If they chose not to believe it, that was their problem, not his.

He was prepared to die at their hands.

The Old One appeared in the doorway, blocking Jackson's exit. "What is the problem?" he asked.

"Get out of my way and there won't be one," Jackson said.

The Old One moved to the side. "Markos? What is this about?"

"Wilhelm is dead," Markos said, "and they want me to bring him back to life. But I don't know how."

"Why do they want you to bring him back to life?" the old Haber asked.

"Ask them," Markos said.

"Cathy Straka? Can you tell me, me why?"

"I can, but I don't see why I should. Will you bring him back if I explain?" she asked.

"It is possible."

"We want him back because we need his presence. We all cared for him. He shouldn't have died, especially under those circumstances. His death is a waste."

The Old One leaked a little violet tinged with white. "You are a selfish people," he said. "I, I have always tried to understand why you have this hatred for a change that has to be. Death is a positive step—"

"I don't hear Wilhelm saying that. Bring him back and we'll ask him."

"Wilhelm means much to me, me, too. This caring does not mean that I, I want him back, though. I, I am glad he has found peace at last. He is no longer afraid of those things he did not understand."

"Sure," she said. "Death does that. He no longer cares about anything. He no longer is."

"You are wrong, Straka. Not only are you wrong, you are selfish. You fear his death was brought about by you. You have no idea of what Wilhelm experiences now. If you did, you would want to let him rest."

"He isn't resting," she said. "He's dead."

"Let him stay that way."

"You won't bring him back?" she asked.

"And you still want me, me to?"

"Yes. You brought back Markos on Gandji. You can bring back Wilhelm, too."

"The Old One might be right," McGowen said.

Straka wheeled around. "Are you serious? Let him stay there, like that? I'd do the same for you, McGowen."

McGowen shook his head. "No thanks. If I get it, I get it. I've lived enough for two people. I'm not greedy."

Straka shook her head. "Have it your way. But I still want him back."

"I don't," De Sola said.

"What's the matter with you two? Are you crazy?"

Markos couldn't be sure, but he thought he saw McGowen grin.

"No, Straka, we're not crazy. And we're not crazed. We don't need to live forever. But I want you to know that if you should get it, I'll do everything I can to revive you," McGowen said.

"I want you to know the truth, too, Cathy," Markos said. "I can't revive Wilhelm. I just don't know how. When it comes to something like that, I guess I'm not really a Haber."

"No, you're not!" she shouted. "You're a freak!"

Jackson appeared in the doorway. "He's loaded on board the wedge. Are you ready?" he asked.

Straka rushed forward, almost knocking Jackson out of the way.

"Wait a minute!" Jackson shouted.

But she kept going.

"I think the plan is off," Markos said.

"What the hell am I supposed to do with the Hydran, then?" Jackson asked.

"What were you planning to do with him?" Markos asked.

Jackson didn't answer. Markos hadn't really expected him to.

"Put him back where he was, Jack. I'll question him in a few minutes."

Jackson looked to the rest of the crew. Markos followed his gaze. They were leaking red from their eyes, nodding slowly. Markos was back in control, for whatever that was worth.

Markos approached Straka's cabin with great trepidation. There was no predicting her mood, and Markos feared the worst. He stood outside the door for a moment, hand touching the strange Terran-made bulkhead, a stress-formed piece of alloy its creators had never imagined would be touched by a creature like him. He wondered what NASA 2 would think if they knew where their ship was.

Markos braced himself as he entered the cabin. Straka was on her bunk lying on her back, hands tucked beneath her head, legs crossed at the ankles. Just like a human, Markos thought. She did nothing to acknowledge Markos's presence.

"I'm sorry. I liked Wilhelm, too," Markos said.

Straka unlaced her fingers and sat up. "About what the Old One said in the rec room . . ."

"Yes?"

"I didn't want Wilhelm to die. I feel responsible for his death."

"Could you have saved him?"

"Maybe."

"Really?"

"There were so many of them, and there was so little time. I keep thinking that he would still be alive if we hadn't gone down there to get that prisoner."

"Perhaps," Markos said, "but there's no real way of knowing that. Sometimes I think I did the wrong thing by changing all of you. I think it might have been better if I'd just given the *Paladin* back to you and forgotten this insane war with the Hydrans.

"There was no need to involve any of you. If I hadn't put you in that pen, Wilhelm might have been alive now. There are just too many 'ifs.' *If* I hadn't been changed myself, *if* I had let you go, *if* I had left Kominski behind, *if* I'd insisted the Old One stay behind. It doesn't do us any good. That's all past. We've got the future to consider."

"All but Wilhelm."

"True. But what about the rest of us? What about the inhabited planets throughout the Galaxy? There are the Hydrans, and they still must be dealt with. You're going to have to put aside your grief and guilt. We've got work to do. This planet has been seeded, and we're wasting precious time here. We either move on or go down to the surface for the Terran. But the decision must be made now."

Straka looked away from Markos, looked at the deck, and Markos knew what he had to say.

"I was wrong, Cathy. And I'm sorry."

"Huh?"

"It's *my* fault Wilhelm is dead. I divided us. I created a rift. If we're ever going to get anything done, we have to work together.

"Let's get that Terran down there. All of us. We'll work as a team. You have my complete support."

She looked at him.

"Really." Markos extended his arms in a gesture he hadn't even considered for years.

Straka threw her arms around him and hugged him tightly. Markos could see that the edges of her eyes were tinged with red. He was never happier to see that color.

The first thing they did was link up. Markos felt it was necessary to bridge the gap that had opened between them all. They stood in a tight circle. Everyone aboard the *Paladin* was there, the bridge unattended. The last real linkup had occurred long ago and, more importantly, had occurred before Wilhelm's death. As the old Haber touched hands with the others, he said, "Watch for our friend Wilhelm."

When the Old One grasped the last two hands firmly, the linkup was complete. At first the strange ceremonial type of communication held nothing new, but as Markos felt the others' barriers melt, felt their thoughts mingle with his, he could see Wilhelm in his mind's eye. He could detect Wilhelm's presence in the group, just as if Wilhelm were alive, standing next to Straka or Martinez. He was still with them.

The grief they each felt mingled and mixed together, diluted and dissipated slowly until it completely disappeared. Markos could feel the difference in Straka. The barriers dissolved completely and their egos disappeared. They were in contact with each other's essences, mingling their selves and raw primal instincts, baring parts of their minds normally hidden. There was no horror felt, nor was there shame. They were what they were—no more, no less—each an individual, unique in countless ways, and yet identical to each other, sharing countless aspects of life.

When the linkup was over, Markos released his grip on the others. He looked around; something was wrong, out of place. He couldn't quite place the feeling, but as he scanned their faces, he saw that they shared the same feeling. And then he realized what it was.

Wilhelm.

Wilhelm wasn't there anymore. But his spirit, his soul, his essence had been so real, so tangible, as solid as anyone's had been just a few moments before. It had felt solid, and when he'd broken contact with the others, Markos had expected to see Wilhelm standing there among them. It hadn't been a conscious thought, but the feeling of his being there had been so strong, so real, that his mind had played a horrible trick on him. He had forgotten Wilhelm's death. A quick scan of their faces had shown Wilhelm's as missing. Markos saw the realization dawn in the rest of their eyes.

"The pain is gone," Straka said. She turned to the Old One. "I'm sorry for what I said. I feel him now, and I understand a little more."

The Old One flashed red.

"Well? I believe we have some planning to do?" Markos said.

30

Markos's ship, H-4, was the last to land. It fell to the ground with a bone-jarring crash, a landing designed to take no time. They needed to take the Hydrans by surprise as much as possible. He and Jackson ran for the bay door even as the last reverberation of the landing traveled through the ship's hull.

Belts switched on, bodies hard, lasetubes in hand, they leaped to the planet's surface. The others were already engaged in a fight.

The ships had settled on a smooth section of land, one of the Hydran launch sites. The prisoner had been to the area where the Terran was kept, and this mental image provided them with an accurate picture of the area. Thanks to a quick linkup before leaving the mother ship, each crewmember shared this picture of the launch complex.

Markos was repulsed by how the Hydran thought of the imprisoned Terran. Virtually every Hydran on the planet knew of him, and some traveled great distances to see him. The image this Hydran had of the Terran was distorted, though, transmitted by word of mouth. It had never seen the Terran itself, so there was no way of knowing just how he was being kept. But there was no doubt that the lost NASA 2 pilot was still alive.

Hydrans were pouring out of the surrounding buildings. The landing party was formed into a small group, lasing down the advancing Hydrans in rapid bursts. Markos and Jackson made their way to the group as quickly as they could.

A quick flash of greeting, a quick flash of encouragement, and they were off, heading toward the largest building. They moved in wedge formation, a wedge with a laser's cutting edge. Markos was on the left flank, directly behind Straka at the point, slicing creatures in half, severing heads from torsos, amputating legs from bodies, slicing, slicing, feeling nothing inside but a need to get this horror over with.

The Hydrans may have been blameless, but they were totally without conscience. He was doing what had to be done. And yet he knew deep down that lasing them down would be another good reason to get the mission over with as quickly as possible and settle into a quick, quiet, meditative death.

A glance over his shoulder showed the rest of the wedge intact, with hundreds of Hydrans swarming over the Haber ships. Let them pry at the seams, scratch at the hull, he thought. They won't do any damage.

Straka was leading them directly for the building that housed the Terran. Markos had to turn his attention to the post as Straka brought them closer to the building. Hydrans were starting to amass a defense of sorts—if a wall of Hydran shell and flesh could be considered any kind of serious defense, Markos thought. Those crewmembers near the front of the advancing wedge helped lase as many bodies as possible.

When they reached the doorway, it was blocked by Hydrans,

most of them dead. Markos stepped over them, on them, around them as if they had always been there. The floor of the building was slippery with their dark blood. Lasers were not always the clean weapons you wanted them to be, he realized. They didn't always cauterize the holes they made, nor did they always make neat incisions.

There was a slight reddish tint to the light in the hallway, and Markos adjusted his eyes to shift the spectrum slightly. The walls were ornate, though not artistic. It was aesthetically unappealing to him, and he had no idea if the uneven surfaces were supposed to be functional or decorative. The floors were not level, but they were covered with something—it was impossible to even hazard a guess with the soles of his rock-hard feet.

Hydrans in the building constantly tried to stop them and accomplished nothing but adding to the piles of corpses scattered about. Markos had learned a lot from the prisoner Straka had taken. The Hydrans in this complex were of a different social level, the elite of the race, those individuals directly concerned with the race's expansion, with the colonization of space. They did research to determine the most efficient ways of ensuring the race's survival.

The ceiling was higher than Markos was used to. He glanced upward and was amazed at the complexity of the building's structure, but had to turn his attention back to their constant advance almost immediately. They were nearing the room occupied by the Terran—this was no time to let his mind wander.

Straka stood before the door, a thick slab of metal slightly recessed from the wall. Fewer and fewer Hydrans were advancing on them, but Markos had no idea why. Perhaps their ranks were thinning, perhaps this area was taboo for them, perhaps for some other reason. He was just glad for the break in the slaughter.

Straka pushed, pulled, then tried to slide the door open. After a few seconds she placed her palms flat against the metal and the door slid to the side.

Straka walked in, and Markos and De Sola followed her a step into the room. It was larger than they had expected. The ceiling was on the same level as the ceiling in the hallway, but the floor was sunken down several meters. They stood on a stairway, waiting for the rest of their party to occupy their defensive positions. Jackson nudged him on the shoulder to signal that it was safe for the leading edge of the group to enter further, that their rear was being properly guarded, and Markos signaled this to Straka.

The room was free of Hydrans. Markos had no trouble recognizing bits and pieces of Terran equipment, no doubt salvaged from Pod 3. It looked horribly out of place in this room, serving an alien purpose for an alien race.

The geltank sat off the floor, raised on a small platform that put its base even with the top of the stairs. Even from that distance, Markos could see what rested inside the tank.

He was sorry they had risked so much, that Wilhelm had lost his life just for this. He wanted to cry.

They approached the tank no longer feeling like heroes. For the person in the geltank it was too late.

They were certain it had once been a human being, though the resemblance was only minimal. The thing in the tank swiveled its head from side to side, an action that was distinctly Hydran. Its flesh was gray and sagging, a mask of infections and sores. Markos made the mistake of looking into his—its—eyes.

The man was clearly insane.

Markos absorbed some of his surface-level hardness and saw Straka and De Sola do the same.

"What's your name?" Straka asked.

The man in the tank did not respond. He continued to sweep his mad gaze over the crew in the chamber. "Cathy? Let's go, okay? There's nothing we can do for him."

"What are you saying?" she shouted, wheeling around. "We have to help him."

"It's too late for him," Markos said. "Whatever he is now he will remain. There's no need to change him into anything. He's so insane, there's no hope."

Straka looked back at the distorted human form in the tank.

"But we have to do something," Straka said.

"There's nothing to be done."

"He's right," De Sola said. "Let's get out of here."

"I'm not leaving yet," Straka said. "Not until I'm sure."

Straka walked closer to the tank. The man in the tank was not a pretty sight. Straka placed her hands on the outside of the geltank while the others watched and waited from a distance, still on the stairs. She took her hands away from the tank, and Markos could see the tinge of yellow in her eyes, reflected off the shiny surface of the tank.

"Are you from Earth?" Straka asked. "Do you understand me?"

The creature in the tank started squealing, making high-pitched sounds, totally alien to human speech patterns. He seemed frightened beyond the limits of human tolerance.

"Come on, Straka! Let's go. He's so far over the edge, there's no way of reaching him. There's nothing we can do for him now."

Straka turned and looked at Markos.

"Let's go. Before this place is swarming with more Hydrans hell-bent on suicide," Markos said.

Straka took one last look at the man they had come to rescue and then turned her back on him, walking back to the steps. "I wish I knew what happened to him," Straka said softly.

"He did what he had to do to survive," Markos said. "He adapted."

"There were some strange chemicals in the tank. I couldn't recognize them."

"Forget it. It's over. Let's get back to our ships and get off of this poor excuse for a planet."

Straka nodded, then made her body hard. Markos and De Sola quickly followed suit. They walked to the entrance, and then Markos stopped. Before De Sola or Straka could say anything, Markos lased the thing inside the tank.

31
.

The *Paladin* circled the Hydrans' planet, its bridge unattended, its defense systems on automatic. The eight wedges had been reattached to its hull, its configuration once again complete and powerful. The ship circled the planet orbit after orbit, waiting for a pair of hands to set a course. The *Paladin* performed the only task that had been set for it and cared nothing about the origin of the hands that issued the order, the motive of the order.

The crew occupied the rec room, their rescue attempt hours old, discussing the questions and issues, the discussion more tangential than paths of light in a mirrored room. Each crewmember had his own course of action, his own goals to guide him, and a vested interest in the outcome of the discussion. Markos was starting to appreciate the way the crew split, rejoined, then scattered again as another point was brought up. The strong Haber part of him found a pattern there, a pattern he could appreciate, a symmetry to the discussion not unlike that of a kaleidoscope.

Like shards of brilliantly colored glass, ideas would mingle; overlay each other, changing the true color of the problem; rotate; then burst apart into their individual idea-colors as a new set of ideas took their place. It was a pleasing experience and it calmed him, removed him enough from the immediate tension of the discussion so that he could wait for the outcome.

He listened to the way the crew said things, paying little attention to the ideas themselves. Their differences were apparent enough in the way the discussion flowed. As long as things did not get out of hand, there was no need for him to really participate.

"I want to go back to Terra," Jackson was saying, and Markos decided to pay attention.

"How long do you think you'll last looking like that?" Straka asked.

"Long enough for them to pump your mind dry, then take you apart piece by piece to find out just what the hell you are," De Sola said.

"Once I explain who I am and what happened—"

"They'll believe you?" McGowen asked. "Be serious, Jackie. They'll take one look and assume the worst."

"Probably not," Martinez said. "By the time we're done seeding all the Hydran planets with the virus, hundreds of years will have passed on Earth. There's no telling what it will be like, or if we'll be remembered at all."

"I don't care. I want to go home," Jackson said. There was a quiet determination in his voice that Markos easily recognized.

"It's your life," Straka said. "Now, me, I want to do some exploring. Get into H-one and do some real traveling. Take a few thousand years to check out this sector of the Galaxy."

"Nothing too big, eh, Cathy?" McGowen asked. "Just stick to the immediate neighborhood? Is that the idea?"

The crew laughed, easing some of the tension.

Once they had finished seeding the rest of the Hydran-owned

planets, they were free to do what they pleased. The way the crew was talking, the seeding would be over soon enough, too. Then Markos would keep his part of the bargain: He would touch and change them permanently, giving them the potential to live forever. With a future that stretched out farther than any of them could conceptualize, there was nothing they couldn't do.

"I'm going back to Aurianta," McGowen said. "There was more beauty there than anyplace I've ever seen. It's probably more beautiful than anyplace I could find in a hundred thousand lifetimes of searching."

Aurianta, Markos thought. It would be nice to have the breathing, living planet beneath my feet again. I miss it, and I'm tired of the lifeless metal of this ship.

"Yes," the Old One said. "It will be good to be home again, to be able to complete the task I, I started many years ago."

"What task?" Katawba asked.

"Dying."

"What are you planning to do, Markatens?" Straka asked.

"Speculating seems premature at this point," he said. "Live my life, die when the time comes. Perhaps do some exploring in between. It is impossible to plan."

"Just like a Haber," Jackson said.

"Yes," Markatens said. "What else are any of us?"

Indeed, Markos thought. What else? They were no longer human, but as Haber as any naturally born Haber could be. The phenotypical change was easier to see, and its effects had been immediate. But the genotypical changes Markos had made were still incomplete and would change them in far subtler ways through the rest of their lives. Straka and even Jackson would find their behavior modified over years, just as McGowen had found his modified by Alpha.

"And you, Markos?" Straka asked.

"Solitude is what I want. I need time to get back in touch with who and what I am. My life over these last years has been dedicated to stopping the Hydrans. Once we're through with the seeding, I'll have time to sit and listen to myself, to the wind. I'll have time to die."

"Have a good time," Jackson said.

"Thank you, Jackson. I will," Markos said.